William Brodrick was an Augustinian friar before leaving the order to become a practising barrister. His novel *A Whispered Name* won the Crime Writer's Association Gold Dagger for Crime Novel of the Year.

D1113647

Also by William Brodrick

THE SIXTH LAMENTATION
A WHISPERED NAME
THE DAY OF THE LIE

the
gardens
of the
dead

WILLIAM BRODRICK

ABACUS

First published in Great Britain in 2006 by Little, Brown
Published in paperback in 2007 by Sphere
Reprinted 2007 (three times)

This paperback edition published in 2008 by Abacus
Reprinted 2010, 2012 (twice), 2013

A CIP catalogue record for this book
is available from the British Library.

Grateful thanks to the Literary Trustees of Walter de la Mare and
The Society of Authors for permission to quote from 'Dust to Dust'.

ISBN 978-0-349-12112-3

Typeset in Baskerville by M Rules
Printed and bound in Great Britain by
Clays Ltd, St Ives plc

Papers used by Abacus are from well-managed forests
and other responsible sources.

MIX
Paper from
responsible sources
FSC www.fsc.org FSC® C104740

Abacus
An imprint of
Little, Brown Book Group
100 Victoria Embankment
London EC4Y 0DY

An Hachette UK Company
www.hachette.co.uk

www.littlebrown.co.uk

For The Passage

ACKNOWLEDGEMENTS

For endless support, patience and guidance, I warmly thank: Ursula Mackenzie, Joanne Dickinson, Araminta Whitley, Pamela Dorman, Beena Kalmani, Austin Donohoe, Victoria Walker, Catherine Browne, Stephen Guise, Sr Jean-Baptiste Koetschet OSB, Fr David Middleton OSA. As ever, I remain gratefully indebted to the communities at Bec.

One of the principal characters is concerned with how evil might be undone. The seed for this question came from a talk given by Metropolitan Anthony of Sourozh.

Finally, my heartfelt gratitude goes to Anne and our three children. They have helped me at every turn, sharing the peculiar weight of a second novel's making.

NOTE

As I hope the Bunyan undertones make clear, much of the landscape in this book is imaginary or serves a symbolic purpose. I ask pardon from readers who note, for example, that there are no 'Four Lodges' at Hornchurch Marshes. The Gilbertines were an English religious order that did not survive the reformation. References in the text to 'The Rule' are to that of St Benedict.

Sleep is well for dreamless head,
At no breath astonishèd,
From the Gardens of the Dead.

Walter de la Mare
'Dust to Dust'

PREAMBLE

Elizabeth Glendinning QC walked purposefully, beside Regent's Canal in Mile End Park towards a trestle-table covered with junk from the houses of the dead. Behind it, his jaw working as if he'd tasted ash, sat Graham Riley, lolling in a camp-chair. To her right, sausages and onions sizzled on a hotplate; steam rose from an urn; clothing hung jammed on racks; bits of houses were laid on a blanket by a sign that read 'Architectural Reclamation'; tools from yesteryear, rusted, robust and manly, stood propped against a dinted van. Elizabeth passed them all, not quite looking, keeping her eye rather on the calm of the waterway to her left, and away from Graham Riley.

Despite years of handling tension, Elizabeth found the strain this morning unbearable: she had devised two grand schemes to bring this man from the camp-chair to the courtroom, that he might answer to his many victims. The first of these, after months of preparation, was about to be fulfilled.

Riley looked up, across the autumn fair, in utter disbelief.

Elizabeth was dressed in courtly black. She wore no make-up. Her hair had been precisely cut at quite fantastic expense. Through anxiety, her skin was pale and her lips peculiarly bloodless.

Riley's jaw was still. He looked like a wasted, frightened boy surrounded by broken toys. But Elizabeth had travelled a long way beyond pity; she'd climbed to the mysterious and airless place where justice and mercy met. Holding her breath, at this the culmination of so much effort and sacrifice, she picked up a set of Edwardian spoons.

Feeling a sudden giddiness and a race of contractions in the heart, Elizabeth stumbled back the way she'd come, beside the smooth, green canal. She slumped in the driver's seat of her lemon-yellow VW Beetle, stunned at her carelessness: she'd mastered the facts, but had failed to consult the law. On the passenger seat was the orange flyer that had led her to Riley's stall. She crumpled it with one shaking hand and forced the ball into an ashtray. She began to sweat and her breath fell short. Feeling a strange sense of moment – as when a train, out of view, hums on the lines – she unhooked her mobile phone off the dashboard and called Inspector Cartwright, being careful to leave only a message. She then rang Mrs Dixon. A rush of wind seemed to come, and Elizabeth dropped the phone midsentence. In the sluggish seconds left to her, Elizabeth found a last, winning smile.

Yes, she was inconsolable. She would never behold Charles, her husband, again . . . he was at Smithfield Market, fretting over the morrow; or Nicholas, her unwary son . . . he was probably on the Barrier Reef, among the brightly coloured fish; or George, her friend and accomplice, who was waiting beneath a fire escape. And, yes, in terms of these grand designs of hers, death had come too soon. It was, as ever, the spoiler. But Elizabeth could laugh, and did. She'd devised contingency arrangements for precisely these circumstances. And there was one scheme left untried – the most far-reaching, and the most grave.

Her heart became wonderfully still.

All at once Elizabeth felt cold. It seemed that she was high above the clouds, coming down to earth at last. As she tumbled in the sunlight, she thought: Now is the hour of the unsuspecting friend, of the puzzled monk to whom I gave the key.

PART ONE

the story of a key

1

Anselm returned to Larkwood, weaving through the apple trees in Saint Leonard's Field. The scooter skipped over tufts of grass, and Anselm bent his head, thinking of Steve McQueen at the end of *The Great Escape*. He could see the fence ahead. In a vivid reverie he saw himself soaring over the barbed wire, away from fiends who would cart him off to the cooler.

Whistling to himself, Anselm pushed the bike into the old woodshed, where he met Brother Louis, the choirmaster.

'Hullo,' said Anselm. 'How was it?'

'Appalling.' He'd been on a ten-day residential counselling course. 'I had to talk about myself. Eye-to-eye stuff.'

'Oh hell.'

Louis sat on a stump. He was tall and seemed to fold himself up. His eyebrows were copper and straight, as if they'd been electrified. Anselm rolled two cigarettes, obedient to a wink.

'From the global perspective,' said Louis, pensively, 'I found some relief.'

'Really?'

'Yes. My parents aren't to blame after all.' He slowly pushed out the blue smoke. 'I am.'

'Don't be deceived.'

Louis tilted his head towards the scooter. 'Where've you been?'

'Buying wood to bank the Lark.'

'I hope you've got a receipt.'

Anselm had thrown it in the bin. 'Why?'

'Cyril's gone round the bend. It's that time of the year, I'm

3

afraid. He's doing the books and he can't account for twenty-eight pence.'

As the cellarer, Cyril was responsible for the financial affairs of the monastery; he was the commercial brain behind various industries derived from apples and plums. An amputee after an industrial accident sustained before joining Larkwood, he had the appearance and character of a one-arm bandit chock-full of fruit and numbers.

'Speaking of madness,' resumed Louis, rummaging in a habit pocket, 'the elderly Sylvester put this in my pigeonhole.'

Anselm unfolded the slip of paper: 'Elizabeth called. Roddy is dead.'

Roderick Kemble QC, Anselm's old head of chambers, a friend and guide from those half-forgotten days. 'Oh, God.'

He ran to reception, where Sylvester struggled with buttons to get an outside line. Anselm hovered, itching to grab both the receiver and Sylvester's larynx – it was a common problem at Larkwood – but shortly he made the call and a growing suspicion was confirmed. 'I am still here,' said Roddy, 'but Elizabeth is not.'

Anselm stepped into the sunlight. He looked towards Saint Leonard's Field as if he'd been warned; and he thought of the key.

Anselm made for a quiet place beside the river – the place he'd brought Elizabeth when she'd turned up, all of a sudden, three weeks ago. A narrow flowerbed ran along a wall to an arch. Passing through, he turned right and sat on a bench of dressed stone – remnants of the medieval abbey, turned up by one of the tractors. The Lark splashed in front between the shoring of black timbers. Elizabeth had sat beside him. 'I need your help,' she'd said, quietly.

Thinking of that conversation now, Anselm recalled an earlier impromptu meeting ten years earlier – their last, in fact, before

4

he'd left the Bar. Within a month he'd be at Larkwood. He'd been at home in Finsbury Park listening to Bix Beiderbecke knock out 'Ostrich Walk' when the doorbell rang (Anselm was a fiend for all jazz prior to an indefinable but tragic moment some time in the 1950s). It was Elizabeth, clutching a box of Milk Tray.

'I don't expect you'll taste such delights in a monastery,' she said.

They sat in Anselm's small garden eating chocolates, and reminiscing, while Bix moved on to 'Goose Pimples'. They talked of the job and its strange compromise.

'We always stand on an island,' she said, 'the cold place of not knowing, and not being able to care.' Her hair fell forward: it was straight and black and cleanly cut, like a queen's in the days of pharaoh. A silver streak marbled one side. It had appeared quite recently, almost overnight. 'We never know if they're guilty, and we can't care if they're innocent. The terms are, of course, interchangeable. And yet, we *do* care; more than most. But we're marooned from our conscience.' She looked at her hands, checking the palms. 'I'm sure there's a trial out there for each of us, which could slip between the not knowing and the not caring and pull us off that beach.'

Anselm reached for the praline and Elizabeth smiled thinly.

Then and now Anselm was struck by her forcefulness, for Elizabeth, like many prosecutors, had been inclined to perceive guilt in anyone who'd been charged. It was a sort of infection, caught through excessive exposure to flimsy defences. 'You're lucky to be called away from it all,' she said, adding cheekily, 'Did you hear a voice?'

'A quiet one,' replied Anselm. 'I've had to learn how to listen.'

Her question had been a joke, but she'd become serious. 'How?'

'It sounds through your desires.'

Elizabeth thought for a while, as though examining the

5

pointing on the yard wall. 'You listen by heeding what you want to do?'

Tentatively, Anselm explained what he'd learned. 'Yes. But it's deeper than any desire. It won't let you go. And even then you need a guide who knows the ways of the heart, in case you're deceiving yourself.'

Elizabeth seemed to snatch a thread. 'Someone to help you understand a voice that won't be stilled.' It was as if she'd decided to become a nun. She knew the score already.

'Exactly.'

'And to ignore it would bring a kind of death?'

Smiling, Anselm studied the curtain of hair with its strands of silver. This was a wind-up, after all. She must have been reading a manual on the spiritual life.

Elizabeth went on, 'So you don't have a choice?'

'Not really.' This was no prank. Anselm wanted to revive the cheekiness that had fled. 'I get the impression God isn't that keen on dialogue. It comes with the territory of always knowing what's for the best.'

She took the praline from the second layer. 'Are they a strict lot, these monks?'

'Not especially . . . Well, they are . . . but about things most people wouldn't care about.'

'So you can pop out on little errands?'

'It's up to the Prior.'

'What's he like?'

Anselm thought of the various things he could say: that he didn't talk much, that he was always one step ahead of you, but he said, 'He pops your illusions.'

At the door she kissed him on the cheek and said, 'I shall miss our little chats.'

It was a truth neither of them had ever named: on a Friday

6

they'd often been the last to leave chambers. For fifteen minutes or so, they'd sit, feet on the table in the coffee room,
going over life, prodding its verrucas. But it showed up a
peculiarity in Elizabeth's personal relations. The different
aspects of her life – the Bar, the family, the Butterfly Society,
and so on – were screened off from each other like beds in a
hospital ward. As far as Anselm was aware they were never
brought together round the one table. He had only heard of
the others. It had made their chats significant while keeping
him at a distance.

Anselm went to bed uncomfortably sure that Elizabeth, like
all examining barristers, had wanted to find out something,
without letting him know what it was. And while he'd been talking, Anselm hadn't been able to dispel the notion that Elizabeth
wanted to speak herself, and that the inclination had ebbed
away. For days afterwards he thought of that silver streak in her
hair. She was, he concluded, very attractive. It was as though
he'd never noticed before.

'I need your help,' she'd said, quietly, ten years later.

Again she'd come unannounced. Anselm brought her to the
stone bench by the Lark. The long flowerbed was bright with
planted daffodils and wild poppies. She'd hardly changed.
Though she was in her late fifties, her hair remained jet black
with that dash of silver, less bright now.

'I once asked if you'd be free to do errands, do you remember?'

Anselm nodded.

She reached into her bag and pulled out a box of Milk Tray.
'You can have the praline in caramel.' Bix seemed to be with
them, blowing 'Ostrich Walk' in the distance.

Anselm said nothing. Monastic life had taught him this much
at least: to know when to be quiet.

7

With a delicate gesture, Elizabeth placed the fall of hair behind an ear. Her profile was exquisitely drawn against the pink blur of Larkwood. Looking towards the river, she began to speak. 'I've been tidying up my life. It isn't easy. But there's always something we can do, don't you think?'

'Absolutely.'

'We can't be lukewarm. That's the only way to mercy or reward.'

'Absolutely.' He'd use that one on Sunday. He waited, silent again. Elizabeth took an envelope out of her pocket, turned to him and said, 'Could you do something for me?'

'Of course.'

'It holds a key and an address.'

Anselm took the envelope.

'If I should die – it does happen – use it.' She looked around, at the river, the herb garden, the arches of the old abbey ruin. 'It opens a safety deposit box. Inside you'll find what you need to know.'

She rose and walked to the bank of the Lark. Anselm followed, keeping slightly back, puzzled by her solemnity and his new responsibility. They listened to the chattering water. It was autumn. Aelred had lined up potted plants on the other bank, as if they might like the view, but most had turned away to face the sun. Quietly Elizabeth said, 'You mentioned once that to ignore a voice would have left you bereft.' She added, with regret, 'You listened. I turned away.'

Lamely, Anselm said, 'It's never too late.' It sounded awful.

'I hope not.'

'We can salvage anything.' That was worse. He didn't even know what he meant, but it was encouraging. He tried a serious kind of joking. 'Don't be lukewarm.'

Elizabeth nodded thoughtfully, her gaze fixed on the Lark.

Lightly, she said, 'You can't always explain things to your children. If need be, will you help Nicholas understand?'

'Yes, of course.'

They walked side by side to the car park among the plum trees. The fruit was soft, ready to fall. Elizabeth quickly kissed him goodbye and rummaged for her keys to avoid his attention. Once again Anselm sensed she'd come to say something but had stepped back. After she'd driven away, he retraced his steps to collect the unopened box of chocolates.

Anselm stayed by the river brooding over these two encounters – impulsive actions, linked it appeared, despite the interval of so many years. Before he could trawl his imagination for the explanation, Larkwood's bells began to peal, calling him to vespers. Nipping through the cloister, he saw a huddle of monks in the South Walk. He paused and listened to their muted conversation. A policewoman – someone called Cartwheel – had arrived a few minutes ago and was talking to the Prior. Sylvester had been putting out leaflets on the table near the door (that was always his excuse for eavesdropping) and he'd overheard the word 'murder'. The considered view of everyone was that Sylvester had, yet again, got it wrong.

2

Nick Glendinning hid in the pantry.

The funeral had flown by but the reception seemed without end. Guests were still in the lounge and corridor, being sympathetic, asking questions about everything but his mother. A tubby executive high up in British Telecom (a client and friend of Charles, his father) was the last to tread the worn route:

9

'I understand you've been in Australia?'

'Yes.'

'Very nice. Hot?'

'Tremendously.'

The tubby executive took a sip of sherry. His eyes couldn't keep still and, as if to match, he had white curls above each ear that wouldn't lie flat. Discomfort made him shuffle. 'Did you see any kangaroos?'

'Lots of them,' replied Nick. 'And koalas – funny fat little things that cuddle you.'

'Good Lord. They live in eucalyptus trees, don't they?'

'Yes.'

'Marvellous.' He looked around, as if for help. 'It's unfortunate you didn't get back in time, given . . . what happened.'

'Yes.'

'I must say your mother was a quite re*maaark*able woman.' He'd shaken his shiny head and Nick made for the pantry.

Where he also shook his head. He'd been away about a year. He'd planned to travel since he was eleven but hadn't actually got on a plane until he was twenty-six. And he was already back, hiding in the family home in St John's Wood from people he barely knew. The endless ceremonial of accepting sympathy required patience and gratitude and he had neither. He had a headache. It had been non-stop movement across time zones: the train to Sydney, the flight to Singapore, the long haul to Manchester, the hop to London – a crazy sequence to get him home as fast as possible. When he had finally embraced his father two days ago, his body was still in Queensland. He'd come home to a fantastic absence in the heart of the familiar. Sitting on a footstool, he wondered how he could ever have been drawn away.

The first impulse to travel grew by the fireside with his father, who, on cold evenings, would read out tales of adventure, of expeditions financed by some committee dedicated to Humanity and Knowledge and Geography. This was the world of men who'd grown beards for the journey, who wore khaki and had machetes. The romance of entering the darkness had filled his boyish soul, and would not be displaced – even by education, an appreciation of colonial oppression and the advent of the aeroplane.

Perhaps it was the spirit of the great philanthropists that pushed Nick towards a career in medicine. In fact, while an undergraduate at Edinburgh, he had considered setting up (eventually) a clinic on the banks of the Amazon – a thought he kept to himself – which itself disclosed that 'ordinary life' held out few attractions for a man whose footing belonged in a canoe. Nick saw his future with Médecins Sans Frontières or at the side of Mother Theresa, and not in a high-street surgery.

The second impulse to travel came from an unexpected quarter: his dealings with his mother. As he'd grown an indefinable tension had crept between them, evident not so much through confrontation as a loss of assonance: that pliability, the willingness of children to rhyme with the lives of their parents.

As a boy Nick had rarely seen Elizabeth before nine in the evening, but she'd sit on the edge of his bed and they'd talk way past a sensible hour. They had no secrets. He would give his verdict on his teachers and she'd pass sentence – like consigning Mr Openshaw, the headmaster, to a week at Butlins with a clothes peg on his nose. This was a time of alliance against Sensible and Prudent, and the Grown-Ups. Unusually the separation didn't begin with a conflict of ideas – although that was to come – but with *his size*. It started when he began lumbering round the house and spilling things at the table because of the glut of adrenalin. As he filled out and rose above her head, she turned brittle. It was as if becoming a man had not been a foreseeable consequence of his infancy. Nick couldn't recall when it first came to pass, but she stopped coming to his room at night, and no comparable ritual took its place. It was what they both wanted, without saying so; perhaps without even knowing it. He'd lie in the dark simply aware that she was still in the Green Room, still between the papers of a brief. During breakfast he could see the courtroom looming in her face. At the weekends, she was forever tuning into conversations halfway through, getting the wrong end of the stick. As he moved towards manhood, her work expanded to meet the space created by his diminishing childhood. It was part of a symmetry that he didn't altogether like. For while he wanted to build his own life elsewhere, he didn't altogether appreciate her concurrence. The night before he went to Edinburgh, she cried: out of loss but with relief, he thought. Most of the friends he made told the same old story.

Comradeship, hangovers and exams were the landmarks of his growing independence. And from that new vantage point he began to see his mother's awkwardness as an achievement, a mighty thing, purchased by little acts of selflessness. She'd managed to let go of her son, knowing that she would drift towards the waterfall. She, too, was an adventurer, he thought. She'd made the heroic sacrifice.

Just when this adult gratitude had shaped his outlook, Nick observed with surprise that his mother was hovering over the terrain she'd abandoned. At one point, he thought she'd lost her sanity. Just after Nick had qualified, she slammed the front door and practically ran into the sitting room. 'You've never had a full medical,' she said, as if he'd been reckless since childhood.

'I'm fine.'

'I don't care.'

They had argued a great deal recently, so Nick seized the opportunity for accord. 'All right . . . send in the doctor.'

Nick had thought of blood pressure and tummy pressing from a buxom nurse. But his mother had other ideas. She wanted every organ screened. They argued some more; they bargained; and she paid. Nick had X-rays, ultrasound scanning and an ECG. Kidneys, liver and heart. When the results came back showing him to be without fault or defect, she burst into tears.

'What else did you want?' asked Nick.

'Nothing,' she sobbed, flushed and radiant. 'I only wanted this.' And they went to a restaurant as if she'd won a nasty case.

After that outburst she began to come at night and sit on the edge of his bed, but it didn't quite work. She once asked about his intentions.

'What will you do, Nick?'

'Dish out prescriptions, hold the odd trembling hand.'

'Whereabouts? I imagine London would be an attractive prospect.'

Without having said anything to his parents, Nick had already approached Médecins Sans Frontières, and various other agencies, all of which had suggested he obtain some practical experience. So Nick was thinking of a couple of years in a surgery, but not one so near to home.

'How about approaching Doctor Ferguson in Primrose Hill?' continued Elizabeth.

Primrose Hill was on the other side of the road from St John's Wood. She wanted him back home. His mother had worked out how to swim upstream, away from the waterfall, and she was determined to survive. At that moment more than any other, Nick recognised that he had to put some distance between her need and his identity.

Nick's father had observed this progression from medical-test frenzy to night-time enquiries after employment hopes with the calm attentiveness that he gave to bookplates and display cabinets. He'd been an unhappy banker for twenty-seven years until they'd got rid of him, an apparent humiliation that had set him free to study butterflies and beetles. He was a simple man who considered work a species of evil.

'Avoid it,' he said firmly.

Elizabeth had just gone to the Green Room. This was the day following the Primrose Hill proposal, and, as if on cue, Charles offered Nick the third reason why he should travel.

'See things. Make notes. Be fascinated.' He was leaning forward, whispering loudly. 'Look at that streak in your mother's hair. That's what work can do to you.'

It had appeared rapidly over two weeks when Nick was sixteen. In fact, as he subsequently learned, there was no medical explanation for the change. But Nick looked to legend if science was found wanting, and something similar had happened to Thomas More and Marie Antoinette before they were executed. He told his father.

'Precisely,' said Charles. 'There's no rush. Have you thought of Down Under?'

Nick hadn't, but he liked the idea. It stirred his soul, for the phrase conjured up the ultimate voyage. He'd be able to wear a hat with corks dangling from strings. He could legitimately have a machete in his belt. A week or so later Charles phoned an old client in Brisbane who, it transpired, had a nephew with a surgery in Rockhampton.

'Where?' asked Nick.

14

'Rocky.' Charles paused as if he were surveying millions of bleating sheep. 'That's what the locals call it.'

'Oh dear, no . . .' Elizabeth underlined a sentence in a brief. She surfaced momentarily. 'Who?'

'Not who,' said Nick, with the relief that comes before a parting. 'It's a place.'

'Where?'

'The land of Oz.'

She was stunned. She'd thought it was all talk. 'Oz,' she said, sinking.

Nick took off from Heathrow in the rain. The plane pushed through the cloud and it was just blue: a wonderful, clean, endless blue, as if he'd entered a sapphire. He caught a night coach out of Sydney, taking the front seat, and the headlights opened up the future. By morning they were cutting through oceans of high green sugar cane. For lunch he stood barefoot on the blistering tarmac drinking fresh pineapple juice. He could smell the sea. There wasn't a sheep in sight.

The nephew was called Ivan and he laboured under the misapprehension that Nick's father had bestowed all manner of financial blessings on his uncle's business – which simply wasn't possible – and so Nick received a sort of reward by proxy. For a modest amount of work, he received immodest remuneration. The world was indeed a different place when things were upside down.

Nick did a weekly stint at a school in Yeppoon where there were fat cane toads in the swimming pool. A sub-aqua club shared the facility once a week. Nick joined them and duly signed up. He bought the gear. He took a course. And he discovered yet another world, but bigger and cleaner and deeper and more mysterious than any place he'd ever known. Out of sight, countless tiny polyps had built the biggest thing on earth: a reef, a barrier, a coral kingdom.

Then the letters from his mother had started to arrive, wistful things, not signed by his father. At first they looked back to his early school days – the time she'd missed. But then her tone became inquisitive. She wanted to know when he'd be returning. For some reason he couldn't write back, so he lunged for the phone on the evening of his birthday. He 'let slip' that he'd be staying another year – something he'd thought of anyway. 'What about Papua New Guinea?' said his father. 'The Bundi do a butterfly dance.' His mother mumbled that Christmas was coming. 'The house is huge and empty without that awful music. Your trainers are still by the door, where you left them. I keep thinking of your feet.'

Then one day when he was diving off Green Island he understood. He was treading water. A queue of small brightly coloured fish was lined up before some sort of plant rising from the coral. It was like a car wash. The leaves, or whatever they were, opened up and a fish swam in. After a moment the leaves opened again, the fish left and the next one took his place. And there, at that depth, watching fish get themselves cleaned up, he realised that his mother wanted to tell him something; that she couldn't write about it; and that she hadn't mentioned it to her husband. Nick sorted out the flight.

A few days later his mother was dead in a parked car. She was sitting at the wheel, eyes closed, with a smile on her face. It was only when a pedestrian knocked on the window that anyone realised that anything was wrong. A paramedic found her mobile phone in the footwell. She must have dropped it as she tried to dial for help. Within reach, on the passenger seat, was a set of antique spoons, marked '£30'.

On the plane to Singapore Nick forced his head against the

16

window. A most awful wave of emotion racked him. He cried desperately. The woman next to him asked for his yoghurt, and he couldn't even face her to say, 'Yes'. His mother was out of reach. He'd travel now for twenty-two hours and he'd get no nearer. By the time he reached Manchester the impact of grief had been anaesthetised around a painful truth: his mother had wanted to tell him something, and he'd left it too late. In the churchyard during the burial, Nick recalled the childhood exchange that had often ended a day of revelations. She'd sit on his bed, stroking his hair:

'No secrets?' she'd whisper.

'None.'

More quietly: 'You can always tell me anything.'

He would study her in the dark with a child's careful eyes, absorbing this insight: his mother received much, but she did not give.

Why did he recognise that only now? Nick slipped out of the pantry. On entering the hall a discreet cough made him turn:

'I'm sorry, but I just don't know what to say. Dreadful business, if you ask me.'

3

Anselm kept his socks in a wig tin. It was large and dinted, a thing from his days at the Bar. His name was painted in gold upon the side. The wig itself rested upon a bust of Plato, part of the miscellany of oddments that he'd kept on becoming a monk (the remainder being his books and a jazz record collection, both of which accrued to the benefit of the community). The tin was still in service. Anselm used it daily, as he'd done in that other life.

After lunch Anselm joined the community for recreation in the common room. It was a relatively important moment because he was wearing glasses for the first time in public. He'd chosen what he thought were modest horn-rimmed frames, but the view of Bruno was that he looked a cross between a futures trader and an owl. He'd been told to wear them all the time. Colouring slightly, he put them on and picked up a newspaper.

No one noticed, perhaps because the alignment of chairs cut him out of three conversations. On his right, Wilf timidly observed that as an entertainer Liszt could reasonably be compared to Richard Clayderman, given his penchant for transcribing other people's good tunes; on his left Cyril expanded (loudly) on the double-entry ledger system; and straight ahead Bernard tried to find a word that rhymed with 'murder'.

'How about "merger"?'

'We're not a company,' said someone.

'"Herder"?'

'We're not a farm,' observed another.

'"Murmur".'

'Ah,' said Wilf, crossing over, 'that is expressly forbidden in The Rule.'

Murmuring. Grumbling from the heart. It could kill a community. Anselm hid behind the raised paper, his mind on the funeral and his wig tin. Elizabeth, he thought, would be buried by now. The key lay in an envelope covered by socks. He'd looked at it every day, until he almost didn't see it any more. Anselm had fished it out that morning knowing the funeral was underway. A brief note recorded the address of a security firm where the safety deposit box was retained. Elizabeth had chosen Sudbury, a town near Larkwood. He'd thumbed the key, pondering her courtesy. Then he'd put it back, firmly closing the lid.

4

'Dreadful business.'

Nick turned towards the voice. A short, oval man bulging out of a dreary suit scooped a fistful of cashews from a bowl and began popping them into his mouth as though they were sedatives. A grey, tangled beard crept up his cheeks to narrow, moist eyes, suggesting a sociable mole on hind legs.

'I'm Frank Wyecliffe, a lowly solicitor.'

'Very nice to meet you.'

'I instructed your mother year in, year out. Family carnage mainly.' He rummaged for a business card. It was dog-eared.

'Thank you.'

'I never knew she had a weak heart, though. Never.'

'Neither did I.'

'Really? You're a doctor, aren't you?'

'Yes.'

The mole popped some nuts, chomping quickly. 'Well, if I had known, I'd have thought twice about some of the stuff I sent her.' He paused. 'First and foremost she was a prosecutor, although she defended on some memorable occasions.' The small eyes brushed over Nick. 'I suppose you knew that?'

'No.'

'Ah.' He sniffed. 'It doesn't seem right somehow. If asked, I'd have said your mother would have died – if you'll forgive the bluntness of the term – on her feet, bringing down the wrong-doer.'

'That would have been more fitting.'

'The East End, wasn't it?'

'Yes.'

'Got family over there?'

'No.' Nick shifted uncomfortably. 'Why?'

'Sorry. Silly question. That's why I keep out of court.'

Nick backed away. 'If you'll excuse me.' The little man's intense manner seemed to have filled the hall. Nick ran upstairs as if on an errand of practical importance. At the open door to the Green Room he paused. With one hand on the jamb he surveyed the familiar chaos.

This was her study. Piles of paper lay scattered on the floor, held down by various paperweights – curious stones or chunks of wood picked up from the Island of Skomer. He saw her in outsized wellingtons, a torch in one hand . . . she cut the beam and called, 'Hurry up.' They'd stood and stared. He could still see the glow-worms and her eyes, wide with astonishment.

Downstairs a glass smashed. Nick stepped into the room, treading between heaps of transcripts and reports. As a child he'd always been picking things off her desk. Now he wanted to hold the fountain pen that had written those letters. By her chair, he stepped over a cardboard box and slipped; a hand flew out and he struck a line of small antique books on the desk – the kind you don't read, but look good. He steadied himself and swore. By his foot was a dark glossy photograph, a shot of a smashed cranium, part of an autopsy report. He knelt down to gather the books. One lay open, its pages fanned against the floor. When he picked it up, a key fell out. Engraved upon it was 'BJM Securities' and a telephone number.

For something like ten minutes Nick sat at her desk, his mind blank. He flicked through the pages of *The Following of Christ* – a tiny volume by Thomas à Kempis, printed by Keating and Brown in 1829. Nick had written all over it when he was five.

She'd never said anything, as far as he could recall; but she must have noticed, even if it was years afterwards, because a hole had been cut into the text. He put the key in his pocket and left the room slowly, like a man crossing a field.

Nick braved out the remaining hour or so, shaking hands and talking of Australian wildlife. When they'd all gone he tapped open the kitchen door and saw Roderick Kemble assaulting the cooker while crunching a mint. Good old Roddy in his red apron. He was swishing onions in a skillet. The cad had prepared for the moment no one had thought about. Nick leaned on the counter, observing his father at the table: the jacket discarded, the rolled-up sleeves. Thin, silvery hair, usually combed back, had been ruffled. The red patches on his cheeks – a harmless liver mal-function – glowed as if he'd been slapped across the face.

He began to speak, and Nick listened, thumbing the key in his pocket. For some reason he felt like an intruder.

'During the reception I nipped upstairs to the Butterfly Room. After a minute there was a knock at the door. Someone called Cartwright.'

Roddy banged the skillet with one hand and threw in some-thing pink with the other. 'She's a police inspector.' He tipped a bottle and threw in a match. The thing almost exploded, as in a pantomime when the genie turns up.

'What did she want?' asked Nick casually.

Charles searched the table, as if for crumbs. 'She asked whether Elizabeth had been troubled by anything.' He was ruf-fled and red. 'Just kindness, you know. Surprised that she's gone the distance too soon.'

Roddy banged the skillet on the cooker, as if it were a gong.

'Plates, glasses and the amenities of joy, if you please,' he said solemnly. 'Even now, at this painful time, we cannot waver.'

*

21

Nick woke in the middle of the night. He went to the bathroom
for a glass of water. The mirror was too low because he was too
big . . . that's what his mother had said . . . so he stooped to look.
Despite the sun, he hadn't gone especially brown. But his skin
was speckled and his eyebrows had turned to straw. As if that
bewildered face ought to know, he asked himself why a solicitor
had quizzed him about the East End, rather than dingos; why
an inspector had gone after a widower; and why a key, his
mother's secret, had been kept not only from her husband, but
also from him.

5

Father Andrew was fond of a saying from a Desert Father:
'Don't use wise words falsely.' Perhaps that explained why he
was always cautious when he spoke. And why it was disconcert-
ing when you sensed he was preparing to speak.

The day after the funeral, Anselm bumped into Father Andrew
crossing the cloister. The Prior paused, eyeing Anselm with an
expression somewhere between expectancy and deliberation.

'Nice day for picking the apples,' volunteered Anselm.

'What?'

Anselm repeated what he'd thought was an amiable observation.

'Eh?' The Glasgow intonation suggested a coming scuffle.

Oh no, thought Anselm. He's changing the community work
rota. The Prior always lost a screw when he was planning to
shift people from one job to another, because everyone complained. Father Andrew waited a moment and then strode off.
In a flush of horror, Anselm thought of the new dispensation:
he might face exile to the kitchen – a sort of limbo where no one

approves of you, except on feast days. But then he settled upon the obvious: that the Prior's ill temper was related to Elizabeth's death, the coming of Cartwheel and . . . an unused key. They were of a piece. And the Prior was waiting for Anselm. He had something to say. But why not call him in? Why the glowering?

Anselm decided that he'd better go to BJM Securities sooner rather than later. First, though, he had to sift through some nagging memories that had gathered around the key. Uneasily, Anselm made his way to Saint Leonard's Field and the sweet ambience of manual labour.

The trees were already peppered with monks. Crates were stacked against a trolley. Ladders and forked poles reached into the branches. There was a hum of contentment. Apple picking always did that, even when community nerves were frayed – which they had been since Cyril had started banging on about missing receipts. And Christmas was coming. That always wound the brothers up.

Anselm chose an unattended tree that was heavy with foliage. He found a wide limb, leaned back and rolled himself a cigarette. And he returned to Elizabeth's remark about 'not knowing and not being able to care'. It didn't sit easily with the vociferous defender of the adversarial system whom he'd known at the Bar.

'Look,' she had said during one of their little chats, 'it's a court of evidence, not truth. We have to forget about the truth, for truth's sake. The truth is out of reach. And we shouldn't pretend when we stand up in court that the truth is what we care about. We don't. We care about what our client *says* is the truth. I can live with that. It's the only way to take innocence seriously when all the evidence points the other way. The truth? What's that? It's something the jury decided after I sat down.'

23

No discomfort there, thought Anselm, blowing a perfect ring.

At the time, ruminating over a Jaffa cake, Anselm had baited her confidence. 'But what if someone got off because the trial took a wrong turn and no one noticed?'

'It can't happen,' she said, glancing at her watch. She was due back in court. 'All the jury hears are competing versions of the relevant facts. Have you eaten the last one?'

'Sorry.'

What quiet voice had seized her conscience? thought Anselm, picking an apple. And what could it seize upon? Every barrister accepted that justice was determined by winning and losing. If you lost, you swallowed disappointment; if you won, you got a pat on the back. As Elizabeth had said, 'what really happened' was whatever the jury decided. And if they convicted an innocent man? Unless you could fault the process or find new evidence, he'd languish in jail. And if a guilty man was freed? No one could bring him back to court. He could chant '*Nemo debet bis vexari*' (or, to be patristic, 'God doesn't judge the same offence twice'). Either way, the truth had gone like the dove off the ark.

Anselm was certain that Elizabeth's crisis had lain in this system, devised over a thousand years to deal with the corollaries of frailty and wickedness. How that was connected with tidying up her life, he hadn't the faintest idea. Having finished his cigarette, he turned his attention to the apple. Organic principles, incompetently followed, meant that most of Larkwood's fruit was technically blemished. He examined a wormhole, feeling a small hankering for the old struggle in the corridors of the Bailey.

In one of those glancing thoughts, seemingly irrelevant, Anselm recalled that he'd only ever done one case with Elizabeth. In many respects it had been an allegory for the law's uneasy accord with the truth. Forensically, it hadn't been anything special. But the client had been awful . . . Riley. That was the name. She'd called him 'a ruined instrument'. Gradually a presence materialised in Anselm's memory: a shaved head, small ears and sunken wounded eyes.

6

Nick went to the Green Room and rang BJM Securities. While waiting, he studied an open trial brief on the desk. A big man had been murdered in Bristol. 'The cranial vault comprises eight bones that surround and protect the brain.' Autopsy photographs reduced him to a one-inch bundle of close-ups.

A Mrs Tippins answered the phone. Nick explained that his mother had passed away and that he wished to collect what had been stored at the premises. She, in turn, described which documents would be required for access to the deposit box.

'Without the probate certificate,' she said, 'you can only look.'

'Fine,' he replied. 'Where are you?'

'Sudbury.' She gave the Suffolk address. After a pause, she said, 'At first I thought you were the monk.'

'A monk?'

'Yes. He's the other keyholder.'

Nick made another call to check train times and then he wrote a note for his father, saying he'd be back late. On rising he looked at the red and blue photographs. His mother had often quizzed him on the building regulations of the body – how it was put together, what would happen if you did this or that to an organ, a tissue. It was an incredibly fragile structure, despite the bones; a staggering, miraculous unity.

'The design is perfect,' he'd once said.

'Not quite.' She'd sounded disappointed.

To Elizabeth, in this chair, the body had been an exhibit, something numbered and sewn up with stitches. Her wonder had been reserved for worms that glowed.

Nick waited in a small room without windows. The only furnishings were a table and one chair. The door opened, and Mrs Tippins entered, pushing a large aluminium box on wheels. She said, 'People bring things here when their houses are full up.' Her skirt seemed to have been made from abandoned hotel tablecloths and the blouse from net curtains. 'It's hard to get rid of things, isn't it? Stay as long as you like. Here's a list of attendances.' He glanced at the single entry, made about three weeks earlier.

Left alone, Nick opened the box. Inside was a single item: a battered red case – a dainty valise for a weekend trip. A seam was split and the gold had flaked from the clasp. He put the case on the table and lifted the lid. Inside it was a ring binder, an envelope and a newspaper cutting.

Nick began with the first. It was wrapped in the characteristic red tape that he'd seen for years on his mother's desk. Typed in the centre was the case name: Regina v Riley. The left-hand corner bore an endorsement:

Coram: HHJ Venning
Prosecution: Pagett
Defence: Glendinning QC
Junior: Duffy
Not Guilty on all counts.

'Duffy' had come to his attention a few moments ago from Mrs Tippins. It was the surname of the monk who'd been entrusted with the second key. Nick had met him, long ago. 'Larkwood Priory isn't that far off, but he's never been here. I've heard that once you're in, you can't get out.' She'd grimaced like a seasoned potholer. Nick considered the name of the instructing solicitor at the bottom of the page. He'd met him at St John's Wood, chomping nuts and thinking twice: Frank Wyecliffe Esq.

Nick untied the tape and opened the binder. The front page was entitled 'Instructions to Counsel' and contained a single paragraph:

Mr Riley maintains that the witnesses, his former tenants, have fabricated a case against him following their eviction for rent arrears. No doubt counsel will be able to advise the client upon the complexion of the evidence.

Nick turned the page and skimmed the typed witness statements. Three young women had said Riley was a pimp. Scattered here and there was another name: the Pieman. The last deposition was that of David George Bradshaw, the manager of a homeless people's night shelter to whom, it seemed, the girls had turned for help. The final page was the defendant's police interview. There was only one reply, 'I'm clean.' Something in Nick's concentration failed and he tied up the brief. It was difficult this: doing what she had done, in the same way.

He picked up the cutting. It was taken from a south London daily newspaper. The paper was dirty and the ink smudged. A coroner's court had returned a verdict of accidental death regarding John Bradshaw, seventeen, whose body had been recovered from the Thames. The report quoted the anger and grief of his father, George – evidently the witness in the earlier trial, even though he went by his middle name. Nick cross-checked the date of the inquest with that of the trial: an interval of five years had elapsed.

Nick turned to the envelope. It was addressed to both his mother and Anselm Duffy. The letter inside was from Emily Bradshaw, the mother of John and the wife of George. It condemned Riley's defenders and blamed them for the destruction of her family. Again Nick checked the date, and then he quickly put everything back in the red case. After a moment's calm he pencilled a chronology to make clear the sequence of events:

End of trial.
Death of J Bradshaw (as per cutting): 5 years after the trial.
Letter from Mrs Bradshaw: 8 years after trial.
Opening of account with BJM: 10 years after trial.

Nick wheeled the aluminium box back to Mrs Tippins. Her look of permanent curiosity prompted him to remark, 'Just some old papers.'

'It's funny what people hang on to, isn't it?'

'Yes.'

She opened a desk register for his signature and then changed her mind. 'Oh, probate's on the way . . . go on, take them. The monk won't be coming, will he? I mean, he's all but locked up, I shouldn't wonder.'

On the train back to London Nick gazed at the evening fields, his mind focused on a small puzzle: how did Elizabeth obtain a cutting from a local newspaper far from where she lived and worked? She was a woman of meticulously clean habits, and yet the paper was dirty and ragged. The only sensible conclusion was that someone had given it to her; and the most likely candidate was either Mr or Mrs Bradshaw. It was unlikely to have been the latter because the

28

cutting didn't fit the the envelope, and in any event, the letter itself was in pristine condition, so that left David George Bradshaw. But how could Elizabeth have met him? She had been defence counsel, representing Riley. They'd been on opposing sides. How could they meet without one or the other, in effect, crossing over? And given that Elizabeth was the one with the suitcase, she was the likely traveller, so to speak. That being so, there was a further curiosity: why would Mr Bradshaw give such a cutting to Elizabeth? Not only did that imply a binding of his mother to the tragic event, it revealed an intimacy that could not have prevailed at the time of the trial: for if Elizabeth had already known Mr Bradshaw, she would have had to withdraw from the case. And, since she didn't, the implication was that Elizabeth had sought him out afterwards, perhaps prompted by the letter from his wife.

So, thought Nick, watching homely lights spread across the fields, you made a friend of your opponent, you stored what you found in secret, and you gave the key to a monk. He felt acutely awake, though tired. He forced his mind to plod on one or two steps and, like a reward, he came to the real mystery. He gazed ahead, as if he'd stumbled on the source of the Nile: Elizabeth had started this collection at the conclusion of the trial, when she could not have anticipated the death of John Bradshaw, or the letter from his mother. Why, then, had she kept the trial papers in the first place?

At Liverpool Street Nick took the Underground to St John's Wood, musing upon a chain of intuitions: there was a link between the evolution of Elizabeth's secret and her desire to keep Nick close to home; at the same time, Nick's father had been urging him to visit Australia. Did he know of his wife's subterfuge? Nick had little doubt: he did not. His father was guileless. His unthinking candour had compromised numerous commercial transactions spanning several continents – the last of which had led to his enforced retirement. He could not be relied upon – least of all with the truth. It made another question all the starker: how might anything be so important to Elizabeth that she could not share it with the man she trusted most?

Once home he walked straight to the Butterfly Room determined to confirm his father's exclusion from the meaning of the key. Charles looked up from an armchair as if he'd seen a well-loved moth. He had an empty glass in his hand.

'Where've you been?' His face was flushed and he was tipsy.

'I just went walkabout.'

'Me too.'

'Whereabouts?' Nick noticed the bow tie, a remnant from his father's banking days. He'd worn a bowler hat to work. His suits had been cut from heavy cloth that made him perspire. But he'd looked the real shilling – as if he were hot with responsibility.

'Regent's Park. And you?'

'Sudbury.'

'Where?'

'Suffolk.'

'Good God.'

Nick studied his father's wounded face. The dear man knew nothing. What had he thought about in Regent's Park? It was easy to surmise: his wife's evasiveness and stealth, which, of late, he had noticed; the manner of her going; and consolation from a police officer whom he did not know. He was bewildered and Nick could not help him – because he held the key. It gave him knowledge, but of a kind he couldn't share.

Nick woke and listened to the rubbish truck and the antics of the binmen. He swung his legs out of bed and reached for his mobile. After considerable hesitation, he rang a monastery.

30

7

Blind George, as he was known, woke up on a traffic island. He was lying on a bench. Marble Arch towered huge and white behind a litter bin. A flag fluttered, its line slapping against the pole. Above, the sky was misty blue. An aeroplane crossed in silence, like an ant on lino. George sat up, with a groan, and opened his notebook. A thumb with a cracked black nail smoothed back the pages. He read out loud:

I am going to Mile End Park to confront Riley.
Wait beneath the fire escape in Trespass Place.
The explanation for Inspector Cartwright is in your left inside jacket pocket.
There's fifty pounds in your right trouser pocket.
Elizabeth.

For years George had kept a record of days gone. Nino, a former traffic warden, had insisted upon the practice. It had been part of his instruction when teaching George about life on the street. Since leaving the world of parking tickets, Nino had moved around the libraries of London, still clutching a floppy pad. He had his own chair in most of the reading rooms. One of them had his name on it – stuck on with tape by the management. He had a habit that drove them to distraction, and kept him on the move: in one place he'd put in a request for a book that was held in another. So all these books were flying about London after Nino, when all he had to do was keep still.

'Don't think,' he'd said. 'Just write, starting at the beginning, and keep going. You'll only understand the story looking backwards. If you start thinking, you'll write the story you want, not the story you've got.'

'Oh.'

'The street is the place of stories,' he'd concluded gravely. Black, tangled hair covered his face and his skin was grey. 'Stories of harm and stories that heal.'

George had obeyed, because traffic wardens have a peculiar authority. When one notebook was full he'd start another. They were numbered on the cover. He had thirty-eight of them. George's whole life was laid out in order, all sixty-four years, as best as he could remember them. Almost every day he'd sat on a park bench or in a café, and he'd scribbled with haste, not pausing to choose his words. Once he'd got something down, he was like an archaeologist with a toothbrush: he gently brushed away the dirt; he'd change a word or phrase, cleaning up what had been saved. It could take months to get it right.

George's earliest memory was of an outing in a pushchair. He was sitting behind an improvised cover to keep out the rain. His mother had made it. There was a polythene window sewn into a sort of waxed cotton tent that covered his upper body. His protruding legs were warm, covered by a blanket; but he couldn't see anything because of the condensation. He could hear only the rain and his mother's feet on the path. They were on their way to see Granddad, whose first name he bore. David. He'd stopped using it a long time ago, out of shame. He'd become George. That burst of anguish took up the first pages of book one, which now lay with all the others in a plastic bag. All them had been filled with a similar, honest desperation: to preserve both the good and the bad. That was something else Nino had said: 'Don't decide what to keep. It all counts. Sometimes it is the worst things that turn out to have delivered what is best.' He'd been solemn again. 'It only appears when you write it down.'

Filling up these notebooks had a dramatic effect on George. It made him a compassionate observer – not just of himself, but of everyone he'd known. But the scribbling had also made him uneasy about the spoken word, because he'd gone through hell choosing the right ones to keep on paper. Ultimately, the precision had brought him close up to his more recent failures, but without the distortion of self-pity. And then, clear-eyed and calm, he'd scrambled into a skip.

He'd seen two black discs among the wood and bricks: a pair of welding goggles. Instinctively he put them on and pretended to be blind. On the face of it he'd gone mad. But it made sense to George. There were things in his life he could not look upon, and he didn't want anyone else to either. The street might be the place of stories, but his was going to remain untold. Once the goggles were in place, hardly anyone spoke to him any more. It was as though he wasn't there. They called him Blind George.

So at first George wrote down his life in order to understand it; but the time came when he did so to keep it together. Long after Elizabeth had found him, and when their project to trap Riley was well underway, George got his head kicked in. His memory was sent flying over Waterloo Station like a cloud of pigeons. The details, with Elizabeth's help, were set down towards the end of book thirty-six. That was after he'd woken to discover that a kind of lake had entered his mind: on the far shore everything was clear, up to the week he'd fallen under those swinging feet; but on this side, where he played out his life, events were like globules of oil. If he didn't confine them on paper, they could separate, drift off and come back when they felt like it – heavily familiar but incomprehensible. He could hold on to faces, geography and snippets of talk, but he'd found himself in a world where everyone else knew all the missing pieces. People would speak, expecting him to understand. And sometimes he did, but often it was a lottery in which he could make no choices. But it was the keeping of the notebooks that saved him and held everything together. Every page helped to bridge the lake. He just carried on plotting the course of each completed day.

Elizabeth had written a great deal in books thirty-six to thirty-eight. She'd recorded everything they'd said and done after his mind went loose. He'd watched her while drinking hot chocolate or whisky. She'd always been careful. She'd treated words like coins. And in her last entry she'd told him to wait.

After Elizabeth had gone to Mile End Park in the morning, George had sat in his sleeping bag beneath the fire escape at Trespass Place. He'd waited until nightfall, counting the hours, his eyes on the arch at the end of the courtyard. But she hadn't come. Then, like a bubble popping at the surface of his mind, he'd heard something she'd said more than once: 'George, if anything should happen to me, don't worry. A monk will come.'

'A what?' he'd said, the first time.

'An old friend. He's forever puzzled, but he gets there in the end.'

George had read his notebook again. She'd written 'Wait . . .' not 'Wait for me.'

The next morning, George looked to the arch, hoping to see a different shape, perhaps someone fat with a white rope around his waist. He watched and waited, through the day and through the night. But when another morning broke, George rose and hurried through the streets. He crossed the river and crept like a thief into Gray's Inn Square.

George stood outside Elizabeth's chambers reading the list of gold names on a long black panel. Men and women slipped past him, flushed and serious. He became paralysed by the grandeur of it all. Then through the glass of a door he saw a round man with an orange waistcoat. The eyebrows rode high above piercing, kind eyes. He stepped outside.

'I'm Roddy Kemble, who are you?'

George panicked. 'Bradshaw, sir.'

Mr Kemble thought for a moment. He didn't move, but he looked like a man rooting through a cardboard box, lifting this, lifting that. Abruptly, he said, 'May I ask your first name?'

'George.'

The man's arms fell by his side. He seemed to have found what he expected and didn't want. Quietly, he said, 'Elizabeth is dead.'

George adjusted his goggles. His mouth went dry and he nodded appreciatively.

'In any other circumstances,' said Mr Kemble, 'I'd offer you a cigarette. But I've given up. Would you like a Polo?'

George nodded again.

Mr Kemble peeled back the silver paper. 'Her heart gave out.'

For a while they stood awkwardly crunching mints, then Mr Kemble said, 'Have you seen Elizabeth since the trial?'

'Yes, sir.'

'Frequently?'

'Yes, sir.'

Mr Kemble looked like a man whose house had just been burgled. He put a heavy hand on his shoulder and said, 'It's time to forget everything, George. Move on, if you can.'

'I stopped going anywhere a long time ago, sir.'

George backed away clumsily. Mr Kemble raised an arm, as if he were giving a blessing or launching a ship. If it weren't for the orange waistcoat, George would have thought he looked sad.

George stumbled up High Holborn and then found his way to Oxford Street, bumping into people and things, until he reached the roundabout and Marble Arch – where he'd last seen Nino, months back, in the summer. They'd sat on a bench and his guide had told him a strange story about right and wrong. George went to the same bench, looking hungrily at the monument, wanting his friend to emerge from beneath one of the portals, his blue and red scarf trailing in the wind. Sleep crept upon him. He woke and saw the arch, the flag and the ant crawling across the sky, and he reached for book thirty-eight.

George left the traffic island and began the long walk to Trespass Place. He thought of Elizabeth, whisky in hand. She'd foreseen her dying and had prepared for it. George had to wait because a monk would come. Another of her phrases floated by; it filled him with hope: 'No matter what happens, Riley can't escape.'

George made haste, and he beckoned Nino's story about right and wrong, but it wouldn't come. All he could recall was the end, because Nino had spoken it with such force. His gaze had been wide as if he were waiting for eye-drops. 'Don't be lukewarm, old friend. That's the only way to mercy or reward.'

When he'd told Elizabeth, she'd scribbled it down on the back of an envelope.

Beneath the fire escape George picked up a sharp stone. On the wall he scratched a few neat lines, one for each of the days he'd been waiting. By extension it was another lesson from Nino: to diligently keep an account of anything that might easily slip away.

8

Perhaps Anselm's sensibilities had been over-roused, but he could have sworn that the woman at BJM Securities viewed him with both fascination and terror.

'You've never come before,' said Mrs Tippins, as if he'd let her down.

'I'm sorry, was I expected?'

'No.'

Anselm couldn't imagine the foundation for reproof. 'Well, I'm here now.'

'I can see that, but you're too late.'

Mrs Tippins explained that the son of the deceased had taken possession of a small red valise.

'That's fine,' said Anselm. He was convinced it was nothing of the sort; that this was not what Elizabeth had wanted. 'I'll just go back home.'

Mrs Tippins seemed uncomfortable, as if the static of her clothing was giving her tiny shocks. She opened the door for Anselm and then seemed to leap at an opportunity. 'Do you mind if I ask . . . but are you allowed out?'

'Every ten years.'

'Never. How long for?'

'Ten minutes.'

'Honestly? You better be making tracks, then.'

'I'm joking.'

Mrs Tippins narrowed her eyes, reluctant to abandon deep-rooted convictions.

Anselm berated himself all the way back to Larkwood. Nicholas Glendinning had opened the box while Anselm had been hiding in an apple tree. It would have appealed to the author of Genesis: Nicholas now knew what he was not meant to know.

Mothers, sons and secrets, he thought. They were an unhappy combination but often found together. As if nudged, Anselm recalled the death of Zélie, his own mother, and the secret he carried. Oddly enough, the circumstances had captivated Elizabeth when he'd told her shortly after joining chambers. That was almost twenty years ago.

They were sitting in the common room on a Friday night. The wind kept triggering a car alarm that seemed to pause when sworn at from a nearby window.

'She'd been in hospital for an operation,' said Anselm. 'Before she was discharged, my father called us all together. He said that she wouldn't be getting better and that we weren't to tell her. I was nine. A few days later she came home. I took her a cup of tea, and she said, "I'll be up and about before you know it," and I replied, "No you won't. You're going to die."'

'Did you tell the others that you'd broken rank?'

'No. They would have seen it as a betrayal.'

'Betrayal?' Elizabeth repeated, as if she were talking to an invisible third party.

'Yes, but from that moment my mother and I were free. We could grieve while she was still alive. We could face what was coming in the absence of lies. I hadn't even realised that obeying my father would have left us trapped.'

'Trapped,' echoed Elizabeth again.

She was talking to an imagined presence, but Anselm hardly noticed because turning over the stone had uncovered forgotten emotion. His eyes prickled and he couldn't speak without his breath staggering. 'Don't get me wrong . . . this is no fairy story about life winning out. Shortly before the end, she said, "I can hear the sounds of a playground." A kid was kicking a ball against our fence. She was drifting off to sleep. But she let slip a confession. "It's been a school for death and I've hardly learnt anything."'

Elizabeth had been spellbound.

Anselm parked beneath the plum trees and wiped his eyes, astonished by the power and freshness of remembered grief. The siren faded, along with the protestations from an upstairs window. Presently, Larkwood's bells found their strike and birds scattered over the valley.

While the loss of his mother remained painful to Anselm, it had opened his child's heart to a very adult truth: what you would cling on to will pass away, like grass. Several times Elizabeth had returned to this subject with a sort of fugitive hunger, but only abstractly, and when they were alone. They'd spoken of honesty between parents and children, of loving by letting go, of this day's importance. Half the time, Anselm was lost in the forest of ideas, but it seemed to help Elizabeth. He sensed she wanted a distant companion while she made a very private passage. She'd always been one for conceptual clarity.

Anselm had recovered by the time he reached the cloister. He always saw things clearly after he'd cried. And he was now convinced that it was back then, on a Friday night, that Elizabeth had decided, one day, to seek his help – long before the 'not knowing and the not being able to care' had become an accusation.

9

Elizabeth had found George before he got his head kicked in. He still didn't know how she'd traced him, though he had his suspicions. The only person who knew about Trespass Place was

Nino. And everyone near the Embankment knew Nino. So George had pictured Elizabeth beneath the bridges, tapping arms, lifting blankets, seeking the whereabouts of a man named Bradshaw. She must have been sent Nino's way; and she must have told him a great deal to make him reveal where George had gone to ground.

A pinprick of light had jigged in the distance, exposing the cobbles like scabs in the asphalt. It grew larger, making her outline darker than the darkness. She lowered the torch and he saw gold buckles on expensive shoes. The beam was cut and she said, 'You walked out of court, George.'

He replied to the shadow. 'Yes, and I let Riley go.'

'We both did.'

Elizabeth sat down on the cardboard beside him. They looked out on the courtyard, the drainpipes and the bins. She produced a flask of whisky and two silver beakers. It started to rain. The drops pattered on the fire escape landing. They didn't speak; they just sipped the warming malt.

She came frequently after that, always in the evening. They fell to talking of old times. George told her what he'd done before the trial: baggage boy at the Bonnington, then one of a team in a night shelter for the homeless, and finally becoming its manager. He'd lost that job for gross misconduct after Riley was acquitted. Elizabeth's story couldn't have been more different: boarding school, Durham University and Gray's Inn. After the trial she was made a deputy High Court judge. Her life had gone up, his had gone down. She too had married; they'd both had a son. Hers was called Nicholas; he was planning a trip to Australia.

'What for?'

'To get away from me.' She laughed. 'He's grown too quickly.' Distantly, she added, 'He's the very image of my father.'

Elizabeth never urged George to find a hostel; she never asked about the home he'd left behind, and the wife who couldn't face him any more. She seemed to understand that sometimes there was no going back; or at least, not until one's connections with the past had been changed. They just sat side by side beneath the fire escape sometimes chatting, sometimes silent. Then she'd go home.

One night she turned up with her work. It brought the ambience of the Old Bailey into this, his hideaway. While she read, marking the page and swearing, he was sure she was ahead of him, waiting. Tension made him fidget. She asked him to keep still. Suddenly he blurted out, 'It couldn't have been any different.'

'I know.' She carried on reading.

'Not after I was asked about my grandfather . . . the dropping of my first name.'

'I know.'

'I never saw that coming.'

'No one did.' She put her files and coloured pens in a bag and pulled out the whisky and the beakers. After they'd drunk several shots, she spoke of John's fall on Lawton's Wharf. The subject had hung in the air while she'd spoken of her own son. George opened out a newspaper cutting of the inquest and gave it to Elizabeth.

'How did Riley do it?'

George couldn't answer because – in truth – it was his fault. He'd sent his son to his death with an aside uttered during *Countdown*. He saw the smiling presenters; and he saw his boy, fearful, stooping through a hole in the wire. He was only seventeen.

'I suppose there's no evidence.'

'None.'

She turned, drawing the fall of hair behind an ear. A diamond sparkled on the lobe. 'I'm implicated in what happened, George.'

41

'No you're not.'

'I let Riley escape far more than you did.' It didn't sound condescending, just private and adamant.

'You can keep the cutting.' It was all he could do to reach her. She had almost left the planet.

When Elizabeth next came to Trespass Place she said her back couldn't take it any more. She was very specific. The problem was degenerative changes at L5 and L6. 'There's a café round the corner.'

They found a table in Marco's by the window. Then Elizabeth went to the counter without having asked him what he wanted. When she came back, he paled. She'd bought hot chocolate and toast. She'd done it on purpose. She'd remembered.

Three girls had given evidence against Riley. It had taken guts, because they'd been terrified of the Pieman. But George had persuaded them to come forward. It had taken three attempts. And he'd done it over toast and cocoa. They'd said so in their witness statements.

'Eat up,' she said gravely.

George looked at the plate and mug in horror.

'Go on,' she repeated. 'Take a sip.'

When he started eating, she said, 'Have you ever wondered how evil can be undone?'

He nodded.

'Me too.'

And that was it. George waited for the follow-up, but they just sat and ate toast and drank hot chocolate.

Elizabeth came back about two weeks later. She stood beneath the arch into Trespass Place and waved. George got up and

42

followed her to Marco's. By the same window they ate more toast and drank more hot chocolate.

Elizabeth said, 'Do you remember Mrs Riley?'

'Yes.'

'Nancy is her name. She listened to the prosecution opening and then left the court, rather like you.'

George remembered the hat – yellow with black spots – pulled down as if it were a steel helmet.

Elizabeth explained that Riley's solicitor, Mr Wyecliffe, was a highly intelligent man. She had asked him to interview Nancy with a view to obtaining a witness statement upon Riley's good character. The difficulty was that no one knew what Nancy might say under cross-examination. Ultimately, it was agreed that Nancy would not go into the witness box: she would only reveal Riley's anger towards women.

George said, 'She's crackers.'

'She trusts him, that's all,' said Elizabeth reprovingly. 'Maybe she sees a trace of something, a remnant of what's been lost.'

Neither of them spoke for a while.

'When I first saw you under that fire escape,' mused Elizabeth innocently, 'I didn't recognise you.'

'I've been sleeping rough for years. It changes you.'

'Even in daylight you looked different,' she continued. 'Something's gone, something you can't catch and put in your notebook. Riley wouldn't recognise you either, if you bumped into him.'

George looked up quickly.

'He's still a criminal, as he always was,' she said, collecting toast crumbs with a manicured finger. 'Nancy is the way to proving it. Maybe we can all make amends. How does that sound to you?'

When Elizabeth had gone, George went back to Trespass

43

Place and wrote it all down in book thirty-five. There'd be one more volume before he got his head kicked in.

George sat beneath the fire escape, his goggles in his hair, reading his account of that meeting. It was the beginning of a calculated scheme – although Elizabeth's plans were already formed. They just required his cooperation. From the moment he'd written down her invitation it was as though every ill that had come to pass since the trial might all be transformed by a greater conclusion. Elizabeth had said, 'If we get the ending right, we'll change everything, right back to the beginning. It's almost magic. A monk told me.'

The monk who hadn't turned up, thought George, looking towards the arch at the end of the courtyard. He hadn't slept for days now. Giddily, he counted the scratches on the wall. Then he hauled himself upright, positioned his goggles and tramped into the sunshine. His shoes were split and the laces frayed. They fell off as he walked. On Old Paradise Street, he slumped forward onto the pavement, one leg in the gutter. He heard the tread of feet: frantic high heels, the measured clip of some army type, the squelch of trainers. Some slowed, some stopped, some spoke; but the river of feet moved on, drawn towards a sea of pressing obligations.

Among the flowing George heard the steps of someone familiar, a dawdling coming close . . . a pat-patting of small red sandals. He was dreaming. The ankles came into view: white skin upon fine bones; blue veins summoned by a wind that lifted off the waves. The boy's copper hair danced. George lifted a hand off the pavement, reaching out, and said, 'Oh, John.'

The waking dream unfolded. It was like watching a family video.

*

George took his son by the hand on Southport Pier. It was a blustery day, with gulls thrown around as though attached to the railings by string. Occasionally they dropped like stones, but landed lightly on discarded crusts of bread. George found a bench, and John clambered beside him, banging one of his knees.

'What's for lunch, Dad?'

George pulled a tin from the plastic bag prepared by Emily. 'Salmon.'

'That's a treat, Dad.'

'You're right there, son.'

They sat side by side, watched by the passers-by. George kicked his shoes off and wiggled his toes. John pedalled the air.

The cold sun tilted towards the west. George checked his watch: it was time to get back to the hotel. Emily was waiting. 'Come on, lad,' he said despondently. He didn't want these moments of happiness to end.

John refused to budge.

'We have to go.'

John leaned away, arms entwining round part of the bench.

George pulled him free and roughed his hair. The boy stomped ahead, along the silver timbers. His voice flew on the wind, 'I like Southport, Dad.'

'We'll come again, son.'

Blind George rolled over onto his back and said, 'But we didn't, did we?'

A passer-by knelt down and placed his hand under George's head. It was a young man. His hair was gelled and spiked like a sea urchin. He wore a T-shirt with WINGS written on it. 'Are you all right?'

'Yes, thanks.'

'You've no shoes.'

45

'I must have left them at Southport.'

The young man sat down and took off his trainers. 'Put these on.'

George couldn't speak or protest. He just watched this prickly helper struggle to fit the shoes onto his feet. They were white with bright red stripes. Seconds later the figure walked briskly away, as if he were embarrassed. Written across the back of his T-shirt were the words: WORLD TOUR.

I wonder where he's off to now, thought George. He jogged back to Trespass Place – with sporty things like that on each hoof, he'd have looked stupid walking.

10

Nick drove to Larkwood Priory in his mother's lemon-yellow VW Beetle. Her red valise lay on the passenger seat. By late afternoon, after several wrong turns, he came upon a line of oak trees straggling towards a set of colossal gates. They were jammed open. Above an incline topped by rhododendrons he saw a spire and patchwork tiles.

The reception desk was unoccupied, although a phone was off the hook. A tinny voice came out of it yelling, 'Hello?' Nick peeked down a corridor but jumped when a hand touched his shoulder.

'Were you ever in the scouts?'

The monk was ageless and aged, dressed in a black habit and a white scapular. A length of frayed plastic twine was tied with a bow round a thin waist. His cranium, while angular, seemed soft as sponge, with a haze of shaved white fluff.

'I was a Sixer,' said Nick proudly.

'When I was a lad,' said the monk, hooking his thumbs onto the belt, 'Baden-Powell told me a secret about the relief of Mafeking.'

'Really?'

The telephone shouted, 'Hello?'

The monk looked at the receiver as if it were an unusual fruit and put it back on the console. 'The Boers were at the gates, armed to the teeth—'

A gentle cough robbed Nick of the disclosure. 'Thank you, Sylvester.'

Father Anselm led Nick outdoors. The monk seemed much younger than the barrister he remembered. As with Baden-Powell's confidant, a life of denial appeared to have disarranged the normal ageing process. He was probably in his forties. They'd met a few times in the corridors of his mother's chambers. A slight hesitation in his gait made him look shy and boyish, as if he were on his way to the podium to pick up the diligence prize after all the clever children had returned to their seats. Short, ruffled hair and round glasses magnified a look of permanent surprise. His black habit was frayed; the white scapular flapped like a long serviette.

'My mother kept a secret,' said Nick. They faced each other across a table in a herb garden. He placed his mother's case between them. 'She wanted to reveal it to me. When I turned to listen it was too late.'

The monk took off his glasses like some patients remove their trousers. He seemed strangely vulnerable.

'By chance,' said Nick, 'I found a key hidden in this book.'

He passed over *The Following of Christ*. 'I'm afraid the scrawl is mine. Biro practice when I was five or so.'

Father Anselm opened the cover and looked intently at the open space. Apparently deep in thought, he closed the book and opened it again, looking at where the key had been kept. Then he turned to the front and read out the dedication:

47

'To Elizabeth, from Sister Dorothy DC hoping that this small and great book will always be a friend to her.'

'Do you know her?' asked Nick. His mother's faith had not been a shared field. It was more of a parallel continent with strict border controls, imposed by both sides.

The monk shook his head.

'I think that whatever my mother wanted to say is tied up with this case. So I opened it, and I'm none the wiser.'

'I'm not surprised,' replied Father Anselm. One arm rested on the table, reaching towards his guest. 'When your mother gave me the other key, she asked me to help you understand what she wasn't able to explain.'

Nick felt a surge of relief. He waited for the account that would make sense of the secrecy and the planning. But the monk just kept smiling benignly. Then Nick realised that he was waiting for the case. Surprised, Nick said, 'Don't you know what's in here?'

'Not at all.'

'She just gave you a key?'

'Precisely,' said Father Anselm, quietly sagacious. Nick had cultivated a similar manner to assure the terminally ill. He pushed the case across the table. Father Anselm placed the contents in an orderly line and then frowned. 'Riley,' he muttered with distaste. Then he started with the ring binder. Without his glasses, he seemed to be wincing. Slowly, he turned the pages. At one point he said, 'Cartwright . . . not Cartwheel.' Then, with a shrug, he read the newspaper cutting, glancing at the trial brief, making the connection. Finally, he opened the letter, saying, 'I've never seen this before.' Leaning his head back, he read out loud:

Dear Mrs Glendinning QC and Mr Duffy,
I thought that if I ever began writing to either of you, I

might never stop. There's no beginning or end to what I want to say. But then I thought, why don't I just tell you what happened when the trial was over, when we went home and you went to a restaurant?

We lost our son. My husband fell to pieces. For what it is worth, along the way I lost myself.

Mr Duffy asked, 'What did David do that George wanted to forget.' I suppose you thought that was very clever. He had no right to ask that, no right at all. Don't think that wearing a wig means you had nothing to do with what went wrong. You're mistaken.

I don't know what type of conscience you must have that lets you walk out of doors. How can you sleep at night having stood up for a man like Riley?

Yours sincerely,
Mrs Emily Bradshaw

Father Anselm placed everything back in the case.

'Well?' asked Nick

Father Anselm put his glasses back on and said apologetically, 'I haven't the faintest idea what your mother wanted me to say.'

'Then why did she give you a key?'

'I assume because I was involved in the case.'

'But why hide it from me and my father?'

'I don't know.' Father Anselm tapped the lid of the case, perplexed but silent. Another monk passed through the gate carrying a wicker basket. He waded into the tangle of herbs and began cutting leaves with a pair of scissors.

'Herbal remedies,' said Father Anselm weakly. 'I'm not sure they work.'

'Who was Riley?'

'He was a docker.' He snatched at random details as if they

were flies. 'He was a crane operator. A docker. An alleged pimp. Three witnesses said he worked for the Pieman.'

'Who was he?'

'Just a name in the papers.'

Nick glanced towards the other monk, who was humming and snipping. A confusion of scents drifted over them. 'Father, what was so special about this trial?'

'Nothing.' He frowned, showing that this was his own question. The monk smuggled each arm into the sleeve of the other until he made a sort of sling across his chest. He looked away, towards a wilderness of healing plants. 'The only memorable aspect of the trial was how it ended.' He fell silent.

'What happened?' prompted Nick.

'I cross-examined the main witness, a man called Bradshaw. He used his second name, George, rather than David, which was his first. In a rather elaborate way, I asked him why, and the case collapsed.'

'How?'

'He just walked out of the court.'

'Because you asked him about his name?'

Father Anselm nudged his glasses. 'It looked like he was refusing to answer for his past. David's past, if you like.'

'What was it?'

'I don't know.'

'Then why did you ask?'

'I couldn't think of anything better.' As though he'd won an unwanted prize, he added, 'It's what's called a good performance.'

Father Anselm's attention shifted to the quiet work of his brother monk. The herb garden was extraordinarily still. It seemed to give emphasis to speech, as if the land and its many plants were listening.

*

Nick left the case on the table and followed Father Anselm to a path of mulch between a stream and an ancient abbey wall. At precise intervals slender pillars climbed from the stone, but most had been smashed at head height. By a pile of black railway sleepers, the monk halted. The creosote was sharp like smelling salts. He breathed deeply and exhaled. 'Something is missing,' he pronounced.

'Like what?'

'Instructions.'

'If that were the case,' replied Nick, 'she'd have given you a letter and not a key.'

'And that,' replied the monk, 'is a rather good point.' His eyes blinked at a mark on the ground, as if Andre Agassi had walloped something from behind an arch.

Nick felt sorry for this puzzled man with tousled hair and flashing glasses. His life among the ruins appeared to have blunted what was once a sharp mind – how else did you win a case by quizzing a witness on nothing more than his choice of name? That was impressive. But now, he felt sure, he needed a little help. Nick said, 'Father, it's a strange story. Of all the trials my mother ever conducted, she kept this one. It just so happens that five years later the son of a witness drowns. My mother finds the grieving father, and it seems they both connect the death to the trial, apparently not accepting the coroner's verdict. Two questions follow: did they suspect foul play? And what did they do next? But I've another: why keep the papers of this particular case? What was so special about Mr Riley?'

Father Anselm's head was angled. Perhaps he looked like that when he listened to sins, or whatever people usually told him. The monk discreetly produced a packet and began to roll a cigarette. He removed a shred of tobacco from his mouth and said, 'She told me she'd been tidying up her life.'

The match sputtered like a damp flare.

They retraced their steps past the great wall with the shattered columns.

'Father, when I was diving on the Barrier Reef,' said Nick, 'I watched fish getting washed by a plant. It was wonderful. They lined up and took it in turns. Somehow, they just knew what to do. There was no need for any instructions.' He looked aside at the troubled monk. 'Maybe my mother thought you were in the same queue, that you'd understand without thinking. Don't worry if you can't help in the way she wanted.'

When they reached the table in the herb garden Father Anselm picked up the case; from there they walked to the car park where the yellow Beetle seemed to quiver against the purple canopy of plum trees. Fruit lay splattered on the windscreen.

'A mad Gilbertine idea,' said Father Anselm awkwardly. 'We forgot that fruit falls when it's ripe.' It sounded like a warning. He asked for time to understand the contents of the case and for Nick's telephone number; and he concluded, 'Don't turn over old stones. Let them lie where they were placed.'

Nick drove down the lane of loitering oak trees, away from Larkwood and the smell of aromatic plants. And as he did so, he reflected, painfully, that he'd never been able to share his mother's deep faith. He leaned more towards his father, who, while adherent, was passive, his true fervour lying in the open fields. When cross, Elizabeth had called him a heretic; in better tempers, she settled for pantheist. Nick had grown up beneath the quirky arch formed where these two types of belief met. He eventually crept away, not quite making sense of the open sky. At university he saw the chaplains and the students, half resenting the consequences of his own choice (if that is what it was), for he would have liked to belong. He eventually found a working credo in science – the purity of facts and verification. His mother had quietly grieved. They'd argued – hopelessly, because he didn't ask her questions, and she didn't want his answers. He could follow loose talk about God, but not to the point where all that type of thing *mattered* – at the meshing of life and ideas.

Shortly before Nick had gone down under, she'd said, 'We should settle on beliefs that are worth the hazards of the race.'

Mildly irritated, because they were watching *Ben Hur* and it was the exciting bit when the chariots were crashing into each other, Nick said, 'Would you fight for yours?'

'I really don't know.' She spoke as if the crowds were waiting, but this was St John's Wood not the Colosseum.

Thinking now of his mother on the edge of the sofa, eyes glued to the screen and worried, Nick decided to ignore the parting advice of a monk. He pulled into a lay-by and fished out Mr Wyecliffe's business card. It was stained with oil from the cashew nuts. He dialled the number on his mobile. The solicitor's surprise was forced and his charm predatory, as if he smelled business. An appointment was made for the next day and Nick resumed the journey home, wondering about the relief of Mafeking.

11

It was odd, but George could remember in his sleep. Sometimes his dreams were like the old films shown at Christmas. He watched with recognition. So when George was slipping away, he would try to switch on what was lost to him while awake. Most of the time it worked. But when he snapped upright it was with the horrible fear that he'd made it all up.

With the sharp stone, George scratched another day of waiting upon the wall. It was early evening. Sheets of polythene wrapping flapped in the corner. He turned on his pocket radio and Sandie Shaw sang 'Puppet on a String'. He became drowsy, drugged by the waiting and the cold. Elizabeth's voice rose in his memory. They'd often sat in Marco's listening to the radio echo from the kitchen. Songs like that were always being dug out. Quite deliberately, George held himself at the line between sleep and wakefulness.

Elizabeth bought more cocoa and toast. 'You really have changed. I barely recognised you.'

'You keep saying that.'

'I'm sorry.'

Elizabeth picked up a triangle of toast with dainty fingers. 'After the trial Riley sold Quilling Road.'

'Did he?'

'Yes. And he left the Isle of Dogs. In fact, he was sacked. With the money from the sale he set up a house clearance business.'

'Did he?'

'Stop asking if he did something, when I just said that he did.'

'Fair enough.'

Elizabeth licked her thumb and forefinger. 'He set up two companies. One of them is a shop run by his wife, Nancy, whom you saw at court. I don't suppose you met?'

'No,' said George. 'It wasn't that type of party.'

Elizabeth dabbed the corners of her mouth. 'The second

54

business is Riley's own concern. He runs it from a transit van, selling odds and ends at fairs and bazaars.'

'Stuff from the house clearances?'

'Yes. So when he buys a job lot, everything is somehow or other divided between this shop and his van.'

'So what?' George wasn't interested in Riley's commercial habits.

'Aren't you ever inquisitive?'

'Not really.' His eye fell on the last triangle of toast. 'How do you know all this?'

'He has to file accounts at Companies House. I've read them.'

Elizabeth pushed the plate towards George, as if it were a donation. She said, 'I'm reliably informed that this business isn't what it seems.'

George threw down a crust. 'You've just said that he's gone straight.'

'No I didn't. I said he'd gone into business.'

'What's the difference?'

'All the figures add up perfectly.'

George couldn't understand lawyers. How could they see a weakness that wasn't there? Mind you, that was what the other one had done. How had he known to ask about David Bradshaw? Duffy was his name. He'd got lots of pages all to himself in book thirty or so.

Elizabeth said, 'To find out what he's really doing we need to see more than a balance sheet.'

'We?'

'Sorry,' said Elizabeth with a smile. 'A slip of the tongue. But now you mention it, I've an idea.'

'Have you?'

Elizabeth glowered at him. 'Yes. Both companies are registered at Nancy's shop.'

'What does that mean?'

'It's their official business address. Riley is obliged by law to keep all financial records for seven years. I doubt if he keeps a filing cabinet at home.'

'So what do you suggest?'

'Nancy is the key. She must have turned aside from so much to have seen so little.'

'Your idea . . . it wouldn't be me knocking on the door and introducing myself?'

'Not far off, George. Imagination and subtlety would have taken you the remaining distance.'

'Would it?'

Elizabeth glowered again and refused to answer.

A loud flap from the polythene nudged George into wakefulness. The present moment gathered density, becoming prickly; he had pins and needles along one arm. The conversation was still complete, like an echo. He listened to the aftershock, understanding – for that moment of rebounding – all that had happened over the following months. But then an awful doubt came over him: had it all been a dream? With a torch held under his chin, he fumbled through his notebooks. He turned the pages quickly, his mind growing dim, Elizabeth's words fading . . . until he paused to smooth out a dog-ear at the beginning of book thirty-six. There was the heading. It brought back her voice: 'George, this is what you are going to do.'

12

After compline Anselm knocked on the Prior's door. It was the Great Silence, but Father Andrew never let a rule, however ancient and secure, take primacy over an insistent worry. A fire had been made. Two chairs had been placed in front of it. The Prior was already seated, arms on his knees. Light flickered upon broken glasses that had been repaired with a paperclip.

Anselm took his place. 'You know of the key?'

'I do.'

By the hearth was a life-size statue that he'd never seen before. Such things turned up occasionally in the fields, or by the Lark near the abbey ruin. Once cleaned up, they stood in for garden gnomes in the grounds. This one had lost its head and an elbow. Whoever it was stood like an observer of sacred things long gone.

'I suspect you know everything else,' said Anselm, grateful to have an ally.

The Prior shook his head. 'All I'm sure of is this: in the nicest possible way, we've been set up.'

They looked at the wrangle of impatient flames. The wood was wet and hissed and steamed.

While Larkwood was a deeply impractical place, its traditions were very ordered when it came to talking – because of the Rule's insistence on listening. Back-and-forth dialogue wasn't the norm with serious matters. You took turns. At a nod from Anselm, the Prior kept the initiative.

'Elizabeth asked to see me – in confidence – the week before you came to Larkwood, which is to say, about ten years ago. Inadvertently, it seems, you had given me a favourable recommendation. Or, at least, the kind that spoke to her.'

Anselm had said that the Prior pops illusions . . . it was all he could remember saying.

'She made an appointment. She came all the way from London. But she couldn't speak. We just looked at each other. And something surfaced while I was watching her . . . anger, helplessness . . . and finally she said, "How can evil be undone?"' The Prior scratched his scalp. 'We spent the next hour exploring this territory, never approaching a specific issue. And yet I was talking to a haunted woman.'

Anselm remembered his own conversations with Elizabeth on those dark Friday nights: she'd been intellectually tireless, searching out the implications of every nuance. When she'd come to Finsbury Park, she'd told of a voice that would not be stilled and Anselm had said that to understand the ways of the heart you need a guide . . .

'Years later she asked to see me again,' resumed Father Andrew, eyes on the fire. 'She didn't want you to know of her visit, so we met while you were away. In many respects it was a re-run of our first encounter, only this time the anger and helplessness had been replaced by despair. As before, she did not speak. So I asked her a question, "Why are you unhappy?" Almost whispering, she said, "I'm implicated in a homicide." And then she seemed to slip away, leaving her body behind. I said, "I think you need a solicitor, not a monk." She replied, "It's not the law that has a claim upon me. It's my—"'

'Conscience,' Anselm interjected. The Prior nodded.

Kierkegaard had called it 'an affair of the heart'. Anselm's rebelled. He'd been in the same position as Elizabeth: they'd both defended guilty men before. And if Riley were connected to the death of John Bradshaw, conscience could not hold either Elizabeth or Anselm to be responsible. There was no link between anything they had done and that outcome. So how had the discomfort become anguish? Mechanically, Anselm surmised that this particular visit to Larkwood must have occurred shortly after Elizabeth had received the letter from Mrs Bradshaw.

'We sat in silence,' continued the Prior, gazing into the fire. 'Gradually, as it were, she came back, and we talked of her

58

work – of revenge and fair dealing, of injury and restoration, of judges and juries: these ideas, and their connections, seemed to fill her mind, and she sifted through them as if she were doing a jigsaw whose picture it was desperately important to complete . . . and keep out of view.'

The Prior leaned forward and threw another log on the fire. Flakes of orange ash burst free and rose and turned instantly to grey.

'The last time I saw her was a month ago. She wanted to talk to you, but only after a meeting with me – which was, however, to remain confidential. She was neither angry, nor helpless, nor desolate. I found her composed; you might even say at peace.' He took off his glasses and fiddled with the paperclip. 'Going back to the jigsaw, I think the gathering of the pieces was over. She said, "I've thought a great deal about our previous discussions and, as a result, I've been tidying up my life." I waited, expecting her to tell me what this had all been about, but she confided nothing. So I said, "If ever I can help again, don't hesitate to ask." She smiled, saying, "Actually, I've a small favour to ask." And at that strange moment, I felt like the first domino in a queue.' The Prior repositioned his glasses and looked to Anselm, as if inviting the next in line to relate the fall.

Anselm said, 'She wondered if I might be free to run an errand on her behalf.'

'She did,' said the Prior. 'And I agreed.'

'She then said, "May I give him a key to be used in the event of my death?"'

'She did. And I agreed.' The Prior pursed his lips, thinking. 'What you will not know are the instructions she then gave me regarding what should happen after you had opened the box. They were precise. As regards myself, I was to wait, otherwise you would not understand what I was to say. As regards yourself,

59

she said, "Firstly, Anselm should visit a Mrs Bradshaw. She wrote to both of us many years ago. She deserves a reply." Does that mean anything to you?'

'I've just read it.'

While Anselm explained what had been written, the Prior went to his desk and opened a drawer. 'She then said, "Secondly, please give him this letter. He should open it when he has left Mrs Bradshaw. After that, everything should fall into place." And she added, "A police officer called Inspector Cartwright will one day thank you, as I do." I'd have called a halt to this drama, if it hadn't been for her resolve and . . . her pain.'

Anselm took the envelope. It bore his name in her small, painstaking hand. 'And then, to evoke the past, she sought me out with a box of chocolates.'

The Prior sat down with a sigh, rubbing the back of his head – a gesture possibly from his younger days in Glasgow. 'Tell me all about it; from when you first met her.'

From when you first met her. The Prior, like Anselm, was already looking further back than appearances would warrant. Accordingly, Anselm began with a conversation on a Friday night long before the Riley trial, a talk about parents, children and dying.

It was late when Anselm finished. Larkwood's owl – heard but never seen – had taken flight, and was hooting round the spire, permanently baffled by the fearlessness of the partridge weathervane.

'I suppose Sylvester told everyone that Inspector Cartwright came here?' asked the Prior.

'Not quite, but the bulk of the message got through.'

'She believes that John Bradshaw's death was a revenge killing linked to the Riley trial, although the mechanics were beyond proving. We decided that Elizabeth must have come to a similar conclusion, because this was undoubtedly the homicide to which she'd referred. This, however, was not the only matter we discussed. It transpired that in the seconds before she died, Elizabeth had made a telephone call to Inspector Cartwright.'

'Really? What did she say?'

'"Leave it to Anselm."'

Anselm frowned and repeated Elizabeth's last words with incredulity. 'What the hell does that mean?'

'She hadn't a notion. Presumably you'll find out after you've visited Mrs Bradshaw and read the letter.' The Prior rose, indicating that the interview was over. 'Inspector Cartwright would like you to call her in due course.'

The cry of Larkwood's owl began to fade as it flew west over Saint Leonard's Field, leaving behind a charged silence, a sense that something strange occupied the night sky above the monastery.

Anselm went to his cell and threw open the window. The night was cool and sharp, softened by the smell of apples. The community had been peeling them before compline, and the skins were in sacks by the kitchen door.

Leave it to Anselm. Was that wise, Elizabeth? What did I say that made you choose me? Or is it something I've done?

Anselm breathed in deeply, wondering why he'd put the key back in his wig tin. Generously, the Prior had not enquired. Perhaps it was that word 'murder', and the hopeless search for a rhyme. Whatever the cause, Anselm was altogether sure that the consequent delay would complicate things considerably. Elizabeth had foreseen many things, but Anselm's hesitation wasn't one of them.

PART TWO

the story of a box

1

The door opened and Mr Wyecliffe's face emerged out of a warm gloom. His brown oval suit seemed to join his beard and run up his cheeks, stopping just below the small eyes. 'Sorry, the light bulb's just blown. There's sufficient illumination, however, in my quarters.' He led Nick to a sort of hole composed of shelves and files. The air was stale and still and seemed to have a colour, as though they were immersed in a yellowish solution carrying a hint of blue from far, far away. Upon a large, chipped bureau stood a yellow plastic air freshener that kept watch over piles of paper in disarray.

'I thought it best we speak outside office hours.' He blinked and nodded with a single movement. 'Can't say much, mind. Client confidentiality.' He slumped in a chair behind his desk and said, 'It was a first-class funeral, if you take my meaning. Very nice reception. Lovely house. Nice to see the clients invited. But I am sorry. Dreadful business, if you ask me.'

'Your clients?' asked Nick.

'Quite a few. One of them ate the ham sandwiches.' He spoke as though he were tempting the outrage of a magistrate.

Nick said, 'You specialise in criminal law?'

'Not really,' he reminisced, scratching an ear as he leaned back. 'I've followed the personal injury market. And family work, of course. I'd always done that. Care, divorce, custody. Always lots to do in that neck of the woods.' His narrow eyes seemed to glaze. 'I sent your mother more dog's breakfasts than I care to admit. But she had a knack with parents not disposed to cooperate with expert assistance.' He blinked in the gloom, regarding the air freshener. 'But why do you want to know about the Riley case? It was a long time ago . . . Best forgotten, I should think.' He almost winked.

'Maybe you're right,' said Nick. 'But I found the papers among my mother's personal things. She kept them for nearly ten years. I wondered if you might be able to tell me why.'

Mr Wyecliffe's eyes enlarged like ink on blotting paper. 'I'll do my best.' He picked up a glass ball containing a log cabin, two fir trees and three reindeer yoked to a sleigh. He shook it and a blizzard swirled against a cobalt sky. It was the only movement in the room. 'Was there anything with the brief?'

'Why?'

'Sorry. Silly question. That's why I keep out of court.' He watched the flakes of snow sinking. 'Maybe I should begin before the trial . . . You don't mind if I put the odd question do you?' His eyebrows seemed to nod.

'Not at all.'

'That's fine.' As if startled by a recollection, he went to a side room. A cupboard door clipped open and then shut. He came back with some envelopes and threw them into a large plastic bin the size of a laundry basket. 'My out-tray,' he explained. 'Where was I? Ah, yes . . . It's probably best to start after your mother took silk. You'll appreciate, I wasn't in the criminal field that often, so what I know was picked up from here and there.' Nick saw him at the funeral reception, eyeing the plates, picking at this and that. 'She'd built a reputation as a prosecutor and was always booked up. But defendants wanted her as well: word gets round. Villains talk while they're on remand. They play bridge and discuss the relative merits of counsel. So, you see, it wasn't surprising to have a client who came in asking for your mother. But with Mr Riley it was slightly different.'

66

'Why?'

'He'd never been in trouble with the police.'

Evening had come and the room was weakly lit by a single central light. A dinted shade hung askew, like a hat on a stand-up comic.

'You mean that Mr Riley asked for my mother?'

'Yes.'

'Did he say why he wanted her?'

'Not right off the bat.'

'Did you ask?'

'Yes.'

Annoyance raised Nick's voice. 'Well, what did he say?'

'That he'd heard she was good; so good that she could win without even opening her mouth.'

'Who'd said that?'

'He didn't say.'

'Did you ask how he'd heard of her?'

'No.' Mr Wyecliffe raised his hands, like he was offering a platter. 'Mr Riley had considered a newspaper article about women at the Bar. He picked your mother because he'd read she could see right inside the guilty. Such an aptitude, he said, would be invaluable for the exposure of his detractors.'

'What's that got to do with her not having to open her mouth?'

'An astute question, if I may say so,' complimented Mr Wyecliffe, 'for that telling phrase wasn't in the article.'

Coldly and with apprehension, Nick considered his interrogator. This mound of hair and cloth had been angling for an understanding of the trial ever since he'd cleaned up the plates at St John's Wood.

Mr Wyecliffe reached for his glass ball and gave it another shake, stirring up the snow. The flakes swirled and began to fall slowly.

Nick said, 'Please can we open the window?'

'Sorry. It's been painted shut.'

The air was still and warm and quietly beating.

'Where was I?' asked Mr Wyecliffe pleasantly. 'Oh yes. I arranged a conference and sent the papers off. Your mother rang up the next day to say the case didn't need a silk and suggested I use Mr Duffy instead. But the client wouldn't agree. So I booked them both – at your mother's insistence. Speaking of the monk – well, he wasn't a monk then – do you know him?'

'Vaguely.'

'Any idea why she might have selected him?'

'No. Why?'

'If I might speak confidentially . . . He was good if you wanted a trumpet on a sinking ship, but to stay afloat . . . there were others. As it happens, I was wrong. He blew the other side out of the water with one question.'

'Something about calling himself George rather than David.'

'Yes.' Mr Wyecliffe twisted the air freshener on its axis. 'How did you know that?'

'Mr Duffy told me.'

The solicitor hitched a shoulder and coughed. 'I trust my nautical metaphor can remain between ourselves.'

'It can.'

'Most grateful.' Mr Wyecliffe scratched his beard. 'All very peculiar really, because the name business came from me – well, I brought it to the attention of instructed counsel – but your mother didn't like it all . . . discouraged it, in fact. I've often wondered why, because it turned out to be our best point. Are you leaving already?'

Nick said, 'Perhaps I might buy you a drink?'

'A most agreeable proposal.'

Mr Wyecliffe opened a drawer on his desk and pulled out a

blue notebook. 'Funny, really . . . if you think about it' – he rattled the drawer shut, toppling the air freshener – 'given Mr Duffy's last question, we did win without your mother having to open her mouth. Even Mr Riley was stunned.'

Nick made for the corridor. Dimly, through a grey pane, he could see the lights of Cheapside.

2

Before coming to London Anselm had suffered a bruising – and inevitable – encounter with the cellarer.

'Are you familiar with the Inland Revenue and its peculiar habits?'

'Yes,' said Anselm humbly. He had presented himself after lauds to obtain the required funds for the trip.

'I thought so.' Cyril was in his office beneath an arcade – an ordered place without ornament, save for colour-coded box files: blue for apples (on the right), and green for plums (on the left). Each carried a date. His one arm was on the table like a cosh. He was large and square. His nose was red and his eyes were yellow. He had a cold. 'They require accurate records supported by all relevant documentation.'

'They do.'

'Can you give me an example?'

'A receipt.'

Cyril sneezed, slamming his nose with a huge polka dot handkerchief. After rattling a box out of sight, he counted out a precise sum to cover anticipated rail and Underground tickets.

'God bless you, Cyril.'

'Don't mention it.'

*

When Anselm came to London he usually stayed with the Augustinians in Hoxton. Sometimes, however, as on this occasion, he booked a guest room at Gray's Inn, his former legal home. The practice kept fresh his associations with the Bar; and it afforded an opportunity to see Roddy, his old head of chambers. Having studied the Riley papers on the train, Anselm trudged up the narrow wooden stairs to his former place of work. It was evening.

Roddy had just purchased what he called a long blue smoking jacket. He sat with his legs extended, looking like a waterbed in a sari. After some chat about hypnotism as a means of trouncing addictions, Anselm said, 'Do you remember the Riley trial?'

'It was the only case you ever did with Elizabeth.'

'Yes, how did you know?'

'She remarked upon it recently.' He reached for a large carved pipe. 'Austrian,' he said proudly. 'Made of bone.'

Anselm hesitated, letting his mind whirr and clank. When it stopped he perceived that Roddy already knew of the trial and its significance for Elizabeth. With this in mind, Anselm explained about the key, the red valise and the letter to be read after he'd met Mrs Bradshaw. Throughout Roddy packed tobacco into the bowl of his pipe, prodding it occasionally with his thumb or a knife. Gradually creases gathered across his forehead, revealing agitation and surprise, as if he'd missed something he ought to have foreseen. Anselm's conclusion snapped into place: Elizabeth's confidence had not been given to Roddy beyond the trial. It was staggering – for Anselm and for Roddy: she'd held something back from the man who'd nursed her career like a father.

'It's been a very long time, Anselm, I've forgotten what happened.' Roddy lit a match as if it were the opening of a ceremony. 'Tell me about Riley . . . that ruined instrument.'

70

'Frank Wyecliffe sent the papers down to chambers for a conference,' said Anselm. 'Three teenagers said they'd met Riley at Liverpool Street Station. He'd offered them somewhere to stay, free of charge. His story was that when he'd come to London, no one had been there to help him, that he'd spent months in a burnt-out bank near Paddington, that he wouldn't wish that on anyone else, that people needed a break. They could think about rent once they were earning, and not before. So they moved into this house at Quilling Road in the East End. All he wanted was the contact details of someone they trusted with their lives – in case they did a runner. Then he gave them a key and he left them alone.'

While Anselm spoke Roddy struck matches, stroking them over the bowl.

'Every now and then he'd come round and ask them how they were getting on, whether they'd found work yet,' said Anselm. 'Then, gradually, things changed. They'd see him at the end of the street, milling around. Same thing at night. He'd just be standing there, rubbing his hands to keep warm. Then he'd be gone. And later, when he came to the house, asking how the search for work was going, he never said anything about having been in the area the week before. That was how it went on: they'd see him outside, near a street lamp, but then he'd be gone, turning up a few days later, and always at the same spot, as if he was waiting – sometimes in the morning, sometimes at night. Eventually they went out to ask him what was going on.'

On the train to London, Anselm had read several times the witness statement of a girl called Anji. She had recounted the confrontation with Riley:

'Why do you keep hanging around?'

'Because I'm frightened.'

'What of?'

71

'Not for myself . . . for you lot.'

'Us?'

'Yes. Each of you.'

'Why?'

'The owner of the house is tired of waiting, and he wants his rent.'

'You said this house was yours.'

'No I didn't, I said I had a house. It's not mine. I'm just the rent collector . . . for him.'

'Who?'

'The Pieman.'

'What?'

'The Pieman . . . that's what he calls himself. He has lots of houses and he likes his rent. I let you use this one because I felt sorry for you. I thought that once you got settled in you'd have the money and we could smooth things over. But you've been slow and he's found out. The Pieman's not happy. That's why I'm worried.'

'How much does he want?'

'What he's owed.'

'What's that?'

'Three thousand three hundred.'

The girls were stunned and angry. They swore and shouted. Riley said, 'I'm here whenever I can to hold him back if he turns up, but this can't go on. The best thing is to start making a contribution.'

They said they were off, that they were paying nothing to no one. Riley told them, 'I wouldn't do anything silly if I were you. The Pieman begins with those you trust. First of all he takes it out on them. Then he comes for you. And he's a way of finding those who owe him. And I wouldn't be standing out here, night and day, if I wasn't worried what he might do. The best thing is to get some quick money, and in the meantime, I'll calm him down.'

Anselm gave the gist of Anji's evidence to Roddy. At its conclusion, Roddy asked, 'Who, pray, was the Pieman?'

'I said it was a load of nonsense, but Elizabeth thought I was wrong. She said this figure was very real for Riley, which was why he could make an abstraction so terrifying.'

Roddy opened his mouth as if to say, 'Ah,' but nothing came out. Anselm continued with his narrative.

'One of the girls ran off and turned up at the night shelter where George Bradshaw worked. They got talking. She left but came back a week later with the others. They told Bradshaw about Riley and the Pieman and he urged them to make a complaint. If we are to believe Bradshaw, he appreciated that these girls would have difficulty persuading a jury to believe them. They'd all committed offences of dishonesty. Their credibility would be an issue. So Bradshaw persuaded them to go back to Quilling Road. Only this time, he joined them when Riley was due to collect the rent. It was a sort of sting: in the event, they said they were leaving and that provoked Riley to make threats within Bradshaw's hearing.'

'Where was he?'

'In one of the bedrooms. Apparently, Riley refused to go up the stairs . . . he wouldn't even go near the bottom step. He always made them come down to the hall.'

Roddy chewed his pipe. 'How peculiar.'

'So Riley was in deep trouble,' continued Anselm. 'A witness of impeccable character would corroborate the girls' evidence. There was no reason to doubt him except for one significant consideration: Riley, too, had no previous convictions. Bradshaw was therefore of central importance.'

Another match flared in Roddy's hand.

73

'When I arrived for the conference, Elizabeth was already there with Riley. She listened while I went through the statements with him.'

Riley came to Anselm with a flash: wiry limbs, the jaw chewing minutely. 'He was calm, even though his defence was based on conjecture: that the girls had framed him when he'd kicked them out for rent arrears; that Bradshaw had been the pimp who'd lost out, which explained his involvement in the scam.'

Roddy examined the bowl of his pipe. 'What did Elizabeth make of that?'

Anselm had found a summary of Elizabeth's words scribbled on the back of a witness statement – made by himself at the time. 'Words to the effect, "Mr Riley, I am very familiar with people who pretend to be one thing when in fact they are another; and with people who lie, and they rarely do it without very good reason. If these witnesses did not know you, if by some marvel you received remuneration arising from their work without them realising it, then perhaps we might find a technical route off these charges. But since that does not apply, in order to promote your defence we are going to need far more than ingenuity."' Anselm paused, as if he were in the room again, stunned by her contempt. 'It was terrific.'

'What was his response?'

'He was smiling.'

'Smiling?'

'Yes, and Elizabeth said, "If I may respectfully say so, you do not appear to appreciate the gravity of the situation in which you find yourself." The smile had gone from Riley's face but he was simmering. He said, "You're wrong there. I know exactly what position I'm in." If Elizabeth had thought he'd buckle and plead, she was wrong. There was going to be a trial.'

Roddy tapped his pipe upon an ashtray. 'He sounds like

many of the gentlemen I've had the honour to represent.' He looked at his watch. 'We'll have to leave it there. I must commandeer a few words to explain away a point-blank shooting. Tell me the rest tomorrow.'

3

'The case started all right but then went badly, although it seems that the decline itself was a strategic decision – because your mother was responsible.' Mr Wyecliffe was lodged on one side of a table in a public house near Saint Paul's. His small head was sunk into the collar of his overcoat. Nick leaned away from the encroaching confidence. 'The first witness was the youngest, a kid under sixteen. I saw her in the corridor, tattooes above each ear. But she ran off.'

'Where?'

'No idea. But that meant that the first charge was in the bin: encouraging a minor or something into the profession, if I might use that word.' He sipped at his pint. 'That was bad news for the Crown and good news for us.'

'I don't follow.'

'It was the easiest allegation to make out because they didn't have to prove procurement or intimidation. Encouragement is enough. The Crown was on the back foot, so to speak, and it was then that your mother seemed – I stress "seemed" – to help their case. The witness in question had, shall we say, a complicated past: not one that would promote trust in her word. But if I wasn't familiar with forensic technique, I'd have thought that your mother reviewed it to evoke sympathy. Take a look yourself. These are my notes of her cross-examination.' He opened his notebook and passed it over. Nick read the surprisingly neat transcription, almost hearing his mother's voice, her reluctance and her understanding.

'Anji, you're seventeen?'

'Yeah.'

'You've been very brave this morning, telling the court how you came to work on the street – I hope you don't mind if I use that phrase—'

'You can call it what you like.'

'Thank you. I'd like to ask you a little about what happened before you came to London.'

'Eh?'

'About Leeds.'

'Whatever.'

'You ran away?'

'So what?'

'You ran away from Lambert House, a care home?'

'A prison.'

'Anji, I'm not going to rake over what happened. This court understands that the places which ought to protect children sometimes fail. Your honour, let me make it plain that—'

Mr Wyecliffe coughed. 'Do you see that bit about Lambert House?'

'Yes.'

'Well, the place was eventually closed down because of its moral failings. Now, the prosecution would have been saving that information about the witness for after the defence cross-examination. That way, the jury's last memory of the girl would be sympathetic – because it gave a handle on the running, the lying and the thieving that was to come. But your mother spiked that by getting it in first. It showed she was being fair even as she was stealing the prosecution's only card. Do you see?'

Nick drew his chair away from the table and continued reading.

'Afterwards you ran away from the Amberly Unit?'

'Yeh?'

'And then Elstham Place?'

'And?'

'Anji, there are nine other projects from which you absconded, aren't there?'

'I never counted.'

Nick let the notebook fall. Mr Wyecliffe was examining his beer glass. 'Tastes mild this stuff but the specific gravity is 5.6. You have to be careful.'

'Why would my mother . . . *seem* to evoke sympathy?'

'Because she didn't want to alienate the jury.' He wiped froth off his moustache. 'The bedside manner would draw them on side.'

'How do you know it wasn't genuine?'

'As a woman, as a human being, of course she felt for the kid,' said Mr Wyecliffe, with mock impatience, 'but as a lawyer that sort of thing becomes part of how you handle a trial. She could make it serve another purpose – to help the client.'

Nick hadn't quite appreciated that this was the sort of manoeuvring his mother had been obliged to perform if she was to win a case. He turned over the page and his attention latched on to an exchange that Mr Wyecliffe had marked with an asterisk:

'Anji, you told the court that Mr Riley said, "The one to fear is the Pieman. I'm just the rent collector." What does the Pieman look like?'

'I've never seen him.'

'Do you know where he lives?'

'Nah.'

'Well, is he in London, or far off?'

'He's just round the corner, like, keeping an eye on us all the time.'

'What makes you think that?'

77

'Mr Riley says so.'

'Have you heard his voice?'

'Nah.'

'Why are you frightened of someone you've neither seen nor heard?'

'Cos of what he'll do if he catches us.'

'What's that?'

'He says that when you're asleep, lying there, with your head all still, the Pieman comes up with a poker.'

'A poker?'

'Yeah, and he'll bash you, just once.'

'He's after you, is he?'

'Yeah.'

'You're in the care of social services at the moment, aren't you?'

'Yeah.'

'You're safe, aren't you?'

'Nah, cos he knows how to find you, no matter where you are, and he always comes at night, after you've closed your eyes. You can't be looked after all the time, you know. He just watches, like, waiting for your eyes to drop, and when no one's looking and it's really dark, that's when he comes.'

'Through a window?'

'Maybes. Wherever there's an opening. He doesn't need no keys or nothing.'

'Anji, from what you've said, it's as though the Pieman is like a bad dream. Is that right?'

'Yeah, but it's real.'

'Thank you, Anji, you've been very helpful.'

Nick closed the notebook and handed it back to Mr Wyecliffe. His mother's work had always been a remote activity: the facts were usually interesting, but it remained on a neutral platform where she'd 'represented' someone in 'a trial' with 'evi-

78

dential difficulties'. Reading the actual questions and answers within their context removed the staging. Each move was determined by one objective: to win. Nothing was sacred, save the rules of the contest. Even compassion was a tool. Nick said, 'Do you know what happened to George Bradshaw?'

'I do not.'

'Do you know what happened to his son?'

'I do.'

'How did you find out?'

'The matter was reported in several newspapers.'

'Who showed you?'

Mr Wyecliffe eyed his beer, admiring the question. 'Can't say much,' he said. 'Client confidentiality.'

They were back to where they'd started from when Nick had first taken a seat in that dim, stifling office.

On the pavement Mr Wyecliffe whistled at the cold. It came funnelling down Newgate Street from the direction of the Old Bailey. The office blocks were slabs of grey with occasional squares of dim light. 'I suppose you know Mr Kemble?'

'Yes.'

'In a class of his own.'

'Yes.' Nick, however, thought of his mother and father holding hands upon Skomer. The sea was often wild and the wind could make you shake. It was a world away.

'Seen him recently?' Mr Wyecliffe's breath turned to fog.

'At the funeral.'

'Of course.' He sniffed. 'I suppose you mentioned your mother's triumphant performance on Mr Riley's behalf.'

'I did not.'

'Ah.' That seemed to be the answer he expected. 'Do you mind if I ask an odd question?'

79

'No.'

Mr Wyecliffe's head sank into his collar until it seemed he had no neck. 'Did your mother ever mention the Pieman after the trial?'

'No.'

'Thought not.'

'Why do you ask?'

He thrust his little hands into capacious pockets. 'Silly question, that's—'

'—why you keep out of court?'

Mr Wyecliffe voiced his surprise. 'Exactly.'

4

George switched on his torch and counted the scratches on the wall. While he'd been waiting for the monk, his mind had kept returning to Lawton's Wharf, for it was there, to the sound of the river, that he and Elizabeth had planned their campaign.

'You are avenging those girls, George.'

That's what Elizabeth had said the first time she'd stood on the landing stage.

'When you walked out of court you left them behind.'

She could be harsh, if she wanted.

The day before, a Friday, she'd said, 'I'd like to see where John fell.'

They'd walked from Trespass Place to the Isle of Dogs. Side by side, they followed a dark, angular lane that ran between tall, silent warehouses, and beneath hoists like old gibbets. Presently, they reached an immense open space fronting the river: the premises of H & R Lawton and Co (London) Ltd. All that remained was a brass nameplate fixed to the perimeter fence with a coat hanger. The railings were loose, held upright by sheets of mesh wiring. George and Elizabeth passed through a large gap, as John had probably done. They picked their way over the remnants of a flattened warehouse into a chill off the Thames. Moving ahead of George onto the landing stage, Elizabeth said, 'You are avenging those girls, George.' The waves slapped against the timbers. 'When you walked out of court you left them behind.'

And then, without waiting for George to reply, Elizabeth set to work telling him what she required.

'There'll be two sets of documents – one for each business: that of Riley, and that of Nancy. They're legally separate papers. They'll be stored separately.'

'Right-o.'

'The first is "Riley's Junk". The second is "Nancy's Treasure".'

'Right-o.'

'Once you've found them, we'll talk again.'

'Right-o. And in the meantime?'

'You introduce yourself to Nancy.'

'How?'

'If I were you I'd sleep on her doorstep.'

'Right-o. But she'll want to know my name.'

'Quite right. I suggest an alias. Mr Johnson. How does that sound to you?'

The bantering vanished at the allusion to John's Christian name. So that's why Elizabeth had come to this wharf, thought George, on a Saturday, and at night. It was to place John at the heart of her planning. She was at it again: evoking a setting for what she wanted to say, like her use of the toast and cocoa. This time it was for what they were going to do. She used these ceremonies to stir up the past and make it present in an unusually

81

active way. George couldn't quite put it into words, but he felt there was something restoring in the revival, even though it summoned his failure. Henceforth, everything they did together occurred among a prickling sense of the closeness of people who'd once been near: the girls whom George had betrayed and the son he had lost.

'Mr Johnson sounds just fine,' George had said.

'Let's get going then.'

A horn beeped three times. It was Elizabeth's taxi, come to take her home.

A few days after this conversation another taxi took George and Elizabeth from Trespass Place to the Isle of Dogs. They had agreed that it would be better if he were closer to Nancy's shop in Bow, which was a short distance from the old docklands.

'Riley comes once a week on a Thursday afternoon,' said Elizabeth. 'He stays about an hour to unload furniture or move things around.'

'How do you know?'

'I paid to have him watched.'

'For how long?'

'Six weeks.'

'I could have done that.'

'No . . . I'd only just found you.'

The taxi idled for an hour while George mooched around the tall abandoned buildings. Barbed wire topped the walls and chicken netting hung across black windows. Planks had been nailed pell-mell across openings, but down an alley, George found a swinging door. It tapped like a mallet, drawing his attention. The room inside was bare like a cell, its walls stained green as if they were soaking up the river. It would do. Elizabeth appeared behind him.

'I can pay, you know.' She sounded grief-stricken.

'I'm not ready.' He didn't understand his own words. Nino did. It was part of the mystery of having lost too much.

She did not press him. Struggling with her voice, she said, 'We'll meet twice a week on Lawton's Wharf.'

'Right-o.'

The taxi whipped through the murky lanes towards the orange lights of Bow, five minutes away. It dropped George at a fish and chip shop near a bridge. Nancy's place – a shack of wood and corrugated metal – was on the other side of the road. Through the cab's open door, Elizabeth pressed twenty pounds into George's hand. Then she was gone.

George scouted around for places where the wind would die – Nino taught him that – and beneath the bridge he found some cardboard. He tracked his way back up the grassy slope and set himself up in Nancy Riley's doorway. He built close-fitting walls against the cold. Then he wrote down the happenings of the day in book thirty-seven.

George met Nancy Riley the next morning. He'd expected to confront someone flinty and impatient. But her face was soft, and she wore a silly hat, a yellow thing with black spots. She gathered up the cardboard as if it were worth something and brought him inside, out of the freezing cold. She put on a gas fire and went to make him tea in a back room. Thick arms filled out the sleeves of a chunky cardigan. She glanced at him, showing eyes that were large and seemed to smile. The kettle was on top of a grey filing cabinet.

Through the dark glass of his goggles, George looked around at the wardrobes, the mirrors and the ornaments. It was like a home; there was nothing of Riley here. He quickly left the shop and rushed back to the docklands. Elizabeth came to the wharf that night.

'I can't do it,' said George. Nancy was vulnerable in the way he was; tired, like he was; hungry for what might have been, like he was. It was all marked upon her face.

Elizabeth seemed neither surprised nor interested. 'You saw a filing cabinet?'

'Yes.'

'And everything else was old furniture?'

'Yes.'

Elizabeth was gratified, like someone ticking a box on a register. 'I'm glad you left.'

'Why?' George was stunned. He'd expected anger.

'Because now you know what you're dealing with. She must be an extraordinary woman to have won Riley's trust without losing something of herself. Perhaps you can help her.'

'How?'

'By drawing her into something she'd never countenance if you asked her directly. Unfortunately, it requires deceit.'

'But why?'

'Can you think of another way?'

George had no answer; he just listened to the river lapping against the wharf. Elizabeth left him with a primus stove and a box full of tins.

A week later George went back to the shop. Again, Nancy let him warm up by the fire. While she was helping a customer load some chairs into a van, George went into the back room. The drawers on the filing cabinet were clearly marked: one for the JUNK, and one for the TREASURE. Within minutes he'd placed two official booklets in one of his plastic bags.

'George,' said Elizabeth that night on the wharf, 'I don't wish to appear ungrateful, but I've already seen this lot. These are the annual returns sent to Companies House.'

Elizabeth took George's notebook and wrote down what she

was looking for: acquisition and sales records for each business. She described what they would look like.

'Stay away for another week, George.'

'Why?'

'Since this is love more than deceit, you have to play hard to get.'

Then she went home in a taxi that was waiting outside the perimeter fence.

When George next turned up in Bow, Nancy seemed pleased to see him; perhaps, even, relieved. Again, she made tea. They talked of the weather. She kept glancing at his shoes. After ten minutes she got up again and came back with a basin full of warm, soapy water. 'Soak your feet, Mr Johnson.'

It was paradise.

In the days that followed, George didn't get a chance to nip into the back room, so he met Elizabeth at the agreed times. In due course, though, he turned up with a couple of canvas ledgers: Riley's were red; Nancy's were blue. George had found them when Nancy went out to get some milk.

Elizabeth sat on the remainder of a low wall studying the books with George's torch. She seemed to be checking individual entries, shifting her attention from one ledger to the other.

'Something's going on,' she whispered, irritated, a finger tapping the page.

'Is it over now? Can I stop lifting things?'

'I don't know,' she snapped. 'I'll tell you tomorrow.'

Elizabeth came back at some ungodly hour while it was still dark. He woke in the abandoned warehouse to find her standing over him.

'These only show half the picture.' She handed back the

ledgers. 'I've copied them but I need something else. There should be individual receipts.' She was speaking quickly out of the darkness, and George was still half asleep. 'You know the sort of books I mean – small with a blue cover. Each page has a number in one corner. The writing is an imprint from carbon paper. The original is with the purchaser.'

George sat up, rubbing his eyes. 'Do I have to, I mean—'

'Yes.' Her voice was raised. She lost control, ever so slightly; just enough to send him back to Bow. 'You're not walking away this time, David George Bradshaw.'

5

Pale morning light described Roderick Kemble QC behind his desk, a revolver in one hand and a document in the other. With savage concentration, he examined the rotation of the chamber while he slowly depressed the trigger. 'Take a seat,' he said after the click. As if there'd been no interval between now and the night before, he added, 'Riley said Bradshaw stood behind the allegations laid against him?'

'Yes.'

'How did you propose to undermine Mr Bradshaw?'

'Frank Wyecliffe's only thought was that it was odd to use your second name when the first one was ordinary. At the time I thought he'd lost his marbles – so did Elizabeth.'

Anselm's mind tracked back to the rest of that conversation with her. They were in the common room. She said, 'Do you think Riley is innocent?'

'No.'

She took the last Jaffa cake and ate it with small bites. 'Would you cross-examine Bradshaw?'

'Of course.' Ordinarily the QC handles the main witness, not an underling. At the time Anselm had attached no importance to the request.

A gentle cough brought him back into Roddy's presence. Anselm spoke softly, searching for the meaning of words spoken long ago, 'Elizabeth said, "This is your chance to do something significant."'

Anselm's problem was that he would have to call Bradshaw a liar – in however polite a fashion – without any justification. There was no evidence whatsoever that he had conspired with the girls to frame Riley. When Anselm rose to his feet, all he had was an intuitive awareness that Wyecliffe had been right: the use of one's middle name was unusual.

Roddy once joked that decisive cross-examinations fell into one of three categories. First, where counsel prevails in a clean argument over facts that will bear more than one interpretation. Second, where counsel is armed with devastating information, which need only be revealed at the right moment to clinch the day. But there was a third: where counsel doesn't know what he is talking about. Anselm put his encounter with Mr Bradshaw into this last category. Elizabeth might have thought the change of name worthless, but Anselm was the one at the wheel. He moved forward tentatively, following the implications of each answer. Most of Bradshaw's replies had been 'Yes.' It had been an entirely civilised exchange.

'You call yourself George, is that right?'

'Yes.'

'But your first name is David?'

'Yes.'

'How did you come to call yourself by your second name?'

'I didn't like the first one.'

Most barristers develop a keen sense of intuition – because they have failed to see the obvious time and again. It's a kind of hunting instinct, a sniffing for a scent. And the dislike of an ordinary first name struck Anselm as unconvincing. Without instructions or vindicating facts, Anselm decided to follow his nose.

'People change their names for all sorts of reasons?'

'Yes.'

'More often than not it is to turn over a new leaf.'

'Yes.'

'One life ends, so to speak, and another begins?'

'Yes.'

'Is that what you did?'

'Yes.'

Anselm paused, letting his imagination loose.

'It meant, I suppose, David slipped quietly away?'

'Yes.'

'And George stepped forward?'

'Yes.'

Anselm didn't make the mistake of asking 'Why?' Instead he shifted ground completely, still feeling his way.

'You are the manager of the Bridges night shelter?'

'Yes.'

'Where you have worked for twenty-three years.'

'Yes.'

'You are there to serve the needs of a highly vulnerable client group, are you not?'

'Yes.'

'Indeed, as I understand it, you've had people in your care as young as nine?'

'Yes.'

'I expect an employee in your position must be of the very highest character?'

'Yes.'

Anselm paused, watching every inflection on the face of the witness.

'Tell me, Mr Bradshaw, whom did the night shelter employ: David or George?'

'I don't understand.'

'What name did you give on the application form?'

'George.'

The next amateur question would have been another 'Why?' Anselm avoided that temptation: the important point to appreciate at this stage was that everything Bradshaw had said might go in one of two directions: innocent or compromising. Roddy often said that with an honest witness, the wider the question the better, because they are disposed to impose relevance upon it – their consciences take them to the crucial, unknown detail. Anselm needed to find out if there was a link between Bradshaw's dropping his first name and his taking employment under the second.

'Mr Bradshaw, have you ever done anything that came to the attention of the police?'

'Yes.'

'Now, would that have been as David or George?'

'David.'

Now Anselm had to make his final move. There was no other territory to explore. Bradshaw was either going to exonerate himself completely by revealing an unpaid parking fine, or he just might divulge something that could be used against his integrity. He said: 'What did David do that George wanted to forget?'

The courtroom makes everyone a voyeur. The witness is often stripped bare, way beyond what clothing can conceal. It is darkly fascinating and can leave the viewer stained with pleasure. These

89

things Anselm had learned long ago. But as he spoke to Roddy, the electricity of this particular spectacle surged through him as if this were the first, forbidden time. Bradshaw stared across the well of the court, his face pale. The jury watched him – as did the lawyers, the ushers, the reporters and the bystanders. Looking down on this exhibition, a judge held his pen above a page. Not a shred of detail would be lost to the official record. Then, as if someone had called his name, David George Bradshaw stepped out of the witness box and walked out of the court. Half an hour later Riley went through the same door, a free man.

Roddy kept his papers and court dress in a tartan suitcase on wheels. It bounced and rattled after him as he pulled it through chambers and onto the stairs that led to Gray's Inn Square. Anselm followed, convinced that Roddy's close examination of the revolver – an exhibit taken out of court with permission – had served some useful purpose, but that the true reason was the commotion that would shortly erupt when he tried to take it back in. Anselm, though, had other concerns. 'Something shot over my head in that trial.'

'Isn't it always thus?' He waddled along the pavement as if he were on the way to Corfu.

'This time it was different. I've been wondering why Elizabeth kept the brief in the first place.'

Roddy bounced his valise over a kerb. 'Sorry, old son. The question never entered my head.' He became studious. 'Forgive me, I must now dwell upon triggers and safety catches. Do you know, in certain circumstances, it's rather difficult to press one without putting pressure on the other? That ought to kick up some doubt.'

They parted and Anselm watched Roddy nod greetings to left and right as he trundled down Holborn towards the Bailey. The rogue never asked the question, thought Anselm, because he'd always known the answer.

6

The memory of Mr Wyecliffe ruined Nick's cornflakes. It was like sour milk. He had never quite appreciated the twilight world of compromise that his mother had inhabited. Nick had woken troubled by three questions. He would deal with two of them over breakfast. His father sat opposite him, examining a boiled egg.

'I wonder what Mum was doing with those spoons?'

'Spoons?' Charles tapped the egg as if it were the door to the MD's office.

'The ones that were found on the passenger seat.'

'Bought them in a shop, I suppose.'

Not on a Sunday, thought Nick. He didn't want to disturb any of the conclusions his father might have framed about Elizabeth's behaviour prior to her death. But the spoons seemed innocuous and important at the same time. She had obtained them, in all likelihood, shortly before her death. There was another incidental detail that remained unexplained, which prompted the second question.

'What was she doing in the East End anyway?'

Charles began dropping the egg on a plate. 'She said it was work. A site visit.'

Nick had in mind the autopsy photographs on his mother's desk. They were part of the last case she'd worked on. The victim had been killed in Bristol, not London. Nick had checked the instructions to every case in the Green Room before they'd been collected. None had referred to the East End.

91

Charles picked at the battered egg with a nail, his face reddening. 'What are you doing with yourself when you're out of doors?' He laughed weakly. 'Going here, heading there. You're getting like your mother.'

'Oh, just friends and unfinished business.'

Charles picked up a knife, eyes narrowed. He looked bullish. 'That's what she said.'

After breakfast Nick went to the Royal Brompton Hospital in Kensington to deal with the third question: a heart condition that had killed his mother. Its presence and gravity had been unknown to him. 'She didn't want to worry you,' Charles had said the night before the funeral. He'd tweaked his tie. 'I'd no idea that she might collapse without warning . . . that the end could come like a bus mounting the pavement.'

There was no point in pressing his father for details. The anatomy of a butterfly he could grasp, but that of a human being left him dazed. Too many pipes. So Nick contacted his mother's consultant cardiologist. He didn't mention it to his father.

On the desk before Doctor Simbiat Okoye was a slim bundle of medical records. Pensively, she leafed through them. Her hair was tightly braided into thick strands and rolled into a loose bun at the nape of her neck. When she spoke, her eyes studied the listener's face. 'Your mother had hypertrophic cardiomyopathy.'

Nick let the words settle. This was a hereditary disorder of the heart whereby its muscles become thick and stiff. In turn, this affects blood flow and valve function. There is no cure; and it's hereditary with a fifty-fifty chance of passing it on to your children.

'You do not have the condition,' said Doctor Okoye. Her eyes were dark with a flush of rose around the whites.

'She had me screened before I went to Australia, without me realising it?'

'Yes.'

Doctor Okoye explained the history and outcome of his mother's consultation. Elizabeth had first developed breathlessness and chest pain about ten years ago. She'd put this down to stress at work: she'd recently found herself frightened of court – not the usual nervousness, but a debilitating anxiety that could make her sick. This had been unknown before. Palpitations and light-headedness were placed at the door of the menopause. And then she'd had a blackout about a year ago. A visit to her GP prompted an emergency referral.

'Surgery wasn't required,' said Dr Okoye. 'I prescribed beta-blockers and anti-arrhythmias. The drug therapy was effective but—'

'—with a small number of patients there's a risk of sudden death . . . like being hit by a bus. My mother was one of them.'

'Yes. Would you like to see my notes?'

'No thanks.' He asked the question for which she was waiting. 'How did my mother get it . . . I mean . . . which parent was affected, her father or mother?'

'There's no way of knowing now,' said Doctor Okoye. 'From what I was told, it may have been her father. I understand he died in an armchair with a glass of milk in his hand.'

'Yes,' said Nick. 'He went out like a light.'

Nick's grandmother had followed her husband shortly afterwards, from septicaemia. He'd never known them. And there were no other siblings, so there was no one else in the hereditary tree.

Doctor Okoye rose and walked to the window. With a gesture she drew him beside her. 'Look down there, in the courtyard.'

A copper sculpture stood in the centre of a pool. Two adjacent basins channelled a watercourse. Exotic plants with fronds like open scissors stood in tubs positioned along the sides.

'It represents a hidden aspect of heart rhythm,' said Doctor

Okoye. 'Apart from muscular contraction, blood movement results from surface waves created by the inflowing stream. It's as though after an initiating shove, circulation could go on for ever, the required energy coming not from a heart, which will one day tire, but through the configuration of cavities and the momentum of blood. Unfortunately, that's not what happens. As you can see' – she pointed towards one end of the sculpture – 'art and nature require a pump.'

Nick looked at the grove, his head against the glass.

'Your mother and I stood by this window,' said Doctor Okoye. 'She had been distressed. But the heart carries a greater mystery than any frailty.'

'What?'

'It's a wonder that it ever worked at all.'

On his way out of the hospital, Nick paused in the courtyard to watch the tumble and splash of water between two scoops of metal. He wasn't thinking of possible worlds but of the inscrutability of this one: his mother had gone to the East End, obtained a set of spoons, and her heart had stopped.

7

As far as George was concerned, after he got his head kicked in he woke up in a very nice garden by the Imperial War Museum. In fact, a lot happened in between. Much of it came back of its own accord, and Elizabeth filled in some of the gaps, as best she could. Her voice released other memories and together they'd put a shape to what had happened.

The preliminaries were straightforward.

George didn't like the docks: the warehouse seemed to wake at night with groans in the bricks: it was resonant with lost activity. More to the point, it wasn't his patch. His territory was south of the river, round Trespass Place. So, a few days after Elizabeth had asked for the receipt books, George walked to Waterloo after nightfall. He was only a few minutes from the fire escape when it happened.

There was no reason for the attack. George didn't go down defending an old lady or tackling a thief. He was just sitting on a bench eating popcorn. Out of the corner of his eye he saw a gangly youth in a padded jacket . . . and then another, with a shaved head. They were laughing and elbowing each other like kids on a school trip. Mischief always ran high when the master wasn't watching. The one with the jacket asked for some pop-corn. George handed it over. The shaved head tipped it over George as if it were a massive salt-cellar. When he stood up they began the kicking, like it was a dance, or a new sport. They panted and grunted and sighed.

And this is where the confusion began in George's mind: he had no recollection of being admitted to hospital or discharging himself or making his way to the garden of the Imperial War Museum. After what felt like a drunken sleep, George simply opened his eyes and saw the trees . . . and clouds like wisps of cream in a light-blue blancmange . . . and his first thought was how delicious the world was. The smell of cut grass was so strong he could almost taste it. This must be heaven, he thought. Overjoyed, George walked out of the gates to discover what was waiting for him. It was only then, ambling down magnificent, strangely familiar streets, that he discovered his mind wouldn't work properly. Instinctively, he'd ran back to Trespass Place like a wounded animal, where Elizabeth had finally found him.

For her part, she'd waited, as usual, on Lawton's Wharf. When George didn't turn up, she went to the police, who traced the hospital; but by the time Elizabeth got there, he'd already slipped out of the ward. 'I knew you would come back here,' she said affectionately. In her hands were his two plastic bags retrieved from the docklands. There and then, beneath the fire escape, she read out the last couple of volumes that covered the known; and together they approached the unknown.

The line wasn't clear-cut. The weeks prior to the attack had been shaken. The events were jumbled and some were missing, but thankfully George's written account was detailed. It provided scaffolding for his memory. With gratitude, he rebuilt the past in his mind around the pieces that he'd saved. When Elizabeth had finished reading she said, 'You have to do this every day, to keep what you've got.' Then they went to Carlo's. They sat down without ordering. There was going to be no toast and no hot chocolate.

'It's over,' said Elizabeth shortly. 'It's time you came off the street, whether you're ready or not; and it's time we let Riley go.'

The mention of that name was like a stab, an injection to the heart.

'I've sorted out a rehabilitation clinic,' said Elizabeth with authority. 'You can stay there for as long as necessary.'

'No thank you.' George went to the counter and asked for toast and hot chocolate. He came back with a tray and said, 'I'm going back to Nancy.'

George didn't go to the shop for a while. He studied his notebooks. By pooling memories with Elizabeth, he brought his own up to date. Then he went to the Embankment, to the other people on the street. He was like a man with a new toy, or a strange weapon: he had to get used to handling his changed mind. He had to learn again how to relate. It took practice and patience. Rather than write events down at the end of the day, he did it soon after they happened. He made lists of things to be done. And throughout the day he made frequent reference to both. It was like turning a timer before the sand ran out. Each minute became precious even though he knew it was ultimately lost. The essential had been written down, so he could let the rest go. Of course, the notebook and the lists covered no matters of importance – nothing that happened to George was important – they dealt only with the commonplace, but in this way George became confident, once more, with the little things. He still slept at Trespass Place, and Elizabeth came in the evening. She tested him on his current list. Gradually, he began to do quite well. If there had been a prize, he'd have won it. And when he'd got the hang of himself, he went back to the warehouse on the Isle of Dogs. And he went back to Nancy's shop in Bow.

On his first day, they sat by the gas fire, and George told her he'd lost half his mind; and that he'd lost his son: it happened naturally, because the recent past had gone, and his loss was ever fresh. But it was also somehow necessary to tell Nancy, because she was close to the man responsible. She listened, forgetting to take off her yellow hat with its black spots. He watched her through his goggles, knowing that she thought him blind, that her expressions of horror went unseen.

The following morning, thinking George wouldn't remember what she was about to say, Nancy told of her life at Lawton's, how she'd met Riley, and about a trial . . . but she left out the details, and kept it vague, just as George had done when talking of his son. That evening, George wrote nothing down of the day's revelations but one sharp fragment survived into the morning: 'He's not a bad man, you know. He's just . . . lost.'

The receipt books were blue, as Elizabeth had suspected. George eventually found them in shoeboxes on a bookcase opposite the filing cabinet. Taking them was difficult, because Elizabeth had been insistent that she needed a selection from each business covering the same period of time. 'Don't just grab them, look at the dates.' So George spent about two weeks snatching glimpses whenever Nancy dealt with a customer or went out to get some milk. One morning he placed four of them in his plastic bag. That night Elizabeth was tense when she took them.

'You do realise that this is your only chance?'

George nodded, not quite following.

'I hope I'm right,' she said anxiously, 'so that you're the one who finally traps him.'

'And if you're wrong?'

'I've another string to my bow.'

George nodded again, utterly baffled.

Elizabeth returned with the books in the morning darkness. 'Well?' said George to the dark outline.

'I need more time,' she said, and the shape vanished as if it hadn't been there.

8

The home of Mr and Mrs Bradshaw stood within a leafy, secluded terrace in Mitcham. Porches and windows were situated in identical positions like enormous stickers. Anselm hadn't knocked, but the door opened slowly, and a slim woman in her sixties with ruffled hair emerged holding a paintbrush. Her skin was freckled with emulsion. The sleeves of a large, shapeless shirt were loosely rolled to the elbow. She looked at Anselm as if he were familiar.

'Mrs Bradshaw?'

98

She wiped paint from her brow with the back of a hand and said, 'She told me you might turn up one day.'

'Sorry?'

'Mrs Glendinning.' She roused herself, like she was about to get to work. 'I suppose you'd better come in.'

Anselm entered the hallway. The carpet was covered with sheets. The rucks lapped against the skirting board like milky floodwater. He followed Mrs Bradshaw into the sitting room. All the furniture was draped and the walls were bare. She'd been painting a ceiling rose. The ladder stood beneath it, with a tin on a stand. They stood regarding each other, Anselm's fingers moving impulsively behind his back; Mrs Bradshaw remained quite still, the paintbrush at her side.

'Mrs Glendinning has died,' said Anselm. 'She left me a key to a small red case, which I have opened. I am brought back to a trial I had forgotten, and a letter I had never seen. And I have learned of your great loss.' Instinct kept Anselm away from John's name. He watched her, willing her head to rise, for a mighty hand to tear away the drapes. He said, 'I want to say sorry . . . to you and your husband . . . only I don't know how to reach the extent of what has happened to you both. If I'd read sooner what you'd written, I would not have waited so long in coming here.'

Mrs Bradshaw began tugging a button on her shirt. It was blue with a British Gas badge on one side. She seemed foreign to her own home. It was as if she'd just turned up to read the meter.

'Mrs Glendinning told me you'd become a monk,' she said. 'I asked her not to tell you.'

'Why?' asked Anselm.

'Because I didn't want to disturb your peace.' She spoke as if he'd found what she wanted for herself. 'And I felt ashamed of what I wrote.' The paintbrush began to swing slightly. 'I showed myself up for what I am. A bitter woman.'

Anselm shrank from the self-loathing. 'You were honest, that's all.'

'I expect like Mrs Glendinning you want to see George,' she said remotely. 'But he's gone, I'm afraid. He's a lost man.'

Anselm could feel the depth of quiet in the house. His chest grew tight and he felt he was drowning. This was the first time he'd met someone from 'the other side' in a case he'd won. Apprehensively, he listened.

'After the trial,' said Mrs Bradshaw, 'George lost his job. He was dismissed for gross misconduct. Not for the fiasco at court, but because he'd got involved with those kids in the first place. He should have kept his distance . . . like a lawyer . . . but he didn't, he couldn't. Afterwards he fell to pieces, here, at home. Then we lost John. I don't know what happened – but George did, only he couldn't tell me. No, that's not true' – she was struggling, as she'd struggled then; with her mind and body she twisted in her big shirt – 'George couldn't have known, but he felt responsible.' She breathed evenly, becoming still. 'One Saturday night John went out. He didn't come back. He'd gone to Lawton's Wharf—'

'Where Riley had worked,' added Anselm.

She nodded, biting her lip. 'But the police could do nothing. A link like that meant something, of course, but it just wasn't strong enough. The fact remains, John was killed because George stood up to that man.' She put the brush on the ladder and knelt, worked her hand beneath a drape that lay upon a sideboard. Without looking, she found the letter from Inspector Jennifer Cartwright.

It was long, detailed and deeply sympathetic but, finally, uncompromising. There was no prospect of arrest, never mind conviction. Anselm gave the letter back and Mrs Bradshaw knelt again, working her hand beneath the drape. She rose unsteadily and reached for the paintbrush and, as if it were a handle, she lowered herself onto a covered chair.

The pit of Anselm's stomach turned. He saw the walls primed with undercoat. Yesterday's patterns had only just been stripped away. Outside rain began to fall, at first gently, and then gathering weight. The low cloud seemed to soak up the light.

'George could no longer live with himself or me,' said Mrs Bradshaw, 'and I could no longer live with him. You cannot imagine the anger that comes between you. It eats up everything. I blamed George. George blamed himself. He blamed me for blaming him. That's what anger does: it makes you hate what you once loved. It finds a way, even if you can't imagine how. And when it finally grows quiet you're empty and changed and you can't get back. You're left with the wrong kind of peace. What can you do? Nothing comes of nothing.'

Anselm looked down, wanting to be on the same level, but he dared not disturb the drapes. Like mounds of snow they couldn't be touched without a kind of vandalism.

Mrs Bradshaw put her hands to her head, the paintbrush sticking up like a feather. 'One morning, five years ago, George walked down the stairs for breakfast, only he walked out of the door. I knew he was leaving. And I didn't even get up to watch him go. It had been exactly the same with John.' Her hands fell. 'I told Inspector Cartwright that he'd vanished. She put the missing persons team on to him. That was a very long time ago.'

Anselm sank to her side but there was nothing he could say. This was the place where everyone's fault was smudged, where 'Sorry' didn't quite work any more. Where something more powerful was needed. On one knee he thought of Elizabeth, her key and her final words: 'Leave it to Anselm.'

In the hallway, Mrs Bradshaw said, 'I didn't understand your job – at the trial or afterwards. But I do now. Mrs Glendinning explained where you were standing.'

On an island, she had said, the cold place of not knowing, and not being able to care.

When Mrs Bradshaw opened the front door, a strong wind carried the sound of shaking trees and rain.

'I asked your husband a question,' said Anselm, feeling queasy, '. . . What did David do that George wanted to forget? . . . . I was being clever within the rules, but I was blind to what it meant . . . I'm sorry.'

'Maybe one day he'll tell you.' She didn't mean it; she couldn't. He'd gone: he was a lost man. 'Here, take this. I found it on the Tube.' She handed him a man's umbrella from a stand.

Anselm stumbled on the sill. He turned, staring past Mrs Bradshaw at the sheets. 'I think that Mrs Glendinning found your husband before she died.'

'Where is he?' She dropped the paintbrush.

'I don't know yet, but . . .'

Mrs Bradshaw's mouth fell slightly open and she quickly closed the door as if she were ashamed.

Anselm strode along the terrace, angling his umbrella towards the rain. He felt a churning violence against Riley and the dominion of his kind, their endless thriving. He would bring them down, if he could, with all the vigour with which he'd once defended them. Of course, Anselm had seen the link between the trial and John's death as soon as he'd considered the contents of the case. So had Nicholas; so had Roddy.

However, meeting Mrs Bradshaw had foreshortened his under-standing and it made him shiver. Riley's presence moved in his mind: arms coiled across a narrow chest, the jaw bony and strangely lax.

Anselm took refuge beneath the first bus shelter and read the letter from Elizabeth. The Prior had been right. She had care-fully drawn them both into a daring purpose.

9

Elizabeth's taxi came along the cobbles chased by kids. George was at Lawton's perimeter fence when he heard the racket. He stopped, one leg through the wire, and watched. These grubby vagabonds crawled all over the docks. They challenged intruders great or small. George had already seen them in action against a fire engine and had kept out of sight ever since. When the taxi pulled up, they danced around it clapping and shouting. The driver sped off, leaving Elizabeth in the street. Unabashed, she walked towards George, followed by a chanting crowd . . . well, there were only five or six of them, but they took over the place . . . and yet he didn't dwell on their antics. Elizabeth was jubilant.

They went through the fence and picked their way towards the wharf. A couple of kids tailed them, but then vanished.

'We've done it,' said Elizabeth. A trial had taken her out of London, so they hadn't met for three weeks. She sat on the rem-nant of wall, glad to be back, her heels tapping like a dancer's. 'He appears to be doing one thing, but hidden within the num-bers is another animal. He keeps it right under Nancy's nose.'

'Would you write that down, please?' George reached for his notebook.

'In due course.' Elizabeth fished in her bag for the whisky and the beakers. 'There's more to say, more that's worth keeping; but now we celebrate.' Out of a carrier bag she produced beef and horseradish sandwiches, and a tub of cherry tomatoes. The surface of the Thames ran upon itself with ripples. On the far bank empty barges hovered in a mist.

'George, there's something you need to remember . . . to dwell on, as I have. The stone you throw is small, picked from his own garden, but it will take away something he values above all else, and behind which he hides: a good character: the gift bestowed by the law upon the righteous, as well as the man who is never found out.'

George frowned. 'Have you got a pen?'

Elizabeth laughed. She put a tomato in her mouth and took the notebook.

'And lay off the stones and gardens stuff. I'd like it in black and white.'

'I'll give you both.'

When she'd finished, Elizabeth fetched out some Greek yoghurt with honey. George was reading the label when an envelope wrapped in plastic blocked his vision.

'Put this in a safe place,' she said. 'Inside is a detailed explanation of Riley's scheme. It's complicated and by no means obvious.'

'What am I to do with it?'

'For now, nothing. Tomorrow he'll be at Mile End Park for an early Christmas fair. In all we have done, I've reserved for myself a small part: to see him face to face once more, and to accuse him.'

'And what's mine?' He looked at the yoghurt pot. Nino had said the stuff was bad for the arteries.

'You will deliver the explanation to Inspector Cartwright. It is the material upon which Riley's conviction will stand. That belongs to you.'

104

George shifted with importance and pride. The moment had become solemn. He felt he should stand up and make a brief speech.

'Have you got a spoon?' he said.

Elizabeth grimaced. 'I completely forgot.'

Elizabeth stayed late that evening. As night fell, lights appeared upon the river, shuddering.

George said, 'You asked me, once, if I'd ever thought of evil . . . whether it could be undone. I wrote it down, but I've been unable to forget the idea. It's impossible. It's greater than anything I can imagine.'

Elizabeth was writing in George's notebook (recording what would happen in the morning, and where they'd meet). Without looking up, she said, 'Many years ago, a wonderful monk told me we could only undo evil to the extent that it has touched us. I can't do it for you; you can't do it for me. It's a wholly personal quest.'

George thought there should be a manual for this sort of thing – instructions with diagrams and a page at the back for troubleshooting. It would make life a hell of a lot easier.

'I was told it's more deadly than vengeance,' she said, narrow-eyed, as if aiming.

'What is?'

'The forgiveness of the victim,' she muttered, making a precise full stop. 'It goes right to the heart.'

George wasn't especially impressed. He'd expected a revelation, something to make you sit up.

'I'm told it's the only way evil can be undone,' she said, closing the book. Becoming practical, she added sternly, 'Whatever happens, wait at Trespass Place.'

*

From beyond the bed of broken brick, outside the fence, a horn beeped three times. Elizabeth stood and faced George. She gave him fifty pounds, and checked that he had understood all that would happen tomorrow, confirming that they would meet in the afternoon at Trespass Place.

'George,' she said, with a sigh, 'even tonight will you not stay inside? How about the Bonnington?'

He refused and she smiled fondly, placing a hand on each of his shoulders. As far as he could recall, she kissed him for the first time. Her hands remained there, heavy and reassuring. Perhaps it was the openness of her face that made George say what he hadn't planned. It seemed to devastate her, on this the night of celebration.

'John's death had nothing to do with you. You didn't bring Riley into court, I did.'

'Yes, I know.' She spoke as if she were haunted; as if she didn't mean what she said. Her arms dropped and she walked carefully along the edge of the wharf. At the far end she stopped and stared for an age into the black water. It chopped around the timber supports like a clock gone wrong, ticking in spasms.

Three times more the taxi beeped its horn.

10

The smooth running of great schemes relies upon the small details. Elizabeth's directions to Trespass Place were rather vague, so Anselm ran to a newsagent, where he checked an A to Z. The fact that Mr Bradshaw was waiting – and had been for over ten days – raised a spirit of urgency that made Anselm fumble and swear. He hurried to the Underground while the wind clutched at the umbrella as if to hold him back.

The train was packed and damp. Wet coats pushed against him. He forced his way to a corner and unfolded Elizabeth's instructions.

Dear Anselm,

Ten years ago I helped Graham Riley to leave the court as an innocent man. He was, I am sure, guilty. I now require your help to bring him back again.

In the first place you needed to be reminded of the trial; to read the letter and the cutting. This prepared you, I hope, for the meeting with Mrs Bradshaw. It was her place to reveal what happened after the Riley trial. It is mine to explain what I have done about it.

Anselm read the first sentence again, not quite believing that an officer of the court would behave in such a way, regardless of any crisis of conscience.

No evidence is likely to emerge which would demonstrate how or why Riley killed John Bradshaw. Something can still be done. George and I have set about taking away from Riley the one thing he does not deserve: a good name.

Anselm ducked beneath an arm to check the name of a station. A territorial shove put him back in the corner.

Riley has remained criminally active. The details are set out in a document retained by George. He keeps it in his inside left jacket pocket. His task is to deliver this, the basis of a future conviction, to Inspector Cartwright. Yours is to bring them together.

107

You will find him waiting beneath a fire escape in Trespass Place, a courtyard off Blackfriars Road. On the street he is known as Blind George, although he sees further than you or me (don't be troubled by the welding goggles). A senseless attack, however, has damaged his short-term memory. He can only retain events by writing them down.

Anselm wriggled into a tight space nearer the doors. Legs and bodies stiffened around him.

This project is of the greatest importance to him. I hope that through its fulfilment he will recover sufficient self-respect to start the journey home. You might elbow him in that direction when you get the chance. He'll need it.

Best wishes,

Elizabeth.

Anselm folded the letter away. His time at the Bar had taught him never to accept any document at face value – you had to scratch between the commas, and, in the final analysis, give the writer a going-over. That last option was no longer available, and was, in these circumstances, unnecessary. The letter corroborated everything Anselm had already concluded about Elizabeth: she had lost her confidence in a system that, perhaps, she had never questioned with sufficient vitality.

Anselm sighed audibly – and not because someone had stamped on his foot. He'd felt an idiot when he'd seen Nicholas Glendinning. Now, at last, he knew what to say – well, sort of, only it was difficult to articulate with accuracy and nuance. How would he explain to him that Elizabeth had been changed by her encounter with Riley? Like a gift, Locard's Principle came to mind. And Anselm, in the secrecy of his soul, felt modestly satisfied with himself, and not a little clever – an agreeable sensation instantly consumed by the recollection of Mrs Bradshaw standing harrowed in a doorway, and that awful phrase: nothing comes of nothing.

The train roared into Elephant and Castle and Anselm burrowed between steadfast shoulders. He stood on the platform hot and wet but triumphant. Through a window he saw a head pressed against the glass examining the handle of Mrs Bradshaw's umbrella.

11

Trespass Place normally protected George from the elements. The fire escape was vast and constructed of sheet metal. But there was a problem when a wind blew. It whirled around the tiny courtyard, throwing the water onto a horizontal plane. George had been wiping his face for ten minutes when he decided to head for Carlo's. He clambered to his feet and grasped his two plastic bags . . . and then he paused, looking down.

In one of them, beneath his rolled-up scarf, was an old carton of milk, a loaf of greenish bread and some tins. This wasn't his bag. He checked the other and immediately understood. He'd picked up Nancy's shopping, misled by the sight of his scarf. He must have put it on top, not noticing. And that meant that he'd left behind volumes one to twenty-two. With growing dread, George checked number twenty-three, to locate himself in his own story. There was no doubt about it. He'd left behind half his life: a childhood in Harrogate, hitching to London in his teens and, of course, his tangled relations with Graham Riley.

The wind moaned and wrestled with the bins and sacks. George grabbed his sleeping bag and the carrier that held the other half of his life. He ran to Marco's and took a seat in a far corner, beneath one of the heaters. Without his having to ask or pay, a plate of toast presently appeared, alongside a mug of hot chocolate.

12

Anselm had forgotten the plan on the A to Z, so at Waterloo Station he went looking for another newsagent. He studied the map, committing to memory the rights and lefts. Then he nipped back into the rain.

Five minutes later he surveyed Trespass Place: its towering walls; its back doors without handles; its signs that read KEEP CLEAR. He walked towards a mammoth fire escape at the far end. To thwart the burglar the bottom section was raised on a cantilever – a measure defeated by the attachment of a long chain that twirled slowly on its axis. Beneath this shelter stood a queue of green plastic sacks with yellow ties. Cardboard was propped against the wall. A shopping bag lay open. The milk was clotted and the bread was furry with mould. Anselm checked the sell-by dates. This lot had been bought before Elizabeth died. George Bradshaw hadn't waited long at all. And who could blame him? Anselm looked at the drainpipes, the tangled tape and the wheelie-bins. A client had once told him that hell was Sunderland Magistrates Court. He was wrong. Anselm moved under the raised steps and pulled back the cardboard. Upon the wall, neatly scratched, was a block of short vertical lines.

Anselm walked briskly out of the courtyard, his head bowed

against the rain. Further up the road he saw the bright lights of a café. He ran and sheltered in the doorway, wondering what to do next.

13

One of the great things about Marco's was the style of electric wall heater. They were high up and old-fashioned – orange bars against curved shining metal. They hummed while they worked, like Marco himself.

George sipped hot chocolate, wondering what to do about his missing books. It would be impossible to roll up, take his bag and disappear again. No, he couldn't see Nancy, not until it was all over – when Riley had been arrested. Then George could explain why he'd vanished, and why he'd deceived her. But that left open the possibility that she might leaf through volume twenty, where her husband made his first appearance. It was a risk he'd have to take. She wouldn't look, though . . . she wasn't like that. She'd been well brought up.

The windows were grey and streaming with condensation. Through the glass door George saw a dark figure swaying left and right in the cold. George stirred milky froth and thought of Graham Riley.

It had been one of the stranger things about the whole trial. Jennifer Cartwright – she'd been a detective sergeant back then – had quizzed him very carefully about Quilling Road. He'd drawn a plan of the house. He'd described the wallpaper. He'd labelled each room with numbers and names. He'd told her of Riley's strange manner . . . his never going up the stairs, his insistence on meeting everyone near the bottom step. And DS Cartwright had written it all down, smoking incessantly.

Months later he'd had a meeting with a CPS solicitor called Miss Lowell. This time there'd been typed-up depositions and a colour-coded floor plan. George had told his story all over again. The details were cross-referred to other witness statements, confirming their coherence with the broader picture. Finally there'd been a conference with a barrister called Pagett, a tall fellow in a morning suit – the kind of thing you got married in. George could almost recite his statement by now. Again, he went over what he'd seen and heard, and what he knew of Riley's idiosyncratic behaviour. But the strange thing was this: neither DS Cartwright nor Miss Lowell nor Mr Pagett thought to ask George if he had met Graham Riley before. None of them wondered why George had been so prepared to help these three girls in the first place. They weren't like the barrister Riley had on his side – the one who'd asked, 'What did David do that George wanted to forget?' If he'd been at the conference with DS Cartwright and Miss Lowell, he'd have rumbled George, of that there was little doubt.

The figure at the door swayed side to side. It had the bulk of a man. George wondered why he didn't step inside. The heaters were just out of this world.

14

Anselm's predicament illustrated the perils of the monastic path. Cyril had given him just enough to cover the cost of public transport. So Anselm, freezing and wet, had enough money to buy what he wanted, but only at the expense of what he needed. A cup of restoring coffee was there, behind his back, but only if he walked to his lodgings in the rain.

Anselm brooded over the choice but finally surrendered his

thoughts to a more serious problem. Elizabeth had failed to anticipate something far more basic than Anselm's delay in using the key. She hadn't given any weight to the reasonable expectation that a man with half a memory might wander off and leave his dinner behind, never mind his role in her scheme. How could he even begin to know where to look?

A flame of protest made Anselm restive. He shifted his weight from one foot to the other, as if he were ready to leave his corner and fight. He recalled Mrs Bradshaw when she dropped the paintbrush, mouth open and appalled at the thought that her husband might come home. Her hope had become too terrible to contemplate.

Anselm blinked at the sodden sky. It was getting worse. He ran to the Underground, dodging puddles and rivulets. In a livid fancy, he grabbed Cyril's remaining arm and chained it to a drainpipe.

15

Beneath Marco's humming heater, George wrote of waiting, a storm and a restless man at the door. (Once George had committed the past to paper, Nino had told him to gather up the present moment. 'It keeps you in the here and now.') When the rain became fitful he made his way back to Trespass Place.

The recollection of Nino's words made his stomach turn. There was something foolish in what George was doing: sitting beneath a fire escape expecting a monk to appear around the corner. It was like pretending that Elizabeth hadn't died, or that her death would have no consequences. In the here and now, Elizabeth was dead. His recollection of all they had done together was a kind of grieving, but also a running away, because it lay back there in the past, when she'd been alive. He shivered with cold and anxiety as if a harsh truth were creeping across Trespass Place: accepting Elizabeth's death meant accepting that Riley would get away after all. They were the two sides of the one coin. Spinning it in the air day after day was just an illusion.

Wrapping his arms around his legs, he remembered that Elizabeth's optimism had been without limit. And it worked backwards as well as forwards: she'd said the past is up for grabs.

16

When evening came, Nick went to the Green Room and opened *The Following of Christ*. On account of the hole it was impossible to read the first page, or indeed, most of the following chapters. Why cut out the heart of a book, unless you knew it by heart? While he tried to complete a broken sentence by guessing the missing words, the telephone rang. Father Anselm was in London, and wanted to meet him that evening. He said, 'I now have at least one of the answers you were looking for.'

An arrangement made, Nick closed the book with the thought that his mother was a comparable enigma.

Nick parked the yellow Beetle facing the old stones of Gray's Inn Chapel. Beneath a nearby street lamp stood Father Anselm, his close-cropped head angled to one side as though he were puzzled by the ingenuity of modern contraptions. Against the arched windows, he would have cut a medieval figure, but for the shapeless duffel coat. They crossed Holborn into Chancery Lane, heading towards the South Bank. The afternoon's storm had cleared the air, and the streets were shining and wet. At the frontage of Ede and Ravenscroft, the court tailors, Father Anselm peered at the wigs, the collars and the sharp suits. Afterwards he was quiet for a while. In the middle of Hungerford Bridge Nick broke step and leaned on the rail, arms folded. The swollen river beneath glittered at its banks, but the central flow was black and mysterious, seeming deeper and magnetic on that account. A small boat jigged on the surface. Nick watched its eerie survival, and a monk's voice sounded at his side.

'Forensic scientists say that every contact leaves a trace.' Father Anselm was also looking down into the silent waters. 'It's called Locard's Principle. The idea is that if you touch an object, you leave behind something that wasn't there in the first place – a little of yourself. By the same token, you take away something that wasn't on you when you came – part of the object. It's an alarming fact. We can't do anything without this interchange occurring.'

Out of the darkness, Nick perceived a rope between the small craft and a buoy. His mother's attachment had been to Saint Martin's Haven. The wind and rain had cleansed her mind for what she had to do. He recognised that now. A busker's flute began to whistle in the distance.

'Locard wasn't thinking of lawyers,' continued Father Anselm thoughtfully. 'Had he done so, had he applied the Principle to conduct, rather than contact, they'd be the exception to the rule, because nothing sticks to their robes. They can prosecute the innocent and defend the guilty and they remain – as they should – altogether blameless. In a way, their sincerity is determined not through principle, but by accident. It can't be otherwise. They stand urging you to believe one thing, whereas, if the other side had got there first, they'd be persuading you to think the opposite – with equal fervour, regardless of any price differential. It has nothing to do with what they might actually believe or, despite popular opinion to the contrary, what they're subsequently paid. Their allegiance is to the evidence and the instructions of their client. For this many would risk life and limb. As for themselves, when they go home . . . they're an island people, isolated by not knowing and by not being able to care. The Riley trial changed all that for your mother. The contact left a trace.'

The monk wormed a hand into a pocket beneath the duffel coat. He passed Nick a letter, and said, 'Having helped Riley to escape, she set out to bring him back to court . . . to take away his good name. In the event of her death, she's asked me to fulfil what she began.'

Nick read the instructions, his mind swimming. Why had she not shared this crisis with him? Why had it remained so very private? He stared at the neat sentences as Father Anselm explained his understanding of events: Elizabeth's faith in her professional identity had collapsed; this was the defence case that had brought down the ardent prosecutor; she'd kept the brief at the time because of what it represented; but then she'd learned of John Bradshaw's death, a killing with a connection to Riley that could never be demonstrated. He paused, and he seemed to reach out to Nick without moving. 'I think she wanted you to understand that she was culpable but without blame.'

They both gazed into the dark river, towards a lonely boat.

'But I would never have accused her,' said Nick.

'Me neither.' Father Anselm seemed melancholy. 'I sometimes wonder if conscience calls us back to a world very different from this one, making us strangers.'

Nick found his eyes filled with tears. She was so remote, now: not only in death but also in life. And, despite his confusion and distress, Nick felt disappointed. He'd anticipated a spectacular explanation for his mother's behaviour – withholding evidence or misleading the court; something that would account for her secrecy, her outlandish actions and the troubled letters that had brought him home. But it had all turned on acute sensibilities.

Nick pulled away, and together they walked back to Gray's Inn.

The orderly streets of St John's Wood were empty. Nick parked the Beetle and sat in the darkness rehearsing Father Anselm's last words. 'Get on with your life,' he'd said, 'I'm looking after your mother's.' They'd laughed, even though his task seemed pretty hopeless with Mr Bradshaw astray. Idly, Nick slapped the dashboard: he'd forgotten to ask about the relief of Mafeking.

Something rattled . . . his mother's mobile phone.

Either a paramedic or the police must have put it back on its stand.

Slowly Nick detached it. He looked at the face. There was a thumbprint on the glass. It could be the last mark his mother had made; all that was left of her. He pressed the redial button and listened.

A knocking sound cut the ringing tone . . . in the background a buzzer rang. Instantly there was applause and cheering.

'Hello? . . . yes?' It was a woman's voice. 'Who is it?'

Nick flushed with heat. But he couldn't reply.

'Are you there?'

The woman waited, and Nick listened, unable to cut the line. She was old, her tone wavering. Nick could hear her breathing. He could imagine a hand shaking.

'Wait . . . is that you . . . is that my lad?'

Nick looked at the phone's screen. The thumbprint was like an etching. Behind it was the dialled number. He fumbled for a pen and jotted it down upon his palm.

'Say something . . .' The voice was far off and desperate.

Nick pressed the off button. His mouth was parched.

17

Anselm caught the last train to Cambridge, where Father Andrew met him on the station concourse. Since the Prior had never quite come to appreciate the relationship of co-operation that prevails between the clutch and the synchromesh gearbox, Anselm offered to drive back to Larkwood. Thus the Prior was free to study, by the light of a pocket torch, Elizabeth's brief account of moral upheaval and her attempt to make amends. When he slowly folded up the letter, Anselm explained what had come to pass with Mrs Bradshaw, how she'd used a terrible phrase: nothing comes of nothing. He concluded by saying, 'And when I got to Trespass Place, her husband had gone. Elizabeth's scheme is already in ruins, within two weeks of her death.'

The car trundled out of the city and it was only after several miles that Anselm, from the smell, realised he'd left the hand-brake on. Discreetly, he released it, and dropped his window by an inch. 'Apparently,' he said, 'Elizabeth had a heart condition that meant she could die at any moment. It must clear the mind wonderfully to know that each breath could be your last . . .'

'It did,' said the Prior. 'She called me on the day of the consultation.'

'When was that?'

'Shortly after she'd come to Larkwood . . . when she'd spoken of a homicide.'

Anselm slowed down to concentrate. Whatever the Prior had gone on to say had almost certainly pushed Elizabeth into action.

'I didn't mention this before,' said the Prior, 'because I felt . . . self-conscious about what I said to her. She began to cry because there was so much that she would change, but it was out of reach.' Father Andrew tugged at an eyebrow. 'I tried to comfort her, saying it's not the beginning that matters, but rather the undiscovered end, because it completely transforms our understanding of where we came from, what we've done, who we ultimately are . . . I said it was never too late, that even last words or a final act could bring about this fantastic change . . . that it was like magic. The line seemed to go dead but then I heard her say, "Thank you." I next saw her on the day she gave you the key.'

'The day,' said Anselm, 'that she prepared for what is now unfolding.'

Gradually, the wide roads narrowed and street lamps vanished. The stars were hidden and the moon faintly lit the edge of a cloud. Beneath it Larkwood appeared like a crowd of fireflies. After parking beneath the plum trees they trudged along a winding path towards the monastery. Anselm could barely see the Prior but he heard his voice clearly. 'You must go back to London, I'm afraid. You owe it to Elizabeth and to George, to his wife and to his son. Perhaps it's owed to Mr Riley; perhaps, also, to yourself.'

Anselm didn't like that final coupling, but he took it as an accident of sentence construction. 'When should I go?'

'Tomorrow night. There's no time left for thinking. As you say, her plan is already falling apart.'

Anselm thought of George in welding goggles, stumbling down an alley. 'How do I find a man who's lost to himself?'

'I'll speak to Cyril's niece.'

'Pardon?'

'Cyril's niece, Debbie. She works with the homeless near Euston.'

Anselm pictured a large, annoyed oblong with clipped hair and a mouth like a post-box. 'An inspired idea,' he said magnanimously.

At the entrance to Larkwood the Prior fiddled with a huge key, wrought from iron hundreds of years ago. As the door swung open, the Prior took Anselm's arm, and they paused on the threshold. 'Find out who Elizabeth was,' he said, 'find the child who grew up to wear a gown that was too heavy for her shoulders.'

He seemed to have vanished, so deep was the darkness.

'Where shall I start?' asked Anselm, sharply awake to the presence in front of him.

'The fly-leaf of an incomparable book.'

Anselm recalled the inscription in *The Following of Christ*, written by a nun, and he smiled at the figure before him as it clanked and fumbled once more with the lock.

By late afternoon the next day, all the necessary arrangements for Anselm's trip to London had been made: a room had been secured with the Augustinians in Hoxton; consecutive meetings had been organised with Debbie Lynwood and Inspector Cartwright (who, of course, knew nothing of Elizabeth's floundering project and the evidence held by George Bradshaw); after a long and entertaining conversation between Anselm and the Provincial of the Daughters of Charity, an appointment had been made with Sister Dorothy – a maverick soul, it transpired, who now endured forced retirement in Camberwell; and, finally, the Prior had produced an envelope containing sufficient funds for a week, a generous act that had spared Anselm a reunion with the cellarer.

After vespers Father Andrew called Anselm out of his stall to the centre of the choir. Following ancient custom, no one left

Larkwood on a journey without the Prior's blessing. He had a little book full of well-phrased send-offs. You'd kneel wondering which one you were going to get.

Anselm bowed his head but, like a blasphemy, he thought of Riley: the bobbing knee, jangling gold on a bony wrist and thin, fixed lips. The image turned Anselm cold, and he woke, as if stunned, for the Prior's concluding words:

'May the light guide your steps, your thoughts, your words and your deeds; and may it bring you safely home, if needs be by a different path.'

18

Night had fallen and George felt a sudden urge to stay in a spike. As institutions devoted to the needs of those without shelter, they didn't compare favourably with the Bonnington, but they had three things in common: a roof, lots of beds and an effective heating system. The combination had its attractions when – like now – it was so wet that the air itself seemed to advance like the Atlantic. The council was responsible for these night shelters. In some you had to lie awake holding your shoes against your chest; if you closed your eyes you'd lose your laces. The first time George had rolled up at a spike in Camden, he'd been given a bed near a white brick wall with posters dotted here and there to add a splash of colour. That night he'd met an old man, who'd told him an old story.

The fellow had matted hair and an overcoat that almost reached his shoes. A scarf with blue and red stripes trailed down his back. He was examining a picture of trekkers following a mountain ridge: the sky was blue and the hills were another kind of blue. In this refuge of chipped bedsteads, of strong odours and shouting, it was ethereal. Written on the bottom in red letters was 'Andorra'. The man muttered, 'You'd think it wasn't there.' He turned around and said, as if mildly surprised, 'What brings you here?'

George said, 'I'm tired.'

'Then you're in the wrong place.'

'So what about you?'

'I like the pictures. You're new to this school, aren't you?' He didn't mean the spike; he meant the street.

'Yes.' George's eyes watered, but he ground his teeth. He no longer had the right to cry.

The man was called Nino. He'd been a traffic warden. After his 'early retirement' he had obtained membership in every library that didn't require a fixed abode. His bed was beside George's. When the lights were out Nino began to whisper.

'Have you heard of Pandora?'

'Yes. She had a box.'

'That's right. Hesiod says she was the first woman that ever lived. Do you know what she was made of?'

'No.'

'Clay. Do you know what was in the box?'

'Worms?'

'No. You're confusing it with the expression "a can of worms", which, I grant you, has considerable bearing upon the matter in hand. Before I go on, let me say at once that Pandora has been much maligned – I've checked every library in north London. The classical mind, like that of ancient religion, tends to blame women when it comes to moral catastrophe. I dissociate myself entirely from that tradition.'

George wanted to cry again. It was like being a boy once more, having a story told at night that he couldn't quite follow. His grandfather, David – whose name he carried and had abandoned – had been a wonderful reader of stories. Listening to Nino, George could imagine big pictures in a big book: a beautiful princess with long, golden hair, her fair hands holding a small, golden casket.

Nino said, 'Now in that box stirred every imaginable evil. Do you understand?'

'Yes.'

'A very foolish fellow lifted the lid. Are you listening, stranger to the road?'

'I am.' George had started to cry. George bit his pillow and his hands gripped the mattress and his leg. Far off there was shouting. Someone cried in a scuffle.

'The evils escaped,' said Nino softly, 'and they caused great suffering. But do you know what was at the bottom of the box?'

George dared not release the pillow from his mouth. But Nino wouldn't go on until George had spoken. 'I've no idea,' he gasped.

Nino's whisper grew fainter, making George raise his head. 'The last thing to rise from that unimaginable quarter was hope.'

George blinked, resolved to wait a little longer. There were tears in his eyes.

PART THREE

a boy's progress

1

'I'm no fool, Arnold,' said Nancy Riley to the hamster. 'It all adds up.'

It was early morning and she'd just slipped into the kitchen, leaving her man groaning in his sleep.

Nancy could see the connections between things. Always had done. When she'd worked for Harold Lawton on the Isle of Dogs she'd once spotted a petty fraud at the hands of the wharf manager.

'When I showed the boss how it was done,' murmured Nancy, 'he said I could've gone places.'

That was a long time ago, but the same sensation of discovery had settled on Nancy all over again: there was a link between things that didn't seem to be connected: the death of that barrister, the photograph that arrived in the post and the change in her man's nightmares.

A couple of weeks back, Nancy had bought a paper. A name on page five caught her eye. Elizabeth Glendinning QC, a well-known barrister, had been found dead at the wheel of a car parked in the East End. She had died of heart failure while trying to call for help. That evening Nancy showed the article to her man.

'What a coincidence,' said Nancy. 'She was just up the road from Mile End Park.'

Riley nodded, staring at the paper.

'Did you see her at the fair?' asked Nancy.

Riley's jaw moved as if his gums were itching.

'They found some old spoons on the seat,' continued Nancy pensively. 'It's sad if you ask me.'

During the night Riley moaned like he was being fried on a low heat. His face was hot and wet. And then, a couple of days ago, the letter came. Well, it wasn't a letter. Riley tore it open and out popped a photograph. The two of them stared at the crimped black and white square on the table. Nancy noticed a booming chest and wide braces, a shirt without a collar.

Riley's hand slammed onto the smiling face as if it were a wasp.

Nancy jumped. 'Who's that?' she asked, shaken.

'No one.' His eyes were trained hard on his fingers as if something might crawl out.

Nancy didn't press her man. She'd learned not to. She could read the signs. He was like hot water in a pan, close to the boil. That night he screamed. In itself, that was no surprise: Riley had suffered nightmares since the trial. ('Occupational hazard,' said Mr Wyecliffe, as if he had them too.) They were always the same: he was running for dear life, chased by something like a dog they'd once seen at the races, and then he was falling . . . but this time it was slightly different.

'What is it?' wailed Nancy. She'd been listening to his muttering but the cry had come like a brick through the window. To her astonishment he buried his head into her neck.

'I'm falling' – Nancy stroked his wet scalp. It was bony like a rock on the beach. His hand covered hers and they stayed like that, as if they were waiting for an ambulance; and then Riley added the bit that was new, the change in the dream – 'I'm just falling down an endless stairwell.'

A stairwell? Strange things, are dreams.

From that day on, Riley's nightmares got worse. To make

128

himself tired, he started walking in the middle of the night along Limehouse Cut, the canal that ran through Bow to the Thames. He'd listen to the foxes in the old warehouses. But that was later. On this night, when he'd calmed down, Riley turned his back on Nancy, and she felt her own stomach fail, for he was always moving away, and she'd never got used to it. And Nancy said to herself, I'm not stupid. This dream, the photo and the death of that barrister are tied up somehow. Mr Lawton hadn't believed her, but in the end she'd been proved right, and he'd said, 'You could've gone places.'

Come to think of it, that was insulting. The boss had let slip what he thought of Nancy: how she'd wasted her life. All she'd done was work for him and marry Graham Riley.

Nancy had gone to the docks when she'd turned sixteen, along with Rose Clarke and Martina Lynch. They'd been together since primary school. They remained a threesome, well known to everyone who worked on Harold Lawton's quay; and they were seen every Friday night at the same pub just outside the main gates, the Admiral – a hole, really, but it was ever so old, and there was this side room made from a ship's cabin. A big plastic sign said the owners had been serving 'seadogs since the days of rigging and sails'. Martina got the nickname Babycham from the landlord because she drank nothing else. True, Nancy was the dumpy one, but it didn't seem to matter when she was jammed between the other two. She dressed nicely and there were always lads wanting to join their table. Thinking of those days, Nancy remembered a small detail about the weekend that followed the night before: more often than not, no one had asked her out. She could admit that now. What did it matter? It wasn't through her friends that she'd met her man, anyway.

Riley used to clock in with all the others at eight in the morning. Back then, everyone had a card that was stamped in a big machine. It was the same at lunchtime. The lads all got one hour off, but they had to stamp their cards again if they'd left the premises, to show they were back on time. It was old-fashioned, but Mr Lawton liked the contraption. He wasn't one for changing with the times. Funny, really, that his business should have lasted so long on the Isle of Dogs, while everyone else went under. Anyhow, one day Riley lingered in the office until they were alone. He'd been taken on a couple of months earlier, after being made redundant just down the road. So he was new, and different from the rest – not a Friday-night man, not a drinker. Quiet. Kept himself to himself. Didn't need friends – didn't want them. His hair was always ruffled and his eyes couldn't keep still. They were blue-green and confused, as if he'd been shaken up in the bottle. And he'd noticed Nancy. He watched her from the driver's cabin of a crane. She knew because he once pulled the wrong lever, and all the stevedores went off it when he dropped a crate of bananas. So, on this day, Nancy sensed him hanging around, edgy and shy. She thought he was about to invite her to that big dance coming up in White City, but he wasn't. Instead he asked her to risk her job.

'Do my card for me, will you? I've got tenants to see.'

Nancy had been impressed. Here was a man with a bit of property. Hardly common among Lawton's boys. A nest egg, he'd explained. He was getting other people to pay off the mortgage.

'I just need about half an hour,' said Riley, looking over his shoulder.

Nancy agreed, and he studied her face like he was looking for spots. Then he said, as if he were handing over something precious, 'I knew I could trust you.'

130

She waited for him to ask her out, but he didn't. A week or so later he suggested having tea in a hotel. She said yes, thinking he meant some place on Commercial Road, but he took her to Brighton, which was a double shock, because he paid for the train as well – first class, if you please. They were married within six months. Babycham and Rose were the only witnesses. There was no reception, just a free drink at the town hall and a cheeky kiss from the registrar. Her man didn't like that. And he didn't like her pals. She still saw them at Lawton's, but the three-some had been split. So the Friday-night sessions came to an end. Nancy didn't altogether mind, because, looking back, she'd never really enjoyed herself.

They moved into Riley's bungalow and set up home. Nancy had always wanted a herb bed but there was no garden, just flagstones. So she started collecting bricks from the towpath by Limehouse Cut – just one at a time, if she happened to see one in the grass. Slowly, as married life got underway, the pile of bricks grew bigger, but the bed was never built. She was a few short. And that mirrored their life together. There were some missing pieces. Within weeks of that free drink at the town hall, the man who'd taken her to Brighton went into hiding – in his own home.

But, of course, he had to come out again. They were under one roof. During the day, he was sharp and brusque, baring his teeth when he felt he was being crossed. His jaw would creep forward, and his eyes would go wide, staring to one side, as if he daren't look at you for fear of what he might do. During the evening, he'd sneer at the television: at politicians, soaps, the news, bishops. His bottom lip would warp, and his bitten nails would scratch the rests of his armchair, catching on the nylon covers. In disgust he'd put on a Walt Disney video, slamming it into the machine. Then his face would light up. He'd weep with

131

Bambi or shake his fist at the queen in *Snow White*. All his feel-ings crackled and popped, like the cereal. But when the film was over, he became pinched, as if it shouldn't have ended. (Nancy didn't like the word 'unstable', but she got the impres-sion that her man held himself together, a bit like a barrel with those iron bands, and that if one or two of the screws came loose, he'd just explode. So she learned to keep well back. She didn't tinker with his ways.) At night he wouldn't touch her. There was a cold part of the bed, right in the middle. It was like that channel in the sea opened up by Charlton Heston, when he was Moses. Both of them were like walls of water, waiting to collapse from the sheer weight of separation. Only it never happened. Not even after that policewoman came to Lawton's and arrested her man at the foot of his crane. At the time, Nancy watched him being led away, waiting for those iron bands to snap; but they didn't.

'It all adds up,' repeated Nancy solemnly. 'I'm no fool.'

Suddenly Arnold froze on his drum. His neck seemed to beat as though his heart was lodged in his throat.

'You think too much,' said Riley quietly.

Nancy let out a cry. Right behind her, an arm's length away, was her man. He was wearing his camouflage parka with the hood up. A high collar almost covered his mouth. He'd picked it up from an old soldier who'd topped himself.

'You scared me,' laughed Nancy. Her pulse found its stride, and she said calmly, 'Don't you want some breakfast?'

'No.' His voice cracked, and his eyes were famished. 'I've got a clearing.'

'Where?'

'Tottenham.'

The back door slammed as if they'd had a row. Standing by

132

the window, Nancy watched her man as if he were on another planet. A dense mist had risen off the Thames and dissolved the streets of Poplar. It would swamp the Isle of Dogs from Canary Wharf to Cubitt Town. Street-lights hung like saucers and Riley slowly disintegrated. When he'd vanished, Nancy turned to Arnold. His little legs started moving and the wheel clinked and whirred.

'How on earth did he get like that?' she asked sorrowfully.

2

As arranged, Anselm arrived at the Vault near Euston Station at seven in the morning. Scaffolds and hoarding covered tall buildings on either side of the day centre. Sheets of polythene flapped and winches clinked in the breeze. A queue of figures shuffled to a gate, evoking the fortitude of travellers bound for the New World. Anselm passed behind them into a narrow, cobbled lane and found the back-door buzzer beneath a nameplate.

'How is Uncle Cyril?' asked Debbie Lynwood, opening the door to her office at the end of a dimly lit corridor.

'Hot and bothered,' said Anselm. 'I threw away a receipt.'

'Cantankerous beast.'

Anselm had expected genetic determinism (bulk in overalls) but Debbie's frame was slight. She wore black trousers and a scarlet roll-neck jumper. A selection of enamel badges revealed an interest in classic motorcycles.

'I can't promise much,' she said, hands in her back pockets. 'Finding someone on the street is almost impossible. But I know a man who might be able to help – someone who knows the ropes.' She moved across the room towards a door that led onto the Vault itself. In the middle was a round window. On the other side Anselm saw the blue haze of smoke. Dark figures crossed slowly as if wading through water. 'When I mentioned what I knew of you,' said Debbie thoughtfully, 'he was eager to meet you. Wait here.'

She opened the door and a low industrious hum spilled into the office. As he waited, Anselm absorbed his surroundings: a wall of box files, posters displaying information, an old school desk, a worn blue carpet . . . and a short, wiry man holding a staff like a curtain rail with an ornamental knob. He wore a green cagoule, his trousers were tucked into his socks, and he shouldered a backpack. His feet, in polished, split brogues, were splayed outwards. A thin, grizzled beard covered an oblong chin.

'May I present Mr Francis Hillsden,' said Debbie.

The traveller made a short bow with his head and shook Anselm's hand. 'A pleasure, with respect,' he said, keeping his eyes averted. They were blue and seemed to be smarting.

Debbie invited Anselm to speak as they pulled up chairs in a triangle. Mr Hillsden perched himself on the edge of his seat, gripping his staff as though it were a pole to a room below.

'I am looking for a man in his sixties,' said Anselm. 'His name is David George Bradshaw. I understand he is known as Blind George.'

'By whom, if I might respectfully ask?' His accent was soft, a cultured voice from the West Country. 'I hope my interjection does not trouble you?'

'Not at all,' replied Anselm. A sense of déjà vu flashed like a weak light. 'That's his name among other homeless people.'

Mr Hillsden gave a brief nod as if he'd made a note of the reply. 'Mr Bradshaw has restricted vision?'

'No. But he wears welding goggles. I don't know why.'

'To hide his face?' The suggestion was directed towards one of the posters on the facing wall.

'Maybe . . . I'm told he keeps his own company.' Anselm felt uneasy, as if he were hiding the part he'd played in the downfall of a man. 'Until recently, Mr Bradshaw stayed beneath a fire escape at Trespass Place. He was waiting there for a colleague of mine who unfortunately died. When I went to meet him on her behalf he had gone. I have an important message for him – in effect, that I will continue what they were doing in her stead.'

'In the first place, I offer my condolences.' Mr Hillsden's eyelids twitched as if troubled by a particle of grit. 'But secondly, with respect, if this gentleman has withdrawn from the company of men, how might one ask questions as to his whereabouts?'

'I don't know.'

'A fair answer, if I may say so. Where is Trespass Place?'

Anselm explained, adding that while Mr Bradshaw might not be blind, his memory had been shattered; that he held time together with a series of notebooks – a detail that somehow seemed to define the man he was looking for.

'A wise practice,' observed Mr Hillsden. He became abruptly stern, glancing round as if he'd heard a voice of contradiction. He banged his staff twice and the severity dissolved. Twitching again, he said, 'I don't wish to intrude, but have you met Mr Bradshaw before?'

'Yes.'

'Frequently?'

'Once.'

'Would he remember you?'

Anselm was stung more by the innocence of the question than its pertinence. His face grew hot: Mr Hillsden was proceeding with him as he had once proceeded with Mr Bradshaw. Neither of them had known what they were doing. 'I hope not,' said Anselm gravely, not daring to look up. He let his eyes rest upon the shining brogues and the socks outside the trousers.

No one spoke after that. Mr Hillsden seemed to be deliberating. Presently he said, 'My colleagues on the street tend to have what might be called a patch. Most of us do not stray from it. When we do, I'm afraid, it is usually for a serious reason. And when we move, it is not to another part of London, but a different corner of England. That, at least, has been my experience.' He stood up, bringing Anselm and Debbie to their feet. 'I'll go over to the South Bank, though I fear the venture will be futile. But should I find him, the most I can do is invite him here. Without his express permission, I would not reveal his location.'

'Of course,' said Anselm. He had the peculiar sensation of standing before a High Court Master in an application for Wasted Costs. He reached into his habit pocket, aware that his coming gesture was ridiculous but necessary: 'Please, may I cover your expenses?'

'Thank you, but no,' said Mr Hillsden graciously. 'I have adequate means which I am happy to place at your disposal.' He looked down at his feet. Briskly, he raised his head and for a split second his blue, watery eyes latched on to Anselm. 'I understand you were once at the Bar?'

'Yes.'

'Which Inn?'

'Gray's.'

Mr Hillsden seemed to breathe in the sound. A ghostly calm changed his face. 'Fantastic forms, whither are ye fled?'

He frowned as if trying to remember what came next. Anselm knew these words of Lamb, but he too was stuck. Suddenly, Mr Hillsden swung to the door with the round window. Without hesitating, he strode into the heavy murmuring and the blue smoke, his stick tapping on the floor.

136

Riley stood at the foot of the stairs in an empty house in Tottenham. It was cold and damp and his heart was beating fast. He stared at the bottom step.

'Who sent the photograph of Walter?'

His eyes moved to the chipped baluster, following the spindles up to the gloom of an unlit landing. The silence opened a door on those shouting voices, the scuffling of feet and whatever it was that ended up smashed on the floor. As a boy in the box-room, he used to beg God to make it stop. And funnily enough, He did. Shortly afterwards things would go quiet and he'd say, 'Thank you, thank you,' his head still under his pillow.

Riley set to work, lifting and dragging. He loaded up the tables and chairs, the mirrors and cupboards, a lamp stand and four candlesticks. His feet stamped out the memory of his child-hood, but others from last week licked him. It was always like this. His head was full of noise. He played arguments like they were favourite records, changing the words for a bit of variety. It was exhausting, but anger made him feel alive. In a full-blooded row, he'd pass through a kind of barrier and float, hardly breathing; he'd think up things to say, and pass them on, as if to someone else. It was a long way from the gratitude of a boy in the boxroom.

He worked feverishly. Puffs of dust made him cough and spit. By the late afternoon he'd finished. The building had been stripped. Panting, he stood in the living room. Sweat touched the nape of his neck like a hand: who had posted the photo-graph of Walter?

He hadn't looked at the picture since the day it had fallen from the envelope. But he could still see the man he wouldn't call Dad, the man no one pushed around, the biggest man in the street. Walter had kept dumb-bells under the bed. He'd done press-ups. He'd boxed the air, snorting and whistling – he'd been a southpaw. He'd smelled of liniment. Riley saw him only in the evenings because he got up at four o'clock to work at the warehouse. After he was made redundant he had to sell pies from a barrow. He was known as the Pieman. And there wasn't a picture of him left on the planet, except the one that had fallen onto the kitchen table. Riley couldn't understand it. He'd burnt them all over forty years ago. Sweat crawled down his back. Who could have posted the photograph? There was no one he could think of. They were all dead.

Riley sat against the wall, hands resting on his knees. Rat droppings were scattered like tiny black seeds along the skirting board. The damp and the quiet closed in upon him.

Major Reynolds at the Salvation Army hostel had always worn a neatly pressed uniform. He had a pencil moustache like that of a Battle of Britain pilot and years of cornet playing had left a small indentation on his upper lip. A shiny square face and prominent black eyebrows completed the impression of military distinction. Riley never learned his first name. He was just 'the Major'.

When this quiet soldier saw the blade in Riley's sock, he should have thrown him back onto the street. But he didn't. Instead, he pulled the runaway into his office, threw the knife in the bin and said, 'You're a grown-up now.'

Riley smiled, like kids do when they're nervous.

'You're a man.'

Riley's eyes glazed, but he kept the smile.

'And a man should think deeply,' said the Major, unperturbed. He folded his arms, and his dark eyebrows made a frown. He measured Riley up and down with a long, calculating gaze, as if to guess the size of his clothes.

The next day the Major called Riley back into his office. He stood with legs crossed, leaning back on his desk. He'd put in a good word to another trooper in the Army, a manager at McDougall's on the Isle of Dogs.

'There's a job if you want it,' he said.

'Doing what?' He stared at the Major's gleaming shoes. Even the soles were clean.

'Stacking crates of self-raising flour.'

Riley had seen the ads everywhere. They made it out to be some kind of miracle when it was just a mix of chemicals. He said, 'Nothing rises on its own.'

The Major narrowed his eyes, like a gambling man, wondering if there was another level to the remark. Uncertainly, he said, 'No, it doesn't.'

Riley never went back to the Sally Ann. He worked hard. He learned how to operate a crane. He saved up. He bought a bungalow. And he bought Quilling Road. The idea was to rent it out and build up an investment, but it turned into something else. No, that wasn't true. It was a choice; a rambling, complicated, murky series of impulses and actions, but, in the end, a very deep kind of choice; something cold and murderous. It was similar to being in one of his rages. It was as if he were watching himself, and he felt nothing at what he saw.

The docks were dying, but Riley survived. After he was made redundant, he found a job the same week at Lawton's, where he met Nancy. Dumpy Nancy with her hungry eyes. He first saw her from on high, looking down from his crane. He seemed to see her close-up for who she was. She walked timidly, as if she'd been hurt. That's when he first thought of selling Quilling Road. He seriously thought of packing up. But he

139

didn't. One lunchtime he went into the manager's office intending to ask her out . . . because there was something about her that had stirred him, that had lit a small flame in his guts . . . But on the day, when he opened his mouth, he'd asked her to stamp his card while he went AWOL to catch his rent. That sudden shift of intention, the deception of Nancy, had thrilled him, as if it were a kind of arson. (Riley understood the excitement of a building on fire.) So that was another choice – an even deeper one, from a frozen place inside himself. Unlike getting married to Nancy. That happened as if it were inevitable. The courting went like a dream. He did everything that he'd seen in the films: aftershave, greased hair, a natty suit – the lot. He took Nancy to a big hotel, ordered high tea and paid with crisp bills fresh from the bank. He left a fat tip. He held out his arm for Nancy. On Brighton beach, he tossed his trilby into the wind. But when they got married, and they went home, and she was there first thing in the morning and last thing at night . . . he felt sick. He didn't know what to do in the day to day. He scoured his past, lifting its slabs, jerking open its drawers, trying desperately to find something that would teach him *what to do*. But there was nothing there, except loathing and disgust, like a warm mist. And there before him, day and night, was Nancy. Dumpy Nancy with her hungry eyes. She was a breathing accusation.

And then help came from a very strange quarter, although he didn't see it that way at the time: a woman in black arrived on the wharf with a few heavies in uniform. Twenty minutes later he was arrested. From that moment, the focus of Nancy's anguish shifted from who he was to what someone had said he'd done. And that gave him space. Not much, but space nonetheless.

*

Riley swept up the rat droppings and put the pan and brush back in a hallway cupboard. As he closed the door he heard that polished voice as if it were on the other side. He saw the scrubbed nails, the white cuffs, the starched trousers.

'A man should think deeply; he should know himself.'

Riley had studied the Major's cap-badge motto, 'Blood and Fire', in a panic, unable to comprehend why this man should care at all.

'I know myself better than you ever will, Major. I've been places . . . in here' – he'd pointed savagely at his head, as if it were a distant continent – 'that you've only heard about.'

'I don't mean what you've done. I mean who you are. The man behind the mistakes and the wrong turns.' The Major leaned forwards, placing a hand on each knee, like the medic on a football pitch. He stared at Riley, his eyes clean and unbearably merciful. 'They're not the same, you know.'

They're not the same. The strange words spiralled down forty years into an empty house in Tottenham. Riley's mind grew dark – even his eyes seemed to drain of light. How could you separate a man from what he'd done? Like a flicker of flame in the grate, Riley remembered himself standing at the bedroom door, a boy in pyjamas, watching Walter punch and stab the air.

4

Anselm was drinking tea in a café ten minutes early for his meeting with Inspector Cartwright. Roughly ten minutes after the agreed time he saw a figure dodging between the cars on Coptic Street. A magenta scarf fluttered against a long black overcoat.

Anselm had first met Inspector Cartwright during the Riley

trial. Afterwards he'd seen her once or twice smoking in the corridors of the Bailey. Their eyes had met; and Anselm, being the sensitive sort, had detected a measure of hostility. That expression, it seemed, had not left her face.

'Sorry I'm late,' she said sweetly, sitting down, 'three kids under five. Don't do it.'

'I'll try not to.' Each ear was weighted with a substantial holly-berry earring, irregular in shape, probably painful to wear and undoubtedly made by one of the under-fives. Her hair was a deep, rusty brown; it had been cut very short, leaving precise lines. 'I think when we last met,' she said kindly, 'you'd just opened the door to let Mr Riley out.'

'And now,' replied Anselm, 'I hope to open another that will bring him back in.'

Inspector Cartwright was, of course, wholly unaware of Elizabeth's hope to 'take away Riley's good name' and her contingency plan should death overtake the fulfilment of her project, so Anselm related what had transpired since the day he received the key.

'Unfortunately,' he said, in conclusion, 'I came to my responsibility a mite later than she anticipated. When I got to Trespass Place, George had gone.'

Inspector Cartwright had listened with fixed attention, a hand at intervals repositioning an earring. She glanced at the cake selection, saying, 'I've already played a part in this business, only I didn't realise it until now. Would you hang on a moment?' She waved at the counter and asked for a date slice. 'Kids. I need sugar.' The waiter returned with a small plate and a small cake. After reflecting for a moment she began to speak.

'A few years ago a friend of mine put a file on my desk. He has an informant in the field called Prosser who trades in

142

antiques at the bottom end of the market. He goes round the fairs and fêtes. He's on a retainer to tell us what he sees and hears. Usually it's handling stolen goods – stuff being moved on for cash without a receipt. Sometimes it's drugs. It happens that he'd filed three reports on Riley.' She leaned on the table, one hand on top of the other. 'Prosser said Riley was up to something, but he couldn't pin it down. But he was sure that people came to Riley's stall, handed over cash and left with nothing.'

'A payment?'

'Apparently.'

'The same people?'

'Not always, but often.'

'Paying protection?'

'We had him watched but he does nothing but empty dead men's houses and sell on what they've left behind.'

Anselm called up the sorts of questions that were once basic to his trade: 'Is the profit margin too high for his kind of business?'

'No. And the accounts are perfect – all filed on time at Companies House.'

'Is he funding a lifestyle beyond his earnings?'

The Inspector shook her head. 'He's got a tatty bungalow, no car and never goes on holiday. So we dropped it.'

'But people still give him money for nothing?' said Anselm.

'Yes, they do.'

Anselm waited.

'A couple of years ago I was at the Bailey for a trial,' said the Inspector. 'One morning I was in the canteen and Mrs Glendinning took a seat right in front of me. Without saying hello, she asked if I'd heard about the death of John Bradshaw. I said I had. And then, like a timetable enquiry, she said, "Will you get Riley in the dock for the killing?" I shook my head and she just made an "Ah," as if a train had been delayed. And then she said, "I wonder if he's gone straight?" That's when I told her about Prosser, but she didn't seem that interested.'

Anselm smiled to himself. With two straightforward questions, Elizabeth had learned what she wanted to know: the state of the police inquiry into John's death, and whether Riley was still believed to be involved in crime. Armed with this information, she'd tracked down George and begun her scheme. In a reverie, Anselm saw afresh its crucial antecedents: her troubled visits to Finsbury Park and Larkwood, where she'd worked out the framework for her actions.

Inspector Cartwright tapped her plate with a teaspoon. 'Hello.' She seemed to be peering into a pipe. 'I'm a police officer. Put your hands up.'

'Forgive me,' said Anselm, blinking. 'I was distracted by a kind of vision.'

'Really? What did you see?'

'That Elizabeth drew you forward; as she drew my Prior; as she drew me.'

For a time neither of them spoke.

'I suppose that makes us comrades,' Inspector Cartwright said at last. She held out her hand. As their palms met Anselm saw Elizabeth leaning over a box of Milk Tray – when it had all begun. Her hair had fallen like a curtain. In his imagination, Anselm peered behind it, and caught her faint smile. 'I've been tidying up my life,' she'd said.

'I never heard from Mrs Glendinning again,' resumed the Inspector. 'On the day she died, she left a message on my answer machine. She just said, "Leave it to Anselm."'

They both now understood what that meant. But Anselm

144

wanted to know something else. 'How would you describe her tone of voice?'

'Supremely confident.'

Standing outside the café, Anselm said, 'Out of interest, did you ever take the Pieman seriously?'

'We ran the name past all our contacts in the field,' said the Inspector, 'and we pushed it through the computer, but nothing came up. When I interviewed Riley, he wouldn't answer a single question, but I kept coming back to that name.'

'Why?'

'I noticed it made him sweat.'

Anselm left Inspector Cartwright on the understanding that he would contact her as and when he heard from Mr Hillsden. Watching her walk down Coptic Street, Anselm recalled Lamb's question to the old benchers of the Inner Temple: *'Fantastic forms, whither are ye fled?'*

5

One freezing morning Nancy had walked from Poplar to her shop. Dumped across the entrance was a pile of cardboard marked FRAGILE in red. She reached over with her keys, glancing down to keep her balance. That's when she saw the finger poking out. She gasped, thinking it must be a body from a gangland war. She tapped the surface with her foot, wondering if the man had been cut up into bits, but the finger moved and a flap opened like a trap door and there was this man, his face black and hairy, his eyes hidden by goggles. She'd thought he must have been a fighter pilot from the First World War.

This man rolled onto his side, drawing up his knees. Then he felt his way up the door, using the handle to lift himself out of the cardboard . . . It was packaging for a fridge.

'Am I in the way?'

'Not at all, but you're nearly in the road. Can't you see?'

'No.'

It was arctic and the man's hands were a dirty blue. Cars whipped over the hump in the road, making them scrape and bang. Nancy said, 'Won't you warm up inside?'

'May I?'

Mr Lawton used to say things like that. *May I?* She opened up and dragged the cardboard through to the back room. It wouldn't feel right, throwing it out. When she came back he was standing inside, his hands on what Riley had called a figurine lamp – a woman with scarves all over and a light socket sticking out of her head. His fingers moved so gently, building the thing in his mind, that it became beautiful.

'I'm Mrs Riley.'

'I'm Mr Johnson.'

Who would have believed it? Over the following months they became friends. He was her one secret from Riley. And then he disappeared. In one sense it was for good, because a very different man eventually came back. He seemed frail and uncertain. He sat down with shaking arms.

'What happened?' asked Nancy anxiously.

'I got my head kicked in.' His goggles moved on a rumpled nose. 'I can't remember much of the present. This morning, last week . . . they've gone down the plughole.'

Nancy lit the gas fire, and she thought of the entertainment Uncle Bertie used to kick off when they were in Brighton. It was called 'Silly Secrets'. Cheerily, she said, 'Shall we play a game?'

'All right.'

'You tell me a secret, and then I'll tell you one.' The idea was that people confessed to daft things they'd done. (Once, in a shop, Uncle Bertie had used a toilet, only to find it was part of a mock bathroom for sale.)

'That's not fair,' said Mr Johnson. 'I won't remember and you will.'

'I'll tell no one.'

Mr Johnson said, 'I once had a son.'

Nancy covered her mouth. He leaned forward, vapour rising off him, his goggles full of condensation, and he talked about summers in Southport with the same longing that she had for Brighton. And Nancy waited, sensing that something awful had happened to his boy, but he never said what. The next day, Mr Johnson turned up and Nancy tipped out things she'd never said and thought she'd never say – how she'd met Riley, the life she'd lost at Lawton's, the children she'd never had . . . the trial. And Mr Johnson listened, warming his grey-blue hands: a gentleman who would remember nothing.

Nancy glanced at the sputtering fire. On her lap was a plastic bag. She'd found it a couple of weeks ago when she went into the back room to pick up her shopping. It was full of notebooks, each neatly numbered on the front. They belonged to Mr Johnson, the gentleman who could remember nothing. Nancy had waited for him to come back, but he'd vanished in the mist, just like Riley on his way to Tottenham. She glanced towards the door . . . and reached into the bag. It was wrong, she knew, but ever since that barrister had died, the trial had returned. Sensations from that time had been prickling her like pins in a doll. The only way to numb the pain was to fill her mind with something else, and the puzzle book was full – she rooted around for number one. On the front was written 'My Story'.

Her mouth was open and her hair tingled. This wasn't right.

I call myself George.

She hadn't known that. He was just Mr Johnson.

I'm a Harrogate boy, a Yorkshire lad. There's a little lane that runs by a bowling green and a tennis court of orange grit. On the other side are houses with mown lawns. At the end of the lane there's a clump of trees and a fence with a gate. It seems that the sun is always shining here and the flowers are taller than me. Foxgloves, I think they're called. But my earliest memory of this place is in the rain. My mother had made a canvas shelter for my pram—

Nancy snapped it shut. This was wrong. But she reached in and opened another number, wondering what had happened to Mr Johnson when he'd grown up.

I'd seen her quite a few times, and always at night. She stood beneath a street lamp, hands behind her back like Dixon of Dock Green. The most amazing thing was her white headdress. It was like a tent without guide ropes.

The doorbell sounded.

Nancy dropped the book, composed herself and presently sold a mirror to Mr Prosser – a dealer in quality second-hand. He was always mooching around, asking how her man found such good stuff. She told him nothing. When he'd gone she tied a knot in Mr Johnson's bag and pushed it into the bottom drawer of the filing cabinet.

148

But that left her exposed. She fell back in her seat, eyes clenched and hands over her ears. In that inner darkness, she sensed the patient 'attendance' of Mr Wyecliffe. It was a word he'd often used. She'd thought he was a sorcerer. How else did he pull off the impossible?

After being charged, Riley was hauled before a porky magistrate with a runny nose, who, between sneezes, sent her man to Wormwood Scrubs on remand. But Mr Wyecliffe got him out within a week. No special keys or dodgy chains. 'Just words, well used, ma'am,' he said, waving a grey handkerchief. 'All that requires my attendance now is the trial.' He sniffed and blinked, as if he hadn't worked out how to do it yet.

The solicitor had brought Riley home and stayed for a 'preliminary conference'. They sat in the living room, drinking Uncle Bertie's 'poison'. Riley was humiliated and speechless and couldn't look in Nancy's direction. He was quaking.

'We'll use counsel,' said Mr Wyecliffe significantly, to break the silence. 'I'll get the best.'

'I know who I want.' It was the first thing Riley had said. He glanced at a spot near Nancy's feet and asked for some sandwiches.

When she came back, Mr Wyecliffe was making notes, and Riley appeared deathly calm. The shaking had stopped. He spoke under his breath while the solicitor stuffed his face as if he'd had no breakfast. Her man stared at the carpet and said, 'How the hell am I to know what the tenants get up to? I'm hardly ever over there. Ask the wife.'

'I will, in due course,' promised Mr Wyecliffe. 'In the meantime, might I have another sandwich?'

Nancy gave him hers.

It turned out the tenants had all been in arrears. Eventually,

Riley had shown them the door. That's why they'd set him up, he said.

Mr Wyecliffe nodded slowly, stubbing the crumbs on his knee. Licking his fingers, he said, 'But what of Bradshaw? He's your real problem.'

'I've thrown his girls onto the street. Now he's trying to make me pay.'

'That's a guess.'

'Why else would he lie?'

'Bradshaw is of good character.'

'So am I.'

'Indeed.' After a moment, as if he'd just finished reading the instructions that had come with a gadget from Japan, Mr Wyecliffe said, 'Okey-dokey. Bradshaw is the pimp.'

Nancy had hated the sound of that p-word. It had been used in her own living room, leaving a heavy stain on the air that she couldn't wipe away. It was still there, even though Riley had been acquitted, even though all those terrible people had been lying. Something ghastly had entered her home. It was like waking to a burglary. The tidying up made no difference.

Thoughtfully, Mr Wyecliffe said, 'The claptrap about the Pieman allows them to say very little about you, makes the story shorter, easier for three of them to learn by heart' – he looked at his empty plate, his features tangled up in his beard – 'but counsel will not advance a guess at trial.'

Riley leaned back, genuinely calm now – Nancy could tell. 'Who said anything about guesses?'

Mr Wyecliffe put his papers in his tatty briefcase and said, 'I ought to observe that no one can save you from the truth or a lie that hangs together. It is a sad fact of life, but the two are often interchangeable.'

'Just get me Glendinning.'

Nancy held back the tears; and her man watched her, approving of the struggle, relieved by it.

Waiting for the day of the trial was awful, if only because of the unimaginable shame. At such times, your mum and dad were meant to rally round, but Nancy's had drawn the blinds good and proper – they'd never liked her man, never. And Riley had no one. Even Mr Lawton went peculiar. He'd always been one for having a good grumble first thing – about the downturn and closures – but he went quiet, all stern, and turned his big tweedy back on her when he had to speak. Everyone had crossed to the other side of the road. One day she looked up and saw Babycham's permed head against the frosted glass of the door. They hadn't spoken for ages.

'Look, Nancy,' she said, after checking the boss was out, 'we've known each other since we were this high. Fair enough, we're not as close as we used to be, but I don't hold no grudges. We all make our own choices, and you've made yours. But still I owe it to you to speak plain. Why do you trust him?'

Nancy was knocked sideways. Not just because she'd implied, all brazen, that Riley was in the wrong. It was that word, 'trust'. Nancy had never quite clocked the obvious: her man was for saying he trusted her when, in fact, it was she who was trusting him.

'Run for it, girl,' Babycham said. 'We'll all rally round, honest. We've had a meeting.'

Confused, angry and feeling sort of cold and stripped, right down to her pants, Nancy gasped, 'Clear off.' Finding some breath, she added, 'Riley always said you were full of wind and bubbles.'

When it grew dark Nancy locked up the shop and walked home along the towpath by Limehouse Cut, past barges and boats moored at the banks of the canal. On the way she found a brick

151

for the herb bed. She dropped it on the pile, had a boiled egg and watched a programme on Liberian shipping regulations. After the news she went to bed and, dozing fitfully, waited for Riley.

The room was pitch black when he climbed into bed.

'Nancy?' He waited, and whispered again. 'Nancy?'

She didn't so much as turn a hair. After a moment he reached over and, for minutes on end, he stroked her nose, her lips . . . each feature on her face, just like Mr Johnson had done with the figurine lamp. Then he shrank back as if he'd done something wrong.

It was often like this. When Riley had done a clearing he didn't come home until after midnight – she didn't know where he'd been, or what he'd done, and she didn't care – but he'd come to bed with these trembling hands. No one had ever touched her so exquisitely (it was a word she'd heard a doctor use to describe intense pain, but when she'd looked it up in a dictionary, she'd thought of these secret moments).

Nancy fell asleep, savouring the aftermath of this mysterious, most secret affection. Beside her Riley started to moan, and downstairs Arnold was running as fast as his little legs would carry him.

6

'You've received another letter from Mrs Glendinning,' the Prior repeated.

Anselm had just finished his breakfast when he was called to the phone. The envelope was marked 'PRIVATE and URGENT', which prompted Sylvester – in a rare burst of competence – to summon the Prior, who'd recognised Elizabeth's handwriting.

'But who *posted* it?' asked Anselm.

'Another friend, I suppose,' said the Prior. 'Shall I read it out?'

Anselm glanced nervously at his watch. An adult life determined in its first half by court engagements and its second by bells had made Anselm (like many barristers and monks) slightly neurotic about time. 'No thanks,' he said. 'Will you fax it through? I've got an appointment in Camberwell.'

The community superior led Anselm through baffling corridors that only an architect could have devised, past various photographs of the congregation's personnel. Anselm noticed the alteration in headdress over the years, from a spectacular construct of starched linen to a simple veil. Entering a walled garden, Sister Barbara pointed towards a path flanked by chestnut trees. At its end, in a wheelchair, sat an elderly woman who wore a woollen hat remarkably similar to a cushion.

Like any sensible interrogator, Anselm had researched his witness in advance. From his initial telephone enquiry, with supplemental details from the superior, Anselm had learned a great deal. Sixty years ago, upon the outset of her religious life, Sister Dorothy had run a London hostel before being installed as matron at a private school in Carlisle. She had been very happy, but her life was to typify the precedence of service over personal inclination. Following a short stint as a prison chaplain in Liverpool, she'd been sent to work as a nurse in Afghanistan. Seventeen years later she'd come home to have her wisdom teeth removed. She never went back to her mountain dispensary. Her one souvenir was an Afghan pakol, the hat that became her trademark.

Anselm approached her, his feet crunching the gravel.

As soon as he was within earshot, Sister Dorothy said, 'I didn't know she'd died until you called.' Her voice was clear but slightly laboured. As Anselm sat on a bench, she added, 'So you're an old friend?'

153

'Yes. We were in chambers together.'

'Tell me, was she happy?' She spoke with the aching concern of an old teacher.

'Very much so.'

'Successful?'

'Oh yes.'

The nun smiled and sighed. Threads of shadow thrown by branches swung across her face. 'Well, well, well,' she sang quietly. Her skin had the transparent whiteness of old age, with a multitude of deep lines. A dint in the profile of her nose revealed a badly healed fracture, sustained (he'd been told) during a prison visit.

Anselm spoke of Elizabeth's professional reputation, of her marriage and her son, while Sister Dorothy listened eagerly, not wanting to miss a single detail. In due course, and adroitly, Anselm observed, 'And yet, after all those years together, I knew very little about her past.'

He waited, hoping. In fact, he prayed.

'Did she ever show you the photograph?' She spoke distantly, one hand raised, as if she were pointing to a wall.

Anselm leaned forward, elbows on his knees. 'I don't think so.'

'The photograph of the family?' continued Sister Dorothy, surprised that her visitor was unsure of her meaning.

'No,' replied Anselm, trying not to sound too interested.

'Well, well, well,' sang Sister Dorothy to herself. She studied Anselm, like one about to break a confidence. 'The photograph tells you everything . . . It's all there in black and white . . . a happy family on a Sunday afternoon some time in the 1940s.'

The part of Anselm's character that trusted in the dispensations of Providence made an exclamation of gratitude. He waited, though he was impatient to learn the history that Elizabeth had kept to herself.

'On the right is her father,' said Sister Dorothy. Wrinkles crowded her eyes as she called up the portrait. 'A tall, thin man with a waxed moustache and shiny black hair. He wore wing collars every day of his adult life. A man fifty years out of his time.' She threw Anselm a glance. 'Did she tell you about him?'

'Not in any detail,' replied Anselm. In fact, Elizabeth had never mentioned him.

'He was an unhappy insurance salesman based in Manchester. After he'd sold his quota of premiums he locked himself in the attic trying to invent an electronic smoke detector. Several times he nearly burnt the house down. He never gave up. He thought if he could only pull it off, the industry would name a policy after him.'

'He didn't succeed?'

'No, he did not.' She paused, looking towards a high wall covered in ivy. 'But he made a fortune.'

Anselm pictured a man with the shade of Elizabeth's face.

'To the left is her mother,' continued Sister Dorothy, like a museum guide. 'A seamstress from Chorley. She's wearing a polka dot dress with enormous buttons. Hair like Maggie Thatcher. A happy, house-proud woman whose only joke was that she'd like to invent a fire extinguisher.'

'And Elizabeth?' asked Anselm.

'She is in the middle. A late and only child. A beaming girl of ten in ribbons and bows. It was an age, she once said, that seemed perfect in every way. She was young enough to appreciate that she was a child, and old enough to consciously enjoy it.' Sister Dorothy swung Anselm a glance. 'That is the photograph of the Glendinning family.'

155

'How did the inventor make his fortune?' asked Anselm roguishly.

'By dying,' she replied.

Elizabeth was born when her mother was nearly fifty, explained Sister Dorothy. Her father was already in his early sixties. It was a late match, and a contented one. They had found companionship after having long accepted that loneliness would take the greater portion of their days. Elizabeth's coming was a boon and, like many boons, unforeseen. But the unforeseen was to lay its heaviest hand upon the child. The year after the portrait was taken, her father came down from the attic grumbling about a trip switch. He turned on a wireless, sipped a glass of milk, closed his eyes and promptly died – as if he'd blown the fuse box. The doctor said he'd reached a fine old age. The fellow might not have had a policy named after him, but he did take one out on his life: his nearest and dearest were amply provided for. A year later Elizabeth's mother died from septicaemia arising from a trivial leg injury. Her father, however, had taken out another, even larger, policy, and Elizabeth, at fourteen, found herself without either parent but the beneficiary of a very healthy trusted income.

'People are odd, aren't they?' observed Sister Dorothy, shaking her head. 'Elizabeth's father had filled in all these forms, but he hadn't made out a will. She had no legal guardian. And there were no relatives chomping at the bit. So the court had to get involved. In the end, it was a judge who sent Elizabeth in our direction.'

The congregation ran a boarding school in Carlisle. (Where, deduced Anselm, you were matron.) So Elizabeth became a pupil, but not without a period of considerable adjustment. The first years after the death of her parents were marked by rebelliousness and grief. She started coming to the dispensary

156

when there was little if anything wrong with her. Headaches. Stomach aches. Splinters. But Elizabeth began talking to this young nun whose veil kept crashing into cabinets and doors – Sister Dorothy would never get used to the contraption.

'But she did very well, in the end,' she said proudly. 'When she went to university, I gave her *The Following of Christ*.'

In a curious way, Anselm felt stumped. He couldn't tell her – as he'd intended – that Elizabeth had cut a hole in its pages. At a stroke, everything to do with the trial had been closed down. He did not feel capable of revealing that the book, her gift, had been permanently damaged. A question left his mouth before he could admire its excellence. 'When did you last see her?'

'Forty years ago.' Sister Dorothy spoke vaguely, as if she were drifting towards sleep. She'd closed her eyes. Anselm watched for several minutes. Then he tiptoed away, altogether sure that the nun in the brown pakol had had enough.

It was only when Anselm was trotting down the stairs to the Underground that he felt the entire interview had been incongruous – but he couldn't reduce the insight to any particulars.

When he got back to Hoxton he found two sheets of paper outside his bedroom door. The first was the fax from Larkwood. The second was a message asking him to call Inspector Cartwright.

Anselm read the letter from Elizabeth by the light of a window.

Dear Anselm,

I would be very grateful if you would visit the following lady:

Mrs Irene Dixon
Flat 269
Percival Court
Shoreditch

Mrs Dixon may not know that I am dead, so please explain, if needs be. Thereafter, listen rather than speak. I suggest you arrive unannounced.

Farewell, Anselm. You have helped me more than you can know.

Warm regards,

Elizabeth

Anselm let his hand drop. This was the final letter, he was sure. He thought of Elizabeth the rich orphan who hadn't quite gone, who wouldn't let go, even in death. Subdued, he rang Inspector Cartwright.

'You won't believe this,' she said, 'but I've received a letter from Mrs Glendinning.'

They arranged to meet in half an hour. Feeling more and more like an ass in a bridle, Anselm set off on this next unforeseen errand. Perhaps it was the act of retracing his steps to the Underground that brought home another veiled truth: the old biddy in the woolly hat had taken him to the cleaners – but he didn't know how, and he couldn't guess why.

7

At breakfast, Nancy said that Prosser had been sniffing around again.

Riley looked up, put his tea down and went bonkers. He grabbed a plate and sent it to the wall, like a frisbee. The pieces went everywhere. Arnold tore from his wheel and Nancy ducked as if it were an air raid (as a teenager she'd hidden in the Underground while London got trashed by the Nazis).

'I'm sick of him,' shouted Riley. His mouth curled like a

boxer's, and he huffed and puffed, pacing the ring in his head. 'He's always watching me, chewing that cigar.'

Riley looked for something else to throw, but Nancy had cleared the table.

'I'll speak to Wyecliffe,' vowed Riley.

'When?' said Nancy, dropping a cup. 'What for?'

'I'll go tonight,' he seethed. 'And he'll bang a writ on Prosser's nose.'

That sounds very legal, thought Nancy, not quite knowing what it meant.

Buoyed up and punchy, Riley set off for work, his boots crunching on the crockery.

When Nancy duly opened her shop that morning she went straight to the filing cabinet. She untied Mr Johnson's plastic bag and pulled out the first volume that came to hand. She sat by the fire, aiming to read, to drive out the memory of that lawyer in his stuffy twilit room. But he was too strong. Nancy let the book drop on her lap. She could almost feel his breath and smell the nuts.

A few weeks after the 'preliminary conference' at the bungalow, Mr Wyecliffe sent Nancy a letter 'requiring your kind attendance'.

She thought solicitors weren't meant to have beards and yet his was like an old toilet brush. She hadn't liked him. Not because he'd been hungry when he should have lost his appetite, and not even because of the grilling he'd dished out (he'd leaned across his desk, tugging at his hairy chin, not taking no for an answer, digging around in her private life: it was like he was after something, but wouldn't say what). No, she didn't like him because she'd said too much. Part of her had gone missing. The room had been dark, the windows jammed, and he'd just bitten his way through her life, as if it were another sandwich. And another thing: his eyes were too close together.

Mr Wyecliffe had said, for openers, 'What you now tell me is completely confidential.'

'Then how does it go in my statement?'

That knocked him one. He wasn't used to women with minds of their own. But he explained himself. He was the professional. He needed to know everything. 'Just imagine I'm doing a jigsaw out of sight. You'll wonder why I pick up this bit or the other. Don't think about the broader picture: leave that to me.' Nancy supposed that that was why lawyers earned so much money – they could see things the rest of us couldn't. And then Mr Wyecliffe got started in the middle of nowhere, and wouldn't let go. 'I suppose your husband goes out with the lads every now and then?'

'Never. He stays at home.'

'All the time?'

'Well, apart from work and that—'

'Every evening?'

'Yes, unless he's doing overtime.'

'Do you ever get unexpected phone calls from a strange man?'

'Of course not.' She folded her arms tight across her chest. 'Why would I?'

'Wanting to speak to your husband?'

'No.'

'Does Mr Riley make calls to anyone you don't know?'

'We're husband and wife.' Nancy had been getting more unsettled than cross, because the questions were like digs in the side, but she was proud to throw that one back. They were man and wife. Till death us do part. For better or for worse.

'Is that no?'

'Yes.'

Mr Wyecliffe nodded like her Uncle Bertie would after he'd

160

checked the odds at Ladbrokes. 'Just as I expected.' He chewed a pencil, smiling at Nancy, his eyes too deep in his head. Not a word had been written down.

'So your husband does lots of overtime?'

'He works for his living, yes.'

'Indeed. This overtime. Is it always on the same days?'

'Not now, what with the downturn on the docks.'

'Of course. But it's frequent?'

'We find out as and when. Mr Lawton's been very lucky, so yes, there's always a lot to be done. The boss has to keep ahead of the game. And my husband's always there, ready to help. He's one of his best workers. Never missed a shift.'

'I don't doubt it. Any cash in hand?'

Nancy felt the coming of a blush. 'No.'

Mr Wyecliffe swivelled the pencil, biting into the wood. He said, 'Do you collect the rents with him?'

'Why should I?'

'Ever met the tenants?'

'No.'

Once again, the solicitor looked like Uncle Bertie with the *Racing Post*. 'Very sensible,' he said. 'Let 'em rest in peace.'

'Exactly.'

Nancy wanted a breather, but Mr Wyecliffe seemed to have her trapped. He said, 'How often does your husband visit the property?'

'Well, I don't know, once or twice a week, if anything needs doing. He does all the maintenance himself. Keeps the costs down.'

'Very sensible. Just let me try some names.'

Nancy thought she'd suffocate if he went on like this.

'David?'

'No.'

161

'George?'

'No.'

'Bradshaw?'

'No.'

Mr Wyecliffe looked at the pencil as though he was a film star with a cigar, and Nancy saw that the lead had snapped. He started chewing the dry end. 'Is Mr Riley in debt to anyone?'

'Absolutely not.'

'Then why the overtime?'

'We'd like a house to match yours.'

'A noble objective that would, however, bring considerable disappointment.'

Suddenly the little man got up and opened the door. He returned and put a plump little hand on her shoulder, 'Sorry, but the ventilation system is somewhat primitive.' He looked at her in a funny way, as if he were hungry again. 'One more name, of a sort.' Nancy closed her eyes. Quietly he asked, 'Have you ever heard of the Pieman?'

Nancy gripped the sides of her head as though it might fall in two. 'Never.'

'Is Mr Riley frightened?'

Frightened? What a thing to have asked. Her man was scared of no one. A flash of heat spread across her chest, face and scalp – that was the menopause, telling her she'd never have a baby, that it was too late. So the doctor had said. Strange even to her own hearing, she replied, 'Yes.'

'What of?'

Nancy didn't want to say. It sounded daft. If she'd been asked was her man angry, she'd have said, 'Oh yes,' and that would have been that. But this question had stirred a new kind of thinking deep inside, somewhere other than her head – it wasn't really thinking; she didn't know what it was, but it happened in

162

her lungs, and lower down, in the stomach. 'Well,' she said, feeling weak, sheets of fresh sweat unfolding, 'he was scared by the hunter in *Bambi* even though you never see him.'

Mr Wyecliffe nodded like the doctor, showing no surprise.

Nancy continued, blinded by salt and mortification, 'And he doesn't like the new queen in *Snow White*.'

Mr Wyecliffe kept nodding, his eyes closed. Then he asked, 'What does he think of the little princess?'

And that was where Nancy went too far – without understanding why, except in her guts. She replied, 'He hates her.' She'd never liked the h-word. It was hard and sharp and somehow dark.

The sweating had stopped and a chill had struck her. Nancy sat with her arms folded tight, feeling like she was in the altogether on the ice-rink at Hammersmith. These humiliating flushes could go on for years, apparently. So the doctor said. Nancy reached for a hankie.

'I don't think we'll be calling you as a witness.' Mr Wyecliffe put his pencil down. And Nancy knew – because she wasn't daft – that he'd never intended to call her in the first place.

The cars struck the bump and swept past Nancy's door. Blinking uncertainly, like she'd just landed, Nancy handled the book on her lap. It fell open naturally in the middle. A spill of coffee or tea had made the ink run and the paper was ribbed and sticky.

. . . and her hair was pulled back ever so tight. Like all female staff at the Bonnington, she had to wear a black dress with a white frilly pinafore. It made her look like a servant in *The Forsyte Saga*. I watched her walk down the corridor pushing a trolley of sheets. That was the first time I saw Emily. And I said to myself, 'I shall marry this woman before the year is out.' I eventually found the manager's office. Sister Dorothy said he would be rude and she was right, but she'd also said keep your eye on his smile, which I did. He said, 'Young man, all you have to do is carry bags, don't speak unless you're spoken to, and don't loiter for a tip. This is London not New York.' I was what an American businessman once called 'the bell hop' – presumably because I came running when I heard a ding from the reception desk.

Unfortunately, Emily had no interest in me.

Nancy was forcefully present to herself now. Eagerly, she turned the page but it was stuck to the next few with something like jam.

and there he was lifted high in the air by a nurse. I said, 'Oh my God, I'm sorry,' because I thought I'd gone into the wrong theatre. But then I saw Emily on the bed. And then I realised that the baby in the air, on his way to the scales, was my son. I'd missed his birth by seconds. I don't remember a sound, not a cry

Nancy slowly closed the book here, at the point that most interested her. This had to be the son who would one day be lost, the boy who'd run along the pier at Southport. Out of respect to Mr Johnson, she would read no further, because in all their many conversations, he'd never told her what had happened.

I'm a dreadful woman, thought Nancy. Mr Johnson had his own tragedy and yet she escaped from hers into his, as if his story wasn't real.

8

George rose, picked up his remaining plastic bag and left Trespass Place. As he passed beneath the arch at the entrance he knew he'd never come back. The waiting was over.

Many people think that the homeless live on the whim of the moment. One minute they are there, in a doorway – as they have been for months – the next, they're gone. In fact, these movements are decisions. Moving on is a kind of obedience – just like leaving home in the first place.

When George found Trespass Place all those years ago, Nino had said that life on the street is like walking round the world. 'It's a turning away; but it can become a turning back.' George had instantly understood the first part, for his arrival beneath Blackfriars Bridge had been an attempt to flee a single conversation.

After the trial, George hardly left his armchair in the sitting room. He faced the window and the treetops of Mitcham. John was fourteen. Of late, he'd taken to roughing up his hair with gel. His skin was raw, as if he scrubbed his cheeks with a nail-brush. He kept coming into the room. He'd sit on different chairs as if he were trying to get a fresh angle on his father. He reminded George of those lifeguards at the swimming pool. They had a way of staring at people who might be in difficulty. They were always young and athletic and confident. John was a small lad, though, with thin arms and long fingers.

One day John was sitting on the rest of an armchair, knotting his fingers together. He was like a man preparing to jump. *Countdown* was on the television and a cheery presenter was adding up numbers faster than George could think. He felt John leaning towards him.

'Dad, I believe everything you said in court.'

The local media had pulled George to pieces. The CPS was considering a prosecution – for some unspecified offence.

'Thanks.' It sounded trite, but his heart had banged against his chest with a kind of gladness.

'You mustn't blame yourself, Dad,' said John. He messed his hair up even more, gathering confidence. 'It doesn't matter that Riley got off. He was just a dogsbody. The police always get hold of the ones that don't matter . . . That's not your fault.'

George allowed himself to look at his son. It was hard, because of the lad's earnestness, the passion to save his father.

'I wonder who the Pieman might be?' asked John coldly.

The lad had been thinking hard, and he'd come to some conclusions. He'd decided who the real criminal was, the one the police hadn't arrested. George looked back to the television as the scores were being read out. George, unthinking, said, 'You'd have to ask Riley.'

The remark must have landed like a pip in the mind's soil, because the boy didn't do anything for years.

When George had walked out of his own front door, he'd been turning away from that remark during *Countdown*. He'd also turned away from the ocean of memories that Emily evoked. But no sooner had he met Nino, than the old man set him on course to face them again – and not just in passing, but with all the detail he could summon to the pages of his notebooks. The turning away, however, had been essential.

And now, with a similar kind of fortitude, he left Trespass Place, and 'a royal scheme to bring down the . . .' or something like that; Elizabeth had often used towering phrases to describe what they were doing. And he'd known why: she, like George, had never accepted that Riley could not be brought to court for

166

the killing of John. All that – a trial and its aftermath – belonged at a still point on the surface of the earth. George moved on, a plastic bag swishing against his leg.

George must have been walking for about half an hour when he noticed he was heading south, way off his patch. He never went south. Mitcham lay down there. He wondered where he was going; and he thought again of Nino, and what the old man had said when they'd left the spike, the morning after the Pandora tale. 'The street is the place of stories,' he'd intoned, leaning on a wall by Camden Lock. 'Stories of how you got here, and how you might leave.' But he'd said something else – and it had frightened George: 'There are stories of how you might stay.'

George didn't want that. All at once, his pace quickening, he wanted to tell the extraordinary story of a man whose turning away had brought him back to where he'd started from: the tale of a man who'd finally made it home.

9

'You can leave everything behind,' the Major said, 'but it'll cost you more than you've already paid.'

He'd come to the court off his own bat, or so it had seemed. He wore his cap as if he were on parade. For the first time, Riley noticed the old shine on the cloth, and the frayed lapels. The trial was about to begin. The witnesses were lined up. The barristers were dressed in all that black. The Major had drawn him into a tiny conference room. Guilt had been assumed, which cleared the air like disinfectant.

Riley played the fish. 'Why should I do that?'

'For yourself,' he said, as if that were something worthwhile. 'And so that you can stop hurting everyone around you.'

Riley glanced over his shoulder. The conference room had large, misty windows from floor to ceiling. On the other side he could see Wyecliffe. He was like a man at prayer.

'You can still turn around,' the Major continued, full of entreaty. 'Anything else is an illusion. If you do, I'll help you. I doubt if anyone else has the inclination.'

Riley laughed in a way that embarrassed him, because his voice squeaked. He saw the lips of the Major harden; the red indentation of a cornet mouthpiece blanched and vanished. He said, 'I needed saving then, not now.'

That was meant to strike a nerve, but it didn't. The Major was more switched on than Riley had supposed.

'We always need saving now,' he said. 'Just stop running.'

Riley shrank more from the repelling compassion than the idea. 'I did. And I turned. Now I do the chasing.'

That hit the spot. The sight of the Major's loathing thrilled him. But the man in uniform still wouldn't give up – Riley could see it in his eyes – he was holding out for redeeming features; what Wyecliffe called 'mitigating circumstances' for why Riley did what he did. And Riley thought, There weren't any. But the Major wouldn't have it. He refused to believe that anyone could be rotten at the core – that a man might even want it. But who else was to blame? Riley's mother? Walter? None of them. Riley was sick to the back teeth of sympathy that gobbled up his identity. The making of allowances – it was daylight robbery. Of course, the family stuff could be used to his advantage in a court, if he'd only plead, if he'd only grovel. But hold it there – Riley felt pride burn the lining of some canal in his guts – I have self-respect. I'm me. In the end, I'm pretty much self-made. He suffered a spasm of sour excitement: this was the one thing no one could harm or take away: the core of himself, the inedible part. A bitter fruit had grown from the dirt of his choices. No one – and he meant *no one* – was going to give that back to his mother.

'If you plead guilty,' the Major said mechanically, 'I might be able to say something on your behalf.'

Riley glanced at his cap-badge motto, 'Blood and Fire', as he'd done when they'd first met. Back then, the Major's compassion had made Riley panic. What had happened? He felt nothing now. He simply observed the man's hopes and intentions. On the face of it, he'd come to wangle a confession out of Riley, urged on, no doubt, by Wyecliffe, who was standing outside, biting his nails. But the Major had his own reasons. He believed in the Lord of how things ought to be, of how they might yet turn out. Riley stood, bringing the interview to a close. He looked down from on high, with a remote, godless pity. The old soldier didn't seem to hear the tune of his own march: you couldn't save a man against his will.

Riley walked out of that tiny room and never saw the Major again. Within minutes, he was in the dock. It was only then, sitting in that box, flanked by guards, that he realised he'd made another choice; that he could still have put his hands up without blaming anyone but himself. It was an example of his actions being one step ahead of his thinking. He hadn't given a second thought to pleading guilty because, in a feverish way, he was looking forward to the trial, to what might happen. No one could possibly know it, but Riley had set up a reunion, and he didn't want to miss it, even though for him, personally, the court process was an unimaginable ordeal. He wanted to see what George would do when he saw Riley's advocate.

Riley was not disappointed. The trial ended exactly as he had expected, but not in the way he'd foreseen. That David/George

169

trick had been baffling. If Riley had been the Major, he'd have thanked God.

On the day of the acquittal, Riley pulled Nancy into the sitting room. He'd sobered up, so to speak. The fever had passed, and he saw with terrible clarity that Nancy had been an observer for years. And when it had been spelled out, she'd fled from the courtroom, just like George.

'Do you trust me?' He stood in front of her, holding her arms, as if she might slap him.

'I do.'

Nancy's eyes revealed a hard decision. Their light was gone, as if a screen had fallen to stop a smash-and-grab. She seemed older and cut off from him – giving away, to Riley, that they'd never really been attached.

I do. It was like getting married all over again. It was a second chance.

On the strength of that vow Riley put Quilling Road up for sale. Then he drove to a place he hadn't seen since the age of eleven: Hornchurch Marshes. He walked down a path of flattened grass until he reached four rectangular ponds, laid out neatly like a window, with a frame made of bricks. It was known as the Four Lodges. His breath grew tight, hurting his chest. Nothing had changed. He wept uncontrollably, looking at the men on stools and the clouds of midges.

10

Anselm passed though the ornamental gates of Gray's Inn Gardens. Here, as a young man, he'd dreamed of standing in the Bailey, of being an old hand, a grumpy legend in a tattered gown. Lying on the grass, he'd cross-examined imaginary foes, breaking them with imperial courtesy. Phantom judges had looked on, mystified by such talent in one so young. Not much later, he'd found himself walking the same gravelled lanes, with their unexpected turns, thinking of a flickering space above a nave, and an attentive silence.

'Good afternoon, Father,' said Inspector Cartwright pleasantly.

Anselm looked to his right, quickly, as if he'd been caught. She was sitting legs crossed on a bench eating crisps. On her lap was a manila envelope. Her ears still carried the weight of a child's affection.

'Have a look at these,' she said. 'Mrs Glendinning is either playing a game or she's being very careful.'

Anselm sat beside her, one hand searching an upper pocket for his glasses. Relieved by the unaccustomed sharpness of things, he withdrew a bundle of papers from the packet. To leave him undisturbed, Inspector Cartwright wandered a short distance away.

In fact there were four bundles, each stapled into a kind of booklet. The first was entitled 'Nancy's Treasure', the second 'Riley's Junk'. Both of them comprised annual returns, covering three successive years, as submitted to Companies House. Nothing had been flagged or underlined. Anselm flicked through the other two enclosures. Each was made up of photocopied receipts. Again they were labelled with the different business names; again the pages unmarked. He glanced at the dates, noting that each pamphlet spanned the same period framed by the formal accounts. Puzzled, he checked the envelope again and then said, 'Isn't there a covering letter?'

Inspector Cartwright licked salt off two fingers and said curtly, 'No.' She dropped the crisps packet in a bin and came back to the bench. She modified her answer. 'Well, there was a

171

signed compliments slip. The explanation of the figures must be with George Bradshaw.'

'But why separate the evidence from its meaning?' mused Anselm.

'My guess is that Mrs Glendinning didn't trust the person she asked to send it.'

'Then why approach whoever it was in the first place?'

'Maybe he or she – like you and I – was involved in the original trial.'

Anselm took off his glasses and returned to a universe that was faintly and agreeably blurred. 'But why send the packet at all? Why not give the lot to George Bradshaw?'

Inspector Cartwright replied instantly: 'Maybe she foresaw that a man with half a memory might get lost before he was found.'

That sounded rather biblical, a thought that might have slowed Anselm down, but he was suddenly close upon Elizabeth's heels and his mind lurched forward. 'Which means that the figures you've received should speak for themselves.'

'I agree, but they don't – at least not to me. I've seen the Companies House stuff already, so I assume the trick is in the receipts.'

Anselm turned the pages with an air of deep concentration. In fact, without his glasses, he couldn't quite make out the numbers. He grimaced significantly.

'Would you examine them?' asked Inspector Cartwright, checking her watch. 'You might have one of those visions.'

After she'd gone, Anselm wondered why he hadn't told Inspector Cartwright about the letter he'd received himself. There had been nothing to suggest that the visit to Mrs Dixon should be confidential. But he knew that he should say nothing. Why? He took a pleasant path between the Georgian buildings where, as a student, he'd dreamed of greatness, and he came to the strange conclusion that he was entering Elizabeth's mind; that he was beginning to sense her will, if not the reason for her calculations.

At High Holborn Anselm bumped into a nun who wasn't looking where she was going. Struck by a sensible idea, he turned round and went back to Gray's Inn. Not knowing quite where to place his enquiry, he went to the library situated on South Square. A short woman behind the main desk, it transpired, was used to helping those who were baffled.

'The archives of the Inn are extensive,' she said, 'and not everything has been stored on computer. We're working backwards.'

'Of course,' replied Anselm. 'You should never start at the beginning.'

He'd meant to be agreeable, but it came out dreadfully. Being wise in small respects, he said nothing more. And she, being perceptive, smiled.

'The point is,' she resumed, 'material on Mrs Glendinning could be anywhere. If you leave me a contact number, I'll dig around this afternoon. In the meantime, I suggest you have a browse through some back numbers of *Graya*.'

This publication covered various happenings in the lives of the Inn's membership. It was an obvious place to look. Anselm wrote down the Hoxton fax number and then settled himself at a table adjacent to the relevant volumes. For over an hour he chased any reference to Elizabeth. He found a small piece upon her becoming a QC, and a longer biographical item following her appointment as a deputy High Court judge. All the background material coincided precisely with what Sister Dorothy had said: birth in Manchester, schooling in Carlisle, university at Durham.

Anselm, however, was disappointed, for he trusted his unruly intuitions. And they had been ruffled. Something wasn't quite right. Standing in a phone booth outside the library, he rang the administration section of Elizabeth's former university. He related the details gleaned from *Graya*. Almost simultaneous with his speaking, he heard a soft tapping followed by the bang of the return key, and then a pause.

'Sorry,' said a man evenly. 'No one called Elizabeth Glendinning attended the university between those dates.' The tapping began again. 'In fact, we've never had a student by that name.'

Anselm crossed Gray's Inn Square as if Father Andrew were by his side. *Find the child who grew up to wear a gown that was too heavy for her shoulders.*

Neither of them had considered switched identities, or a burned history.

11

The closer George came to Mitcham, the heavier his body became. He pushed himself along his own street, past the lit windows of Aspen Bank. The televisions were on and the curtains were drawn against evening. Opposite George's home, across a patch of grass in shadow, was a children's play area. A low fence and a tiny gate gave it a sense of shape and importance. George sat on a merry-go-round, one leg trailing on the asphalt. He watched Number 37 as though it weren't really there; as though it might vanish if touched. Emily was upstairs. George could see her shadow, thrown large across the chimney-breast wall. She was moving about quickly.

A quite extraordinary stillness settled upon him. It was a

solemn moment – one he would like to have shared with Nino: his life on the street was about to end; he'd walked around the world and made it back to his point of departure. With a shove of one foot, the merry-go-round began to spin, wobbling gently on its axle. George saw his home, the trees, the distant tower blocks, the lights on Aspen Bank and then his home again. Round and round he went, slowly building up the courage to cross the patch of grass and the empty street.

The light upstairs went off.

The light downstairs came on.

George dragged his shoe as a brake and the merry-go-round clinked to a halt.

The front door of Number 37 opened and Emily stepped onto the garden path. She walked a few steps, threading a handbag along one arm. Her hair was different, but the movements of her body, its tiny hesitations, were the same.

George stood up and quietly cried, 'Emily.' He couldn't get his mouth and lungs to work. He was spent. He could only lift and drop his feet.

Suddenly the light from the open door was blocked. A large man appeared, jangling a set of keys. He angled them to the light, to find the one he was after.

'Have you got everything?' he said wryly.

Emily nodded. She was looking up at the stars.

George couldn't stop his legs. His eyes swam and his hands were joined. He was still in shadow and about to enter the pale orange light.

The door banged shut and the big man placed a heavy arm around Emily. His keys jingled again and two headlights flashed. George stepped off the grass but veered aside with a groan. He tripped on a paving stone but kept his balance, heading back along Aspen Bank – the way he'd come, a few minutes earlier, and the way he'd gone a few years before.

An engine coughed and tyres began to turn. A few moments later they drove slowly past him and for an instant George saw his wife. She was straining forward in the passenger seat, her face framed in the wing mirror. But he couldn't read the expression because the car moved on, gathering speed. He watched the indicator blink at the end of the road and then he was alone.

Where do I go now? he thought. Nino had said nothing about this sort of thing.

12

All those years ago, Mr Wyecliffe had called to tell her the good news.

'We've won,' he exclaimed, and his beard scratched against the receiver.

Feeling sick, she waited on the doorstep for her man. When he arrived, he wasn't smiling and he said nothing about how the case against him had fallen to bits. He just pulled her into the sitting room and asked her if she trusted him. Staring back, she said, 'I do,' with all her soul and with all her might, and he quickly kissed her on the cheek, as if there were people waiting to clap. Then he drove off.

Riley put Quilling Road on the market. He decorated the bungalow. He quit his job. Within the week, Mr Wyecliffe was in the sitting room dishing out advice over a spam fritter: 'You might give constructive dismissal a run.'

Riley did. He took Mr Lawton to court *for sacking him*. It was another triumph and the company had to pay him thousands. Nancy never got her head around that one, but Mr Wyecliffe knew his onions. No one seemed to realise that this second victory was Nancy's loss. She could hardly stay on as Mr Lawton's bookkeeper. She handed in her notice. Mr Wyecliffe deemed it 'prudent but outside the compass of economic redress'.

With all that money, her man bought a shack on a bed of crushed cinders opposite a crummy fish and chip shop.

'What do you want that for?' asked Nancy.

'We're going into business,' said Riley, as if they were emigrating. He was edgy. It was as though he were destroying everything behind him . . . except for Nancy. He didn't even ask her what she wanted. She was part of him, like his hands or feet. They were man and wife.

As for Riley, he bought a big van without windows. He lined it with thick plywood – floor, roof and sides – and he put up shelves and straps. He put an advert in the local papers offering to clear houses. And he made good. In fact, two years on he'd had to rent some garages for storage. If you came with a voucher from the Salvation Army, you could take what you liked. He was a good man, was Riley, in his own way.

So that was where all the pieces landed after her man came back from the Old Bailey. Day in, day out, Nancy sat by a gas fire, working her way through a bumper book of puzzles. It was a long way from the banter with Babycham at Lawton's. That was when she'd started thinking of a house by the sea in Brighton, going back to the place of childhood holidays on the pier, back to the bright lights of the Palace, to the magicians and the rousing bands. But her man wouldn't hear of it. They had a new life: Riley on the road, and Nancy in the shop. He had to keep moving, and she had to keep still. If this is what it means to win a trial, she often thought, I can't imagine what it's like to lose.

*

A few months later, feeling guilty but resolved, Nancy bought Stallone, her first hamster: guilty because she was satisfying an ache in her heart; resolved because Riley couldn't heal the injury. He had, after all, caused it. As she stood at the counter, with her new friend, a cage and a bag of dried corn, she didn't even feel humiliated. On the contrary, she almost trembled with excitement, because something so small, so unnoticed, was going to receive the *simplicity* of her affection. The complex stuff would go to her man.

The trouble was, Riley was no fool. He sensed the division of Nancy's warmth. And he was jealous . . . *jealous of a hamster.* Nancy would have enjoyed being the nub of competition if she hadn't known, deep down, that the situation was pitiful. It was also, in practice, distressing because unfortunately hamsters don't last that long. (Stallone made it to three, but Mad Max and Bruce dropped tools at two and a half.) And you can't let on that you're grieving, not without looking a fool. Pretending she felt nothing, she'd attend to the burial and then pop down to the pet shop for another one. It was unseemly. But there was nothing else to be done.

Riley watched the hamsters come and go without saying anything – except once.

After Nancy found Bruce on his side, she said wistfully, 'Aww. Where've you gone?'

'Nowhere,' said Riley from a rocking chair in the next room.

'What do you mean?' said Nancy sharply. She didn't like this kind of talk.

'We came from nowhere, out of nothing, and we end up nowhere, back to nothing again,' he replied, like an old-timer whittling wood, 'and in between we're alive.'

Nancy glanced at Bruce, wanting him to survive in another place . . . along with Uncle Bertie, her mum and dad, everyone she loved . . . even though none of them had been on speaking terms.

'What's the point?' asked Riley quietly.

There was an odd excitement about him, and Nancy wondered what he could do — what anyone might do — if it were true, if you didn't have *any* beliefs that made sense of being alive (not necessarily the whole package, of course, but at least the wrapping). But that was Riley. He didn't really mean it. He said one thing and did another. He loved Nancy — though he'd never said it, though he couldn't show it.

Riley stomped off to work and Nancy went and bought Arnold. Thinking of her man, she said (not for the first time), 'How did he end up like that?' But she asked the question mechanically, without any real interest in the answer. It wasn't important to her. If there were a book called *The Secret to Graham Riley*, she wouldn't have bought it. The contents would have nothing to do with why she actually loved him.

And why did she love him? There weren't answers to questions like that. If there'd been a list of 'reasons', Riley's conduct would have torn it up years ago. Lists were for the likes of Mr Wyecliffe. Ultimately, nothing could explain why his constant testing of Nancy's attachment had opened her heart rather than closed it. It was very simple: what she saw she loved. Babycham hadn't been able to understand her — and she'd said so (she'd always spoken her mind). Sitting in the Admiral on a Friday night, at one of their last gatherings as a group, Nancy had struggled to find the words, fiddling with her glass. She'd blushed and a slot machine went ding. Finally she'd said that to see Riley as Nancy saw him, you needed Nancy's eyes.

179

13

Anselm walked from Hoxton to Shoreditch, and to a tower whose hotchpotch of lit windows rose like Braille against the night sky. Here and there, laundry dangled across a balcony. The lifts were out of order, so Anselm trod cautiously up a concrete stairwell, past confessions of love and hate, persuaded that the whole damp edifice was being sucked into the ground.

Mrs Dixon peered above a door chain. She was stooped and suspicious, squinting through large glasses. 'Are you from the Council?'

'No,' replied Anselm gently. 'I'm a friend of Mrs Glendinning.'

The door closed, and the latch rattled and slid. It opened again, letting loose the sweet and sour of meals on wheels.

'When's she coming back?' said Mrs Dixon anxiously. 'I've missed her . . . The stories, the cakes and all that . . .'

Mrs Dixon fell back into an armchair before a crowded coffee table. A dinner plate with swirls of gravy lay in the centre. A button nose and pink cheeks suggested a rag doll. Her hair was curled and faintly blue.

Anselm said, 'I'm here to tell you that Mrs Glendinning won't be coming any more. I'm very sorry.'

Mrs Dixon lined up her knife and fork. 'She's dead?'

'Yes.'

'Her heart?'

'Yes.'

Anselm sat on a wicker stool. Unsuccessfully, he tried to picture the exchange of confidences. Glancing around, he noticed there were no pictures or clocks, no postcards propped on the mantelpiece. Streaks of Polyfilla split the ceiling like forked lightning dried out. A settee from a missing three-piece stood adjacent to the coffee table. Elizabeth must have sat there, relating what the consultant had said, before going home to gin-and-it with Charles and Nicholas.

While he was half-French, the part of Anselm that was English emerged forcefully in moments of strong emotion. 'Can I make you a cup of tea?' he said warmly.

Mrs Dixon shook her head. Her mouth worked and she rearranged a salt cellar, a napkin ring and a side plate. 'She was my friend, you know.'

Her face crimped with emotion, as if there was something she wanted to say. Finally she blurted out, 'I'd been here for so long on my own and then she came along out of nowhere.'

'When did you first meet?' he asked ingenuously.

'Just over a year ago,' she replied, finding a hankie in a sleeve. 'I'd been on to the Council about being lonely, you know. But it feels like I'd known her all my life.' She became fervent. 'Do you know what I mean?'

'Yes.' He looked across at Mrs Dixon, remote behind her table, eyes tightly closed with a tissue at her mouth. Her hand dropped and a lip twitched. She coughed. 'Did Elizabeth tell you about me?'

'No,' admitted Anselm. 'She simply asked me to come here if she died.'

'Wasn't there any other message?'

One of her legs began to bounce on its toes. Anselm watched it, and he frowned.

'Didn't she . . . say anything about my lad?' Her eyes fixed on him.

'Who?' asked Anselm gently.

'My son.' Mrs Dixon began to shuffle forward, her hands

fidgeting. 'He went missing years ago, as a boy, and Elizabeth said she might be able to find him, what with all her contacts and all that . . . I've never known what became of him . . . He was a good boy, you know . . .' The desperation had changed her face. She was someone entirely different. Her voice became metallic. 'Did she leave a message for me?'

Anselm moved to the sofa, within reach of this frightened, vulnerable mother. 'In a way, yes.' He spoke quietly. 'Elizabeth asked me to listen to you.'

'What?'

'Elizabeth thought you might like to talk to me,' he replied gently.

'But I don't have anything else to say,' said Mrs Dixon, shrinking back in her chair. Confusion and caution changed her features once more. 'Has she told you anything?'

Anselm didn't reply. He searched her face, willing her to release what she was holding back.

'Did she tell you?' Mrs Dixon's voice quaked and rose.

The lawyer in Anselm would have done anything to discover what Elizabeth might have told him, but something like mercy made him say, 'I know nothing. But you can tell me anything in complete confidence.'

Mrs Dixon looked as if she had been manacled. With sudden dignity, she said, 'Would you go now, please, I'm all upset. I never thought she'd not come back and I'm too old for this . . . Look, just go, go . . .'

Anselm explained that she had nothing to fear; that he would leave immediately and never come back; that he'd write his telephone number down, in case she changed her mind. 'After I've gone, please remember, I was sent by a friend – yours and mine.'

In the hallway, Anselm paused before a creased picture in a

frame painted gold. It was one of those nineteenth-century images found in sacristies and second-hand shops: a man with beautifully sculpted muscles bearing the cross of Christ, his head raised high, to something dark and wonderful in the watching clouds.

'Simon of Cyrene,' said Mrs Dixon. Her composure was still fragile. 'It was my mother's.' As Anselm stepped away, she said, 'Ask the Council to send someone else, will you?'

14

Riley sped along Commercial Road, up Houndsditch and into the City. He parked in a loading bay on Cheapside, near Wyecliffe and Co.

'How very nice to see you,' said the solicitor, stretching a moist hand over columns of paper. His face was dark and grey and hairy; his eyes glittered. It had been years since Riley had entered this room, but Mr Wyecliffe seemed to be expecting him. 'Do take a seat. How can I help you?' He was a silhouette against a jammed sash window. Like the Four Lodges, nothing had changed. Not even the air. It was like a warm tomb, but Riley was shivering.

'Someone's after me,' he blurted out.

'I often have the very same sensation.' He picked up a glass ball with a log cabin and some reindeer inside. He shook it and snow began to fall.

'I'm serious,' snapped Riley.

'So am I,' Wyecliffe intoned, leaning forward, his chin resting on stubby fingers. 'Tell me what brought you back to this worrisome place.'

That was Wyecliffe. He referred to things but never said

them. Riley had last come here when Cartwright was trying to pin the death of John Bradshaw on him. He'd been sick with fear.

'A guy called Prosser keeps hanging round Nancy, asking questions.'

'First name?'

'Guy.'

Mr Wyecliffe scraped his moustache along one finger. 'So what?'

'*So what?*' breathed Riley. 'He wants to know where I get my stuff from, as if the business wasn't clean.'

'Is it?'

'Completely.'

'Well then,' said Mr Wyecliffe reassuringly, 'there's nothing to worry about.' He paused. 'Mr Riley, we've known each other a very long time. Just hand over the other pieces, I'll look after the larger picture.'

'Someone's trying to scare me,' he whimpered.

'In what way?'

'I received a letter.'

'Saying what?'

'Nothing.' Riley couldn't say any more, but he needed help. 'It was just a photograph.'

'Of whom?'

'It doesn't matter,' said Riley, his voice rising. 'I thought it might have been Prosser, that's all.'

'Most unlikely,' observed Mr Wyecliffe confidently. 'Someone clever enough to let a photograph speak for itself doesn't blow their cover by asking stupid questions.'

Pushed by fear, Riley almost let slip what he'd held back for most of his life. 'I just want to know if you can stop someone digging around.'

'That rather depends,' said Mr Wyecliffe. One of his hands covered the glass ball. 'Who else might be handling the shovel, so to speak?'

'I don't know,' barked Riley. He'd asked himself day and night. If it wasn't Prosser, there was no one. John Bradshaw had come with a question and a promise, but he never got an answer. Riley said, 'There's no one alive that I can think of.'

'Anyone dead?' The lawyer shook the globe.

Riley held his breath, feeling heat descend like a crown. 'Don't play around with me, Wyecliffe.'

'I've never been more serious.'

Riley's temples began to throb. 'The dead?'

'Yes.'

Riley couldn't think straight. Only the living could reach him. He jerked his head, as though to shake off some flies.

'Very well,' said Mr Wyecliffe, with a long sigh of disappointment. 'If you don't have any more names – likely or otherwise – I cannot act. You'll have to wait and see what they do with what they know.'

'They?'

'A figure of speech,' replied the lawyer. Hooking his thumbs into his waistcoat pockets, he added, 'That said, perhaps your correspondent has primed several people to act on his or her behalf.' He examined Riley with something between pity and wonder. 'You know, everything always comes down to facts.'

'Facts?' The change in subject threw Riley off balance.

'Yes. Those known and those not known.' Mr Wyecliffe waved his palms over the desk as if he were incanting a spell. 'We lawyers assemble the known ones for the jury. You'd be surprised how many different pictures a clever hand can make out of the same pieces' – he chuckled at the thought – 'and if it were a game, I'd say that was value for money. But after forty years in the courts, let me tell you something.' He was no longer merry and the lights seemed to go dim. 'No one can change the shape of a fact that makes sense on its own. It's like a photograph.'

Riley tugged at his top button. Wyecliffe hadn't changed subject at all.

'Tell me the name of the man in the picture,' said the lawyer soothingly.

'I never said it was a man.'

'Quite right.' He nodded a compliment.

'If I tell you, can you help?'

The scratching began again, high on his hairy cheek. He sighed and whispered, 'That rather depends.'

Riley kicked back his chair and yanked at the door. Everything always 'depended'. Wyecliffe had been like that last time, hinting and sighing and never looking surprised.

On Cheapside, Riley found his van clamped. In a frenzy, he kicked the huge yellow bracket and tore the notice off the windscreen. He nearly cried. Someone was after him, and he couldn't get away. Then, in a moment of sickening calm, the obvious hit Riley like a backhander: whoever it was already knew what John Bradshaw had wanted to know.

15

George wasn't sure, but he probably followed the exact route back to the river that he'd taken when he'd first left Mitcham. As he walked, Nino's story about right and wrong came to mind. Elizabeth had loved the ending, but George had never been able to catch the beginning. And now, after she'd gone, it had popped to the surface.

'I've had a very odd dream,' Nino said, while they sat on a

bench near Marble Arch. 'I was standing on a road between heaven and hell writing parking tickets. A reporter came along. "What are this lot waiting for?" I asked. "Nowt," he replied. "They can't go to heaven because they didn't do anything good, and they can't go to hell because they didn't do anything bad. Hardly a scoop, but it's still a good story." He showed me the headline on his pad: "*They lived without praise or blame.*"'

Nino didn't say anything else.

'What's that supposed to mean?' asked George.

Nino became resolute, as if he had been quizzed about the value of double yellow lines. 'Don't be lukewarm, old friend. That's the only route to mercy or reward.'

George had told Elizabeth, and she'd written it down, asking him to repeat every word.

But to what end? Where was she now? And where was he?

George crossed Blackfriars Bridge with a glance towards Trespass Place. On the north bank of the Thames he turned east, following the road to Smithfield and Tower Hill – the route to the Isle of Dogs, and a wasteland of padlocks and chicken wire. The river flowed oily and magnificent on his right; traffic swept along to his left. George's mind tracked back to the night he'd pulled open a wrought-iron gate at three in the morning. He'd given no thought to praise or blame.

Three made-up girls stood shivering on the other side.

'Come on in,' he said. 'I've a kettle and a toaster.'

He followed them down the alley to the door he'd left ajar, looking at their bare legs, the blue veins and the goose pimples. This was late November, the month of biting rain and short days, the month when shop fronts twinkled with the approach of Christmas. George made cocoa. He didn't tell them that all the beds were taken, that they'd have to leave.

187

Let them have the length of a hot drink, he thought, it's not much. George left them so he could make the usual telephone calls. Every project was full, although the Open Door in Fulham could see them at half eight: that was five hours away; five hours to lose heart. George had learned long ago that with some kids you only got one chance to offer them a hand, and even then they didn't take it. But some did – that's what brought him to the gate night after night: some did. While waiting for the toast to pop up, George overheard the first name: Riley, and then he caught the second: the Pieman. When he appeared around the corner they stopped talking. He said, 'After this lot, you'll have to move on.' There was no protest.

He followed them back towards the gate. Their shoes clattered on the flags like dropped marbles and George felt – as he'd often done – like an accomplice to murder. One of them – the youngest – had a tattoo of a dragon above one ear. Her head was shaved. The three girls must have been a good fifty yards up the pavement when George came running after them.

'If you want to fight back, I'll help you.'

Two of them stared; the other laughed. They backed away shrouded by rain.

That should have been the end of it. But a week or so later they'd returned to the gate, again at God knows what hour, wanting to know what he'd meant. George stood on one side, they on the other, separated by bars. There was so much that did not need to be said: about who they were, what they did, even the where, when and how: everything, really, except for the why – those impossibly intimate histories that would not be reduced to a common badge.

George said through the bars, 'What happened at the Open Door?'

188

'Getting away is one thing,' said the one with the dragon, ignoring the question. 'But you said we could fight.'

He turned the lock and yanked back the gate.

George made more cocoa for Anji, Lisa and Beverly.

'I believe you,' he said.

'About what?' asked Anji. She spoke for the others; she was the eldest, a kind of leader at nineteen.

George saw the resentment in their eyes and their obstinate vulnerability. 'I not only understand,' he said heavily – for he knew this look; he'd felt the same once – 'I'll do something about it.'

Without invitation they started talking about Riley, fighting one another for the right to give details of his appearance and habits. George listened with glazed eyes. This man, when a boy, had been a kind of brother to him. In the years since, he'd often wondered if Riley was one of those for whom the helping hand had come too late, or if he'd turned away. No doubt it was this heavy reminiscing that made George slow on the uptake. When the three girls stared at George, drained and expectant, he said, 'I'll call the police tomorrow.'

'Police?' Beverly asked, her mouth open, like that of her dragon.

'Yes.'

'Us?'

'Yes.'

And then George understood what had brought them back. 'Hang on,' he said in disbelief, 'you didn't think I was offering to whack him over the head?'

The three conspirators threw glances at one another. Unmasked, they appeared younger still, and more awkward. Lisa stood, putting on her bomber jacket. 'We fight back by filling in a complaint form?'

'No. By taking Riley to court.'

'That's easily said. We'd pay and it would cost you nothing.'

Anji followed Lisa to the door while Beverly, still slouching, looked George right in the eye. 'They'd tear us to pieces.'

If precision matters, this was the moment when George lost his senses, when two teenagers stood at the door and a third was about to pull away. 'Yes. But they can't do that to me.'

'What's it got to do with you?'

George wasn't going to answer that question. 'If I support what you say,' he persisted, 'Riley will be convicted. There's nothing they can throw at me. Nothing.'

'What will it cost you, then?'

'If it goes wrong, my job.'

'Why do it?'

Again, he sidestepped the question. 'It can't go wrong.'

The next day George woke up profoundly grateful that Beverly had joined her pals at the door. But a week later – again at three or so in the morning – the buzzer had torn George out of a deep slumber. It had been a bad night, with a punch-up over queue-jumping. He stumbled angrily to the gate with such a weight upon his eyes that he could barely see. He heard Anji's voice:

'We'll risk it, if you will.'

In a stupor, George leaned his head on the bars. The wisdom of these kids, he thought. They trust only the person whose outlay matches theirs. The gate swung open for the last time; and George made more cocoa and toast.

'If I do this,' he said cautiously, 'will you go to the Open Door?' They all shook on it while George's gaze rested upon a tiger's head that snarled behind Beverly's other ear. It hadn't been there last time.

Funnily enough, it was the tiger and the dragon who fled on the day of the trial. Anji and Lisa kept their side of the bargain. And then George was called. If he'd even sensed what might be waiting for him in the courtroom, he'd have joined Beverly on the pavement. In the corridor, Jennifer Cartwright grabbed his arm. 'Where the hell are you going?'

'Home.'

'Where?'

'Back home.'

'Why?'

He didn't reply.

'Two girls have just had their heads kicked in.' She was seething. 'You can't go home.'

George took the bus to Mitcham knowing that Anji, Lisa and Beverly wouldn't be going to an open door in Fulham. That was George's fault. In the long run, she'd been right, that police-woman.

Much later George had written in his notebook, 'Who'd have thought that a question about my grandfather would have set Riley free?' And it was only then that George realised that his downfall hadn't begun at the night shelter's gate, when he was a man, but with a secret, discovered when he was a boy.

And now, walking by the Thames, George asked himself where lay the praise and blame? That was a tricky one, because things couldn't have been any different. Mercy or reward? Well, that was trickier still.

George followed the cobbled lane that ran between the warehouses and the hoists. He ducked through the mesh wiring onto a quilt of broken brick. A bitter wind swung off the Thames, pulling at his hair and stinging his nose. He stood upon Lawton's Wharf, his long walk ended. He'd been homeless without knowing where he was going, but now he'd arrived – at the place he'd visited more frequently than any other. He spied a ladder built into the dock wall. He took off the bright new trainers he'd been given on Old Paradise Street and laid them to one side. Slowly, he lowered himself into the river. His clothes gathered weight, and the cold clasped his legs and stomach. A painful thought passed across his mind: for Emily he was already dead.

16

Anselm went to bed with the accounts and receipts that had been sent to Inspector Cartwright. Even with his glasses on, he couldn't make head or tail of a single column (at the Bar, he'd steered clear of cases that had numbers in them), so he put the documents on the floor and gave his attention to something more promising: a cornucopia of intractable problems. A lawyer's habits made him divide them into two groups.

First, why had Elizabeth sent him to see Mrs Dixon without any clue as to what she might say? What was the point of leaving him powerless, and her powerful – in the sense that she could refuse to talk, which is precisely what happened? Why take another risk that could only harm her prospects of success – for just as George Bradshaw (predictably) had gone missing, so Mrs Dixon (not surprisingly) had refused to talk about her missing son. The only answer Anselm could muster was this: at the heart of Elizabeth's bid to make good the past was a complete respect for the free choices of the other actors. There would be no cajoling, no forced outcomes.

The next group of problems was, for Anselm, the most intriguing. How did this second mission connect with the first?

What was the link between the missing boy and the bid to bring Riley back to court? While listening to Mrs Dixon, Anselm had noted the vowels resistant to life in the South; the northern intonation in the word 'cake' had survived completely intact. It had shone like a tanner in a heap of decimal currency. Who, then, was the missing lad? He'd been a good boy, a good son. Reviewing the cornucopia as a whole, Anselm came to a sensible though uncomfortable conclusion: both of the matters that had been entrusted to him by Elizabeth were now well on the way to monumental failure.

Success, however, had come Anselm's way earlier that evening, albeit from another direction. He had, of course, begun looking into Elizabeth's past, while she had only expected him to move forward on her behalf. And initial results were interesting.

After leaving Mrs Dixon, Anselm paid a visit to Trespass Place, hoping that George Bradshaw had returned to his patch, but it was silent and bare; so, discouraged, he went back to Hoxton, where he found a bundle of faxed documents from Gray's Inn. He leafed through them while his shepherd's pie revolved in the microwave. The librarian had organised, in reverse order, various notices covering legal responsibilities assumed by Elizabeth. It was only when Anselm reached the final sheet that he appreciated his earlier, decisive mistake. It was obvious why this particular Glendinning hadn't gone to Durham University. Looking down, he read again the list of names. It was a register of those called to the Bar by the Honourable Society of Gray's Inn on the fifteenth day of October nineteen hundred and fifty. The librarian had marked the relevant entry: Elizabeth Steadman.

Glendinning was, of course, her married name. Anselm had never known her as anything else. On marrying, most women barristers kept the names under which they began their careers because they carried their reputations. Elizabeth, however, had dropped hers and started all over again. Anselm sat down, suddenly excited because someone else had made the same gaffe as himself, only she didn't have the excuse of not knowing any better. His thoughts becoming tangled, he picked up the telephone and called the Prior.

'Sister Dorothy reeled off the history of Mr G, the frustrated inventor, and Mrs G, his uncomplaining wife.' Anselm paused. 'But she got the name wrong. It should have been Mr and Mrs Steadman.'

'Teachers follow the fortunes of their pupils,' replied Father Andrew confidently. 'Perhaps she learned of Elizabeth's marriage and switched the names by accident.'

A monk can always contradict his prior. But it has a taste all of its own. 'My first thought too,' said Anselm warmly. 'However, she hadn't had word or sight of Elizabeth in forty years. She shouldn't even know the Glendinning surname.'

It was hardly caviar, but the hiatus was delicious. Anselm said, 'But why would Sister Dorothy lie?'

'Perhaps, like you, she'd given her word,' said Father Andrew distantly, as though he'd turned to the fire. 'And perhaps,' he added, 'that was the first of the many promises that have been sought and obtained.'

17

Riley took the bus home because the fascists who'd clamped him weren't answering the phone. He came in the back way, pausing to glance at Nancy's bricks: she'd been collecting them all her married life. She rummaged in the grass by Limehouse

Cut and brought them home one by one. Exhausted by the bout with Wyecliffe, defeated by the Council, and cold to his bones, he felt suddenly weak: affection stirred inside him like a shot of Bertie's poison.

There was an irony about Riley and Nancy: prior to the trial, he'd pushed Nancy back, but she'd kept returning; after the trial, he'd wanted her to linger, but she kept away. So when Riley told her what had happened to his van, she was very understanding; she said all the right things; but she was far off. She didn't even ask what he was doing in Cheapside. Later, Riley lounged in his rocker, listening to a very different kind of chat. As Nancy cleared away the plates, she asked Arnold how he was getting on, whether he was tired of his wheel, whether he got lonely in his cage. Riley's chair creaked as he moved more quickly, as his envy grew.

After Nancy had gone to bed, Riley stayed up watching the fire decline. In the stillness of the night he took out the photograph of Walter from his pocket. Without looking he dropped it on the fading coals. He heard it snap into flame. When he glanced into the grate, all that was left was a curl of ash.

Who posted it? Until that evening, Riley had confined his thoughts to the living, but the lawyer had turned to the dead. Who'd he been referring to? Or had he been having a dig, trying to tell him that he'd never believed him about John Bradshaw?

Suddenly, Arnold started running in his wheel.

Years after the trial, Riley was doing a clearance when his mobile started the nerve-racking tune that he didn't know how to change. He stabbed a button to make it stop.

'Will you help me find the Pieman?'

Riley was stunned. 'Who is this?'

'Someone who knows you weren't the only one to blame.'

Riley couldn't reply. He sank onto a thing the relative had called a *fauteuil*.

'If you tell me,' said the young voice, 'I can inform the police. I'll be like a cut-off. And when they've found their own proof, they can act without bothering either of us. You've nothing to fear.'

In the corner, a budgie hopped from bar to bar, tinkling a little bell. He'd come with the job lot. 'Who is this?' said Riley again.

'I'm the son of George Bradshaw.'

Riley watched the bird pecking seeds, its green-and-yellow head jerking like it was being shocked at intervals from the mains. Riley said, 'Who else knows that you've called me?'

'No one.'

'Will they find out?'

'No. I promise.'

Much later Riley concluded that some big decisions aren't as simple as they might appear. Like a wall, they're built from the bottom up. You stand on the top course, laying bricks, not daring to look at where you'll end up if you carry on. Finally, you're too high and you can't get down. And yet, from the outset, there was always a kind of knowing; and recklessly it was broken down into manageable bits, and put together.

It was therefore without having reached a decision as such, but irresponsibly, that he said, 'I need to think. Call me back in six months.'

The next day, on impulse, Riley went to Lawton's Wharf. Everything had been sold off or flattened. The whole place was falling into the dark-blue river. Suddenly moved, he stood on the cracked plinth that had held his crane and he searched the pale evening sky for Nancy's window.

What was he going to do about Bradshaw's son? He gazed at the wharf, sentimental for the days he'd never really enjoyed. His eyes settled on the DANGER sign attached to a barbed-wire fence that blocked access to the main quay. Farther on he noted a line of plastic bollards. The timbers on the other side were black and green.

Four times over the next six months Riley came home late and told Nancy that his van had broken down. He complained about it to Prosser and the rest. He bought spare parts, kept the receipts and went through the motions of an unnecessary repair. He was getting higher and higher, never taking his eyes off what his hands and feet were doing.

Arnold's wheel rattled and raced.

Riley had hoped that George's boy would drop the matter, but he rang back, as arranged. Wobbling, but keeping his nerve, Riley said, 'Meet me on Lawton's Wharf on Saturday night.'

Why there of all places? It wasn't just because it was secluded and dangerous. Riley hadn't thought it out, but his instinct wanted to stamp upon the world of fluffed chances, to wreck it good and proper. Accordingly, broken down into bits: Riley left a fair in Barking at six, cursing the rain. Half an hour later he rang Nancy and told her that the van had stalled. At seven he cut down the barbed wire. At ten past, he set about the bollards. (They'd been filled with concrete, so one by one, he dragged them to the edge of the wharf and tipped them into the river.) Since the planking was rotten, Riley crept along a supporting beam, and was at the end of the platform by seven-thirty. At eight a figure appeared.

Riley never once looked directly at the boy. He kept his eyes down and began a conversation that had no purpose because he was too high up to listen properly.

'I only want to vindicate my father,' said John Bradshaw. The drizzle pattered on their shoulders.

'Vindicate'. What a hauntingly strong word. This boy would never give up.

Fear played its part, for sure – not the kind that gripped Riley in his childhood, but something organic, a condition that he could feel all the time if he'd checked for it (like an irregular heartbeat). It pumped ink into his intentions – and he shoved with all his might . . . hoping and not hoping that it would happen; that he could console himself afterwards by saying he didn't really mean it.

The boards cracked. A whole section of planking gave way and Riley was abruptly alone. There was a cry, but after the splash, there was no noise . . . none at all . . . just the slapping of the river and the patter of the rain.

Riley waited for half an hour, checking the side of the quay. Then he went home and thrashed Nancy at dominoes.

The following morning, as usual, he went to work. The weeks passed and he did the things that he always did. But just as Arnold's whiskers got wet every time he licked the milk, so a kind of suicide happens with a murder. Sitting opposite the Major, Riley had been bitterly proud of his home-made identity. He'd sought no mitigation. He'd scorned salvation now, never mind the hereafter. But with the death of John Bradshaw all that posturing fell slack. He felt strangely sick of himself, in a new way, and of the world. He tried to doubt that he'd shoved him. Some big decisions might be made up of small choices, but what Riley couldn't work out was why, in another world, he wouldn't have chosen the end result in the first place. Why he recoiled from it in this one? And with that insight, Riley teetered towards an abyss of self-pity, for he wondered if he'd been acting freely, if he'd *ever* been free; if he ever would be. Within a couple of months, after years of clean living, Riley began his new scheme.

And then, out of nowhere, came an envelope containing a photograph. The image sent Riley flying back to the times he'd done his best to forget. He was overwhelmed by his powerlessness – either to annihilate that face or to hinder whoever it was that had sent it. Stranded, he felt a need for Nancy, far stronger than anything he'd known since the trial. It seemed incredible, but it was true: standing in his way was a *hamster*. It was humiliating.

The spool fell silent. Arnold had been running for ages. If he'd been a man on the road he'd have reached Penzance.

Riley went to the kitchen, bit an apple and threw it in a plastic bag. Still chewing, he opened the cage and dropped Arnold onto the fruit. Then he followed the lane that led to Limehouse Cut. The bins were out. A crowd of polystyrene pellets skittered along the pavement, white and vibrant in the darkness. He swished the bag across his trouser leg, like a boy with sweets from the corner shop – sticky things out of tall jars held out by Mrs O'Neill. She'd only ever been kind to him – but with a pity that had guessed everything, that had stripped him down to the contusions. 'He has tempers.' That's what his mother had said of Walter. Tempers. It sounded like something Babycham would have ordered with lemonade and a cherry. 'Not to worry, son,' his mother once said. She wiped her own split lip as if she'd just finished her fish and chips. 'You fell off your bike, all right?' Her eyes had dried like a desert, centuries before.

When he reached the canal, Riley halted. The bag swung by his leg. Hesitating, he began to think. In a way, Walter, John Bradshaw and Arnold belonged together. Each of them, in very different ways, had been so much stronger than Riley. And with that terrible thought, he let go.

18

Despite expectations that he would sink quickly under the weight of wet clothing, George had remained afloat. An action somewhere between swimming and treading water led him away from his point of entry. He felt a colder current around his feet; the smack of small waves made him spit. He was being pulled now, towards the full flow of the river. The final supporting pillars rose out of the shadows to meet the abrupt ending of the wharf's run. George turned into the water.

In so far as this moment had received any planning, George had intended to give his final thoughts to John. To his surprise he found himself upon the tracks of his own childhood, running down a winding path, at the back of a string of council houses in Harrogate. It was a sunny day; the ground was ribbed and dry underfoot. To his right were fences and small gardens with sheds . . . windows framed white in walls of red brick . . . A shining cat lay sprawled upon warm slate; to his left there were trunks and branches, screening a tennis court of orange grit . . . and then a bowling green . . . a velvet stage for men in white coats with bald heads or big caps . . . He was skipping and hopping, for the sheer joy of being alive, feeling his heart ache with the strain. He was ten. And he wanted to stay that age for ever. At the end of the path was a thick patch of dock leaves at the base of a tree by his home. George began to sink, just as he remembered kneeling down, panting and curious, to taste a bright, crisp leaf as though he were a rabbit.

Something made of metal hit George on the head. Instinctively, his arms flailed and he surfaced with a gasp. Bobbing in the water was a tin can. Looking up, he saw a boy sitting at the end of the wharf, his legs idly dangling. A small shaved head cut a fine serrated hole into the sky. Suddenly, he vanished. Rage ran hot through tired old veins. 'The little brat . . .' George was panting now. Cold had seized him as though it were a weight. Panic gripped him. The boy appeared again at the edge of the wharf. George shouted for help. A thin arm swung out, and something angular swiftly cut a fine arc against the sky, like a shooting star without light. It struck the water with a deep thud. The arm flashed again.

'What the *hell* do you think you're doing?' yelled George. In a frenzy he shook off his coat. Enraged, he began moving towards the side. The boy, relaxed, followed the swimmer's progress, walking along the rim of the wharf, tossing chunks of broken masonry. They landed around him casually. George hauled himself up the rusted ladder and collapsed, spewing water, onto the quay. His teeth worked in unison with a vivid memory, and he began to weep. The sun was warm upon his neck, and he was a lad again, on his knees at the foot of a tree, tasting a leaf. It had been surprisingly bitter, when he had wanted it to be sweet. He arched his head, opening his streaming eyes: the boy was sauntering towards the perimeter fence, hands in his pockets.

George tried to shout, but nothing came from his throat. He clambered to his feet and stumbled after his persecutor. Several times he fell, cutting his hands and knees. The pain quickened him. Frantically, George continued his ridiculous pursuit, driven by a senseless desire to express an elemental, livid gratitude. Beneath the radiance of a street lamp, the boy stooped, working his way through a hole in the netting. By the time George stood dripping in the road that ran adjacent to Mr Lawton's fallen kingdom, the assassin had gone.

A couple of hours later George swayed beneath the fire escape and was stunned to find his bed made. As consciousness became pain and a deep, immense shivering, delusion eased away his last waking moment: he could have sworn he saw a figure coming down from the steps above.

19

When Nancy had gone to bed, leaving Riley in his rocker, she'd tossed and turned, annoyed by questions as if they were lumps in the mattress. Where was Mr Johnson? What should she do with his notebooks? Who was the man in the photograph? With this last, Nancy had, in fact, made some headway: it might be Riley's father, she thought, because he never spoke of him. Or maybe his mother had sent it: he didn't speak of her either. That was Riley. He was so different, you wouldn't be surprised to hear that he'd never had parents. She laughed at her own joke, changed sides and plumped her pillow. Listening to Arnold, she finally became drowsy.

Nancy woke up. Something in the house was slightly different, but she didn't know what. Riley wasn't beside her . . . but she could hear him in the kitchen. The back door opened and closed. A tug of sympathy took Nancy out of bed and to the window: her man couldn't come to bed; he had to walk himself like a dog, until he was so tired that his mind couldn't worry him. This is what British justice had done to her man – to a man who'd done nothing wrong.

202

She moved the curtain an inch or two. At first she couldn't see anything. Some of the windows on the other side were lit round the edges . . . and the bins were out. Her breath steamed the glass. She gave it a rub with the sleeve of her nightie, and then she saw him. Riley was at the top of the street. She knew his walk, by the way his arms swung like loose ropes.

Nancy climbed back into bed and twenty minutes later, Riley slipped between the sheets. She didn't stir and he didn't move. Almost at once, he began snoring with his hands behind his head. Nancy couldn't get back to sleep because she was distracted: something had been altered in the house, and she couldn't put her finger on what it was.

20

In his sleep Riley was running down a dark corridor towards a window, its frame blurred by light. His footfalls were silent. All he could hear was the breathing of the Thing behind him. Blinded, he broke though the glass as though it were tracing paper. His stomach spilled out and he began to fall.

Even as he fell, he knew this was the old dream – the dream that had begun the day of his acquittal. And even as the stairs appeared, he recognised that this was the development – like a turning of the pages in his mind – that had started after he'd received the photograph. He was observing himself, and yet experiencing the rise of terror.

All at once the nightmare cut location. Riley was no longer falling. His stomach was in his belly. He was walking along a small corridor in a silent terraced house. Upstairs there were three bedrooms. Outside, at the back, there was a small garden with a gate that led to three trees. He didn't know why he knew all this, or why he was aware that the front door was green, or that the kitchen floor had been laid with fake marble. It was simply part of the sensation of being in this empty house. He moved slowly, like an underwater diver. Sunshine lit the floating dust. To his right, through a doorway, he saw an iron fireplace. The grate was clean. By the hearth were a pan and brush on a stand; the poker was missing. A kind of barking started in Riley's guts – a juddering sensation brought on by the recognition of his surroundings: this was home. He noticed that he was not a man, and not a boy; that he was in between the two. Ahead and to the left he saw a hand on the carpet. It hung off the bottom step of the staircase. The bystander in Riley vanished. Riley became Riley, in his entirety. Slowly, bravely, his eyes moved along the arm, up the shoulder and onto the matted hair.

A lifeless, loveless face looked back. So great was Riley's horror at the sight of himself that he didn't even scream.

PART FOUR

a girl's progress

1

Anselm faced Mr Hillsden. Between them, in a hospital bed, lay George Bradshaw, a frown holding one side of his face like a paralysis. Clippers had neatly removed his hair and beard, leaving a ragged stubble. The skin around his eyes was pale, as if he'd just returned from two weeks on a sunny alpine piste.

'I don't recognise him,' said Anselm quietly. The man in the witness box had been tall and imposing. Where on earth had he been after he'd walked out of court? What manner of journey could so reduce a man? He said, 'How did you find him?'

'With respect,' said Mr Hillsden, 'I lodged at Trespass Place.'

'All this time?'

'Indeed, on the upper platform of a fire escape.' He stood with both hands resting on the ornamental knob of his curtain pole. 'He chose an agreeable location, if I may say so. South-facing and close to all local amenities.' There was a heavy irony in his voice – that of the commentator who can't adequately explain what he's known and seen. His watery blue eyes never strayed higher than Anselm's folded arms.

It transpired that Mr Hillsden had secured an ambulance by halting it on Blackfriars Bridge with his raised staff. He'd then waited at the hospital all night until the Vault opened, when a sympathetic nurse had made a telephone call to Debbie Lynwood. She had immediately contacted Anselm, who, in turn, had left a message for Inspector Cartwright. It was nine in the morning.

Anselm examined the twisted shape in the bed. According to

his witness statement, David George Bradshaw was a married man with one child, a careworker by profession, in the employ of the Bridges night shelter. 'When you wake,' said Anselm, detached from his surroundings, 'please tell me what I did wrong.'

The sound of feet and bustle announced the approach of a consultant weighed down by a stethoscope and students. 'Are you a chaplain?' he asked. The tone was kindly, but implied a treatable deviation from the norm.

'No.'

His eyes moved onto Mr Hillsden. 'A relative?'

'With respect, no.'

'If you don't mind,' he said hastily, 'I'll proceed.'

'Go ahead,' said Anselm, stepping back.

The doctor flicked through the medical notes on a clipboard while his young audience formed an arc around the bed. Mr Hillsden did not move and stood among them, head bowed, hands on his staff.

'Male, sixtysomething,' intoned the consultant. 'First admitted after a beating at Waterloo Station. Multiple blows to the cranial vault. No patient history' – he glanced towards an industrious young man with a pad and pen – 'Edgerton, stop writing and listen. Just think. It's far more difficult. Outcome: ruptured aneurysm. Louise, a definition, please.'

'A sac in a major artery or vein that burst,' said the young woman, 'causing a leak of blood into the brain.'

'Correct.' The doctor hung the medical notes on the bedstead. 'The required surgical procedure is rather like patching the inner tube on your bike, but rather more difficult. You may record that for posterity, Edgerton. In the instant case, no post-op complications. One hitch: short-term memory loss. Treatment?'

Glances fell on Louise.

'In effect, there is none.' The doctor eyed his patient with pity. 'To anchor events a routine and supported life is essential. Unless he writes things down, the recent past will draw back like the tide on Dover Beach. In the circumstances, that may not be a bad thing. Last night someone found him soaking wet. He's now got mild to moderate hypothermia. Treatment, Gardner?'

'Cover with blankets at room temperature.'

'Precisely,' he replied. 'What you see now is a pandemic condition characterised by static posture and reduced but reversible sensitivity to external stimuli. Diagnosis?'

No one spoke.

'With respect,' said Mr Hillsden apologetically, 'the term "asleep" has the advantage of economy.'

Outside the ward, by a door marked EXIT, Anselm and Mr Hillsden once again faced each other. This time nothing lay between them, save for the kind of awkwardness that might befit separated friends. Anselm looked at the lowered head, the green cagoule and the polished, split brogues. Casually, as he might have done on a rather stiff social occasion, he said, 'Might I ask, to which Inn do you belong?'

For an instant, Mr Hillsden's washed eyes caught Anselm's gaze. A faint smile moved beneath the grizzled beard. 'The Inner Temple.' The words were barely audible.

'Which chambers?' asked Anselm carelessly.

'3 Vellum Square.'

'Ah.' Anselm knew it well. 'Facing that glorious magnolia tree?'

Mr Hillsden nodded. 'There's a sundial, too . . .'

Footsteps echoed, moving swiftly. Anselm glimpsed the

magenta scarf of Inspector Cartwright at the end of the corridor. He called out and she paused, retracing a few steps. With a brief wave, she came towards them.

'She will be as grateful to you as I am,' said Anselm, turning back to Mr Hillsden . . . but he was gone. Anselm ran through the EXIT door into a stairwell. Leaning over a railing, he could see nothing but a shadow thrown across the steps, descending.

'Come back,' he shouted.

The staff sounded on the stone like the tapping of a patient carpenter. A door closed out of sight and Anselm found himself alone with Inspector Cartwright.

'Who's that?' she enquired. A breath of lavender came with her approach.

'Just another member of the Bar,' he replied.

Anselm and Inspector Cartwright chose window seats in the cafeteria. Down below the Thames seemed not to flow. It flickered with light around a reflection of Parliament and Big Ben. The sky was immense, cold and blue.

'Did you make any sense of those accounts?' asked the Inspector, stirring foam in a mug of hot chocolate.

'No,' replied Anselm. 'No matter how hard I looked.'

'I don't suppose it matters, now that Mr Bradshaw has turned up.'

Anselm examined his toast. This was soft, additive-packed, white sliced bread. None of your grains and nuts, like the breeze blocks at Larkwood. It should have been a moment to relish, but his appetite had gone – with Mr Hillsden. 'The letter from Elizabeth has been destroyed,' he said shortly. 'George's clothing was binned at three in the morning. The waste disposal truck came at six. I arrived at half eight. I think that just about explains what's transpired in our absence.'

'We're stuffed, then,' observed Inspector Cartwright.

'Not quite,' said Anselm. He measured his words with care, sharing a thought that had come to him earlier that morning. 'All manner of fowl are drawn to the monastic life. Some are very talented but for years these guys have to follow the same routine as the rest of us. And then one day . . . the Prior gives them a job. Suddenly, all that unexercised talent breaks out on the laundry, or the kitchens, or – and I have a concrete example in mind – the priory's accounts. It's hell for the rest of us, of course, but in that one quarter we have levels of efficiency the Bundesbank couldn't dream of. All of which persuades me we should send the accounts to Brother Cyril. This is a man who spends the night hours chasing pennies, and he finds them.'

Inspector Cartwright had the original papers: she would fax them to Larkwood as soon as she got back to her office. Anselm wrote out the number, explaining that he'd prepare the way with a call to Father Andrew. 'In the meantime,' he said, 'I shall wait for George to wake up.'

What was Riley doing? The question was unspoken but it bound them together. Inspector Cartwright sipped her hot chocolate and Anselm nibbled his cold toast.

2

Riley glared at Prosser, at his felt hat, at the cigar jammed beneath a handle-bar moustache. They'd both set up their stalls in Beckton Park. The air was sharp and a frost had made the grass ribbed and hard. The 'dealer', as he called himself, had ambled over to Riley's patch and was nosing through his goods. He stood with his hands behind his back, picking up this and that with a nod of approval.

'Keep away from Nancy,' said Riley.

'Whatever do you mean?' Smoke came slowly from Prosser's nostrils.

'You heard me.'

Prosser stepped away but then hesitated. 'Look, Riley, we're both men of business, so I'll be honest. I'm interested in the shop, not your good lady. You've a prime location there. No offence, but I'd say the building requires the sort of investment you can't afford.'

'Push off.'

'I'd give you a good price.' He walked backwards, winking.

'I'll never sell.'

Riley held himself tight, arms wrapped across his chest. A chill had reached his bones and he squirmed, thinking of Wyecliffe's questions. They'd burrowed into his head and eaten away at what was left of his peace of mind. He'd wanted the solicitor to weave his magic, to do something startling with the law that would protect him. But he couldn't pull it off, not this time. Instead, he'd made it worse – deliberately – with that remark about the dead being on to Riley's trail. For the first time, there was no Wyecliffe twitching by his side: he was on his own. Riley hugged himself more securely, feeling more exposed than ever. Someone was after him. They were watching and waiting and they would come. A familiar racket began deep in the tissues of the brain: he heard bangs on the wall and screams on an upstairs landing. Riley covered his ears with gloved hands and stood to shake off the sound. Violence swirled inside, making his eyes glaze and dry out.

Riley blinked. Beckton Park appeared as if it hadn't been there. Trees, grass and people became solid. Prosser was watching, legs crossed on a commode as if it were a throne, puffing on his cigar. Despite the cold, Riley felt sweat sting the corner of his eyes. When his head grew quiet, he sat down, slightly out of breath.

As if someone had turned on a radio by his ear, Riley heard himself talking to Nancy over his breakfast.

'It was me,' he said honestly, feeling grubby. 'I oiled the wheel and I must have left the cage open.'

Nancy leaned on the counter almost dazed and unable to speak. Riley couldn't understand it. She'd had three hamsters. When one died, she bought another. It was a routine. But this time it was different. She'd never been so winded.

Riley turned aside to escape the recollection. At once, his eye snagged on a billboard showing a smiling woman with a bottle of milk. Her lips were red and her teeth were as white as the sky. There were lots of children in the background looking at the bottle, as if it would make them happy. He swore and looked the other way. But he saw a mother tabbing by a pram, and beside her a man, hungover, lean and yellow. He closed his eyes to escape . . . *everything*. When he opened them he saw a newcomer thirty yards away. He was reading the name on Riley's van.

Major Reynolds had once said, 'You've made lots of choices, and you can make others.' That one idea had stuck to Riley like pitch. He'd never been able to scrape it off. All he'd wanted was a warm bed for the night, but the Major had given him words that burned. *You can make other choices.* The idea was horrendous . . .

The man drew close. He was middle-aged, dressed in a bomber jacket, jeans and a cap. Uncertainty made him fidget with the zip on his jacket. He moved it up and down, and said, 'Can I buy a number?'

Riley charged his eyes with disgust until they stung. Did he really want to do this any more?

213

'Sorry,' said the man fearfully, 'I've made a mistake . . .'

Riley summoned him back with a flick of the hand and took out a notebook. He flicked through the blank pages until he came to a calling card, picked up from a telephone booth near Trafalgar Square. Slowly he read out the number.

The man seemed to wake up, patting his pockets, trying to be normal. He took out a crumpled envelope and a pencil.

'I'll read that again,' said Riley, his attention shifting to Prosser. The dealer had sidled from behind his stall and was watching every movement. He lit a new cigar and studied the glow of red ash.

After jotting down the number, the man said, 'I understand it's fifteen quid?'

'We don't talk,' said Riley, taking the money. 'It's the only rule.'

The man walked quickly away, between the trestle tables and the moochers, tracked by Riley's contempt. When he was out of view, Riley went through the motions (his mind returning at intervals to the sight of Nancy, winded by the counter). He selected a vase from his table marked for sale at '£15'. He wrapped it in newspaper and put it in a crate – for transfer to the shop in Bow. Then he opened a pad labelled 'Van Sales'. He made out a receipt to record a fictional transaction: 'One Vase. £30 received in Cash.' Carefully he detached the original from the blue duplicate beneath. Ordinarily, this would go to the customer, but since there wasn't one, Riley tore it to pieces. He then opened another pad marked 'Acquisitions' and wrote out a second receipt – for an imaginary purchase: 'One vase. £15 paid in Cash.'

When he'd finished, Riley dropped the pads into a cardboard box at his feet. He looked at them, at the bones of his system. Not since his childhood had he felt so strongly the desire to run away: from the voices, the billboards, the sheer filth of his existence. But he'd learned long, long ago, there was a most unusual pleasure that came with the staying.

Prosser ambled along a path puffing smoke. He was pretending to stretch his fat legs, to get some heat into his toes. In fact, he was trying to work out what had taken place before his eyes . . . just as Riley, that morning – feeling queasy – had tried to make sense of Nancy.

3

'Don't use wise words falsely,' quoted Father Andrew.

Anselm had rung Larkwood to forewarn the Prior that a fax would shortly arrive for Cyril's kind attention – it was an unlikely outcome, admittedly, but it was important not to hold a man to his past. In the background he'd heard a bell, and, feeling abruptly homesick, Anselm had opened his heart: he didn't know what to say to George Bradshaw; he was ailing with a strain of guilt. And that had provoked the familiar quotation from a Desert Father.

Anselm put the receiver down. Thoughtfully mouthing the phrase, he returned to the ward, where a nurse informed him that George was not only awake, but in a chair and anxious to meet him.

Anselm paused at the entrance. From a tinny radio, Bunny Berigan was playing 'I Can't Get Started'. The trumpet soared while Anselm examined the bandaged feet and dinted legs. Then Bun gave it voice:

I've flown around the world in a plane,
I've settled revolutions in Spain,

The North Pole I have charted,
But still I can't get started with you.

Remembering Emily Bradshaw in Mitcham, Anselm entered the ward.

George had been conducting, but instantly he rose, his wrists quivering on the armrests as they took the strain. 'Elizabeth said you'd come,' he exclaimed, hand outstretched. 'Funny thing is' – he laughed quietly at the coming joke – 'I can't remember why.'

Anselm smiled thinly, and he flinched at the old man's grip. Mumbling how nice it was to see him, he sat on the edge of the bed, still wondering how to approach what had to be said. He couldn't look at George, any more than Mr Hillsden had been unable to look at Anselm. Something tied them together, though, because they were both held spellbound by Bunny Berigan's trumpet solo.

'Even Louis Armstrong wouldn't touch that number,' observed Anselm, at the end of the song. It was hardly wise, but at least it wasn't false.

George gave Anselm a friendly shove, as if they were pals sharing half a pint of mild. 'These days,' he said, 'I've no choice about what I remember. Tomorrow, if we meet, don't expect to pick up where you left off. Begin all over again. With me, I'm afraid, you're always starting afresh . . . That's not so bad, is it?'

Anselm raised his eyes, suddenly aware that a kind of pardon had been given to him. George's thoughts seemed to mark his face like stippling on a reef, as though one might understand him by watching. There were no barriers left: the surface was the depth. Anselm was staring at George – right into him – and there was no anger, no resentment, no pride, just a certain

shining quality, which might be the brightness of the light . . .
and yet, which might not. Fumbling for confidence, he said,
'Mr Bradshaw, about the trial, I asked you a very particular
question—'

George raised a hand. 'I'm no longer troubled by anything I
can remember,' he said simply. 'I've let it fall away . . . like a
stone in the Thames.' He patted Anselm's arm, signalling the
end of that particular conversation.

Anselm was disorientated, for this broken man spoke an
idiom whose meaning he could barely follow (he'd had a similar problem with a traffic policeman in Czechoslovakia). On
the one hand, the forgiveness had been given quickly and
comprehensively; but on the other, it had come from a spirit
of detachment that Anselm had never met before, save in
some of the older monks at Larkwood. Anselm had no time
to ponder either mystery, because George had already moved
on.

'We went after Riley, and I got hold of the works, like
Elizabeth told me to.'

'Yes.'

'And she discovered what he was doing – it was there, in the
numbers, plain to be seen. Once she'd cracked it she went to see
him.'

'Who?'

'Riley.'

This was not something Anselm had anticipated. 'What happened?'

'She died,' replied George. 'I'm not saying he did anything,
it's just that death follows him around.'

Tentatively, Anselm said, 'Did she explain Riley's scheme to
you?'

'Several times.'

'Do you recall what she said?'

There was no doubt about it: George's facial expressions revealed his thoughts. And at this moment it was evident that he considered Anselm to be rather slow. 'What do you think?'

'No,' replied Anselm apologetically.

'Exactly.' George, however, was not especially troubled. 'Elizabeth wrote it down. It's in my jacket.'

Gently, Anselm explained what had happened to George's clothing, and, therefore, the letter, but the old fellow just made an 'Ah'. That, it seemed, was just another stone in the river. Anselm was astonished. He said, as though to comfort himself, 'But there's still hope. Inspector Cartwright received all the business records through the post.' He was struck by an idea. 'Did you send them?'

'I can't remember.'

Anselm fetched up a grin. 'Of course not. Sorry.'

'I doubt if I posted anything, somehow.' George rubbed a finger into his brow, trying to knead a splintered thought to the surface. It wouldn't come. He shrugged at the deep itch and said, 'Can the Inspector understand them?'

'No.'

'Ah.'

'But someone with an eye for these things will be considering them shortly.'

'Very good.'

'You've done your part,' said Anselm, wanting to give something back to this man who'd given so much. 'Now you can rest.'

George raised his legs, looking down at the bandaged feet. 'I lost my shoes, somehow, and I got terribly wet and cold.' He became confused, his mind in suspension; he seemed to have heard a noise, like a scratching behind the wall. Quietly, he said to himself, 'No . . . no . . . It's gone.'

218

Later in the day, Anselm would ring Inspector Cartwright to recount the conversation that revealed how little George knew, and how much. But first, there was something else to be done. He reached deep into the oldest part of anyone's memory, saying, 'Would you like to go home, George?'

4

Nick Glendinning sat in the sitting room at St John's Wood twirling a piece of paper between his fingers. Written on it was the telephone number of the woman who'd asked about 'her lad', the woman who'd probably received his mother's last words. She hadn't rung Charles, or the police or the medical services. She'd rung this stranger. What had she said, before dying?

At first, Nick told himself that Father Anselm was handling Elizabeth's final dispensations – she'd planned it that way – so he tried to forget the question: he signed up as a locum, and he tried to assume a normal life – until it dawned on him that he'd stumbled on another secret, his mother's last; and that whatever she'd said was more important than the key or anything retained in its box. This realisation haunted him. It made him pick up the telephone.

'My name is Nicholas Glendinning,' he said. 'I understand you know my mother.'

He pressed the receiver against his ear, to stop his hand from shaking. All he could make out was laboured breathing.

'Can I meet you?' said Nick, pressing harder.

The air whistled in his ear. 'Did she tell you about me?'

'No.'

'What do you want?'

'To talk about my mother.'

The breathing grew calm. 'I'd like that very much.'

Having noted the address, Nick rose and swivelled on his heels. Framed by the doorway was his father. His arms were almost raised. He looked like one of those entertainers in Covent Garden who don't move until you give them some money.

They looked at each other, both utterly still. Abruptly, Charles grimaced and flicked a finger in the air, as if he'd remembered what he was looking for. Then he quickly shuffled upstairs.

Nick sat on the sofa adjacent to a low table in the Shoreditch flat. The old woman was dressed in a yellow floral dress as if she were off to church or a summer garden party. She wore earrings, a necklace and creaking leather shoes. The room was conspicuously tidy but very cold, even though a radiator clicked with activity. She'd had the windows open, and an air freshener had been used. Nick found the assembly of images and sensations unequivocally surreal. He could not imagine his mother traipsing up that filthy stairwell, or sitting here, before this apparition with silver hair and tragic eyes.

'I don't even know your name,' he said awkwardly.

'Mrs Dixon,' she said, clearing her throat at the same time. 'Refreshment?'

'Yes, please.'

The low table was covered with a white cloth. It had been laid for a small reception. Mrs Dixon poured tea into ancient china cups. 'Milk or lemon?'

'Milk, thank you.'

A whole ritual unfolded, as if he were a vicar, or the squire. She offered Nick sugar, a teaspoon from the Isle of Man and a jammy dodger from a cake stand.

'Your mother was my friend,' she said proudly. 'The Council sent her along when I got lonely.'

'The Council' had evidently explained that she was dead. The flat vowel in 'lonely' disclosed that Mrs Dixon was not a Londoner. Her accent had been softened, but the northern intonation in that one word was unmistakable. Before Nick could think of what to say, Mrs Dixon spoke again.

'She came here every week, on a Friday, and we talked . . . mainly about me, and my family.' Delicately, Mrs Dixon raised her cup. 'She was full of questions, but it did me good to get things off my chest. It's not good to keep things in, that's what I say.'

'Absolutely.'

'You're a doctor, aren't you?'

'Yes.'

'Well done,' she exclaimed.

Nick sipped his tea, wondering how soon he might reasonably make his exit. But Mrs Dixon's confidence had grown. There was something predatory about her delight. 'A biscuit?' she said, pointing at the stand.

'Thank you.'

Mrs Dixon settled back in her chair, her teacup and saucer resting in the middle of her chest. Looking over the top, she said, 'I told her so much about myself, but I never asked about her . . . Do you mind telling me a little?'

'What would you like to hear?' asked Nick.

'Well . . . anything really. Something that explains where she came from . . . Like I did, with her.'

Nick surrendered to the circumstances, as his mother must have done, when she'd first realised what she'd let herself in for. Mrs Dixon's question, however, was so broad that he didn't know where to begin. And then he thought of the photograph.

'We have this family portrait at home,' he said thoughtfully. 'It shows my mother as a child with her parents.'

The picture was in the sitting room at St John's Wood. As a boy Nick used to study the sepia faces of the solemn man and his proud, buxom wife. They were stiff and unsmiling, in a happy sort of way, obedient to the formality of their time. His neck was bound in a wing collar, and she was packed into a polka dot dress. Elizabeth was in the middle, her long hair scraped back and held by ribbons. An affectionate hand from her father had strayed onto her knee, unnoticed by the camera- man. There was a clock in the background and a tall dresser. Elizabeth used to say that her self-understanding – where she'd come from, who she'd become, her dispositions and their prove- nance – had been captured in that one photograph, with one explosion from the flash. It was her way of explaining to Nick why, as he'd grown older, she'd become more reserved; and why there was a melancholy even in her smile. As a teenager, her quietness, her lack of bounce, had sometimes irritated him and, being a teenager, he'd told her. It made him sad, now, to think he could ever have held her to account, given the tragedy that overran that prim family in the photograph.

Nick found himself explaining to Mrs Dixon how events had wiped clean his mother's expectations before she was fifteen. That her father had died suddenly before her eyes.

'What happened?' asked Mrs Dixon, blinking over her teacup.

'He just passed away, like a light going out.'

'But how?'

'A weak heart.' Nick understood now, because Doctor Okoye had made the diagnosis.

'What was her father like?' asked Mrs Dixon after a moment.

'My mother rarely spoke of him,' replied Nick. 'She once

told me that not a day passed without her calling him to mind.'

Nick sipped his tea – it had gone cold with his talking – and then he said, strangely moved, 'She said I was just like him . . .' In saying that sentence to this dolled-up stranger, Nick, for the first time, understood his own adolescence, and his mother's anguish as a parent. She'd tried to tell him why they'd fallen out of kilter, but he hadn't understood.

'And what of Elizabeth's mother?' said Mrs Dixon. 'How did she fare?'

'Not very well.'

'I'm not surprised.'

'That's not what I meant.' He paused, not wanting to divulge much more. 'She died too – shortly afterwards, from septicaemia.'

Mrs Dixon seemed visibly shocked, and Nick felt a stab of irritation, fearing that his mother's life had become an episode in a kind of soap opera.

'Thank you for telling me what happened to Elizabeth,' said Mrs Dixon, placing her cup on the table. 'I now understand why she came to look after me.'

'Really?' asked Nick, curious now.

'Yes . . . You see . . . I, too, have had my mishaps.' She picked up a paper napkin. 'And I know what it's like to lose someone and want them back. Of course, the Council had all this information in their files, and they'll have told your mother. So when she knocked on my door, thank God, she didn't bring just pity, she brought . . . herself.' The napkin tore in her hands.

Nick was ashamed of his earlier irritation with this poor woman who was genuinely distressed. He would have liked to leave, but now was the obvious time to put the one question that had brought him here. He said, 'Before my mother died, she made a telephone call . . . to you.'

223

Mrs Dixon nodded. Her mouth was set, and her eyes were suddenly vacant.

'Do you mind telling me what she said?'

'Not at all.' Mrs Dixon appeared tragically isolated in her chair, the only one left at the garden party. 'Elizabeth said . . . "I'm very sorry, but I won't be coming any more."'

Nick was dumbfounded. The latter part of his mother's life had been devoted to a scheme wholly personal in its objectives and significance. But her last words had been said to a forgotten woman halfway up a tower block who dressed up for a cup of tea; to the person who probably needed her most.

5

At the mention of going home, George whispered, 'Can I?'

'Are you ready?' asked Anselm.

'Yes.' His features showed both desire and dread. He shifted in his seat.

'If you forget my going,' said Anselm confidently, 'I'll surprise you when I get back.' No truer words, he thought, had ever passed his lips. He was sure that Emily Bradshaw would be with him.

More out of excitement than impatience, Anselm banged the knocker to the terraced house in Mitcham. A figure came to the door, fragmenting in a globe of dimpled glass.

Emily Bradshaw stood at the bay window while Anselm, by the arm of a settee, felt the rigour of hesitation. She'd walked to her post without a word, without offering a seat. When the past comes to an end, thought Anselm, you panic. He knew exactly what he was going to say. He'd chosen his words carefully on the Underground. 'You told me last time that nothing comes of nothing.'

Emily moved a net curtain with the back of one hand – just an inch. 'I got it from *The Sound of Music*.'

'Sorry?'

'*The Sound of Music*. The Captain and Maria sing it in the garden when everything falls into place.' Emily spoke with immeasurable sadness. The hand fell to her side.

Anselm became strong; these moments could be overcome. He sat down and spoke towards a happy ending. 'I have seen George. He's ready to come home.'

'Yes, I know.'

'Pardon?'

'He came back.' She raised a net curtain once more, looking out hopelessly.

'And he left?'

'Yes.'

'But why?'

The gate tapped shut and the front door opened. Anselm's empathies dropped. They'd been tailored for a happy ending in Salzburg. He felt the coldness of real compassion. In the hallway, feet stamped, shaking off the week. 'Bloody hell, it's cold. But it's Frida-a-ay.' It was a reassuring sound, kindly and rooted. A zip hummed down its line.

Emily moved to the middle of the room. She did not sit, so Anselm remained standing. She said, 'George's place isn't filled. Don't think that, please. I can't understand our life together, that's all. And if you can't understand something, it's . . .'

A round freckled face, smudged with grease and surprise, appraised Anselm. 'Oh, hullo, sorry about the swearing, like—'

'Don't worry. It is cold, I entirely agree.'

225

'Peter, this is Father Anselm. He knows George.'

The man's hand was large, stamped with work and decency. Anselm reached over. It had looked like an anvil, but when touched it became a fat sponge.

Emily said, 'Father Anselm was just about to go.'

Peter stood in the doorway like a roadblock. His blue overalls were parted, revealing the V-neck jumper, the shirt and tie. A slight paunch stretched the patterned wool. He took a shallow breath while practical, no-nonsense eyes seemed to weigh up a fractured joint, something basic that couldn't be fixed. Peering through a sort of spray, he said, 'How is he?'

'Fine. Not so bad,' said Anselm, trapped between honesty to Peter and sensitivity to Emily.

'Well, that's good news, isn't it?'

'Yes, it is.'

Anselm pictured the arrival of the big man, his ordered life folded up in cardboard boxes: a few pictures, his dad's tin mug, some Corgi cars, mountains of underpants, a shoe-cleaning box. Anselm said, 'George makes no claims.' It was a strange announcement. He didn't know why he'd said it.

Peter rested blue arms on each pillar, his head aslant. He was balding. The remaining hair had been creased by a regulation hard hat. 'Emily, let him in. Take him back.' He drew up the zip of his overalls, as if he'd just emerged from the locker room. 'It's his home.'

Emily was crying. She pushed past Anselm and said, 'Peter, would you make some tea?'

'You'll have one, Father?'

'No, he won't,' sobbed Emily.

At the door, one foot on the flags, Anselm said, 'Is there anything you'd like me to say?'

'Yes.' Emily searched her pockets nervously.

Anselm said, 'I think I'll be able to explain without saying anything.' He was looking at Peter, out of earshot.

Emily said, 'Tell him . . .' Her face crumpled. She fetched out a biro that had leaked and a receipt. With a slap at the air, she threw them against the wall and slammed the door.

Anselm entered the ward. George was dressed, his knees crossed, one leg bobbing. He was like a granddad in a waiting room, ears cocked for an announcement. He'd been smartened up. The hair hadn't quite taken to the parting, but the comb lines stood out. Someone had found an old blazer. It had a crest over the breast pocket with a motto: '*Legis Plenitudo Caritas*'. Love fulfils the law.

Before Anselm could move, George swung him a quick look and grimaced. His feet slipped, despite the shoes, and he locked his wrists on the armrests. Bony shoulders took the strain of standing. Before Anselm could stop him, George was upright, a hand outstretched. 'Elizabeth said you'd come,' he exclaimed.

Anselm felt the grip. It was reassuring; it was strong. He looked aside from cloudless eyes that revealed nothing but the sky.

'Funny thing is' – George laughed gently at the coming joke – 'I'm not quite sure why.'

6

Riley unscrewed the box casing that concealed the water pipes in the kitchen. Nancy stood behind him waiting for the news.

'Not there,' he said.

'But he can't get out,' moaned Nancy. 'You said so yourself.'

Riley replaced the casing, thinking he shouldn't have said

that, because she'd latched on to it. He'd only expected a ten-minute look-around. But Nancy was ready to dismantle the building. She'd already made him check the washing machine, the dryer and the fridge. She wouldn't give up. That glow of expectation in her cheeks was like the fog lights at Lawton's.

'I'll check the bedroom.' Her voice was tight with the strain.

'This is a waste of time,' he said, thinking of the dark around Limehouse Cut.

Nancy got down on all fours, one cheek flat on the carpet. Riley stood behind her, looking down. Her fastidious concentration was ridiculous to him.

'Where are you, Arnold?' whispered Nancy.

Riley knelt beside her, as if to drink from a stream. 'Not there,' he said. These were bitter waters. He tasted one thing, and she another. His stomach turned, like it did in his dream.

This charade was played out in every room until they returned to the kitchen and faced the empty cage. All at once Nancy slumped into a chair, pushing a hand through her hair, one elbow on the table. 'He's so small, and so weak.'

The phrase threw up the days when Riley wore shorts. He'd been a small lad. Everything was heavy, even the shopping. He'd hated his weakness. Coming round, he noticed that Nancy's shoulders were shaking. She's laughing, he thought, with relief, and it brought a nervous giggle out of him. Like a thing on a ratchet-wheel, Nancy slowly looked up, and showed her tears.

'How could you?' she whispered in disbelief.

Riley paled, thinking that she'd known all along; that she'd led him round the houses, giving him the chance to admit what he'd done. He panicked and sniggered again.

'Go on, laugh,' she howled, proud and defiant. 'Join the rest of them who think that Nancy Riley's such a joke.' She hid her face with her hands.

Riley waited for her to stop, but she didn't. She moaned gently into her fingers, shaking her head, and he watched her, as if his mind were on a shelf, while his body, against him, still wanted to laugh. The more he listened to Nancy's grief, the longer he observed her covered face, the more he seemed to become separate from himself. He was retreating from this awful sight – he'd never seen her cry like this – but his lungs were ready to explode. Unable to stop himself, he began to laugh.

Nancy lowered her fingers. Impassively, she watched him – as he had watched her. With a pink tissue she dabbed each cheek as if she were putting on her make-up.

Riley's laughter wouldn't end. Shuddering and out of control, his voice grew loud. He tried to stop it with a cough and a whistle, but it was no use. It was like being stripped down, and Nancy could see him for who he was. She didn't storm out; she just kept crying and dabbing her cheeks, watching him like it was a sad film, a tragedy. It turned into a sort of game: who was going to stop first, him or her? The thought allowed him to recover, because he didn't want to win: he couldn't bear to watch her any more. The hysteria was over. And yet . . .

Riley didn't know what was happening. He touched his cheeks . . . they were wet, like a rock on the beach. Nancy rose as if someone had banged at the door. She came towards him, curious and frightened, while Riley backed away. His tears kept spilling out. The muscles all over his face ached terribly, and yet part of him felt nothing, because he was distant, like a balloon, bobbing against the kitchen ceiling. Then, as if punctured by exhaustion and a will to resist no more, he felt himself sinking: coming down to a distraught man with a wet, contorted face.

'It's not your fault,' urged Nancy, appalled. 'You only left the cage open.'

Sobbing with a sound just like his laughter, Riley yanked open the back door. Cold air bit his face. He was still falling, but more quickly.

'I'm here,' said Nancy, softly, at his shoulder. 'I'm always here, Riley.'

At those words, he caught himself up. He felt weakened – dreadfully – by the realisation that he wanted to live like other men; that he'd had enough of the twisting, the breaching and the wrecking of everything that passed before him. He'd gone out of his way to smash whatever might break. Nancy was in the yard, at his side, and Riley saw her as he'd first seen her at Lawton's long ago, at their bleak beginning. She was still the same old Nancy, still dumpy, still hungry.

A frost had fallen with a faint mist. The yard was crisp with tiny crystals. It was dark and Nancy's pile of bricks glittered with rime. Closing his eyes, and through a growing headache, Riley thought of snow . . . fields and fields of fresh fallen snow, as it's seen at night, practically glowing from the inside – not a leaf, not a flower, just snow. That was his wife. He knew it. And with a savage certainty, he knew that he didn't want to spoil what he'd seen, not with a single careless footprint. Stunned, Riley recognised that he . . . *loved her*.

He looked up to the misty night sky. There were no stars, just this ghostly breath off the Thames.

They were sitting at the kitchen table. Nancy had fished out Uncle Bertie's poison and filled identical tumblers.

'To Arnold,' she said.

They clinked glasses and downed their drinks in one.

Nancy coughed, and Riley's lips ignited. To the blotches of purple light, he said, 'I've had enough.'

Nancy nodded and put the bottle back in the cupboard.

Because the poison was illegal, she always hid it, even though no one would ever come looking. That was Nancy all over. He said, 'I've got a Christmas Fair coming up.'

'Where?'

'Wanstead.' Riley conjured up those fields of snow spreading out before him as far as the eye could see – beyond the Weald and on to the South Downs. 'I'll do this last one.' He could do it; he could take a first step, as long as Nancy knew nothing of what lay behind.

'What do you mean?' Nancy stood with hands on her hips. Her face still blotched from the tears.

'I'm going to pack it in.'

'What, the business?'

'Yes.' He could walk away and keep going. Every step would be new. He need never turn around. Riley's eyes glazed before a sort of darkness. He didn't understand his own thoughts. This was the Major's country.

'You've had too much of Uncle Bertie's poison,' said Nancy. She smiled, and was, to Riley, very pretty. 'Your sort never give up.'

7

Anselm slept fitfully, waking at intervals to be tormented by George's calm, and his own folly. The old man's repetition word for word of their earlier conversation had been a device of mercy, but in the giving George had revealed the activity of his memory: he'd known that Anselm had been to Mitcham; and he'd understood that Emily wouldn't take him back.

When morning came Anselm acted without hesitation: whatever Doctor Johnson thought of London, Anselm was tired of it. His life lay elsewhere, as now would George's. He rang Larkwood to say he was coming home, and he asked Wilf – the guestmaster – to prepare a room for a weary pilgrim. At the hospital, George warmed to the proposal immediately, volunteering that he'd never been to a monastery, and that *The Sound of Music* was his wife's favourite film. On the train he kept breaking into 'Doe, a deer' while Anselm studied the badge on his blazer: *Legis Plenitudo Caritas*. It was a warning and a promise: the law would be fulfilled, but only by love. What would Elizabeth have made of that?

By early afternoon George had been installed in a room overlooking the valley of the Lark. The stream sliced through ribbed fields, drawing down the winter sun. On the far side, oaks and chestnuts crowded on the slopes. Anselm leaned on the sill, beside George, longing to get among the blue shadows, to kick the acorns and conkers.

'I knew a strange man called Nino,' said George, searching the treetops. 'He told me that at the bottom of every box is hope. No matter what terrible things jump out, he said, we have to wait.'

The old man hung his hands on the lapels of his blazer and talked to the valley about this Nino, a guide who told stories that George had rarely understood first time around. It was a patchy reminiscence, of sayings uttered near Marble Arch or King's Cross, on a bench or by a bin. His memory hadn't held on to the parts that would have made the whole easy to understand. But as he spoke, Anselm thought of Clem, his old novice master, long dead, who'd taught through mysterious tales of the Desert Fathers. And slowly, like warming up, Anselm felt close to George, as he'd been close to Clem, and yet – as with Clem – he remained so very far away. For with every word, it became clear: George understood Nino's stories without being able to explain

232

them. George had come to that point of stillness and detachment that Anselm was hoping to reach through monastic routine. This mendicant beside him was already home: he'd reached the same strange uplands stalked by two strange masters.

'Here's a small present with many pages,' said Anselm, taking his leave. It was a notebook with Larkwood's address and phone number inside.

He moved briskly down the corridor, intent on grabbing the Prior just before compline, when authority was both tired and indulgent, to beg that George might live out the remainder of his days at Larkwood. For the moment, another task required his attention.

Anselm went to the calefactory, a side room off the cloister with a huge fireplace, some armchairs and a telephone. In the Middle Ages, it had warmed up rude and ready monks; now it was one of the monastery's many hideaways, a place in which to thaw and think. It was empty. Anselm sat by the inglenook and made what amounted to a preliminary call.

The Provincial of the Daughters of Charity remembered him from his earlier enquiry about Sister Dorothy and the account of a hidden key. Anselm wanted access to any records that touched on the background of Elizabeth. They were held in the congregation's archives, he assumed, at Carlisle. Fearing a refusal if he approached the school directly, he wondered if the Provincial might sanction his appeal for help.

'Why, exactly, do you want to know?' she said. 'I don't see how your question is linked to your objective.'

'Because I think it's only a matter of time before her son wonders why his mother cut a hole into that particular book, which will bring him to Dorothy,' replied Anselm. 'And as this business reaches its end, I fear everything will unravel. I want to get back

233

to the first dropped stitch – if there is one – so that I might help him.'

The Provincial told Anselm to wait one hour and then he was to ring the school and ask for Sister Pauline.

When Anselm duly dialled the Carlisle number the phone was picked up instantly. And just as promptly they set to work. There was only one sheet of paper in the file, said Sister Pauline. 'I'd rather not release a copy, Father, but I can read it out. Is that all right?'

'Yes.'

Laboriously, she described the format of the page and the brief details recorded on it. Anselm listened, eyes closed, picturing the document in his head. When she'd finished, Anselm decided to repeat back the particulars that mattered for confirmation.

'So, am I right, Elizabeth Steadman was born in London, not Manchester?'

'Correct.'

'No parental details are recorded?'

'None.'

'Her home address is given simply as Camberwell?'

'Yes.'

Anselm wondered why such an important matter had been left so vague.

'Because we know exactly what it means,' said Sister Pauline. 'Camberwell refers to our hostel. It means she was based there before being given a place at the school.'

'Hostel?' asked Anselm, thinking of the convent where he'd met Sister Dorothy.

Sister Pauline explained that the Camberwell hostel had been their biggest London project, offering accommodation and help to anyone and everyone, so long as they were female. The building had been converted years ago to provide affordable housing, a part of the ground floor being retained for the community. Anselm had already been there.

He could imagine Elizabeth's journey north, far from the big city; but something was missing. 'If she came to Carlisle through the hostel, without parental involvement, then there should be a court order . . . a legal document that defines her status and yours. Are you sure there's nothing else in the file?'

'Absolutely.'

And that, he inferred, means it's either been destroyed, or it never existed.

Anselm thanked Sister Pauline and put the phone down. His thoughts fell neatly into place: if no court order had been made, then Elizabeth's presence at the school would have been with parental consent – that of Mr and Mrs Steadman. So why had no address been recorded? And why had Elizabeth been linked to the hostel? The only person who knew was Sister Dorothy, and she, Anselm decided, would receive another friendly visit – only this time they'd get beyond the figures in a photograph.

The calefactory door swung open with a bang. Anselm bristled – a common enough experience in monastic life, for sensibilities were always colliding, especially on the little things, like how to open a door – and there, standing like a slot machine, was Brother Cyril.

'At last,' said the cellarer. 'I've been looking all over.'

'I'm sorry.' That was another aspect of existence in a habit. With some people you had to apologise when you'd done nothing wrong. Guessing Cyril's mission, Anselm said, 'I've put all unspent money – with receipts – in your pigeon-hole.'

'I know,' he snapped, 'That's not why I'm here.'

Anselm prepared himself for a harangue on the theology of internal audit. 'Do continue,' he said wearily.

235

'I've worked out what this Riley man is up to.' Cyril's one arm swung proudly.

'Already?' asked Anselm, astonished.

'Yes.'

'You'd better tell Inspector Cartwright.'

'I have done. She's coming here tomorrow afternoon.'

Anselm stood up, distracted by all that must now be done. He would have to tell George; and, instinctively, he knew that this was the moment to draw Nicholas more closely into his mother's doings.

'Shall I explain the trick now?' asked Cyril impatiently.

'No, I'll wait, thanks.'

'Pah!'

Anselm almost ran down the trail that led to a narrow bridge over the Lark. The sky was clean and shining like metal – as it was, no doubt, over Marble Arch or King's Cross. Anselm sensed he'd be going back to those bustling streets, but for now he wanted to be alone, to enter the far wood and pray among the acorns and conkers.

8

'Nancy, is that you?'

It was Babycham. She hadn't changed. Well, she had, because of the hair extensions and a fur coat. And her lashes were false. And ten years had made a difference. Those pink cheeks had fallen a bit and the powder looked like bruises; or maybe it was the cold.

'It's been ages . . .' The fur ruffled magically, leaving windy paths like those corn circles. It was the real thing. You could tell.

Nancy had just got off the bus. With worked-up hope, she'd

gone east this time, into West Ham, hoping for a glimpse of Mr Johnson. She'd sat by the buzzer, her eyes latching on to every uncertain step among the flow of jackets and prams; she'd checked a bench by a newspaper kiosk and a heap outside Currys. He was blind. He couldn't have gone that far. She'd stepped out to buy some Polos, when that voice had made her jump.

Nervously, Babycham said, 'Lovely hat.'

Riley had found it in a drawer at a clearance. It was yellow polyester with black spots.

'How's things?' asked Nancy. When they'd last met, she'd told her she was full of wind and bubbles.

'Altogether nice,' said Babycham. She turned to a newsagent's, to the paints and pens and toys with stickers on. The glossy mags were on display – happy faces, baring their teeth. *Woman's World* had a couple of answers. 'Take Control: Tell Him What You Want in Bed'; and, in bigger letters, 'How to Stop a Yorkshire Pudding Falling Flat.'

Nancy admitted, 'I didn't mean what I said.'

'Course you didn't.'

Nancy waited, but Babycham didn't reciprocate. It was to be expected. She never dealt in returns or cast-offs. She'd always gone top drawer. Knew her mind. She'd told Nancy to run. They'd had a meeting.

Babycham looked hard into the window again. The glare from the shop made her cheeks redder. Forty-denier tights. All you had to do was tear a number off the bottom and ring up whomever it was. Only one had been taken.

Nancy said, 'So what's been up, then?'

Babycham pulled out a hankie. It had a blue 'B' on one corner and lace round the edge. 'Well . . . I ended up with Harold . . . You know, the boss.'

'Mr Lawton?' Nancy's surprise made it sound ridiculous.

'Yes.' She carefully touched the corner of one eye.

'So it's easy street for you then, Babs.' Mr Lawton must have made a packet, what with the development of the docklands.

'Well, he held on to his turf, so he could negotiate, sort of thing. That was the idea. And you?'

'Antiques.' Nancy felt a punch of self-hatred for the lie, for the lack of pride in what she did, for who she was.

'Oh, very nice.'

'Well, you know, second-hand. I've a small shop.' Before Babycham could ask whereabouts, Nancy said, 'I suppose you've got tons of kids?'

'Three. And you?'

'None.'

'Sorry.' She dabbed the other eye. 'It's arctic.'

Riley had said, 'No children. No talk of it. It's just the two of us.' He'd spoken like it was a deal before they hit the sand. They'd make it out of this hell together. Confident and romantic, he'd ducked like John Wayne on Iwo Jima. Nancy had agreed, not knowing that Riley never changed, that he'd come out of the packaging ready made and complete, all the screws in place. There was nothing to add on, no expensive extras. Whereas she'd been incomplete, with gaps, so many gaps. She'd always wanted to be a mother, and the nearest she'd got was Arnold. Shame and a kind of hatred – again, of herself – twisted in her stomach, like when she'd been starving after a day on grapefruit, part of a diet that was meant to transform her shape in two weeks. It hadn't worked.

Babycham said, 'Harold didn't sell up when he wanted, you know.'

'Why's that?'

'He had to. After he got fined.'

'What for?'

'Health and safety.' The hankie went up a sleeve. Her eyes were fine now, and her cheeks not so red. 'Did you not hear? A lad drowned off E Section.'

'No.' Nancy shuddered as something fell inside her – like one of those metal shutters that could stop a car, never mind a smash and grab. Her voice failed.

Years back a woman had come to the shop and handled a mirror – checked her lower teeth and a spot on her chin. She'd been sociable and asked how business was going. Then she'd shocked her by using her name: 'Nancy, I'm not a customer. I'm a copper.'

Feeling sick, she'd said, 'What have I done?'

'Nothing. Can we have a talk, just us two, going no further?'

'Well, I suppose so.'

She'd tried to win her round, with talk of the poor mother, and that man Bradshaw, the father, who'd walked out of the court. Cartwright, that was her name. Jennifer. She'd made insinuations. It was like being trapped in Wyecliffe's office all over again.

'Where was he last Saturday?'

'The car-boot fair at Barking.'

'It rained.'

'He went.'

'What time did he get back?'

'I was asleep.' That hadn't been true. But lying awake was her secret.

'What time did you go to bed?'

'Elevenish'

'The fair would have wound up by six or seven?'

'Yes, but his van broke down.'

'Where?

239

'How would I know?' These police and their daft questions.

Babycham said, 'A lad went through some of the planks. Harold had put up a notice, a fence, bollards, but they'd all been moved. Dumped in the river.'

'Really?'

'Yes. He'd checked them on the Friday at seven o'clock, but they'd gone by Saturday night.'

Nancy said nothing. Babycham stepped closer. Fur tickled Nancy's wrist.

'And that was when the lad drowned, the Saturday. They said he was a trespasser.'

'And Mr Lawton got fined?'

'Because of the holes in the fence and the missing bollards.' Like she had an itch, she repeated. 'They said he was a trespasser.'

'I suppose he was, then.'

'Well, I don't think so. And neither does Harold.'

A slow-moving HGV had snarled up the traffic. It crawled past, heaving a trailer with a huge shed on it, more like a fairy-tale doll's house, painted red and white. There were two windows and a door in the middle. Someone's moving home, joked Nancy to herself, her eyes smarting. The idea stung every-where at once, as if she'd crunched a nest underfoot; wasps, angry and purposeful, swarmed around her.

Jennifer had said, 'Where was the van fixed?'

'On the spot.'

'Who by?'

'He does it himself . . . He keeps everything he needs in the back.'

'Why?'

'Well, it's been breaking down a lot recently.'

'For how long?'

'Six months.'

'And he always does the work himself?'

'Yes.'

'At the side of the road?'

'Yes.'

'Have you seen him do it?'

'Once.' She'd said it with a gusty success, as if she'd swatted a big one.

'When?'

'At home. About three months back.'

Jennifer had looked inside a wardrobe and checked the joints. 'Does he always tell you when the van breaks down?'

'Well, if he doesn't tell me, there's no way I'd find out, is there?' These police. No wonder they didn't catch anyone. 'We're man and wife, you know. That's why we talk.'

'Of course, Nancy . . . But there are people who say things . . . and your husband won't help himself, you know that. That's why I've come to you.'

'Saying what sort of things?'

Babycham said, 'We think it was deliberate.'

The doll's house had gone, and Nancy hadn't noticed. She hugged herself, gripping her elbows. 'Deliberate? You mean the lad jumped in?'

'No. I mean someone pushed him. Or let him fall. Got him out there. When it wasn't safe.'

'Why do that?'

'I wonder.'

'Who'd do a thing like that?'

'There's no knowing, is there?' It was a real question.

Nancy stepped back, away from the tickling hairs. 'Then Mr Lawton should've fixed the fence.'

Babycham dug out the hankie and prodded the corners of her mouth. A matey tenderness from the yard made her voice

241

suddenly hoary – like when they'd told Carmel Pilchard to get knotted, that she couldn't join in – 'You haven't changed.'

'Neither have you.' For one brief, terrible moment they were both barelegged in knee-high socks, with bruises on their knees. Pilchard's mam had one eye and her dad was doing time. 'Serves him right with a name like that,' Babycham had said. Nancy had thought that a bit on the harsh side.

'Best be off,' said Babycham, checking her watch – it was small and gold with trinkets dangling off the strap: a horse, a pig and a penny. 'I'd stay, but I've a plane to catch. Winter break.'

'Very nice.'

'Who'd've thought there'd be an airport between the King George and the Royal Albert. The place was dead.'

With a quite awful longing, Nancy wanted to go back to those days of heavy morning mists . . . when they'd first arrived at the docks, when she'd tramped up the iron stairs to the office with a view of the river. On some days, you wouldn't be able to see it until lunchtime. As the sun burnt through the sodden cloud, the waves would appear, here and there, like silver chains. She wanted to wind back time some more, into the yard, by the toilets, when they'd changed their mind about Carmel. They'd felt sorry for her mam. Exclusions weren't so bad, then, although it had felt like it. She said, 'And who'd've thought you'd be cooking dinner for Mr Lawton.'

Babycham pressed a button on a key and a nice car winked. It was like magic.

Nancy said, 'I'll see you around, then.'

'No. You won't.' She didn't deal in returns, Babycham. And she always spoke her mind.

'Ta-ra, then.'

'Yes, ta-ra.'

*

When the bus pulled into the depot, Nancy changed numbers and followed another route, her face set against the window. It was useless, but she kept looking for Mr Johnson, while her mind kept turning to Arnold. Her breath steamed up the glass. She gave it a rub with the sleeve of her coat . . . and out of nowhere, she remembered seeing her man at the top of their street at two in the morning. Nancy knew it was him from his walk, and the way his arms swung like loose ropes.

9

As Nick drove through the pinks and thatch of Suffolk, he continued to brood upon the tall figure at the window of the Butterfly Room. Charles had been watching as Nick pulled away on yet another solitary jaunt in the Beetle.

Ironically, since Nick had left Australia, a great distance had fallen between them. Nick had been making short expeditions: from Larkwood, to Mr Wyecliffe, to Dr Okoye, to Mrs Dixon and now, coming full circle, back to Larkwood again. And he had said nothing to his father – not since he'd concluded that the dear old buffer hadn't the faintest idea what his wife had been up to. Driving through the monastery gates, Nick resolved to buy some red mullet and white Burgundy. He would cook the meal that his father had planned on the day Elizabeth had died. And, when they were warm and tipsy, he'd tell him all that had been happening while they'd both been far away on different continents.

Nick couldn't take his eyes off his mother's accomplice: a solemn man in a school blazer that was far too small for him. The white cuffs of an ample shirt stuck out from the sleeves. A blue-and-yellow-striped tie suggested membership of an exclusive cricket club. His eyes were dark, like rings in pale saucers.

Apart from Nick and Mr Bradshaw, seated round the table were Inspector Cartwright and three monks: the Prior of Larkwood, Father Anselm and Brother Cyril – a man whose pinned sleeve would have evoked Admiral Nelson, had it not been for his defining squareness. He seemed to have lost his neck, never mind an arm. They assembled in a cool room of thick white stone. Arched windows threw sunshine across the old flags like banners of yellow cloth.

'It's all very simple,' said Brother Cyril, as if it were a complaint. 'In a nutshell, it's a scheme to sell information, but it's hidden within a legitimate business. I became suspicious because if you look at the receipt numbers and the dates and the description, on one and the same day, Mr Riley sometimes sells an object but then buys it back again. I'll give you an example. Let's take that ashtray. Imagine it's on Mr Riley's stall. There's a little sticker on it marked '£15'. *But he sells it for £30.* Then he buys it back again for £15. It's a crazy way of accounting for the fact that he's made £15 and the ashtray hasn't left the table.'

'But that isn't what we've been told,' said Inspector Cartwright. 'Our understanding is that people arrive, give him money and then leave.'

'Of course they do, because that's exactly what happens: they buy some information.' Brother Cyril scanned his audience. 'The shenanigan with the receipts is done afterwards. It only occurs on paper. The ashtray doesn't even move. But the receipts show that a different kind of sale has occurred. They prove that Riley pocketed £15.'

'But why do you think he's selling information?' asked Father Anselm tentatively.

'Because otherwise,' snapped Brother Cyril, 'someone's giving him money for nowt.'

Nick was amazed. Neither of the other monks was in the least discomfited by the ill temper of their confrere.

'And why go to such lengths?' added the Prior. Each eyebrow was like a chewed toothbrush, and his glasses were lopsided, with a paperclip on one side for a screw. He had received Nick with surprising warmth.

'There's only one explanation,' said Brother Cyril, raising a thick index finger. 'If he got rumbled, he could trace every transaction, just like I've done. He can account for every penny received. There's no cash in hand. So he can show that when all's said and done, he's paid tax on the lot. In fact, he's in breach of all manner of accounting rules because this is a completely separate business – and he wouldn't pay any tax at all if he'd set it up properly. And that brings me to the heart of this completely barmy system.' He laid his arm flat on the table, fingers splayed. 'On the one hand, he must think that what he's doing is legal, because he could have sold his information over a pint of beer. Instead, he fills out all this paperwork to demonstrate what he's doing. On the other hand' – he shrugged the shoulder with the missing arm – 'he's obviously hiding something. And that suggests it's an illegal activity.'

'But who, then, is he hiding it from?' asked Inspector Cartwright.

'Nancy,' replied a husky voice.

Everyone turned to Mr Bradshaw. During Brother Cyril's explanation, he'd been kneading a temple, but nodding with increasing conviction. Nick couldn't expel the notion of a gentleman chairing a team of selectors for the England XI.

'Elizabeth thought he was hiding it from Nancy,' he said, both hands straying to the lapels of his blazer. 'And himself.'

245

Nick just caught Father Anselm's half whisper, '*Himself*?'

'George,' said Inspector Cartwright, 'is this system all about information?'

'Yes . . . Something Elizabeth told me has come back, while I've been listening.' He pulled at one of the short sleeves, trying to lengthen it. His mouth sagged, and purplish shadow crept up to his eyes. 'She said Riley had gone back to where he'd started from, that he was selling . . . introductions.'

The long banners of light faded with a movement of cloud, and the stone vaulting seemed to contract. No one spoke. Almost everyone, except Brother Cyril, was leaning on the table, arms folded.

'And that,' said Inspector Cartwright finally, 'is called living off immoral earnings. However convoluted the system, and whatever his motives, it's illegal.' She thanked Brother Cyril and Mr Bradshaw and then said, 'I shall arrest Riley tomorrow morning. He, in turn, will want representation from Wyecliffe and Co. All things being equal, the interview will begin at two o'clock' – she looked to George – 'I'll have to reveal how I obtained this paperwork, so Riley will know that you've brought him down. There's an observation room with a mirror-window, so you can attend unseen, if you wish – in fact, any of you can.'

Father Anselm coughed deliberately. 'Cyril, you said if he'd set this up properly, he wouldn't pay any tax . . . What's the turnover? How much are we talking about?'

'Peanuts.'

'I'm thinking of a likely sentence when it gets to court,' said Father Anselm, turning to the Inspector. Reluctantly, he said, 'A judge may think the offence is not the most serious of its kind.'

'I appreciate that,' she replied. 'But in my book, it could hardly be worse. Do you know why? Because he doesn't give a toss about the money; *he only cares about what he's doing.*'

Outside the monastery, Nick made hasty goodbyes and set off down the track for the car park. Father Anselm came running after him.

'Nick,' said the monk, out of breath, 'you didn't speak in the meeting . . . Are you all right?'

'There's nothing to say,' he replied. Nick didn't want to linger; he didn't want lunch in the guesthouse; he didn't want a chat with Mr Bradshaw. His mind was on his lonely, troubled father, a shifting shape behind a tall window.

'Will you attend the interview?' asked Father Anselm.

'No.' The whole sordid business had thrust him back into Mr Wyecliffe's fetid burrow. He faced the kindly worried man. 'When I first came to Larkwood you said, "Don't turn over old stones. Let them lie where they were placed." You were right. I should have left things be. And now, I just want to go home.'

It was late afternoon when Nick cut the ignition in the back lane at St John's Wood, thinking of his mother, not wanting to diminish her achievement. But he couldn't help himself: a key in a book, a letter to a monk, a parcel for the police and all the conspiring with Mr Bradshaw: such effort expended to the moment of her dying, but for what? A fixation with a two-bit crook peddling a two-bit crime. In a liberating moment of self-realisation, Nick let the whole matter drop, as if it were someone else's suitcase. This was his mother's life, not his. He was free. He always had been.

As he reached for the key, Nick's eye caught on a small orange triangle. A paper dog-ear had been trapped in the closed ashtray. He tugged out a flyer for an antiques fair. The various participants were listed beside their phone numbers. Towards the bottom, circled in biro, he saw a name that he knew: Graham Riley.

Nick pushed open the back gate, remembering Mrs Dixon, who shared one thing in common with his mother: they both knew what it was like to lose someone.

10

Nancy was bewildered. There was a spring in Riley's step like she'd never seen before. Over breakfast he'd rung Prosser and offered him the business, there and then, if the price was right. That had led to a bit of swearing, but the two men had agreed to meet.

'It's going to happen, Nancy,' said her man, heading out. 'We're off to Brighton.'

'For the weekend?'

'For good.'

He'd driven to Wanstead Park laughing at the wheel. That had never happened before. Nor had the stunning experience of the night before. They'd been lying in bed, side by side, discussing Uncle Bertie's liver. Nancy's arm had strayed into the narrow corridor between them. Still talking of poison, Riley's hand lightly touched her fingers, and then her wrist; he'd held on, like in the films when someone tumbles over the edge of a boat or a cliff; but there was no panic or hollering, he just carried on talking in a husky voice about percentage proof and damaged organs. He let go as he fell asleep, and he didn't dream. Intuitively, Nancy was worried. She'd always seen her man as a barrel, wrapped with iron bands, and wondered what might happen if they fell off. And, in a way, they had . . . and there had been no explosion. Somehow, it wasn't quite right.

That said, the notion of a house in Brighton made Nancy excited beyond measure. But there were two hiccups, one small, the other large: Arnold hadn't turned up, and neither had Mr Johnson. The bigger problem took her to the plastic bag in the shop that would soon belong to Prosser. For once she had a reason to leaf through the pages – to find the address of Emily. Nancy would give her all the books that her husband had written. What else could she do with them?

Sitting on a stool, listening to traffic fly over the bump, Nancy flicked through some pages, until her eye caught on a name. She caught her breath and read from the top:

. . . wouldn't believe me. She said Grandad was a war veteran. He'd survived the Atlantic convoys. He'd been given a brass lamp by the shareholders when he'd retired. You carry his Christian name. You're David George Bradshaw. What could I say? That was all true, but it had nothing to do with what I'd found out. So I told my father. He kept puffing on his pipe. After a while I noticed, that his neck was red. He was like that when he was angry or frightened. For a good ten minutes I didn't know which it was. In the end he said, 'Have you any idea what you're saying? What it means?'

George Bradshaw. The man from the trial. Nancy went dreadfully still. She'd been played upon . . . something had happened, under her nose, and she didn't know what it was. But that's not what made her breath pull short. No, it was Mr Johnson. He'd been *genuine*. Their times by the fire had not been makebelieve – she knew that, in her bones. She'd made friends with an old gentleman who'd lost his son, and half his mind. The man in goggles who'd stumbled out of a cardboard box had been homeless, for real: it was in his skin, that deep grey with black speckles like asphalt. But he was still . . . that other man

Bradshaw. Her head began to beat, and she hastily checked the other books, getting nowhere, until she paused at the inside cover of Book One: there it was, an address in Mitcham.

When the front door opened, Nancy held up the plastic bag as if she were making a delivery for Tesco. 'Your husband left these in my shop.'

The woman made no response. It was as though she had been anaesthetised.

'Are you Mrs Bradshaw?'

The woman nodded, staring at the bag.

'I know George,' said Nancy, all friendly, but wanting to shout and cry. 'I sort of looked after him.'

'Come in,' said Mrs Emily Bradshaw. 'I'll make some tea.'

What a nice house, thought Nancy. There was a faint smell of fresh paint. All the wallpaper was new – expensive stuff, too . . . a soft corn yellow with silver lines, straight as cheese wire. None of it had been scuffed yet. Pictures had been hung close together, not one of them askew: a cathedral rising out of some trees, a field with cows by a river, someone praying by a windmill, ducks taking off. The settee had matching armchairs. Nancy sat down, noticing that the covers were stiff and the cushions were firm. Yes, it was very nice and new. But something was missing. There was an immense hole that the catalogue hadn't been able to fill or paint or cover.

'Milk and sugar?'

'A cloud and two lumps,' said Nancy.

It was very quiet, like a dentist's waiting room.

'How is he?' asked Mrs Bradshaw automatically.

'Not so bad.'

'Oh.' She kept her head down, eyes in her mug.

'Well,' said Nancy, 'he's blind, and he wears these massive

goggles, and he can't remember much because someone bashed his head in.'

Nancy hadn't wanted to speak so bluntly. She'd planned a few nice phrases, but here, before his wife, she abandoned niceness. It seemed more kind.

Mrs Bradshaw didn't drink her tea, and she didn't look up. She was stuck on the end of her chair, her knees held tightly together. Nancy liked the checked slippers. One of them had a hole in it, near the big toe.

'His memory works, mind you,' said Nancy. The plastic bag of notebooks was on her lap. 'He talks of his days in Yorkshire, of the Bonnington, of you, and your son. All that is bright and clear. He can recall your white pinafore . . . even the frills. It's what's happened recently that he can't hold on to. He once said that he wished it was the other way round. But he didn't mean that for a minute. He's a clown, your husband.'

Nancy had seen wine tasters once, on the television, and they looked just like Mrs Bradshaw: a frown, concentration and a mouth barely moving. Any second now, she'd spit.

'What happened?' asked Nancy. She shouldn't have asked; it was prying. But this woman's husband had played on her, despite his battered brains, and she didn't know why he'd done it. And she was confused. She'd come to Mitcham thinking she might go mad, because this was George Bradshaw's house, the man who'd played on Riley. But she'd found an ordinary home, with a big hole in it, and an ordinary woman, who was empty.

Mrs Bradshaw said, 'Our son was killed by a bad man.' She held on to the mug like it was a rope on a winch, wanting to get away from Nancy and her simple question. 'But I blamed George.'

An obvious fact hit Nancy like a swipe from a rolling pin. The son Mr Johnson had spoken about was indeed lost: he'd died off

Lawton's Wharf, and Inspector Cartwright had made insinuations, and Babycham's husband had been fined by the Health and Safety, and Riley's van had broken down. Nancy, too, wanted to escape. She stood up, putting her mug on the shiny table, but something in her soul held on to the memory of Mr Johnson, steaming by the fire, his hands raised in surrender. 'Here's your husband's notebooks,' she said generously. 'He's written everything down, from his birth onwards. I hope you don't mind me saying, but if you dip in, as I've done, you'll see him as he was: the brave boy who left Harrogate and made it to Mitcham.'

Nancy walked quickly along Aspen Bank, hounded by noise. It came from the hollering in her mind, and a low voice that shoved hers to one side. 'Some men are like a coin,' yawned Mr Wyecliffe confidentially at the Old Bailey. 'He shows you his head. But give him a spin and, if you're lucky, you'll find his tail.' Nancy had gone cold, because he could have meant Bradshaw, or her man. She'd left the building half an hour later.

At the end of Aspen Bank she broke into a run, because an even quieter sound was growing louder: a tap-tapping at the window.

Having left the court, she'd hidden at home and wouldn't answer the bell. Then the tapping had started, moving round the house. On and on it went, like someone needing help, until she'd opened the door to a smartly dressed man from the Salvation Army.

'I've got no money,' she'd said through a crack.

'Have you a plate?' He'd held up a cake from Greggs. 'I'm Major Reynolds.'

He knew Riley from way back. They talked of Lawton's and the loss of jobs left, right and centre. He'd been watching her, giving her the chance to cry. But she'd kept a good grip, taking note of things that didn't matter: that his uniform was smart but old; that his polished shoes had split, that the laces were new. At the door he shook her hand and wouldn't let go. 'Nancy, maybe your constancy will save him. But what about you?' He waited, his black eyebrows knitted with worry. 'If you ever want my help, call this number.' She'd taken the slip of paper and thrown his cheek in the bin.

'Constancy'. She'd looked it up in the dictionary, knowing that with every second the trial was unfolding. While all those dreadful things were being said out loud, she'd folded back the corner and marked the definition in red biro.

When Nancy got back to Poplar there was a policeman at the gate. The hems on his trouser legs were far too high, but he was very polite. A radio kept talking on his shoulder.

'I was hoping to go to Brighton,' said Nancy distantly, when he'd finished.

'I'm sorry, madam.' He gave her a note with an address on it. 'Inspector Cartwright would like to speak to you as soon as possible.'

After he'd gone, Nancy crumpled the paper, thinking of constancy and that kind man tapping on the window long ago.

11

Anselm sat beside George facing a tinted window. Ahead, through the weak bluish haze, were a table, four chairs and a tape machine. A door banged shut. Inspector Cartwright walked to her place, followed by another police officer and Mr Wyecliffe – more aged to Anselm's eyes, but still in his brown suit. Suddenly Riley appeared at the window, his nose against the glass. He checked his teeth as if in a mirror and he smiled rage and impatience and . . . Anselm thought it might be exhilaration.

Inspector Cartwright began the litany of warnings prescribed by the Codes of Practice, while Riley searched the window with the flat of his hands, his face wet and sallow. Unblinking, he backed towards the table.

'Now the preliminaries have been completed,' said Mr Wyecliffe, twitching, 'there's the technical issue of intentional trespass and the theft of my client's property, grave matters which—'

'Belt up, will you,' said Riley. He slouched in a chair and smiled. 'Hurry up, Cartwright, I want to go to Brighton,'

Step by step, the inspector presented the system disclosed by the financial records. She invited Riley to confirm her explanation, but he turned aside, gazing back towards Anselm and George. His fingers tapped erratically on the table, and he said, 'Come on, get on with it.'

Judiciously, Inspector Cartwright said, 'I suggest that you are receiving remuneration arising from prostitution.'

Riley crouched, angry and bored. 'Correct.'

Mr Wyecliffe, who'd been absorbed in the blank pages of a yellow notepad, put down a chewed biro, and said soothingly, 'Can we just pause there for one moment . . .'

'Shut up, Wyecliffe,' whispered Riley.

Inspector Cartwright said, 'You have a list of telephone numbers?'

'Correct.'

'You provide contact details in return for a payment?'

'Yep.'

'How long have you been doing this?'

'Yonks.' A frown displaced the resentment and laughter. An agony of confusion seemed to hold him. He shouted towards the ceiling light, 'I should be on the Brighton road by now.'

'You've had a long enough holiday.'

'Have I?' The swing from euphoria to despair was complete, and menacing.

'Graham Riley you are charged with living wholly or in part on the earnings of prostitution contrary to section—'

'It's all legal.'

Inspector Cartwright turned on Wyecliffe, 'Can you enlighten me?'

'Certainly not. How dare you.'

Riley stood up, looking down upon his interviewer, 'I get the numbers from magazines and phone booths. They're already in the public domain. I sell them to people who think I have a special connection.'

'That is still an offence.'

'Is it?' Riley seemed to rise higher. He appeared mighty over a domain of dirty facts. This was his patch. He didn't take lessons. 'I sell numbers that anyone could find if they knew where to look.' He swaggered on the spot, bony hands on his hips. 'Whoever's on the end of the line doesn't know me. I don't know them. They don't know I've been paid. They don't know *nothing*.' He spat out the word as if it were a failing, something that should be punished. 'They just do what they do, and I get paid . . . for *nothing*.' Glaring outrage and disgust, Riley swept Mr Wyecliffe's papers off the table.

'Sit down,' ordered Inspector Cartwright.

'No. I'm off to Brighton. You can check the law.'

'I will.'

'Make sure it's a silk—'

He bit his lip, not finishing the jibe, and Anselm's mind reeled back to that first conference when Elizabeth's poise had failed. Instantly – and horrified – he understood: Riley's system had grown from the seed of Elizabeth's words: she'd said that if he'd

255

received payments linked to the girls' activity, but without them knowing, then there would be a technical defence . . .

Anselm heard a soft noise behind him. The door opened and a woman entered wearing a peculiar yellow hat with black spots. Her red, trembling hands were crumpling and reopening a small piece of paper. Timidly, she checked the room, until her attention settled on George. Then, her mouth open, she looked into the blue haze.

'If I can help in any other way,' said Riley, 'don't hesitate to contact me.'

He made to leave, but halted before the window. Confused and deliberating, his eyes shot towards the door, as if the cry of gulls had carried from the seaside, calling him to another life of deckchairs and ice cream. Instead Riley turned back to examine his reflection.

It was an awful scene, because Anselm knew that Riley had sensed their presence – at least George's – and he was staring through the image of himself at what he thought was on the other side: but, in fact, he was looking directly at this haunting woman in her yellow spotted hat.

'When you came, Inspector,' said Riley faintly, eyes on the glass, 'I thought it was about John Bradshaw.' His face was a like a mask, thick and oxidised.

'I'm bringing this interview to a close,' said Inspector Cartwright. She rattled off the date and time and the names of those present and hit the tape machine, turning it off. She walked up to Riley's shoulder, seething, 'You have blood on your hands.'

They were both staring towards the poor woman who was crumpling a scrap of paper.

Very clearly, Riley replied, 'Yes, I know.'

Inspector Cartwright blinked a few times, not quite believing what she'd heard, and George, who did, stepped towards the window, pressing both hands to the glass. The woman moved beside him and together they watched what was about to unfold.

Inspector Cartwright switched on the tape machine, reamed off the necessary details, and said, 'I would like to confirm the exchange that has just taken place. You have blood on your hands?'

Riley circled the room, his arms swinging like chains. 'Yes, but not much.'

'Does the quantity matter?'

'No. It was still innocent.'

Mr Wyecliffe patted his hands on the table, as though to calm a family spat. 'Stop the tape please. I'd like to discuss matters with my client.'

'Forget it,' said Riley, falling into a chair. 'It's too late now.'

Anselm had seen this sort of thing before: it was part of the psychology of wanting to be caught. Conscience was elemental: a small quantity could produce an explosion of truth that could obliterate a lifetime of deceptions. The change in Riley, a moment ago strutting and now cowed, was shocking.

Inspector Cartwright said, 'How did you kill him?'

'I knew he couldn't swim.'

'Go on.'

Riley leaned on his knees, his head angled down, showing the spine bones of his neck. 'In the middle of the night I put him in a plastic bag with an apple.'

'This is no time for jokes.'

Riley shook his head. 'Then I threw him into Limehouse Cut.'

'Who?'

'Arnold.'

'Arnold?'

'Nancy's hamster.'

Cartwright turned off the tape, without the usual formalities. 'You are a bastard,' she said.

Riley looked up and said, 'Inspector, that's the first thing you've got right today.'

The hands of the woman crumpling paper became still and George said, 'I'm sorry, Nancy.'

She nodded and quietly left the room.

The door behind Anselm swung open and Inspector Cartwright entered, saying, 'I'm sure he's wrong, George, but I need to check this out, all right?'

'Of course.' He coughed like a patient who didn't believe in doctors.

'Is there anywhere you could wait?' she said to Anselm. She was weary and angry and upset. 'It could take the rest of the day.'

After a phone call had been made to Debbie Lynwood, it was agreed that they would meet that evening at the Vault Day Centre. Anselm took George's arm. He felt as if he were guiding a man who was so much older than before, a man who could no longer see.

12

Riley pushed open the swing door, leaving Wyecliffe flapping behind. At the end of a corridor he kicked another and strode past the custody desk, barging aside people and things to reach the pavement. There, in the street, he saw Nancy.

'What are you doing here?' His jaw began to work.

'An officer came to tell me you'd been lifted.'

'Have you been inside?'

'I've just arrived. What's happened?'

He groaned with relief. 'They've been chasing me again. For nothing.'

'What do you mean?'

'They've never given up, not since that trial. Come on.' He pulled Nancy's arm and they walked down the street. He turned a corner, any corner. He didn't know where he was going. He swung on her, 'Cartwright's been looking at my business, but I've done nothing wrong.'

'What did she say you were doing?'

'The same as last time.' Riley didn't use the words that would hurt her.

'Oh God.' Nancy sat down on a low wall. The railings had been cut down during the war, leaving black stubs in the stone.

'But it's nothing, Nancy. Nothing.' Riley plucked at his jacket and shirt. Sweat itched his stomach. Inside, behind that wet lining, he was ruptured with anxiety and rage. The lot of them had put Nancy through the mill for nothing. That was meant to be all gone. He'd put himself out of reach. He said, 'Look, we're off to Brighton, right?'

Nancy pulled off her hat, disarranging her hair. She looked faint. 'It's too late, far too late.'

Riley watched her, as he'd once gazed into the waters of the Four Lodges. If you kept still, you could see the perch dart around in the green-black water. They were like torn scraps of aluminium foil. Something seemed to move in Nancy's face. 'I really wanted to go to Brighton' – she looked down at the flag-stones, the weeds in the cracks, the fag ends – 'I really fancied the sound of the sea. A walk on the beach. And maybe a stick of rock. It wasn't too much to ask, was it?'

'No,' urged Riley, taking her hands, 'and it still isn't. We can still make it.'

'Can we?'

'We're selling up, we're moving out. We'll leave this place behind.'

Nancy normally didn't stare. She'd always been demure, one step back, a bit scared. At Lawton's her shyness had kept her head to the page, even when he'd tapped on the counter. Now she faced him with wide, tired eyes. They were like polythene bags from the tackle shop, full of clear water. Something orange flickered, wanting to get out.

'Nancy, head off home, I'm going to see Prosser.'

Riley moaned as he ran. He knew that Elizabeth had worked out what he was doing when she turned up at Mile End Park. She held up a set of spoons and went through the same routine as Cartwright.

'But you taught me how to do it.' He was mocking her.

She frowned – a bit like Nancy a few moments ago – while he reminded her of that conference in her chambers. 'You can keep the spoons,' he said, and she sagged as if he'd squeezed her heart.

He ran even faster. All that manoeuvring, that hunger to win back something, belonged by a stream of deceit – the one he'd tasted with Nancy. He just didn't want it any more. It lay behind him – with every stride. 'I'm going to Brighton,' he shouted, knocking into some codgers by a newsstand. His arms flung out: they were in his way. The whole world was in his way. He crashed against a bin, and spun, thinking Nancy had dropped a notch: she wasn't in the usual place, and it terrified him.

13

There were no red mullet left, so the fishmonger at Smithfield Market suggested tench, a freshwater fish which, when duly cooked at St John's Wood, turned out to be utterly disgusting. But they'd already drunk a bottle and a half of Mâcon Lugny, so it didn't matter. Charles was laughing like a schoolboy because he'd spilled half a glass on his tie when Nick said abruptly, 'Did Mum ever mention the Pieman?'

It was meant to be an introduction to what Nick had prepared himself to reveal. He was seeking a small piece of common territory upon which to build.

Charles carried on laughing and dabbed his chest with a napkin. Lining up his knife and fork, he replied, 'I'll thank you kindly never to mention that name in this house again.'

The laughter had ceased, and Charles's face was bitten, his lips pursed. He moved his plate an inch.

'Is he for real . . . this bogeyman?' asked Nick, incredulous.

'This conversation is over.' Charles had that pale, helpless look that must have driven them all mad in the bank when explanations were in demand. He said, 'You don't need to know. Your mother's dead. It's over.'

They both became completely still, hands on their laps, concentrating on a half-eaten fish. This, I suppose, thought Nick, is what passes as a moment of truth. He'd been convinced that his father knew nothing of his wife's crisis; but in that opening Edwardian rebuke he'd shown that he must know everything, that he always had done, and that he'd held back even the barest of explanations from his son. He'd watched Nick scuttling around in a yellow Beetle; he'd stood at doors and windows clocking that a parental secret had been breached: and he'd said absolutely nothing – and never had done, except to commend the merits of a trip to Australia . . . and Papua New Guinea.

Something like rage and love and fear swooped upon Nick: anger at the antics of his parents, passion for their protective concern, but a certain dread at what had driven them to behave like that in the first place. His mother had wanted to bring him home, to tell him; but his father hadn't agreed: he'd been scared. 'The Bundi do a butterfly dance,' he'd said.

And Charles was still scared. But of what? And who? And why?

Nick folded up his napkin and went upstairs to the Green Room. This was where she'd planned it all, and this was where it would end – for him and his father. The only person who knew what the hell was going on was a half-wit crook, whose grubbing around had demolished Elizabeth's self-respect.

Nick took the orange flyer out of his pocket. The wine had made him foolish, he knew, but also perceptive. Colours were slightly brighter than usual – like his insight; things wouldn't keep still – like his resolve.

He dialled the number and listened.

He'd been a fool. He hadn't seen the true crisis, even though he'd found the key and opened the box. The 'not knowing and not being able to care', Locard's Principle (as applied), the 'responsibility without blame' – it was all good stuff, but these had only pointed towards a rarefied conscience. And yet there'd been something else in the box, right from the outset.

An answer machine clicked into action. Nick stubbed the button and dialled again. He waited, getting jumpy.

Nick had actually hit upon the critical question long ago, in a dingy pub near Cheapside. He'd ignored it, wanting to turn away from the idea that Elizabeth's compassion had been a commodity for the client, a bonus thrown in with the brief fee.

But now he wanted to know what had really happened when his mother had risen to cross-examine Riley's pitiable victim. For Anji, who'd had the guts to step into a witness box, the Pieman had been a dread presence, a reality that still exercised Mr Wyecliffe's fascination ten years later. And what had Elizabeth done? She'd skilfully – and *compassionately* – made the Pieman into a figure from Anji's tormented mind; she'd explained him away, she'd made him *a dream* . . .

The phone was answered.

It had to be the wine, but Nick shrank from the voice, for it was otherworldly in its harshness. He pictured his father before a half-eaten tench . . . It was safe downstairs . . . and there was another half bottle of Mâcon Lugny waiting . . . but he wanted to know the answer to his question.

'Who was the Pieman?'

Nick had to ask because he felt, obscurely, that his mother had known all along, even as she'd taken Anji by the hand; that he had found the secret spring of Elizabeth's disgrace.

Twenty minutes later Nick was at the wheel, over the limit, and driving east towards Hornchurch Marshes. He'd expected a reluctant conversation, not a demand for a meeting.

14

The Prior frequently reminded the community in chapter that, as the Rule made clear, there are times when good words are to be left unsaid out of esteem for silence.

With this counsel in mind, Anselm guided George to the Vault, saying very little. Before withdrawing, Debbie Lynwood led them to a simply furnished bedroom away from the bustle of the day centre. On a sideboard was a selection of games and puzzles in battered boxes. George studied the lids meditatively. 'Riley knew I was there,' he said. 'He was speaking to me.'

Anselm nodded at the rounded back of this lean, honourable man in his honourable blazer and tie. Adam's sin, said Genesis, was that he wanted to be like God, to direct the great arrangement of things into which he had been wonderfully born; to know why good was good, and why evil was evil; maybe to make a few discreet changes. There are occasions, thought Anselm, when I would like to be God: long enough to understand this man's fall, and to do something about it.

George chose a jigsaw – a medieval map of the known world.

Anselm left George and took a bus to Camberwell. Once more he was directed to the garden and the corridor of chestnut trees. Sister Dorothy was in the same place, at the far end. Tartan blankets kept her warm; the brown pakol had been pulled down to protect her ears. She glanced at Anselm as he sat down beside her on a stone bench, and said, 'She was a very clever girl, but naughty. Didn't take to the rules at first. She spent her first months in detention every Sunday afternoon. I used to visit her with parcels from the tuck shop.'

'I take it you mean Elizabeth Steadman, and not Elizabeth Glendinning,' said Anselm.

'What a *very* silly mistake,' she replied, closing her eyes. The fracture in her nose caught the low, slanting light, and it appeared dark and grotesque.

'I was completely fooled,' said Anselm.

Sister Dorothy might have admitted defeat, but she was shrewd enough to wait and see just how much territory had been lost. Anselm smuggled an arm into each wide sleeve, taking hold of his elbows. It was cold. Three ravens watched him from the branches of an oak beyond the convent wall.

'I imagine that it was in the evening,' said Anselm, 'and that it had grown dark outside. Elizabeth was alone in the Green Room at St John's Wood. She opened *The Following of Christ* – a book that went back, perhaps, to her last meeting with you – and she cut a hole in the pages deep enough to hold a key. Much later she came to Larkwood with a duplicate and asked me to use it if, by chance, she were to die. Her last words to me were, "You can't always explain things to your children. If need be, will you help Nicholas understand?" At first, I thought she meant help him come to terms with grief. Then I thought she wanted me to explain that you couldn't be a lawyer without a sort of innocent compromise. But now I fear she meant something very different—'

Sister Dorothy made a low groan of surrender. 'Mr Kemble said you might come.'

The ravens hopped onto higher branches, and then flew off in different directions.

'You know *Roddy*?' Anselm had the sort of sensation that might occur if you turned a corner in a familiar street, only to find you were in a different country.

'Oh yes, we're old friends,' said Sister Dorothy. 'I met him during a prison visit. My veil charmed him. In those days it was like a marquee. He wanted to know how it was fixed, whether it was comfortable. I rather thought he was jealous.'

'He's never mentioned you.'

'I should hope not.'

'Why?'

'Because that is what we agreed.'

Anselm tried to stop his intuition racing ahead of his questions. 'Sister, did you introduce Elizabeth to Mr Kemble?'

'Not quite.' Sister Dorothy seemed proud of her own machinations. 'I told Roddy all about Elizabeth when she began her studies for the Bar. He wangled several accidental meetings and eventually urged her to apply to his chambers. Elizabeth never found out.'

Anselm's inkling was like a rush of blood. He said, 'You didn't meet Elizabeth in Carlisle, did you? You met here in Camberwell . . . This is the hostel where you were based . . . before the architects put in those corridors . . .'

Sister Dorothy gazed high above the convent wall, as if she could see ridges, peaks and snow. 'Wheel me inside, please, and tell me about the key,' she said.

As happens in November, darkness had come like a thief, and quickly.

15

When Riley got to Hornchurch Marshes the light was dwindling. Gingerly, he trotted down a sloping path that led to the Four Lodges. Years back, a cooling tower had been demolished and all that remained were these rectangular pools. The Council had put some fish in and left them to it.

On the site of the old tower, Riley scoured the grass. Whimpering and swearing, he kicked free some rocks and a blackened two-by-four with rusted nails protruding like a row of buttons. Then he sat on the remnants of a wall, hugging himself, his eyes fixed on the path. He was up a height, feeling nauseous, watching his actions run ahead of him, like they'd done with John Bradshaw. At his feet were the weapons, and a torch.

This was only the third time Riley had been here. The last was after the trial, and before that he'd been a boy.

Very early one morning the man Riley wouldn't call Dad had put the remaining kitten in a sack. The other eight had found good homes. 'Put your coat on, Graham,' he said. There was a smell of aftershave – something brash and fiery.

Without speaking, they walked through Dagenham's empty streets towards the pale light over Hornchurch Marshes. Presently, the flats of the Thames opened out like a damp blanket and there, in the middle, were four panes of water, framed and criss-crossed by slippery bricks.

They walked to the edge and Walter's arm began to swing. His chest blew up and his mouth went firm. Sick at the idea of unwanted life, Riley grabbed the big man's sleeve, but a backhand sent him flying. He was on his hands and knees for the splash, with blood on his lip. The bag turned in the water and sank. Riley watched, transfixed. He'd expected a scream – not from the bag, but from above and all around. But there was no sound . . . none at all. After the ripples had run off, the surface carried nothing but colour snatched from the brightening sky.

That evening, they came back to the Four Lodges. Midges clung like hats around the fishermen. They sat on boxes and stools, maggots on their bottom lip. That's how it was done: you warmed it in the mouth. When it hit the cold water the thing wriggled on its hook, attracting the perch and the carp. Walter kept his supply in a Tom Long tobacco tin.

'Go on, Graham,' he said distantly.

Riley wanted to please Walter, so he did as he was asked, and Walter looked on, midges circling his head. Riley gazed into his high, tormented eyes: the big man didn't really want to be like this, but he couldn't stop himself. However, there and then, Riley's understanding shrivelled up. Somehow, this couldn't be right . . . feeling this thing writhe between his lips. It was the taste of decay.

Riley didn't trouble himself with questions like why the man he wouldn't call Dad did what he did – he already knew the

267

answer: Walter had a child of his own; Riley was in the way. The big man had lost his job and his self-respect. He wanted a life different from the one he'd got. Those huge lungs were bursting with complaint. The braces weren't strong enough to hold it in. When Riley lay awake that night, after two visits to the Four Lodges, such thoughts didn't even ruffle the surface of his mind; no, Riley was more confused by the senseless parade of death: in one day, he'd seen a fish taken out of water, and a cat thrown in.

When Riley next came, after the trial, he thought of the Major, who'd never lost faith in the boy who'd turned up at the hostel, who'd seen someone else behind the flesh and blood in front of him – someone lost to Riley's eyes. Leaving the conference room, Riley had glimpsed something like agony on the old soldier's face. The Major was asking himself how this beast had turned out the way he had. It was a good question, but who'd have thought that the die was cast when Riley, still a boy, couldn't make sense of a brightening sky?

On that glorious day of acquittal, midges gathered around Riley's head; and he wept as a man on the grass where he'd wept as a boy.

The temperature was dropping fast with the light and Riley shivered. Before him lay the Four Lodges and, on their far side, coming down a sloping path, was a big lad . . . a lad who was on to Walter.

16

Nancy stood in the yard by the pile of bricks that she'd been collecting for the herb garden.

268

'You could have gone places.'

Mr Lawton had said that because Nancy saw the connections between things. It was insulting, she'd thought, because he was implying she'd wasted her life, when all she'd done was work for him and marry Graham Riley.

'We've had a meeting.'

Babycham had been fiery and protective and a friend – her oldest friend, in fact. There'd been a meeting of the clerical staff and everyone was ready to support her. 'Run for it, girl,' she'd said.

'I once had a son.'

Mr Johnson had steamed like a tea bag on the draining board and Nancy had listened with a hand over her mouth. She'd been desperate to know what had happened, but her friend in the goggles had never been able to put words on it.

'Our son was killed by a bad man.'

Emily Bradshaw had said that to Nancy, not knowing who she was; just as Nancy had spoken to George Bradshaw not knowing who he was. She'd listened to neither of them. She'd run out of Aspen Bank chased by the sound of tapping on the window.

'Maybe your constancy will save him. But what about you?'

That kind man had refused to give up. He'd circled the house, knowing she was inside. He'd come with a cake from Greggs. He'd left his phone number.

They'd all come – even Mr Wyecliffe, with his quip about tossed coins and their tails – but Nancy hadn't seen any of the connections. No, it was worse than that, far worse. She *had* seen them. And she'd turned away in the name of trust.

'My life rests on a heap of lies,' said Nancy. She felt no emotion whatsoever, though she was crying all the same. Her soul was like an arm gone dead, as when you wake up at night and find this heavy thing, limp by your side. All you can do is wait for the tingling to come and bring it back to life.

Nancy knelt down and started counting the bricks, to see how many more were needed.

17

Nick paused at the bottom of the slope. It was almost dark and extremely cold. In the distance he could see the Thames like a black vein. Above it and beyond glowed the lights of south London. To the west stood the motor works, immense and silent. Directly before him, like pools of oil, were the Four Lodges. On the other side, stamped against the skyline, sat Riley. He was utterly still; his breath appeared as a coarse mist.

Skirting the water's edge, Nick suffered a primal desire to run away. He subdued it, because the hunched figure had scared his father and possessed his mother. He stopped by the end of a pool, well back from Riley, but close enough to hear his words.

A low voice came out of a small fog. 'Didn't your mother tell you about me?'

'No.'

Riley's elbows were on his thighs. His face and body were completely blacked out. 'Who gave you the photograph?'

Nick angled his head, trying to see into the dark shape ahead of him, the moving arms. The questions seemed planned, as if they were a test.

'I don't know what you're talking about.'

'Did you post it?'

'No.'

After a few moments Nick heard something fall to the ground near Riley's feet with a thump. A long exhalation of mist came from the lowered head. The voice became curious and quieter. 'How old are you?'

'Twenty-seven.'

'What do you do for a living?'

'I'm a doctor.'

'A *doctor* . . .' It was as though he'd never met one, but had heard of them from magazines and television programmes. 'What's your father called?'

'Charles.'

'What does he do?'

'A banker.'

'A *banker* . . .' They were another species from the same glossy pages, off the same screen. Riley stood up and purposefully crossed the five yards between them. As he passed Nick he slowed, saying, 'Forget about the Pieman.'

Nick turned on his heel, watching the stooped figure tread quickly along the lodge bank, towards the path. 'Where are you going?' he called stupidly.

'Brighton.'

Nick stumbled after him, unable to see where he was going, aware only of a sheet of glinting black water to his left. He grabbed Riley's shoulder, sensing the sheer physical difference between them. Nick was a big man, towering over a bantam. 'Tell me what I came here to find out.'

'No.' Riley pulled free with a swing of his elbow.

'Who was he?'

'Go home . . . just go home; go back to your patients.' Riley began to trot, heading up the slope, towards the night sky.

Nick gave up. He cast an eye around Riley's chosen meeting place: at the cold marshes, the scattering of small lights, and, upstream, the brooding hulks. A spasm of rage made him rebel against this embodiment of his mother's conscience – at the thought that she felt responsible for Riley's twisted actions.

'Before you came along, she was happy,' he bellowed. 'You shattered what was left of her life.' His voice bounced off the motor works, falling quiet as if the air had soaked it up.

Riley seemed to strike a wall. Slowly, he turned around, and came back along the brick ledge beside the water. When he was close, he halted, treading the ground, his head bent and angled. Gusts of fog escaped his mouth as if he'd just run a race.

'Let me tell you something you don't know.' He seemed to be struggling, as if a shred of pork were jammed between two teeth. A faint light touched his face, and Nick finally glimpsed his features, judging the man to be not just ill, but profoundly sick. 'Before she met your father,' said Riley, as if he were forcing out the words, 'before she got her chance, she was on the street. I might have kept the money . . . but she earned it.' Riley looked up with pity, a far-off emotion gathering like water on limestone. Quietly, almost gently, he said, 'She was no better than me.'

Riley stepped back and groaned.

All at once a bright light struck Nick's face. Terrified, he raised his hands . . . Slowly, he let his arms drop. Stunned, feeling light-headed and sick, Nick glared back at the unseen presence behind the torch. Riley must have been observing him intently because he didn't cut the beam, and, for a very long time, he didn't move. Then, after a snap, it was dark again.

The last that Nick saw of Riley was of a sunken head, and limp arms against the sky on the brow of a slope.

18

'When the university term was about to begin,' said Sister Dorothy, 'I drove Elizabeth to Durham. We strolled down a cobbled lane near the cathedral and she stepped into a charity shop and bought a picture. I thought it was the frame, but I was wrong.'

As in many religious houses, the living room seemed to have been furnished exclusively from the type of place where Elizabeth had bought her picture. A mismatch of chairs were grouped around a fifties glass-top table. At its centre, having a status somewhere between that of a relic and an ornament (said Sister Dorothy), was an ashtray that had once been used by a pope. The carpet was hard, without a pile, creating the durable look of a car showroom.

'We found a bench on Palace Green,' said Sister Dorothy, pushing stray silver hair beneath her pakol. 'There was a market with people milling all around, but Elizabeth didn't seem to notice. She couldn't keep her eyes off the three people in the picture. Rather sadly, she began to imagine who they were, and what their stories might have been. I joined in. Elizabeth came up with the mad inventor dreaming of a smoke detector, and I added the wife, with her one joke about a fire extinguisher. We both laughed . . . among all these real people, with real lives.' She sipped a glass of milk, resting it on her lap and the tartan blanket around her legs. 'And what of the little madam in the middle? I said. Elizabeth touched the girl's hair . . . as if she might reach through the glass to the ribbons . . . and she said, "She's got the whole of her life ahead of her." Even then, I didn't see what she was planning. It was only when we reached the gates of her college that she told me her decision . . . that we could never meet again.' Sister Dorothy sighed. 'She wanted a fresh start. The story we'd made up would become hers, because she could live with its tragedy. She would take the girl's life and make something *wonderful* of it ... Those were Elizabeth's words ... something wonderful.'

With permission, Anselm rolled himself a cigarette. Licking the paper, he said, 'And what of the girl whose tragedy was too painful to bear?'

Sister Dorothy nodded knowingly. She recognised the unlimited scope of the question, Father Anselm's plea to be told everything.

'I met her shortly after I came to Camberwell.' She paused while Anselm's match flared. 'In those days this place was a hostel for girls, an open door with no questions asked. But it was one step removed from the street, and I wanted to reach the kids who would never look in our direction, who might not know we were here. I wanted to change the world with ... *acts of mercy*' – she sang the phrase with a raised fist – 'so we tried something different. I'd jump in a taxi – driven by Mr Entwistle, a friend of the community – and he'd drop me off at Euston, so I could keep my eye out when the trains pulled in ... You see, there were lots of kids coming down to London from up north, to the pavements of gold, to a better life ... and we hoped to get them off the street as fast as possible.' She dropped her little fist and sipped her milk. 'So, Mr Entwistle would come back after half an hour and take me to King's Cross, and then Liverpool Street, and so it would go on, to all the mainline stations. I'd mooch around, plucking up the courage to approach anyone I thought might have nowhere to go. I confess in those days, we had our eye out mostly for girls. And yet ... Elizabeth's story begins with a boy I met at Paddington.' She glanced sideways and said confidentially, 'Would you roll me one?'

'Of course.' While Anselm made the cigarette, Sister Dorothy finished her milk. Then she lit up with the panache of Lauren Bacall.

'I saw this boy in a man's trousers stealing fruit from a barrow,' said Sister Dorothy sternly. 'I called to him, and, strangely, I suppose, he came. We got talking and he explained that he'd just left a burnt-out bank round the corner, a squat run by a lad, a hard lad. When Mr Entwistle turned up, I took the fruit thief to an hotelier I knew who kept a bed free, and then I went back to Paddington, to a lane that ran by the tracks.' With determination, but control, she slowly blew out the smoke. 'I stood beneath a street lamp watching these garden statues at intervals along the pavement. That's what I thought at the time. They were like ornaments that could no longer spout water in the grounds of . . . a terrible place. One by one, they drifted down the road, but none of the cars that came ever stopped. So I remained there, too scared to step forward and too angry to move back. A lifetime later, Mr Entwistle took me home. I went to the police. They told me that so long as I frightened off the business, the kids wouldn't work, and without any evidence, there was nothing they could do. It was a terrible irony. All the same, I put myself beneath that light every evening, from eight until ten, and that was how I met her.'

Sister Dorothy reached for the ashtray on the coffee table and placed it between them, on the arm of Anselm's chair. 'That's how I met Elizabeth', she repeated. 'At night, a fifteen-year-old with white legs, long black hair and no socks . . . bare feet in black, boardroom shoes. She was the only one who came anywhere near me – about as far away as that chair. Close enough to deter any business, and far enough to catch my voice. Every night I came to that lamp, and every night she

275

hovered within talking distance. That's how I learned her name. She taught me to smoke. Can you picture it, the two of us, by the kerb, sharing a cigarette? We talked of the weather – anything, except why she was there and where she'd come from. When Mr Entwistle arrived, I'd open the door, and she'd just look at me and shake her head. And then, one night, she came.'

Anselm felt his mind crowding with images of Elizabeth, none of them remotely similar to the description he'd just heard. He saw himself as a pupil in chambers, sharing a box of Jaffa Cakes with the best silk in her field. She'd picked him out, in a way, and started their conversations . . .

'She was standing closer to me than usual,' said Sister Dorothy, leaning towards Anselm. 'At her feet was a small red suitcase, like you'd take on a weekend break. And over her shoulder I saw someone edging along the pavement. He was neither boy nor man, a wiry thing with his hands in his pockets. At that moment the taxi pulled up . . . Elizabeth turned around, as if she'd known all along that this creeping thing was there. "I've paid you in full," she said, very deliberately, "and now I owe you nothing." I opened the door, and she picked up her little suitcase and climbed in. That hollow, haunted thing on the pavement was Riley. When I came back the next night, the street was empty and the squat had been abandoned.'

Anselm rolled fresh cigarettes for them both, fumbling with the paper. He could hardly keep up with Sister Dorothy's rolling narrative. She'd gathered speed, speaking towards the empty chairs in the common room. Elizabeth had stayed at the hostel for months. Refused to go home. Wouldn't eat. Wouldn't talk. Finally, she was prepared to let Sister Dorothy act as a messenger. But she was very clear that if steps were taken to send her home, she'd disappear once and for all.

'So I knocked on the door,' said Sister Dorothy, slowing as if she'd just tramped across London. 'I told Mrs Steadman that her daughter had run away but was safe' – she glanced at Anselm, her eyes narrowed and moist – 'I did this kind of work for years, and I always had to manage hysteria and anguish . . . the lot . . . But this time, and neither before nor since, I met with instant and complete resignation.'

She motioned for a light, because the cigarette had gone out. Anselm struck a match. 'What of Mr Steadman?' he asked, after a short silence.

'Accidental death,' she replied, through a breath of smoke. 'Mrs Steadman wouldn't speak of it, but the coroner's certificate was required when the authorities were convened to plan Elizabeth's future – that's how I found out. In all the years to come, Elizabeth never referred to him. *Not once.*'

With court approval, it was agreed that Elizabeth would attend the Carlisle school, and Sister Dorothy would act as a go-between to Mrs Steadman. The court order was kept in an office upstairs because, technically speaking, Camberwell became Elizabeth's home address.

'After she went to Durham, I never saw her again,' said Sister Dorothy, 'but I received a postcard when she decided to become a barrister.' With the cigarette between her teeth, she wheeled herself across the room to a sideboard. She returned with a bre-viary on her lap. Wincing at the smoke, she leafed through the pages until she found her bookmark.

The picture showed Gray's Inn Chapel on a summer's day, beneath whose tower Anselm had waited for Nicholas. Written on the other side were these brief words:

Tuesday week I shall be called to the Bar. Thanks to you alone, I am happy. The girl we found in ribbons shall spend her days on the heels of the wrongdoer.

With my love,

Elizabeth

'That same day I gave Roddy a cold call,' said Sister Dorothy, taking back the card. 'I hoped he'd remember me from my veil.'

'Did he?'

'Oh yes.'

They both smiled, quiet for a moment at the recollection of Mr Roderick Kemble QC, who'd wheedled his way into Elizabeth's aspirations, and fulfilled them.

Darkness had fallen completely outside. The rush of traffic on Coldharbour Lane sounded like the tide, sure but fitful. When George had accused Riley, thought Anselm, Riley had turned to Elizabeth. The three of them met in court. The symmetry was appalling. And I stood among them, unseeing.

Sister Dorothy stubbed out her cigarette and said regretfully, 'I'll tell you now about the boy who sent me towards that street light.' (Anselm had wondered about him. A sympathetic hotelier had given him a bed for the night.) 'He was named after his grandfather – a revered man in the household.'

'To use the language of the day,' said Sister Dorothy wearily, 'the lad discovered that his namesake had *interfered* with a neighbour's child. It was the word he used when he told his mother, who didn't believe him . . . and when he told his father, who couldn't . . . so the lad went to the police. The victim denied it, so the lad was ostracised. Then, one morning, Granddad took a train to Scarborough and walked into the sea, leaving his medals on the beach.

'That's why he left home,' mumbled the old nun, 'why he had

278

to.' She was heavy with remorse, not wanting Anselm to see the place into which he'd stumbled (the place where, unknown to her, Anselm had found the lawyer's grail: a win against the odds). 'He wouldn't tell anyone who he was,' she admitted, quietly. 'It's Elizabeth's tale all over again. Start afresh, I said. Use your other name. I've often wondered what became of young George.'

19

Charles Glendinning's interest in Lepidoptera did not extend to catching examples for display. They belonged out of reach. And because they rarely kept still, occasions of extended observation were rare, always unforeseen and thereby, on each count, prized. Perhaps, then, it was out of respect that Charles had acquired several antique collections: long, shallow boxes lined with green baize, fronted with glass. The specimens were laid out in neat rows, each with a label bearing a name in brown copperplate. These cabinets lined the walls of Charles's study. It had always been known as the Butterfly Room.

After parking the VW in the back lane, Nick moved through a dark and silent house to find his father. His lungs were tight, as if they were too small for the job. With a shaking finger he pushed open the door to the study. Charles was leaning over a display cabinet, hands behind his back, his face artificially bright from phosphorous illumination.

Nick let the door clip shut. He wanted to be a child again, to sit on someone's knee, and to be told it was just a dream; to be ushered back into a world without demons. The leather armchair was cold to the touch.

'That tench was nauseating,' said Charles, without shifting his gaze. 'The wine, on the other hand, was divine.'

'Dad,' said Nick, 'I've just met Graham Riley.'

Charles placed an arm on either side of the cabinet under review. His knuckles turned white. The examining gaze, however, remained intact. He is a man preparing himself, thought Nick, wanting him to be strong and bigger than his own revelations.

'That,' said Charles faintly, 'was a remarkably foolish thing to do.'

Yes, it was, thought Nick. And now I know what I do not want to know. It did not belong in the garden of their shared memories. Every year they'd gone to their cliff-top cottage at Saint Martin's Haven, facing the Jack Sound and the island of Skomer. As a boy he'd follow his father in the dark of summer nights, shining his torch on the island's protectors, a militia of toads. They'd sat on the paths, fat-necked and smiling. Once, his mother had come. They'd gone looking for these lazy squaddies but had halted, awestruck before a patch of heathland lit by glow-worms.

'He said Mum was no better than him . . .' Nick was pleading for the innocence of Skomer, the Barrier Reef, Christmas Day . . . all of it. He wanted the lot restored. He wanted his father to tell him something that would put things back into position.

Charles had closed his eyes. He was like a man praying, horribly fervent and yet *strong*. Nick had always seen the duffer – the gentleman with raised eyebrows in the provincial museums of half-term holidays – but never *this*. This was a different kind of strength, and it was not the kind he was looking for or wanted.

'Did I ever tell you how I met your mother?' asked Charles ingenuously.

'Of course,' said Nick, wanting to scream. Charles's employer had retained Elizabeth to bring a claim for money paid under a mistake of fact – that is to say, Charles had authorised payment of a cheque to an individual notwithstanding the countermand of the person who had drawn it. Elizabeth won on a technicality. The same day Charles rang her chambers, he sent her flowers . . . he did all the things that he'd thought he was constitutionally incapable of doing. Such was the transforming power of forgetting yourself, and being unable to forget someone else. Such was the received wisdom.

'Well, let me tell you another version,' said Charles. He motioned to his son with his hand – warmly, like he'd done upon the heath on Skomer.

Nick came to the display cabinet and looked down at the specimens, lined up and labelled. His father's arm was suddenly heavy on his shoulder.

'See this one, top right?' With his free hand Charles pointed through the glass to a butterfly with large, dark reddish-purple wings trimmed with a buttery gold. Reserved but ardent, he said, 'This lady came to be known as White Petticoat and Grand Surprise. The labels suggest that she's naughty . . . a shameless gal, a trickster. She's had lots of names. They tell you something, but they never quite capture her.' He glanced at Nick, as he used to do in those fusty museums. 'She's not a city girl. She likes the woods . . . willow, birch and elm.'

'Where's she from?' Nick scarcely heard himself, because he thought his father had gone raving mad.

'Another land, far away . . . she's a rare vagrant.' He looked more closely, drawing Nick down with him. 'She has another label: the Mourning Cloak. But when she was first sighted in Cool Arbour Lane' – his voice dropped, as if he'd come to the secret – 'she was called the Camberwell Beauty.'

Charles was holding his son tightly across the shoulder, but all the time he looked down into the cabinet of phosphorescent light. His grip was almost fierce. There was no escape.

281

'Your mother was a Grand Surprise,' said Charles, confidingly. 'She moved warily, as if she'd been netted once . . . and was forever mindful of where she'd been. When I first saw her at court, I had to follow her. There was something about her eyes, the movement of her arms. So I tracked her progress. Nothing could keep me away, neither nettles nor thorns, and I went through the lot, barelegged without a net, never wanting to trap her, only hoping to be near by. That's how it was when we got married. I had to keep my distance, all scratched and swollen.' His grip on his son eased, but only slightly. 'But when I least expected it – many years later – she came to me . . . I could barely breathe; I could only look at her broken wings with wonder, with astonishment, that she could still fly, and that she had deigned to rest on me.' His blue eyes began to move, checking labels. 'Nothing Riley told you could come between me and the love I have for your mother.'

Gently, Charles pulled Nick round, placing a hand on each of his son's shoulders. 'The mother you knew has vanished, I know, and I grieve for you. But if you just wait' – he was distressed, but strong in this newly discovered way – 'the labels – those tabs that hang on what we've done, that can never sum up who we are – they'll all fade and find their place. And then someone infinitely more wonderful will appear.'

Charles strode across the room to a drinks cabinet and poured two glasses of scotch. 'Will you drink to that?' he asked.

20

'At any one time,' said George distractedly, 'there were roughly ten of us living in that squat.'

He picked up a jigsaw piece and angled it towards a small

lamp. The map of the known world was almost complete.

'News of a place to stay travels on the street,' said George, 'and that is how I met Elizabeth. I first saw her huddled by a fire in the manager's office. On her lap was a small red suitcase with a gold lock. We became friends, though I never heard her story, and I never told her mine. Riley was kind . . . helped her settle in . . . he *watched* her. At that stage, he seemed no different to anyone else. But then a change occurred.' George knitted his fingers on the table. 'I don't know whether Riley started it, or whether he moved naturally with the downward drift, but talk moved from cold and hunger to quick money. Either way, Riley became a leader . . . feverish . . . and, in a way, *ambitious* . . . and that's when I left. For reasons I will never understand, Elizabeth refused to come with me.'

Anselm sat very still, arms folded on the edge of the table facing George. The room was dark, save for the pool of light thrown between them.

'After Sister Dorothy found me a place for the night,' George continued, 'I came back to Paddington. What I saw, I've never forgotten. There she was, beneath a street-light, completely still. Ahead, and to the left, in shadow, stood the squat. On the right, behind a wall topped with broken glass, ran the railway line. Against the sky I could see a footbridge leading from the station. The street was empty. And then I saw some movement on the bridge . . . two people . . . one larger than the other. They paused midway, and I knew it was Riley, looking over towards Sister Dorothy. Even back then, he was bony and stooped, strangely angular. He was leading someone by the hand. They came down the steps and onto the road. Again he stopped, facing Sister Dorothy . . . with Riley holding a hand, and carrying a bag. Slowly, with side-steps, he moved into the squat, tugging the arm of another runaway.'

George returned to his jigsaw, tapping edges that wouldn't stay down. He wasn't concentrating, because some pieces became detached and he left them misaligned. Remotely, he said, 'It was . . . awful . . . you see, Riley went to the station *because* Sister Dorothy had come to the street. It's as though he'd taken her place on the platform, and, coming back to the squat, he'd let her see the consequences of her choice.' George found Anselm's troubled gaze and said, 'That night I vowed that if I ever got the chance to name Riley for what he was, to bring him down, then I'd seize the day.'

The room grew darker, and the lamplight grew harsher. The walls seemed to have vanished. All that existed was this table, this jigsaw and an old man with careful fingers. Anselm sat back, almost in shadow, listening to what had happened to a boy who'd made a solemn promise.

George had got a job at the Bonnington and there he'd met Emily. They saved pennies in large bottles and 'did without' until they could afford two rooms in a boarding house. Emily went to night school, did a typing course and landed a job with the National Coal Board. George couldn't forget the quiet street that ran by a railway line in Paddington. When he got the chance, he started work at the Bridges night shelter, first as a helper, and finally as manager. It played havoc with married life, because George was out four nights every week and permanently on call: no one seemed to know the system quite so well as George; no one seemed to solve a crisis quite so deftly. But, as Emily well understood, this wasn't 'work' for George. The Bridges was his way of reaching back to where he'd come from. It was therefore fitting, observed George, that he should have heard the name Riley from the mouths of children: Anji, Lisa and Beverly. 'But I let them slip over the edge,' he said.

Anselm stared at the map's illustrations. Monstrous creatures of the imagination inhabited the extremities; radiant apostles stood upon the lands to which they'd brought the Good News. It was difficult to conceive how such a chart could have served any navigational purpose. He let his mind study the robes: he knew that the unfolding narrative was moving inevitably towards his cross-examination.

'After leaving Paddington, I never saw Elizabeth again,' said George. 'Not until that day at the Old Bailey. We'd been told to address our replies to the jury, so I hadn't noticed her . . . and it had been over twenty years, so a glance told me nothing. It was only when you began your questions that a glance became a stare. And then I realised: Riley had picked Elizabeth to silence me.' He breathed heavily through his nose, and leaned back into the obscurity behind the light. A slight agitation raised his voice and his hands began to move with his words. 'As you were asking your questions, I was trying to work out what was happening. I was sure that this confrontation was a threat . . . If I stuck to my evidence, then Riley would expose Elizabeth. She was gazing at me, pleading with her eyes, but telling me what? To spare an old friend who'd made a new life? Or to get on with it and condemn Riley . . . to bring him down while she was watching?'

Anselm knew the answer, because Elizabeth had told him the night before. 'Do you think Riley is innocent?' she'd asked him, feet on the table. And when he'd said no, she'd invited him to cross-examine Bradshaw the next morning. 'This is your chance to do something significant.' Outwardly, Elizabeth had been mildly bored. But inside she'd screamed with fear that George might fail, without dreaming that Anselm might succeed. He stared at the map, with its strangely beautiful but false proportions, and said, 'And before you could determine if it was mercy

285

she wanted, or sacrifice – for it would mean her public humiliation – I asked you the one question you could not answer.'

George did not reply.

'Because if you told the court about David,' said Anselm, 'it
would undermine your own evidence.'

George still did not speak.

'And, of all people, it would fall on Elizabeth to argue that
the word of George Bradshaw could not be trusted, because
he'd made false allegations once before.' Anselm paused. 'It
must have been a dreadful moment, George, when I pushed
you out of that witness box. I'm far sorrier than I can express,
all the more so because I gloried in not knowing what I'd
done.'

The sounds of feet and low voices were at the door.

No one is more familiar with the varieties of forensic disappointment than a police officer. Sometimes she knows that a
man has committed a crime but she can't bring him to book,
either because a witness won't speak out (unlike Anji) or the
assembled facts wouldn't convince a jury of guilt (as in the case
of John Bradshaw). And even if she rolls him through the court
door, a wheel can still fall off (as happened with George
Bradshaw). But, curiously, the greatest disappointment of the lot
is the one reserved for objectionable conduct that falls short of
an offence.

These sunless thoughts settled upon Anselm as he greeted
Inspector Cartwright, noting that she did not smile or look at
George, and that she kept her coat wrapped tight despite the
rampant efficiency of an institutional heating system. They
formed an apprehensive triangle. The main light had been
switched on, but the bulb cast a weary glow, as though it were
fearful of what might be revealed.

286

'There is a simple legal problem,' said Inspector Cartwright bluntly. 'Riley's scheme doesn't constitute a recognised criminal activity. He's no different to someone using a telephone directory. He sells a number, that's all. And in his hands, it's neutral. If there was an arrangement between Riley and the girl, then it might be different. But there isn't.'

With the back of his hand, George brushed unseen dust off his sleeve. Anselm gazed again at a schoolboy's motto: the law will be fulfilled by love.

'Even if charges could be framed,' continued Inspector Cartwright, 'it would be a weak case, a case that we couldn't reasonably pursue.' She slowed her delivery, hating her role, her obligations. 'George, this means that Riley is out of my reach, and yours. I'm sorry to say this, but it looks as if he always was, even before you and Elizabeth set out to catch him.'

It struck Anselm that the last observation belonged to the category of things that need not be said, even though true.

'Would you mind writing that down for me?' asked George appreciatively, as if he'd received complex travel directions. 'I'll need to remind myself in the days to come.'

With a frown of concentration, he tapped his blazer pockets, not quite sure where he'd left his notebook.

Anselm had foreseen that the lateness of the hour might preclude a return to Larkwood. Accordingly, after Inspector Cartwright had gone, George was left in place poring over a table, and Anselm was directed to a narrow storeroom with a camp bed that snapped shut when he sat in the middle. Surprisingly – and in the morning, he thought, indecently – Anselm fell asleep easily. He began compline, but didn't get beyond the first verse of the opening psalm. When daylight came, he knocked on George's bedroom with all the worry and

287

regret that he'd thought would keep him awake. The door was ajar and swung a little at his touch. Entering, Anselm found the bed unused and the jigsaw completed.

David George Bradshaw had gone.

PART FIVE

of beginnings and ends

1

Anselm joined Father Andrew in the cloister. They sat on a low wall beneath one of the arches, looking onto the garth. At the insistence of an MCC benefactor the square had been laid with turf from Lord's cricket ground – 'Father, we'll lay a sand-based, fast-draining outfield' – but rank disobedience to the maintenance regime had permitted this corner of the English soul to be eaten by moss. The square was now a deep emerald sponge that held on to water.

The Riley business was, they both concluded, a sorry affair. Their involvement left the bitter aftertaste of shared failure: as if they might have done something to prevent the outcome – the dereliction of a dead woman's hopes. She had set out to alter the appearance and effect of the past. That her entire project should founder on a mistake of law was unfortunate. That the correct legal analysis should have come from her mouth in the first place was a tragedy.

Learning of Elizabeth's background ought to have surprised Anselm, but it did not (he said, letting his eyes rest on the crisp, frosted lawn). The manner of her living now made sense: a life in compartments, the zeal for prosecuting and, like an arch, her inventiveness. In retrospect, Anselm could see her quietly working out the knots of her history, as when she, who had lost her father, had drawn from him the loss of his mother. They'd discussed its manner and meaning, but she'd applied its lessons elsewhere. From the outset childhood grief had bound them together, though he'd never known it. Perhaps that's why she

291

turned to him – instinctively – when she saw 'Riley' typed on the front of the trial brief; when she read the name of David George Bradshaw on the witness list. She must have seen what Riley was hoping to do: that he might well succeed; that he could do so only if Elizabeth sacrificed the identity she had so carefully constructed. Professionally speaking, in that one trial, unseen by the public and her peers, Elizabeth had committed suicide: she should have withdrawn from the case; she should probably have gone further, and revealed what she knew of her client, 'this wounded instrument'. There were lots of shoulds, but they were not enough when weighed against her need for self-preservation. Or – to be just – was it yet another murder that could never be laid at Riley's door? As he had been from the beginning, Anselm was linked to Elizabeth by a kind of grieving that he didn't fully understand. Her dying words to an answer machine seemed preposterous, now: 'Leave it to Anselm.'

'What was I supposed to do,' asked Anselm, drawing breath, 'sweep up the pieces? Explain to George the limitations of the law – as if he didn't know already?'

'No,' said the Prior patiently, 'the message related to a project she knew had failed, otherwise she wouldn't have called the police. They're words of hope, urging Inspector Cartwright to remain confident, despite appearances.'

'The point remains,' said Anselm, with mock testiness, 'what is it that I'm meant to be doing?'

'It sometimes helps to shift tenses,' said the Prior, nudging his glasses. 'What are you meant to have *done*?'

'Find George,' replied Anselm smartly, for there he had succeeded, before he'd lost him again. (Before coming home, he'd checked Trespass Place, left messages at homeless shelters in London and written a letter for the kind attention of F. Hillsden Esq.)

'What else?' asked the Prior routinely. He seemed to be slipping away, drawn by adjacent thoughts.

'Visit Mrs Dixon.'

Anselm pondered these twin duties while the Prior fiddled with the paperclip on his glasses. Slowly, like water clearing in a stream, Anselm began to understand Elizabeth's last wish. Answering the Prior's questions had placed George and Mrs Dixon side by side. And, seen like that, their link grew strong.

Mrs Dixon, with her drawn-out rogue vowels, hailed from the north of England. She'd lost her son. She'd remarried. She was utterly extrinsic to Elizabeth's scheme of retribution.

George had run from a good northern home, leaving behind a truth that wouldn't go away. But George's father may well have died by now. The burden of loyalty on the mother would have been lifted. Perhaps she'd built a new life with another man. That woman could be Mrs Dixon . . . it *had* to be.

Leave it to Anselm, he thought excitedly, gratefully.

Who better to bring George back to that place of first departure, than Anselm, whose question had reached so deep into the Bradshaw history? Elizabeth had prepared the means by which Anselm could reclaim his own regret.

Leave it to Anselm.

Why say this to Inspector Cartwright? Because Elizabeth foresaw that this tireless policewoman would be devastated – because she was a servant of the law that would once again disappoint an honourable man.

Leave it to Anselm.

'Can I visit Mrs Dixon?' said Anselm keenly, turning to the Prior.

'Yes.' He'd taken to examining the garth, as though the benefactor had demanded a written report with several appendices. 'What were Elizabeth's stipulations?' he asked, rising.

'To call uninvited and to listen rather than speak.'

'Sound advice,' replied the Prior. He smiled benignly, and then shuffled through the cloister, hands thrust behind his belt.

Anselm went to check for mail in the bursar's office, expecting to find some fresh tobacco, obtained by stealth at the hands of Louis, who'd had business in the village. On the way Anselm fell to thinking about Nicholas Glendinning. There was no need for him to know what Sister Dorothy had disclosed. It all happened a long time ago. And since then Elizabeth had become someone totally different. The truth need not be told, he thought awkwardly.

Brooding on this conundrum, Anselm reached into his pigeon-hole. There were two items. One was a manila envelope from Louis wrapped in tape. The other was a letter from an unknown hand, postmarked London. He opened it and read:

Dear Father Anselm,
Please bring George home as soon as possible.
Yours sincerely,
Emily Bradshaw

He folded up the paper and mumbled a prayer – giving God several options, like a multiple choice – that George would make his way to Mitcham, or that someone would read Larkwood's address in his notebook, or that Mr Hillsden would strike lucky once more. All the same, Anselm felt uneasy when he should have been edging towards jubilation. It was the image of the Prior staring at the garth, thinking tangential thoughts.

2

Nancy had the day to tidy up the shop because Prosser was coming to barter with Riley at the close of play. This room of bumper puzzles would be sold. The sound of cars bashing the hump near the bridge, the sight of the flints by the railway embankment, the clang of the bell over the door: all this would pass. Riley was with the estate agent, arranging the sale of the bungalow. The world she had known was coming to an end. They were going to the seaside.

For most of Nancy's life Brighton had been the object of her dreams. Even the word shone. It was the place of childhood memories of her mum and dad, of fish and chips wrapped in newspaper, of warnings about Uncle Bertie's wayward habits. And now it was as though the pier had broken away and drifted out to sea, with her memories giving chase, like dwindling gulls. She covered her face, defeated: so much remained unresolved, undone and unspoken.

The bell rang, and she turned.

'I've come to say goodbye, Nancy.'

Mr Bradshaw's overcoat was stiff and creased with frost. His beard had thickened since she'd last seen him at the police station. There were no goggles and his eyes were pale and defenceless.

'Not just yet, please,' she entreated. 'Warm yourself, one last time.'

Mr Bradshaw sat in a small sewing chair while Nancy lit the gas fire. As the heat drugged the air, the windows streamed, and George said what he couldn't have prepared (for, as Nancy well knew, he could do that sort of thing).

'When I first came here,' he said, rubbing his hands, 'it wasn't to deceive you. I just pretended to be someone else, but I've only told you the truth about myself. There've been no lies between us.'

'Thank you.'

Mr Bradshaw inched his boots towards the fire and vapour rose off the caps. This is how I shall always think of you, thought Nancy: steaming as if you'd been hung out to dry.

'An old man once gave me a golden rule,' continued Mr Bradshaw. '"Don't be lukewarm, old friend," he said. "That's the only route to mercy or reward." It's the reason I came, Nancy. I'd walked away from the trial, and this was my last chance to go back, to make up. I might have failed, but something happened that I hadn't thought possible, and it has made losing worth the candle: I didn't expect to become your friend.'

'Thank you,' said Nancy again, warmly. Emotion wouldn't let her say much more. She glanced back at her life, at its many candles, and the burnt-out stubs. It was like one of those big stands with tiers in a church. Was this really the Golden Rule: to keep on lighting another wick, when the wax always melted? To keep on hoping, no matter what? She mastered herself by making a confession.

'You left behind a plastic bag full of notebooks,' announced Nancy. 'I'm afraid I read some of them.' To show that she'd made good the wrong, she added swiftly, 'I also took the liberty of returning them to your wife.'

At first Mr Bradshaw didn't reply – he nodded at the first part and then shook his head at the second, which Nancy took as a sort of quits, since one cancelled out the other, like in the ledger at Lawton's – but then he said, 'I hope Emily reads them.'

With a slap of each hand on a knee, Mr Bradshaw stood up, and said, 'Well, I'd better be making tracks.'

'Where to?' asked Nancy, surprised by the worry in her voice.

'I don't know.'

'Have you ever been to Brighton?' she blurted out.

'No,' said Mr Bradshaw, checking his buttons, 'but I've heard of the pier.'

'There's two,' stammered Nancy. 'The West Pier, which is falling into the sea, and the Palace.' She wanted to share it with him, while it was still good, before it was altered. She raced like a guide in a tourist office, telling Mr Bradshaw what she'd told him many times before. He always listened as if it were new, as if it were fresh. 'I went there every summer, with my mum and dad and Uncle Bertie. We stopped going after I got married. There was all sorts . . . magicians, jugglers . . . the helter-skelter . . . a clock tower . . . and right at the end a funfair with a ghost train. We'd walk around eating rock, wasting pennies in the one-armed bandits. But it was the sea I liked most, now grey, now blue, stretching away, lonely. Long ago, I heard that the whole lot was slowly falling to bits . . . like me' – she smiled, looking down at her legs, the strong veins behind the tights – 'but it's been completely renovated. Nowadays the deckchairs are free.'

'Magnificent,' whispered Mr Bradshaw, sitting down again.

Boldly, but decisively, Nancy said, 'Would you like a holiday by the seaside?'

Mr Bradshaw's agreement was far more emphatic than his surprise at the forwardness of the question. Nancy drew some directions that would take him along Limehouse Cut to the agreed meeting place. She wrote down the time he should be there, and she gave him her watch. Throughout he made a show of impatient nodding, as if the mastery of such details was child's play. After Mr Bradshaw had gone, Nancy tenderly thought: The great thing about someone who's lost their memory is that they're so used to forgetting answers that they don't ask too many questions. And that was a help, because Mr Bradshaw hadn't asked what Mr Riley might think of her invitation; or what Nancy proposed to do with the options that remained open to her; or how she, too, might take the route to mercy or reward. It would have taken Nancy a very long time indeed to explain.

3

Perhaps Nick's father had dropped a hint along these lines: 'He hasn't come to terms with the passing of his mother. He could do with a treat . . . something to take him out of himself.' Or maybe it was simple generosity of spirit. Either way, the tubby executive at British Telecom – last seen sipping sherry at the funeral – had offered Nick a treat closed to the general public for donkeys' years: a view from the top of the BT Tower. The executive was called Reginald Smyth.

'One hundred and eighty-nine metres high,' he said, reverently, on the thirty-fourth floor. 'Sways twenty centimetres in a high wind.'

Reginald was a plump and ponderous man with active eyes, and a commiserating manner. He'd lost all his hair save for white curls above each ear. Standing with joined hands, he ushered in fact after fact as if they might soothe the bruised and broken. 'As you can see, there are no walls, just windows and, of course, the floor rotates, obtaining a full circuit in twenty-two minutes . . .'

Nick missed the details about tonnage, nylon tyres and speed. He was already gazing at the sprawling majesty of London. Sitting down, he picked out St John's Wood, hazy under the threat of snow and, with an alarming shudder, the floor began to move.

From this suburban pinnacle Nick looked upon recent events

as if he were detached from their happening and significance. It was calming; it was a treat. He listened and watched while the world seemed to go round. Reginald, being a man with a sense of moment, kept a respectful distance.

'We had a long-drawn-out argument,' Charles had admitted, clinking more ice into more scotch. After the visit to Doctor Okoye, Elizabeth wanted to tell Nick about Riley and his place in her life.

'I didn't know about the heart condition,' said Charles, handing Nick a glass. 'Your mother only said that maybe it was time to retire, that the cut and thrust was all getting a bit much for her valves.'

Husband and wife toyed with selling up and fixing the tap in Saint Martin's Haven. Led by Elizabeth, they talked of all the things they agreed about, until Charles realised she was trying to seduce him. Snapping a thumb and finger, he said, 'No.' He was against any disclosure of the past, not because he was ashamed, but because he was frightened: for Nick.

'There was no need for you to know' – he hunched his shoulders and squinted – 'You'd be shocked. You'd been protected. And what did it matter? She'd moved on, *wonderfully*.'

That notion of *protection* irritated Nick. It was demeaning. It was a kind of pity that insinuated measurement: it cut love down to size – for Nick, not knowing all, had therefore not *loved* all. He'd loved only partially. His father failed to realise that Nick's heart was greater than his needs or expectations; that the woman of his dreams was Sonia, the prostitute in *Crime and Punishment*. But he hadn't said that out loud.

The revolving deck groaned suddenly on its rails, sending a stab of fear through Nick. He threw his eyes to work, spying the Inns

299

of Court, and further on, the Isle of Dogs, where towers were being raised from the mist at Canary Wharf. Nick's attention shuddered to the east, to things known but out of sight, to Hornchurch Marshes and the Four Lodges. He thought of the cold wind, the small shaved head, the lingering torchlight; and he heard again the unnerving pity in that voice.

Nick's parents had never fully resolved the disagreement, though Charles won the first round on points. While Elizabeth urged Nick to find a practice in Primrose Hill, Charles pushed for paid indolence in Australia. (He wanted his son out of the way, while Elizabeth went after Riley. If it came to nothing, then Nick would be left *unscathed*. Should an arrest become imminent, then, perhaps, the matter could be re-examined.)

The word 'unscathed' also irritated Nick, because it was the twin of 'protection'.

The second round began when Elizabeth turned to letter writing, those lures of affection and melancholy, while Charles (guessing the stratagem) countered with more temptations of distance and wonder. This last had been a subtle ploy, for Charles was drawing on what bound father and son together: the dream of escapades and foreign peril.

'In the end, she was several moves ahead,' said Charles affectionately, spilling whisky as he poured from the decanter. He was weary, his sleeves rolled up and a tartan tie askew. A shirt-tail hung out like a waiter's cloth. 'I knew nothing of the key, or Father Anselm's role as her unwitting understudy.' He paused as if ashamed by the complaint in his own voice, the hint of resentment. 'For your sake, I'd hoped that this business would pass you by; as still it might.'

'For your sake,' repeated Nick quietly. 'As still it might?'

'Let's get back to normal,' said Charles, with a sudden note of beseeching. 'Let's . . . let's go to Skomer.'

Nick laughed, not so much at what Charles had said, as his appearance: the red face, the clothing in disarray and the precariously sinking glass. Charles took the laughter for assent and joined in heartily.

London kept turning and Nick kept watching, high above all that had happened, glad that it was over, perhaps grateful – if he were honest – that he had a protective father. When the twenty-two minutes had elapsed the floor stopped, and Nick was facing St John's Wood.

'The lift moves at six metres per second,' said Mr Smyth, more relaxed, hands in his suit pockets. Nick guessed that he was the sort of executive who liked to don the hard hat and chat with the lads about the tricks of cable installation.

As the narrow compartment plunged down to ground level, Nick ignored some more statistics, marvelling rather at his father's determination, his refusal to compromise with his wife, the captain of matters practical. This time Charles had taken the lead and called the shots, forcing his mother's hand. It was the sort of bull-headed drive the bank had wanted and never got.

'Who's Mrs Dixon?' Nick had ventured, before going to bed.

'I haven't the faintest idea.' Charles had rolled down his sleeves, pulled his tie up and dabbed at the spillage with his shirt-tail. Nick watched him carefully . . . and he just couldn't be sure: was this the truth or another species of protection?

The lift doors opened and Nick showered thanks on Mr Smyth. It was, he replied, the *least* he could do, adding, as if he hadn't been heard the first time:

'I must say, your mother was a quite re*mark*able woman.'

301

4

'You're a hard man, Riley,' said Prosser. He puffed on his cigar and nudged the peak of his cloth cap.

'A fair one.'

'Twenty-five grand it is, then.'

The figure wasn't quite accurate, but it was in keeping with the outward show of honesty. Prosser would pay that handsome figure into the Riley bank account first thing next morning. An extra five thousand was due now, in cash – an exchange that would trouble neither the conveyance deed nor the records of the Inland Revenue.

Prosser had a worn leather pouch of Spanish origin. Having tugged it from the inside of his heavy overcoat, he opened it slowly, lowering his hands to show how much he'd brought. Then he counted out the bills, licking his fingers, making it painfully clear that he was handing over far less than he'd expected – that he was a harder man than Riley.

'Wyecliffe will do the paperwork,' said Riley, and he tossed high a bunch of keys.

Catching them, Prosser replied nobly, 'The traditions of your business will continue.'

'I doubt it.'

Prosser was jubilant. He sucked air through his teeth, breathing in a mix of furniture wax and butane.

'When you're ready,' he said, 'I'll lock up. I bid you good day, ma'am.' The last affectation came with a bow for Nancy, after which he swaggered outside to linger on the pavement. He winked to an imaginary audience, and licked the butt of his cigar.

Cars smashed over the hump in the road. It was nearing the

end of the day, so everyone was impatient, even Riley. As he checked the limp notes against a light bulb, he became scatty – he was looking at the pictures and not the watermarks – because every action was a movement away. Every breath was one less among these standing ruins. He was going to walk with Nancy on Brighton Pier. Something rustled at his elbow.

Nancy was holding out a plastic bag as though it were Riley's turn for the lucky dip. It was empty and she looked severe.

'Let me carry the money,' she said, pronouncing each word distinctly. 'It's my shop, remember.'

Riley didn't have the guts to refuse – Nancy had been acting funny. Not that she'd said or done anything. It was just a sense that she'd already gone from Poplar and left him behind. He wanted to catch her up. Without a word he wrapped the notes in an elastic band and dropped them into the bag.

'You can trust me, you know,' said Nancy under her breath.

She was being funny again, though Riley couldn't put his finger on how. But she made him think of trust: it had held them together, even in the breaking.

Nancy lifted up her skirt and stuffed the money beneath her tights, across her stomach. Then she went into the back room and came back with a grey canvas rucksack. Riley had found it in the cellar of a mountaineer.

'I want to pick up some bricks by the canal,' said Nancy, adding proudly, 'for my herb bed.'

Riley was aghast. 'You want to go along the Cut with five grand in your tights?'

'No one will look.'

'Nancy, have you ever heard of muggers . . . villains?'

'It's never happened before.'

Prosser called out, 'Oi! I'm freezing out here.'

'I want to finish the bed,' said Nancy flatly.

303

'All right, fine,' sighed Riley, giving up. He'd follow Nancy to hell, never mind Limehouse Cut.

They walked side by side, Riley shouldering the rucksack. The sky was reddish brown like a bruised fruit. Beneath it, in the near distance, a bonfire kicked sparks into the air. Smoke billowed and a smell of rubber drifted along the towpath beside the Cut. The hush was a trick. Somewhere ahead was a den of foxes. When it grew dark, they'd scream and it was like a feast of murder. Nancy broke step. She'd seen a brick. Examining its edges, she said, 'It all begins with Quilling Road.'

'What does?'

'Our trouble.'

Riley closed his eyes and stumbled slightly. He didn't want to hear of that place. An old voice came out of him, and he listened, 'How was I to know?'

He hated the weakness and the whining and the cowardice. But they were weapons, and he'd learned how to use them like an automaton.

'Of course not,' said Nancy sympathetically. She stepped behind Riley to struggle with the toggles on the rucksack. She dropped the brick inside, and left the flap open.

They walked on, coming closer to the fire. Riley wondered, Could it really be that easy? Was the future an open field? He felt a shudder of excitement. With Prosser's money he'd buy some new shoes. He'd chuck away that camouflage jacket.

Nancy bent down, complaining about her old knees. With more groaning about her limbs, she picked up two bricks, and said, 'It was terrible when that boy drowned and the police tried to pin it on you.'

The comment was like a smack in the teeth. Nancy had

never referred to that before. Like Quilling Road, it was another crater in the dark. They walked around them. But now she spoke as if she were in the laundrette with Babycham.

Smarting, Riley said, 'Cartwright has never let me go.' He whistled quietly, because he'd strayed to the edges of truth, close enough to fall in.

'I kno-o-ow,' sang Nancy, sharing his indignation, and he could just see her, nudging Babycham's ribs.

Nancy put the bricks in the rucksack and Riley shrugged the shoulder straps into a more comfortable position. After that drowning, he'd expected the Major to turn up at Poplar – to target him with that old, quiet urging. But he never came. Their last meeting had been at the Old Bailey, when he'd said, 'They can lock you up, but they can't stop you taking that first step.' The Major had been brittle and despairing. Where was he now? What would he tell him to say to Nancy?

It was dim now, and the edges of the canal had blended into its banks. The sky had lost its colour and joined the slate on the straggling warehouses. Nancy's puzzled voice was muffled while she rummaged near a hedge of barbed wire.

'So that's why they hauled you in again?'

'What do you think?' Riley made it sound like a 'Yes'. He didn't know what else to say. They hadn't spoken of the arrest since the day he'd been released without charge. She'd been off-colour afterwards, and he hadn't been able to read her. Suddenly, she was tugging at the rucksack.

'Are you all right?' asked Nancy, as though she were anxious for his health.

'Fine, absolutely fine.'

Carefully, she laid three bricks on top of the others.

'Steady on,' he rasped. 'I'm not . . .' – *Stallone, Mad Max,*

305

Bruce: the hamsters' names ran into one another like a furry pile-up but a name popped out, like it was shoved – '... Mr Universe.'

Riley leaned forward and increased his speed, as if to get away from that reminder of Arnold. At the fire, a gang of youths brandished flaming branches. They danced and whooped and stared. A car tyre lay smouldering near the bank. It was almost dark now. The path narrowed and Nancy dropped back, leaving Riley to move on ahead. He looked aside into the dull, smooth water. And then he thought, as if tripped, Why do I keep remembering what the Major said? Why can't I just forget an old soldier's hopes, his insane confidence?

'I wonder what happened to Arnold,' asked Nancy faintly.

'God knows.'

There was a long, withering pause. Then Riley heard Nancy's feet in the grass, as if she were swishing a scythe. His thoughts became bitter, remonstrating: the journey from Paddington to this point by the Cut owed a great deal to John Bradshaw – for that death had marked his soul – but who took the laurel? The Major? No, that honour went to a *hamster*. Even in conversion, if that is what it was, I'm a contemptible specimen.

'That's the lot,' she said with resignation. One after the other she placed four bricks into the remaining space.

'Bloody hell, Nancy,' he gasped, 'what are you trying to do?' He fastened the clips across his chest, linking the arm straps. After a few steps, he glimpsed the hunched figure of a man by a wall ... someone who was watching him. Riley swung around, wanting Nancy's help. 'I'm sorry, there's too many,' he whispered, genuinely sorry, 'I can't carry this lot.'

'Neither can I.'

'What?'

Riley couldn't see her face. She walked slowly towards him.

306

He knew what was going to happen. Nancy pushed him with a finger and he fell backwards. As he left the towpath, he wondered why it was that he felt relief.

5

At school, Anselm had met a Jesuit teacher who considered familiarity with the life and work of John Bunyan to be a valuable adjunct to the onset of adolescence. First, that exemplar, in his youth, had been haunted by demonic dreams; second, he'd suffered a strange sickness that had made him blaspheme atrociously and want to renounce the benefits of redemption. To counter these inclinations, so often manifest in the young, the amused Jesuit would read choice excerpts from *Pilgrim's Progress*, the allegory of a burdened man, fleeing a burning city.

This warm memory touched Anselm because he was sitting on a bench near the author's tomb in Bunhill Fields. At his side sat Mrs Dixon in a long overcoat of russet tweed. She wore sturdy shoes and thick socks. A paisley scarf had been tied around her head with a knot under the chin. She'd brought Anselm to this garden of peace without a word. Thousands of tombs stood crowded among the planes, oaks and limes. The light came to them through the rafters of these winter trees.

'I had already decided to speak to you about my son,' said Mrs Dixon finally.

Anselm presumed he would now learn why she hadn't mentioned George's name at their first meeting. A jitter of excitement made him impatient. Leave it to Anselm.

'I told someone recently that Elizabeth's last words to me were that she wouldn't be coming any more. That wasn't true.' Mrs Dixon examined the backs of her hands. 'Elizabeth said a lot more: that she'd found Graham; that the time of the lie was over.'

For a second or so, Anselm didn't understand what had been said. His mind lay with George Bradshaw, not Graham Riley. When he clicked, it was as though he'd stepped out of a musty matinee into the chilling daylight. 'Your son?' he asked foolishly.

Mrs Dixon nodded. Her face became blank, as if all her emotions had been drained into a jar for safe-keeping. Decisively, she said, 'But that was not the lie.' Mrs Irene Dixon spoke softly and resolutely. 'I wish I'd stayed in Lancashire, but I went south, to start over. All that I knew had changed, because Graham's father died in the pit, under thirty tons of coal and rock.'

Mother and child came to London, encouraged by an aunt – a seamstress – who had a house with rooms to spare, and a business with more work than she could handle. These were hard times because Mrs Dixon was a widow at barely twenty. But then she met Walter, a big, handsome man with responsibility and a house of his own in Dagenham. He was the manager of a warehouse in Bow; he hired and fired. He ruled the roost. After courting for a year, they were married, and by the end of the second year, there was a child on the way.

This is the beginning, thought Anselm. From this moment onwards, it is all an unfolding. He understood everything, but with such speed that his insight into what would happen became foreshortened, and he lost the detail. He was left with the first simple realisation that Walter Steadman was Elizabeth's father; that Riley was her half-brother.

The two children grew up under the one roof, but did not enjoy equal favour. Walter didn't mean it, said Mrs Dixon, but he was hard on Graham, who was not his own, and soft on Elizabeth, who was. The inequality of affection was ever present and Graham simply couldn't understand why: they were, after all (he thought), the same flesh and blood. As Graham grew older, it became obvious: he was not a Steadman.

'The boy became the shadow of his father, my first love,' said Mrs Dixon. 'And Walter was a jealous man, even of the dead. It was pitiful that a boy so small could pose a threat to a man so big.' She hesitated, as if she'd come to a defining moment. 'And then the warehouse closed and Walter lost his job.

'It might not sound much,' said Mrs Dixon, after another break, 'but the big man who'd told everyone else what to do for ten years was unemployed. The only work he could find was selling pies from a barrow on the pavement. He lost his self-esteem. The men he'd sacked mocked him. He drank what he earned, and I had to work twice as much. And when he was in drink, he didn't control himself any more. The small things loomed large in his head. You could say he was the same; you could say he'd changed.'

Walter hit Graham and Mrs Dixon. But he never touched Elizabeth. He wanted to be someone else with her – the person he could have been – and that longing survived even the sickness that came with beer. Graham, however, became Walter's target.

'When things go wrong in your life,' intoned Mrs Dixon, 'you look for someone to blame. And you always settle on someone who's *different*. Graham was different, in every way, and all of them small.'

According to his teacher, Graham was clever. He asked questions that didn't have easy answers. He shrank from the rougher games, preferring to collect things – all manner of rubbish that he thought interesting, like pebbles and bottle tops. His arms and legs were thin. When he tried to help with the shopping, it was always too heavy. It showed up the sheer difference between

309

him and Walter. And on one fateful, drunken day Walter mocked him, just as those sober men had mocked Walter.

'No son of mine would collect bottle tops,' said Walter, swaying.

'But I *am* your son,' snapped Graham defiantly.

'No you're not.'

'What?'

'You heard.'

'That was how he found out,' said Mrs Dixon. 'He seized hold of me, wanting to know who his father was, his real name, what had happened, why he'd never been told . . . endless questions . . . It was as though Walter's rage – all of it – had infected him. From that day, Graham refused to call Walter his father. He dropped Steadman and became Riley. And the rage I'd seen . . . It simply vanished.'

While Mrs Dixon was speaking, Anselm began to recover a fraction of the insight that had struck him and gone. He remembered the conversation with Elizabeth about the death of his mother, knowing that she'd been harvesting his experience. He said to Mrs Dixon, 'What happened to Walter?'

'We were at the top of the stairs,' she replied, as if she were dictating a statement to the police. Her eyes were to the front, her back straight. 'There'd been a lot of shouting. He swung out but keeled over on the step and went down, like a tree. I fell back, trying to keep my balance, so I didn't see; I just heard him tumbling down, and then, after a second or so, a bang. When I looked, there was a large heap on the floor. I called the ambulance and they took him away, but he was dead.'

'I'm sorry,' muttered Anselm.

'Don't be,' she replied. 'I was relieved . . . glad that he was gone.'

Staring ahead once more, Mrs Dixon resumed what she'd planned to say: the opening up of a lie. Again, she seemed to be recording a deposition.

'A week or two later a policeman knocked on the door. He knew Walter. He knew about his temper and the violence. He told me the doctor had found a long wound on the head. He examined the stairs. He took measurements of a tread, and its edge. I said nothing about the bang that I'd heard after the fall, that Graham had been downstairs, that the poker was missing. In due course, the police concluded it had been an accident. My son, however, had stopped eating. He was sick. One night, I held his hands in mine and asked if he'd seen the poker. He pulled himself free, hid behind a pillow, and said, "I've thrown it in the Four Lodges." The next day he was gone. He was seventeen. I haven't seen him since. Everyone said it was because he'd lost his dad.'

Bunhill Fields is a wonderful place, thought Anselm, wanting to flee those stairs, that hallway. The Pieman must have taken shape among its shadows and blood: a name coined from other people's contempt, an engrossment of rage and abuse, tame to Riley, but towering over those whom he would terrorise. Elizabeth had walked along the same corridors, among the same shadows. Anselm felt her presence. She'd worn a delicate perfume that didn't seem to fade. She was always very *clean*, in strictly tailored clothes, with sharply cut hair.

Elizabeth blamed herself for Graham's running away, for Walter's treatment of him. And Mrs Dixon, against herself, blamed Elizabeth: not with a single word, but with a host of manners. On a cold night Elizabeth made a fire. Looking for the poker, she asked her mother where it might be.

'Graham threw it away.'

'Why?'

311

Mrs Dixon didn't answer the question directly. She let the silence do it for her. A month later Elizabeth disappeared. Everyone said it was because she'd lost her dad and her brother.

Anselm knew what had happened next. Sister Dorothy had come to the house of Mrs Steadman. Her decision to do what Elizabeth wanted had been instantaneous and heartbreaking. Mother and daughter, without saying so, had agreed to hush up a murder. You can't do that sort of thing under the same roof.

'I next saw my daughter a year ago,' said Mrs Dixon, without emotion, enunciating her words. 'She traced me through my national insurance number, because I had remarried . . . to a wonderful man, who would have been a wonderful father to anyone's children.' Mrs Dixon swallowed hard and carried on with the job in hand.

Elizabeth had learned of her heart condition, and that it was hereditary. Mrs Dixon underwent the tests with a Doctor Okoye, who pronounced her clear. Big, strapping Walter, it seemed, had been a fundamentally weak man. But that was not why Elizabeth had come.

'She told me that Graham had built a new life,' said Mrs Dixon, 'but not a nice one.'

Not for the first time in his life, Anselm marvelled at the word 'nice', and the wonderful uses to which it was frequently put.

'She told me that the only way to save him was to bring him to court to answer for the murder of her father. It wasn't revenge she wanted, I knew that. She was talking about . . . what was right. But I refused.'

'Why?'

'Because if it was anyone's fault, it wasn't Graham's, or Elizabeth's, it was mine. I failed to protect him. I thought that if

312

I stick by Walter, then maybe he'll change back to who he'd been – who he *was* with Elizabeth – that his anger might boil dry; that he might wake up and see Graham as . . . different, yes, but not a threat. I'm the one who put that poker in Graham's hand. All I ever said to him was that Walter has tempers.'

The quietness of Bunhill Fields filled the pause. Nothing moved, not even the trees, which were so full of life. For once, it seemed strange.

'Elizabeth came each week, trying to persuade me. I refused. Then, on the day she died, I received her last call and her last words.'

'The time of the lie is over,' Anselm said to himself. To this he added the final message for Inspector Cartwright, uttered seconds before: Leave it to Anselm.

'Mrs Dixon,' said Anselm, 'as I'm sure you know' – he watched her nodding, because Elizabeth had already told her – 'I will have to inform the police. They will interview you. Graham will be tried for murder. You, too, may well be charged, because of your silence. Do you realise this?'

'Yes,' she replied, as if she were already in court.

Anselm regarded her with compassion and said, 'Why did you change your mind?'

'Because,' said Mrs Dixon defiantly, proudly, 'I have met my grandson, Nicholas. And I do not want his life to rest on a lie – on a false understanding of who he is and where he comes from – as Graham's did. One day he might learn the truth about his family. I do not think he would thank his mother for the story she dreamed up in its place. It is, of course, what she wanted, what she'd asked of me. I didn't appreciate why until I saw Nicholas . . . He looks just like Walter.'

*

Anselm took Mrs Dixon's arm, and they walked slowly, like mother and son, along the lanes of Bunhill Fields. In their shared quiet, he thought of Riley's early life, and of murder, undetected and forgotten, and what it might do to a man. And he thought of Bunyan, whose youth had been marred by four chief sins: dancing, ringing the bells of the parish church, playing tipcat and reading the history of Sir Bevis of Southampton.

6

For the fourth day in a row, George ordered a full English breakfast (with Cumberland sausage). Nancy opted for the kipper (from Craster), explaining, 'You only live once,' which was very true. They sat in a bay window of the Royal Guesthouse, looking at the waves trimmed with foam. Far off, daft gulls dipped and rose like kites. It would be another windy, wonderful day.

The entries in George's notebook would have told him that Nancy had withdrawn thirty-six thousand, four hundred and twenty pounds and fifty-two pence from the Riley bank account; that facing rooms had been booked in Brighton for a week (meals included); that she had bought a two-for-the-price-of-one packet of envelopes from Woolworths. However, he didn't need to remind himself of their comical project, any more than he needed to be told of Nancy's horror and guilt over all that Riley had done, or of her remorse for the murder of John. It was, as they say, written on her face. She was not to blame, by any stretch of the imagination. And yet, on their first night, over Hereford beef with Yorkshire pudding, Nancy had said, 'I share the fault, because I share the disgrace' – a stinging phrase which revealed that Nancy accused herself because she'd known what her husband was like, and she'd turned away.

When breakfast was over they prepared some envelopes, put on their coats and set about the business of the day. They strolled along the esplanade towards the Palace of Fun.

'How about that one?' asked Nancy.

George nodded.

Coming towards them was a young girl, pushing a pram against the grain of the wind. Her knuckles were blue. Judging by the noise, the child was not happy.

'Excuse me,' said George, 'we represent a secret society whose object is the benefit of humanity.'

The girl's eyes flicked from George to Nancy and back to George again. She said, 'Sorry, I don't need anything.'

'I'm afraid the steering committee does not agree,' said George severely. 'Here's a thousand pounds.'

Nancy pulled an envelope from her handbag, and held it out. The young mother stared, as if it were a warrant from the bailiff.

'The only condition is this,' said George, suddenly kind, 'under no circumstances are you to spend it *wisely*. We wish you a very good day.'

And with that, the delegates crossed the main road, heading towards the forecourt of Brighton Pier. Near the entrance, a Salvation Army brass band was playing carols. The cornets and trombones glittered in a semi-circle, pointing down slightly. Nancy approached them respectfully, walking round the arc of bonnets, caps and polished shoes.

'Hark the Herald Angels Sing' . . . the words rode on the back of the hymn, melancholy and joyful.

George mumbled the rest of the verse, gazing at the turrets of a dome and two flags fluttering against a clean blue sky. Suddenly, Nancy was at his side. Ceremonially, they walked onto the long quay as if it were a nave, as though the world itself were a cathedral of unutterable magnificence.

George's spirit soared higher and higher with the brazen gulls. There were no clouds, no shadows, just the harsh seaside light. The wind carried the smell of sand and bladderwrack, shells and salt.

'Peace on earth and mercy mild, God and sinners reconciled.'

Nancy handed out ten-pound notes as they walked along, as if they were flyers for Unimaginable Warehouse Bargains. People stopped and stared. An old woman in black with bowed legs waddled towards them, head down like a bull, her hair harnessed by a net.

'Excuse me,' said George, 'here's five hundred pounds for your trouble.'

'Are you mad?' she replied, straining to get her neck upright.

'I was, but am no more.'

She glanced around warily. 'Is this *Candid Camera*?'

'Indeed not, madam,' said George, like a magician. 'This is real life.'

'Thank you, but no.' Her head went down and off she went, burrowing through the wind to the town.

At his side Nancy was laughing. She pulled off her yellow hat with its black spots, and forced a hand through her hair. Breathing deeply, she closed her eyes and threw back her head. Her nose was bright red at the end.

'Let it be known,' cried George, raising his arms like Charlton Heston, 'that for one week a kind of justice ruled on Brighton Pier.'

'Joyful all ye nations rise, join the triumph of the skies' . . . the sound was fading. As they walked on distributing their leaflets, George glanced over his shoulder: he could still see the caps, the bonnets and the glitter of instruments.

'. . . Glory to the new-born King.'

*

316

In the Palace of Fun, Nancy bought tickets for the dodgem cars. The till was wrapped in tinsel and a Christmas tree was chained to a bracket. A girl in the booth wore a Santa hat and she called the management when George gave her two hundred pounds. The police turned up and particulars were taken. When everyone in a suit or uniform was happy – actually, not so happy – George and Nancy climbed into a rather small Rolls-Royce. With a crackling of sparks, the music started and they were off.

Driving always made George thoughtful, and present circumstances proved no exception. Nancy had pushed her husband into Limehouse Cut; George had witnessed the fall, and made a note of the details that night on the train (first class). With a glass of champagne in one hand, and a pen in the other, Nancy added an important postscript to explain that Riley's point of entry had been adjacent to a boat, moored by the canal wall. George, however, was still troubled on his friend's account: what would she do when all the money was gone?

'Where will you go, Nancy, when this is all over?' he asked.

'I haven't a clue.' Her hands were folded on her bag and her knees were squashed against the dashboard. 'What about you?'

'No idea,' said George. He turned to Nancy, wanting to thank her for their time together, for this brief, shining . . .

George thwacked a yellow Lamborghini. It was his fault. He hadn't been looking. The jolt was so severe that stars twinkled behind his eyes. When he could see straight, he saw a police officer – the same one as last time – talking to his radio and summoning George with a gloved hand. Thinking the world had turned upside down (leaving aside his and Nancy's efforts in this regard), he drove to the rubber kerb. Ten minutes later they were taken in a squad car to the station. George was left in the waiting room and Nancy was taken to an office with a panel of frosted glass in the door.

Twenty minutes later George and Nancy had been released. For a long time Nancy did not speak.

'George,' she said evenly, 'when they checked us out for giving money away, my name caused a stir on the computer.' She sat down on the low wall of someone's garden. 'I was reported missing two days ago, and yesterday Inspector Cartwright charged Riley with the murder of his stepfather. Without being asked, he confessed to the murder of your son and to everything that happened at Quilling Road. He'll be going to prison for a long time.'

George felt as though he were back in the Roller, seeing stars; that the world must right itself at any moment. He lowered himself onto the wall and took his friend by the hand.

'What will you do, Nancy?'

With her hat pulled down over her ears, she looked resolved.

'I've two days left in Brighton,' she said, as if doing her sums. 'I've got ten thousand pounds in my pocket. And I've got agreeable company for the duration. What else could a girl want?'

George studied her face, its softness.

'And when my time's up and I'm broke,' she said, gazing at George as if it might be wrong, as if he might never understand, 'I'll go back to Riley.'

Side by side, they walked into the wind and the sun, heading back towards the band, with the music growing stronger.

'Someone has to love him,' she said simply.

7

Nick came to Larkwood not so much because Roddy had urged it upon him, but because it was fitting. He'd begun a kind of journey with Father Anselm, and now it was over; there were no more secrets. It was the right time to say goodbye.

'Because I'm a monk,' said Father Anselm, wrapped in a long woollen cloak, 'I am a creature of ritual. Symbols help me understand things.' They were sitting on a bench of dressed stone – a chunk of the medieval abbey. It faced the Lark and a row of empty plant pots. 'Your mother and I sat here at the outset of her endeavour,' he continued. 'Perhaps it's not a bad place to examine where it ends.'

A week ago, Nick had felt irritated at his father's desire to *protect*, the energy spent on leaving his son *unscathed*. He'd found it patronising. Nick was a grown man, a doctor. He'd swum with cane toads. But now he knew that Walter Steadman had been his grandfather, killed by a boy who'd grown to kill as a man and who, for good measure, was Nick's half-uncle. Roddy had come round to explain these niceties because, following Riley's confession, a trial became inevitable and Nick would soon find out – if not from him, or his father, then the national press, who would probably be competing with one another for the most punchy by-line to describe his mother. It transpired that Roddy had known of Elizabeth's short time on the street, but no more. He'd learned the rest from Father Anselm.

After Roddy had tumbled into a taxi, Nick finally appreciated his father's bullish resistance. Even after Elizabeth's death, Charles had clung on to a slender hope: that Father Anselm would fail; that Mrs Dixon would enjoy a long and private retirement. The matter of Walter Steadman had been the issue upon which Nick's parents had been most divided. And Nick wholly endorsed his father's reading of the compass: what was the point in bringing it out into the open? Why had she set up this dreadful, public annihilation of the living? For whose benefit? Only that of the dead. Nick wanted to be protected, frankly, and left unscathed. He had said all this to Father Anselm on the way to the bench of dressed stone. Worn out, he slumped down, arms on his thighs. He looked ahead at the river and the teetering plant pots.

'Your mother ran away from a house in which her father had been murdered,' said Father Anselm steadily. 'She didn't admire the man, although he'd made a claim upon her affection. That must have been difficult for her: to see his brutality, and his gentleness; to wonder how both could rise from the same soil; to try and give credit for one while condemning the other. She was, of course, just a child. And it was as a child that she turned her back on the gravest offence known to the criminal law. She'd made an unspoken agreement with her mother to remain silent, as though it were a payment she owed to her abused sibling. Elizabeth could do this only by wiping out her past – every memory, every smell, every taste, every sound – and by creating a new history of imagined sensations. And she succeeded. She launched a career, she married and she had a child. But then the half-brother she'd protected appeared in this wonderful universe of her own making.'

The monk reached down and picked up some twigs. He snapped them, while he thought himself into this other livid experience.

'When Riley instructed your mother to represent him, he did so, in the first place, to silence George. But there was more to it than that. He wanted to destroy an achievement that, to him, must have been an unbearable sight. Since their last meeting, she had changed beyond recognition; while he, the other run-away, could only look upon the same squalid reflection. So it's worth pausing to consider what Riley now demanded from your mother. In the first place, he was holding up, like a mirror, her silence over Walter's murder. He was saying, "Look well, look hard: your position as an officer of the court is a sham, it always has been; and your likeness is just as soiled as mine." And nowhere could that have been acutely felt than when Elizabeth was obliged to cross-examine Anji, staring – as she must have been – at the unhappy face of her past.'

Father Anselm looked to Nick, inviting him to speak, but his mind had drained of everything save what he now heard. It was of course a fancy, but there was something in the monk's manner, his choice of words, that seemed to speak truly of Elizabeth, a mother who'd wanted to speak to her son.

'Now, what did Elizabeth do in that terrible situation?' Father Anselm reached for more twigs. '*She surrendered*. But why? This woman had given her life to the law, she believed in due process. How could she suffer his *winning*, and the *defeat* of everything she had valued? That is the most taxing question. I think I know the answer.

'Riley asked for your mother, believing this: She helped me once; she'll help me again. That was a huge error of judgement. Elizabeth had changed in more ways than he could imagine. Her attachment to the law was so great that I think she would have *seized* the opportunity to expose the facts of her life, regard-less of the personal cost. But she didn't. What Riley didn't know, and this is what saved him, was that Elizabeth now had a son. Nick, I think she cooperated with Riley for you. To protect you. To leave you unscathed. To keep intact the world she'd created for you with Charles.'

Nick didn't like Father Anselm using the words of his own

321

complaint, but the monk did so kindly and tentatively, as if he were passing them back across the counter. Nick looked to the river and a strange mist rising on the other side, stretched thin like a silver table. In a kind of daze, he listened to Father Anselm's exposition.

The price paid by Elizabeth was high, he said reluctantly. By continuing the case, she broke the rules of her profession. By asking him to cross-examine George, she hoped, nonetheless, to lose the trial. Even that went awry because, unfortunately, the stooge had been lucky. Throughout the following years, nothing unsettled Elizabeth's resolve to remain silent – not the letter from Mrs Bradshaw, not the death of that poor woman's son. The strong spirit of her childhood had returned. And being so resolved, she lost her faith in the law – just as long before she'd lost faith in her family.

'But then,' said Father Anselm, 'something of capital importance happened. Your mother learned that her days were counted – a moment which, I am sure, has a stillness all of its own. And in that quiet she recognised that a great lie had been allowed to take root, and that unless she acted, it would define her life. The problem, of course, was that it was too late. Your mother had already made her choice. She'd done Riley's bidding. And it is at this stage, I think, that Elizabeth's story becomes what my father used to call a corker. She decided to alter the past by changing how everything would end.'

The monk was smiling encouragement. He stood up and with a tilt of the head suggested a walk. They quietly followed the Lark and crossed a small footbridge. On the other side, they entered a field that was hard underfoot. Without a path, they tracked a furrow towards the table of mist.

'As you know,' said Father Anselm, 'your mother devised two schemes. The first was for George: to let him take away the good character of the man responsible for the death of his son. She went to extraordinary lengths to succeed because she hoped to restore his self-worth. But a great part of her energy, I am sure, arose from a blinding desire to see Riley convicted of any offence of this kind, however trivial in the eyes of the courts; to have him proved a pimp. That outcome was denied her. She failed.

'The second scheme was for herself: to bring Riley to court for a murder whose evidence she had helped to suppress. To succeed, Elizabeth had to convince her mother to reveal what she knew to the police. She failed again.'

They had reached the centre of the field and stopped. The mist was just above head height, rolling within itself.

'It might reasonably be said,' observed Father Anselm wryly, 'that I was the contingency plan. And I too failed, comprehensively.' He fixed Nick with an enquiring, kindly gaze.

'Who persuaded my grandmother to speak?' asked Nick. Whether he liked it or not, he felt himself a part of the narrative; as if it were his proper concern.

'*You did*,' said Father Anselm, quietly fervent. 'She didn't want you to live a lie – as she had done; as her children had. For no one knew better than your grandmother the cost of a lie.'

The monk started walking aimlessly, his hands moving with suppressed animation.

'It was only when I met Mrs Dixon that I understood the importance of what Elizabeth had set out to do,' he said. 'Once she'd decided to reclaim her past, the only available means was the legal system that she'd abandoned. So through each of these schemes, she was hoping to restore justice itself. She saw afresh – I'm sure of it – that the rule of law *matters,* that our attempts to punish *matter*, that to show mercy, however clumsily, *matters*.' Father Anselm turned to Nick, wrapping his cloak around his body. 'A man had been killed – your grandfather. Brute or not, his life had been taken from him. The irony is that he was a man ready to die at the drop of a hat. But that's of no consequence: a murder is a murder – be it Walter's or John's. To bring this truth to light was your mother's endeavour. She succeeded – but not through her own efforts.' He paused to reflect. 'Nick, if I can say anything to you that I'm sure I'll stand by tomorrow morning, it's this: isn't it fitting that *you* have achieved this on her behalf . . . and not some bumbling oaf like me?'

Nick agreed, reluctantly smiling.

'And who better to help your father understand,' continued the monk, 'than the son he sought to protect?'

The table of mist had spread across the valley. It caught the sunlight, bringing it within arm's reach. Walking beneath it, they passed the bench where Elizabeth had given Father Anselm the key. Slowly, they followed the track to the plum trees and her yellow car.

'Can I ask a favour?' asked Nick.

'Of course.'

'What's the secret of the relief of Mafeking?'

'After "the Boers were at the gates",' said the monk, 'the story changes all the time. I'm not sure even Sylvester knows, not any more. He makes it up as he goes along.'

When Nick was in the car and the engine was running, Father Anselm knocked on the window. Diffidently, he said, 'Did you ever look inside the hole where your mother kept the key?'

Nick had only ever examined the outer cut pages.

'Have a peep when you get home,' said the monk. 'It tells you the route your mother tried to follow.'

When Nick got back to St John's Wood he went to the Green Room and opened *The Following of Christ*. He hadn't noticed before, but the incisions had created a window around a quotation:

> The humble knowledge of thyself is a surer way to God,
> than the deepest searches after science.

Nick closed the book. He didn't know about God – or science any more – but he was convinced, with gratitude and joy, that his mother had known herself intimately, that she must have found her heart's desire.

8

It was completely by chance that Nancy spotted the monk's entry in the notebook. They were in the Snug Room at the end of a busy day. Having put the remaining five thousand pounds into ten envelopes, she glanced at George, who, true to his routine, was refreshing his memory. Nancy picked out: 'If you meet this gentleman, please contact . . .' It was like one of those tags put on a family pet. Nancy smarted at the condescension, but quickly discovered that she couldn't come up with a better alternative. When George excused himself to answer a call of nature, Nancy noted the number. And when he came back, she retired to her room, ostensibly worn out by the rigours of the day. Apprehensively, Nancy rang the monastery, and a sort of hell broke loose. The monk on the switchboard lost his marbles, another one said, 'Hang on,' and then a fellow called Father Anselm turned up panting. He took Nancy's number, saying he'd contact Mrs Bradshaw, but rang back in a tizzy, saying there was no answer. He said he'd go here, there and everywhere, on a train or in a car, and Nancy, being a decisive woman, told him to calm down and stay put. 'We have our own steam,' she said. 'When we've completed our business, I shall bring him to your premises.'

Nancy went to bed quite sure that something good was about to happen. At breakfast, she had another kipper, but said nothing of her intimations. Her time, and that of George, was given over to hearty meals, long walks and senseless giving.

On the morning of the seventh day, using funds set aside for the purpose, Nancy paid the bill. She rang Inspector Cartwright for a chat, and then, by train and cab, and with George at her side, she went deep into the Suffolk fields.

The monastery was like something from a fairy tale. The roofs were higgledy-piggledy, with russet tiles and slate tiles. There were pink walls, stone walls and brick walls. It seemed as if the ancient builders had made it up as they went along. Nancy was overwhelmed by the sight of the place . . . because it was holy. So she asked the driver to pull over. 'Let's say goodbye here, George,' she said, 'I don't want to go any closer.'

They stood awkwardly on the path, and she appraised her friend, with his coat over one arm, and his small blazer all buttoned up. The blue and yellow tie – and she'd told him – was too bold.

'Thank you,' she said cheerily, 'for a wonderful week by the seaside.'

He took her hand and kissed it. 'I shall never forget it.'

Uncle Bertie had always said, don't hang around saying ta-ta. Get it over and done with. So Nancy urged him on, with a shove. It was a painful sight, looking at his back, and those white cuffs peeping out of the sleeves, for Nancy knew that this would be the last she'd ever see of George Bradshaw.

Nancy asked the man in the taxi to cut the engine, just for a moment. She'd seen a wooden sign for the information of visitors.

Following the arrow took her closer to the monastery, but the temptation was too strong. Behind a broken gate Nancy saw the wildest herb garden she'd ever seen. She was so entranced by the mess, by its abundance, that she didn't hear the monk's approach. She only heard his voice.

'Hello, Nancy,' he said. 'We've met once before, many years ago – in my old calling. I represented your husband.'

Nancy wasn't quite sure what to say. But you have to be honest with a monk, so she said, 'Well . . . no offence, but you didn't do him any favours.'

'No, I didn't,' he replied, moving beside her. He, too, looked at the tangled herbs. 'But this time – if he wants – I will.' He became shy, but forceful. 'Is there anything I can do for you?'

Glancing at the taxi, and getting itchy feet, Nancy said, 'When it's all over' – her heart began to run, and her face became warm; she'd turned all serious – 'if I stick by my man . . . will God turn him away?'

The monk seemed mildly stunned, like Uncle Bertie when he checked the final results against his betting card. He reached for a pair of glasses and, thinking better of it, put them back.

'Surely I can't be less constant than God?' she persisted.

'No, you can't,' he said. He was staring at her, thinking through his own answer.

Nancy was surprised: she hadn't expected to give a monk some guidance on his own turf. I mean, she thought, it's all fairly obvious, isn't it? But then again . . . Babycham had said, 'He's not worth it,' and her dad had said, 'There has to be give and take, and he doesn't give.' They were both right. But no one seemed to understand. It wasn't about her gaining or him deserving.

Nancy wished the monk a very merry Christmas and clambered into the taxi.

'Wormwood Scrubs,' she said, leaning forward.

The driver frowned his disbelief. 'The prison . . . in London?'

'Yes,' said Nancy gaily, 'my husband's a guest on D-wing.'

'It'll cost you a bomb . . . it's hours away.'

'I've got my problems,' said Nancy with a sigh, 'but money isn't one of them.'

They pulled out of the monastery and Nancy's chauffeur began to chat, just like Cindy at the hairdresser's. Nancy was a 'somebody', of course. She was the wife of a villain. He wanted to know what he'd done, but was too scared to ask outright. But he'd get there, like Cindy, long before they got to London.

According to Inspector Cartwright, Riley had already received one visitor: a lieutenant-colonel in the Salvation Army.

9

George didn't look back after leaving Nancy. He followed the path towards Larkwood with a growing sense of loneliness and loss. It was blinding, for he trudged on, losing sight of his surroundings, save for the small stones underfoot. Birds whistled in the trees that were banked tight against the verge.

When George looked up, he saw a woman coming towards him. At first he didn't recognise her because she was out of place. A monastery was not her normal stamping ground, although, that said, *The Sound of Music* was her favourite film. He became confused in a terrible way, a way that had come with the beating to his head. For there were times, now, when he doubted what he experienced, when he tramped through a world that he didn't fully understand. Such is the importance of memory, and the things it saves; for, as George well knew, it's only by remembering the lot that we can hope to grasp the lot. And when you cannot grasp the lot, you become very circumspect indeed. But Emily was there, right in front of him, advancing along the same imaginary line as if they were on the top corridor of the Bonnington. Father Anselm appeared behind her . . . he ran past him, asking of Nancy, and George mumbled something, keeping his eyes on this apparition from his past that was crying.

In the same drunken spirit of doubting – and of terror that someone would shortly explain what was really happening – he said goodbye to a parade of monks as if he were the Pope. The boot of Emily's car was open . . . robed figures carried a crate of apples, two bottles of plum brandy and some preserved pears. He was mumbling to himself while someone took his arm by the elbow. The passenger door banged shut. He opened the window as if he needed the air to breathe. A small crowd smiled and waved and Emily was at his side unable to get the key into the ignition. Someone did it for her, and she laughed into a handkerchief. A long corridor of oak trees passed slowly, as if the car were standing still. The lane opened out onto gentle hills with a scattering of houses, and the place that had given him shelter was gone.

'Emily,' said George, very sure of himself now, 'are we going home?'

'Yes.'

He looked at the hedgerows, thinking of the other man he'd seen in Mitcham. 'I tried to come back, once.'

'I know,' said Emily. She understood. 'No one has ever taken your place. Peter was nothing more than a friend. He was to me what Nancy was to you. And God knows, George, we have needed friends, if only to bring us back together.'

329

Emily explained that the house would look very different, that it was new and clean. The neighbours hadn't changed but someone round the corner had bought a dog that they let loose at night.

'Why do you want me back?' asked George, pulling at the sleeves of his blazer.

'Because I found you again, in your notebooks,' she replied, reaching for the gear stick, but not changing gear. 'I don't know how I could have ever let you go. Maybe I lost sight of the right and left of things, the front and back, the top and bottom . . . everything that brought us together. I didn't only find you, George. I found myself.'

George slept – not the sleep of exhaustion through labour, or the fatigue of strong emotion. A great weariness had taken hold of him, as though a whole life had ended. He woke somewhere in London, unsure again of his senses until the car parked outside the home he'd left so many years ago. It was very dark.

'Can we start again?' asked Emily, her voice heavy with hope.

'No, I don't think so.'

They both looked through the windscreen at the antics of a stray dog. George had strong views on dogs – especially those that barked.

'Can we carry on from where we left off?'

'That makes a lot of sense,' said George. 'Of course, I can't remember what's happened in between.' He took her hand. 'It'll be as though nothing ever happened.'

That, of course, wasn't true. It was a joke to bridge the distance between honesty and expectation. Emily unlocked the front door and George came home, as he'd gone, without any luggage. What did he have to show for it? Nothing you could put your finger on, he thought merrily, except apples, plum brandy and some pears in a jar.

10

A long-forgotten Gilbertine once had the wild notion that Larkwood's dead should be broken up by aspen roots. The proposal had been enthusiastically endorsed without a mole's breath being spent on the implied logistics: the need to dig *through* the roots for each internment. But perseverance with the shovel won out. And so, years later, white wooden crosses lay sprinkled between the slim trunks, as if they'd grown with the dandelions. A railway sleeper had been sunk into a facing bank for the comfort of visitors. Anselm and the Prior sat in the middle, wrapped in their cloaks.

'When I look at everyone involved in this case,' said Anselm, 'Mrs Dixon, Walter Steadman, Elizabeth, George, Nancy, me . . . we're all, in varying degrees, responsible for what happened; but in varying degrees were not to blame.'

'You left out Mr Riley.'

The omission had not been deliberate, which, thought Anselm, was telling. It showed that Anselm was undecided on something of great importance. Inspector Cartwright had, with a marginal lapse of propriety, shown the text of Riley's interview to Anselm. There were hardly any questions. He just spoke into the tape machine, sometimes so fast that the transcribing typist couldn't catch the words. Each page contained multiple ellipses. It was (in their joint experience) a unique mixture of honesty, insight, right thinking and, fundamentally, a defining self-regard. At the end, when he'd recounted all he'd done, and how and (most strangely of all) why, he said to the officers at the table, 'Look, I'm crying.' With a hand he'd touched his face as if it belonged to someone else. Inspector Cartwright said he kept saying it, looking around the room. It was as though he were announcing an achievement.

'The passages that unsettled me most,' confided Anselm, 'were those where he seized the blame. Repeatedly, he said he'd made his choices, that no one had twisted his arm, that he was his own man. It read like vanity, or a kind of vicious pride; as though he was holding on to what he could of himself, however ghastly it might be. And yet, in one place – almost inaudibly, I assume, because the typist had put questions marks on either side – he seems to have said, "I never had a chance." He strangled his own mitigation before it could see the light of day.' Anselm wrapped his cloak tighter, hugging his knees. 'Was he free, even though he claimed his actions for his own? Can you be responsible if you're so injured in the mind? I'm filled with dread at the thought that today's capacity to choose might already be forfeit to yesterday's misfortune.'

'Well, it might be,' said the Prior simply. 'But it might not. When I first went into the confessional, I believed that all evil, at root, was a wound and never a choice – and I still hold on to that, when I can. But I've met charming people who tell me they've done unconscionable things, quite freely, without the benefit of yesterday's misfortune. And I believe them. The wounded and the free: they both break windows. But there's one narrow piece of ground upon which they have an equal footing. It might seem unfair, but forgiveness is available to each – not because they can prove they deserve it, but because they can both say sorry. I used to think it scandalous that each could be reprieved on the same basis, just as easily, when the deserts of one so outweighed the other.'

'What changed your mind?'

The Prior's eyes twinkled. 'A little knowledge of myself.' He stood up and brushed the back of his cloak. 'As for Mr Riley, who knows where he stands? We can't discern who's truly free, and who isn't, or where the difference might lie. We have to muddle along, all of us, remembering, I think, that in the end, the giving of mercy is not our lot.'

Resolutely, Father Andrew followed the track away from the aspen trees towards Larkwood. He had a meeting organised by Cyril. Gazing at graves, he'd said, was an excellent means of preparation.

The winter sun was low and clouds were moving over St Leonard's Field. The air was charged with precipitation, and the light curiously pink.

The court system, thought Anselm, would handle the question of Riley's intentions and deserts with bracing clarity. He would receive censure, a certain amount of sympathy and a lengthy custodial sentence, which, on reflection, would be merciful to Nancy. But despite his many crimes, Anselm felt pity for Graham Riley. He could not easily dismiss the image of a boy collecting coloured stones and bottle tops; of such a boy casting a poker into a lake that it might never be seen again. In a sense, he thought, Elizabeth had successfully recreated herself; and so had George. They'd run away and started again. But Riley had failed hopelessly. He'd never left Dagenham. The courts could no longer punish him. It would just be window-dressing, however severe. He was, in several disquieting respects, beyond the reach of the law. But not Nancy's . . .

That ruined instrument, Elizabeth had said of him. She, too, had finally settled on pity.

Anselm looked up, his attention caught by a small, roundish figure hurrying along the track. He wore a brown overcoat with the collar up and a red woolly hat with a bobble on top.

'Frank Wyecliffe,' muttered Anselm, astonished.

The solicitor bowed, shook hands, looked around warily and sat on the railway sleeper. He wanted to raise a delicate matter, he said. He'd asked for Anselm and a monk had given him fault-less directions to the graveyard, which, given the errand in hand, was a most appropriate location. He sat blinking at the aspen trees.

'So . . . is this how you spend your free time these days?'

'Some, but not all,' replied Anselm.

'Very nice.'

Mr Wyecliffe rubbed his hands, blowing into them. His head had almost vanished below the high collar. He said, 'Our mutual friend Inspector Cartwright is of the opinion that my old client, Mr Riley, could not have devised his harebrained scheme with-out contemporaneous informed assistance. She thinks it came from me. But I don't give that kind of help – not on legal aid . . .' He glanced over the collar. 'That's a joke . . . all right?'

'Yes,' replied Anselm.

'I could do without another complaint to the Law Society,' he said, wincing at the cold. 'Would you explain to the good Inspector that I'm not responsible for the workings of Riley's mind? That I limit myself to its effects?'

'Of course.' Anselm considered the huddled figure with warmth and something like admiration. For thirty years, Frank Wyecliffe had represented Graham Riley's interests – from con-veyancing to homicide; he was that most adroit of guides: a scout in the maze of the law. If there were a turning he could take to his client's advantage, he'd take it, with a bow. He was a necessary man, a dedicated man; a good man, though, inevitably, such work leaves its mark.

'Frank . . .' Anselm began to smile. At last, he'd worked some-thing out. 'Did you post letters to me and Inspector Cartwright on Elizabeth's behalf?'

The hairy head appeared above the collar again. The narrow eyes were asking if this matter was on the record or off. 'Consider this a species of confession,' he said, to cover both alternatives.

It transpired that Elizabeth had come to Cheapside not long after she'd visited Larkwood for the last time. Just as Anselm had been entrusted with a key, so Mr Wyecliffe had been given two letters. They'd each been asked to act in the event of her death. They'd both of them delayed (in Mr Wyecliffe's case, because he'd lost them in his office. It was the phone call from Nick that had him on his hands and knees).

Anselm could not suppress a smile. There can be a grim humour among lawyers. And he saw wit in Elizabeth's allocation of duties:

'You ought to know,' he said, 'that you posted to me the means by which your client now stands charged with murder – for that was how I met Mrs Dixon. And if Elizabeth hadn't made a mistake about the law, you'd have posted to Inspector Cartwright the evidence to convict him of living off immoral earnings.'

Mr Wyecliffe blinked at the aspens, and said, 'I wonder what the Law Society would make of that one?'

'Don't worry, Frank,' said Anselm. 'We're all in the same boat. She gave everyone a part to play, depending on what they'd done: me, George, you, even Inspector Cartwright. We were all meant to get what we deserved. Especially your client.'

Mr Wyecliffe hurried back along the track, a figure so very different to the Prior, and perhaps, in his own way, just as important.

The branches trembled and snow began to fall. Instantly, the whole valley of the Lark became speckled. The greens of winter began to fade and the woods turned white. There was so much activity, and so much silence. Pensively, Anselm thought, What will grow in the space I leave behind? Something for the delight of others, or pain? He didn't know; and, he felt, he ought to. 'Now is the time to decide,' he said out loud. On that note of homage to Elizabeth, he rose and sought refuge in the small tool-shed propped against the enclosure wall. As he rattled free the door, a yellow butterfly skipped past him and left the grove. It vanished as quickly as it had appeared.